CRY FOR JERUSALEM

BOOK TWO: 66–67 CE

AGAINST ALL ODDS

WARD SANFORD

PUBLISHED BY STADIA BOOKS LLC

WWW.CRYFORJERUSALEM.COM

D1082236

CRY FOR JERUSALEM

BOOK TWO: 66–67 CE

AGAINST ALL ODDS

WARD SANFORD

CRY FOR JERUSALEM
BOOK TWO: 66–67 CE
AGAINST ALL ODDS
WARD SANFORD

PAPERBACK ISBN: 978-1-950645-02-2

PUBLISHED BY STADIA BOOKS LLC
WWW.CRYFORJERUSALEM.COM

CRY FOR JERUSALEM is a work of fiction that has been inspired by eyewitness records of historical events. Some characters, many scenes, and most of the dialog have been fictionalized for dramatic purposes.

Front cover artwork created by Tony Foti.

WHAT PROFESSIONAL REVIEWERS ARE SAYING ABOUT CRY FOR JERUSALEM BOOK ONE

"The story sweeps across a first-century world that's diverse, gritty, and laced with tension. Majestic and colorful landscapes such as Jerusalem, Rome, and the many places in between, both on land and sea, are richly detailed. I loved the maps that are included at the beginning. Sanford uses his characters well. Men and women have strong influence on the plot, including women who interacted with and changed their circumstances despite social constraints. Everything is supported by an incredibly well-researched foundation. The time period and social customs are delightfully developed... there is political and religious strife, moments of ancient beauty, and well-developed characters to carry the plot forward. Sanford is a talented author with an exciting new series to get lost in."

--Historical Novels Review Issue 91 February 2020

"In this first installment of a series, Yosef comes to realize what a tinderbox the political situation has become. As Roman leaders become increasingly authoritarian and hungry for tax proceeds, Jewish militancy increases, setting the stage for a brutal confrontation, a historical predicament vividly and intelligently depicted by Sanford. And Nero, looking for an excuse to rebuild Rome, raise taxes, and consolidate his power, takes Florus' advice to burn the city to the ground, starting the "most extensive and destructive fire that Rome had ever experienced." The plot is as gripping as it is historically edifying, remarkably authentic, and rigorously researched. At its conclusion, readers will be left impatient for the book's sequel. An impressive blend of historical portrayal and dramatic fiction."

--Kirkus Reviews June 2020

ABOUT CRY FOR JERUSALEM

A four novel—historical fiction—series based on the writings of Yosef ben Matityahu (Titus Flavius Josephus). Yosef's (Josephus's) work as a historian provides valuable insight into first-century Judaism and the background of early Christianity. He has specific details on the First Jewish–Roman War, which he not only witnessed but took part in at a high level. The story takes place from late 63 to 70 CE, a little over one-third of the way into a 200-year period of increased and sustained internal peace and stability for Rome, though not without lesser wars, conflicts of expansion, and revolts. This *Pax Romana* was first broken by the Jewish (Judean) first war of rebellion.

First-century Judea was a time of new belief systems, persecution, and economic upheaval. Ruled by Rome's puppet-King Agrippa, the Judeans had fragmented into three factions under the Romans: the status-quo pro-Romans; the Zealots/nationalists, who wanted Judean and Jewish independence; and the Sicarii, a violent splinter group who not only wanted independence from Rome—once the revolt intensified—but also had a goal to kill pro-Roman collaborators.

SYNOPSIS OF BOOK ONE: RESISTING TYRANNY

Yosef, Nicanor, Sayid and Lady Cleopatra's (Cleo's) shared experience forms an unlikely bond of friendship tested throughout the four novels in the series. Was it fate, destiny, or some divine plan that brought these four very different travelers together to survive a shipwreck while traveling to Rome?

In Rome, the reader meets Emperor Nero and is introduced to the intrigue that permeates the empire. Nero—at the suggestion of Gessius Florus, and to serve his own purpose—sets Rome afire while shifting the blame onto the Christians. This sets events in motion to replenish Rome's depleted treasury by igniting a war in Judea to steal the vast treasure believed held in the Jewish Temple in Jerusalem.

Yosef, Nicanor, Cleo, and Sayid experience the Great Fire of Rome and its aftermath. Then each separately returns to Judea, where their fates further converge: Yosef to report the release of the Jewish prisoners and to attempt to stave off the increasing militancy of the anti-Roman factions, hoping to find a peaceful resolution with Rome; Nicanor—having avoided the Praetorian Guard duty he did not want—to return to his beloved legion duties in Antioch; Cleo, now married and accompanied by her husband; Gessius Florus, who is to become the new Procurator of Judea; and Sayid, glad to return to auxiliary duty in a land where he feels at home, is assigned to Lady Cleo and often thinks of Yosef and Nicanor.

In Jerusalem, the reader meets Miriam, Yosef's sister, who survives a tragic attack by Roman soldiers that changes her forever, turning her into something and someone she could never have imagined, which becomes a dark secret she must hide from her family.

In Judea, Gessius Florus shows his true colors. His oppressive actions are designed solely to squeeze more tax revenue and to heighten tensions between the factions within Jerusalem and Rome itself. He creates situations and events—including a massacre in Jerusalem shortly after Passover—that lead to chaos of conflict and the birthing of a full-blown war. All were intended as justification to steal the Jewish Temple treasure and to further his plan to keep a large part of it for himself and send the rest to Nero.

In Antioch, the reader meets Cestius Gallus, governor, and commander of the 12th Legion. Circumstances and the actions of the rebels forced him to lead his legion and allied forces into Judea for an ill-fated—ultimately aborted—attack on Jerusalem and one of the worst defeats of any Roman legion during their retreat through the pass at Beth Horon.

Yosef, Nicanor, Cleo, and Sayid, along with their family and friends, play critical roles at a focal point in the history of Western civilization. For as the winds helped to spread the great fire in Rome, they also carried embers to Judea, where they threatened to ignite a conflict that would forever change the world for Jews and Christians. In between the recorded historical events of that time, there's the story of the people involved. The reader gets to meet them in Book One of *Cry for Jerusalem: Resisting Tyranny,* and in Book Two: *Against All Odds,* their epic saga continues as the war begins.

CONTENTS

DRAMATIS PERSONAE

YOSEF BEN MATHIAS

A young, upper-class, educated Jew, sent—in Book One—to Rome as an envoy to free imprisoned priests. Returns to Judea, and when the war begins, in Book Two, is assigned to become military commander of Galilee.

REBECCA

Yosef's mother, who has a lineage of Jewish royalty from the Hasmonean dynasty.

MATHIAS

Yosef's father and a leader in the Sanhedrin, the governing body of the Jews in Judea.

MATTHEW BEN MATHIAS

Yosef's older brother, an officer in the Jewish Temple Guard, who also plays a vital role in the plan to save the Temple treasure from the Romans by hiding much of it.

MIRIAM

Yosef's younger sister, her betrothal broken off due to tragic events in Book One. Her personal tragedy and transformation continue in Book Two.

LEAH

Yosef's cousin, mutually attracted to Yosef at age sixteen and afterward, but married to an abusive man.

YONATAN

Leah's husband, a rebel with a dislike of Roman collaborators.

RACHEL

Leah's younger sister, Yosef's cousin, who develops feelings for him.

I

YOHANAN BEN ZACCAI

Member of the Sanhedrin, respected by both moderates and rebels, who becomes Yosef's chief advisor in Galilee and courier to and from Jerusalem.

ELAZAR BEN YAIR

Member of the Sicarii, and Menahem ben Judah's chief lieutenant, who replaced Menahem ben Judah on his death.

YOHANAN BEN LEVI (OF GISCHALA)

A rebel leader in Galilee, often at odds with leadership in Jerusalem. His refusal to accept Yosef's appointment as commander in Galilee results in death and disruption in the region.

LEVI BEN ALTHEUS

Judean rebel, a native of Yotapta, who becomes Yosef's chief lieutenant in Galilee.

ARIELLA

A Galilean woman, daughter of a veteran Jewish soldier, who comes to Yotapta to help prepare to fight the Romans. She becomes a valued person in the effort and falls in love with Levi ben Altheus.

ESAU BEN BEOR

A leader of the Judean province of Idumea (which has a troubled history with Jerusalem and Judaism) whose secret hatred of Jerusalem enables Florus to leverage him to become his spy within the Sanhedrin.

EHUD BEN MESHULAM

An old friend of Matthew and Yosef's who is also Miriam's former crush. His family had left Jerusalem years before and has business connections with the Romans in Alexandria. Gessius Florus forces him to become another spy in Jerusalem, or his family will lose all, including their lives.

HANANIAH

Recruited through Capito—Gessius Florus's military aide—and his connections in Alexandria. A master metal craftsman and killer-for-hire who hates Jerusalem.

ELEASAR BEN ANANIAS

Captain of Jewish Temple Guard, a rebel leader, though not an extremist. He is assigned responsibility for Jerusalem and southern Judea's defense against the Romans.

ZECHARIAH

A craftsman living in the Lower City, virtually blind, who befriended Miriam in Book One and is killed saving her in Book One.

SIMON BAR GIORA

Top rebel leader from Judea and a competent field commander. He led the rebel force that—in Book One—defeated the 12th Legion and took their *aquila*, battle standard, at Beth Horon.

YEHUDAH ISH KRIOTH

A respected member of the Sanhedrin, formerly a prisoner in Rome, who also became Gessius Florus's first spy in Jerusalem. Killed in Book One.

MENAHEM BEN JUDAH

The leader of the Sicarii (Jewish assassins) who hated all Romans and collaborators. His efforts to further drive a wedge between Jewish factions in Jerusalem led to his death in Book One.

NICANOR

A Roman centurion who befriends Yosef. His father was also a Roman legionary, and his mother was Greek. Beginning in Book One and continuing in Book Two, he becomes entangled in the intrigues of Rome and the agendas of powerful men in the empire.

CLEOPATRA (CLEO)

A young Roman woman of high social standing who—in Book One— marries a newly appointed Judean Procurator Gessius Florus. An admirer of Jewish culture, she had toured the eastern Roman provinces before their wedding. In Book Two, she has remained in Judea married to a man she is coming to fear and hate.

SAYID

A young man from Syria, a volunteer Roman army auxiliary whose father was a Roman soldier of African descent who fell in love with

III

his mother, a Syrian. He is assigned to Lady Cleo's retinue in her travels. After Cleo's marriage, he is attached to the 12th Legion and—like Nicanor—finds himself drawn into helping his friend, Lady Cleo.

GESSIUS FLORUS

A Roman tax collector who marries Cleo and becomes the Judean Procurator, then Nero's Imperial Tax Collector in the region, who also plans to steal much of the Jewish Temple treasure. Empowered by that assignment, he becomes even harsher toward his wife, Cleo, and deadly to anyone in his way.

NERO

Despotic Roman emperor who has brought the empire to the verge of bankruptcy. Under his reign, Rome was nearly destroyed by a great fire (Book One). Now he pursues his plan to replenish his treasury by stealing from Judea under the guise of war.

CESTIUS GALLUS

The Roman legate (governor) of the eastern Roman provinces, including Syria and Judea. Commander of the 12th Legion. He attempts to alert the emperor to concerns about how the war was provoked, and how that resulted in events in Book One (his aborted attack on Jerusalem and defeat at Beth Horon).

VESPASIAN

A formerly victorious but out-of-favor and retired Roman general recommended to Nero by the Praetorian Prefect Tigellinus to take over the Judean campaign to crush the rebels.

TITUS

Vespasian's son and field commander of three legions moved into Judea and Galilee as part of his father's campaign.

ELIAN

A young slave boy, part of Lady Cleo's new household in Ptolemais.

QUINTUS

A mercenary sea captain, known by Capito, who becomes another henchman/killer for Gessius Florus.

GLAUCIO

Florus's *major domus* and his watchdog over Cleo. He also has another role kept secret from Gessius Florus.

ERIS

A maidservant, and Glaucio's other set of eyes on Cleo.

OCTAVIA

Wife of Cestius Gallus, a friend of Cleo, who sympathized with provincials over which Rome rules.

GALERIUS SENNA

Senior Military Tribune of the 12th Legion. Becomes its commander when Cestius Gallus is relieved of his duties by Nero.

GRAIUS

Lady Cleo's retired former *major domus,* introduced in Book One, who helps Nicanor in Rome.

TYRANNIUS PRISEUS

Camp-prefect of the 12th Legion and made so after the sudden death of his predecessor in Book One.

POPPAEA

Nero's wife, Cleo's best friend and former sister-in-law. Killed by Nero in Book One.

AGRIPPA II

Rome's loyal client-king of Judea descended from Herod the Great, Jewish by heritage and religion.

BERENICE

Sister of Agrippa II, who sympathized with the plight of the Jews, her people, in Book One.

HISTORICAL BACKGROUND

By the fall of Jerusalem in 70 CE, the culmination of *Cry For Jerusalem*, Rome had much of the known world under its control. The empire reached its largest expanse in 117 CE under Emperor Trajan.

THE ROMAN EMPIRE CIRCA 117 CE

The empire encompassed an area of three-million square miles and stretched from the British Isles across western, central, and southern Europe, northern Africa, and western Asia. Its estimated 60 million inhabitants would have accounted for between one-sixth and one-fourth of the world's total population. It was the largest unified political entity in the West until the mid-19th century. More recent demographic studies suggest the population could have risen to 100 million at its peak. Each of the three largest cities in the empire—Rome, Alexandria, and Antioch—were almost twice the size of any European city before the 17th century.

The Romans had occupied greater Judea since the invasion of General Pompey in 63 BCE. Many large buildings and a grand Temple complex in Jerusalem were constructed by King Herod the Great from circa 20 BCE until well after he died in 4 BCE. After Herod's death, the greater province was divided up into four tetrarchs ruled by Herod's descendants, who functioned as Roman-controlled governors.

Map 1 – Eastern Mediterranean Coastline

MAJOR CITIES, TOWNS AND ROADS IN THE FIRST CENTURY CE

MAP 2 – JUDEAN PROVINCES

THE JUDEAN PROVINCES IN THE FIRST CENTURY CE

MAP 3 – GALILEE

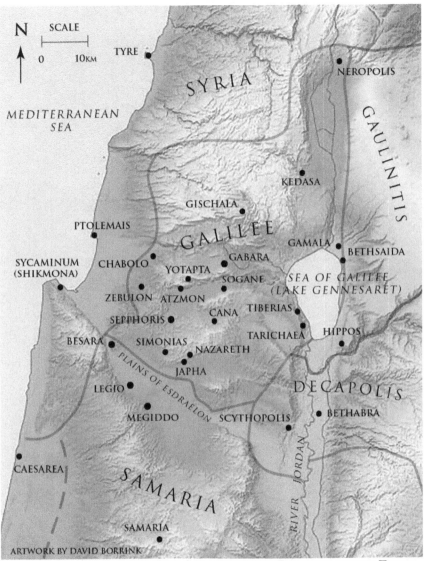

CITIES AND TOWNS AND THE SURROUNDING REGIONS IN THE FIRST CENTURY CE.

MAP 4 – YOTAPTA (AND ITS SURROUNDINGS)

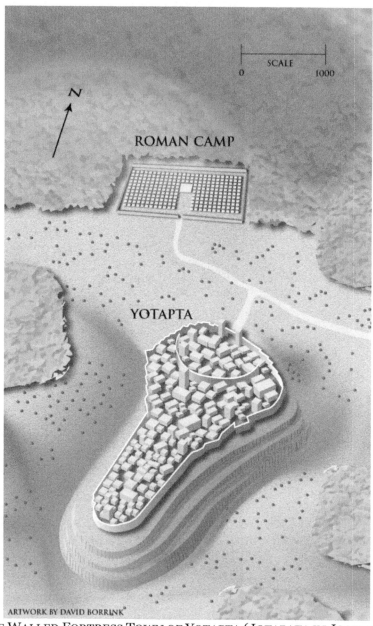

THE WALLED FORTRESS TOWN OF YOTAPTA (JOTAPATA IN JOSEPHUS, MODERN DAY YODFAT) IN THE FIRST CENTURY CE.

Map 5 – Jerusalem

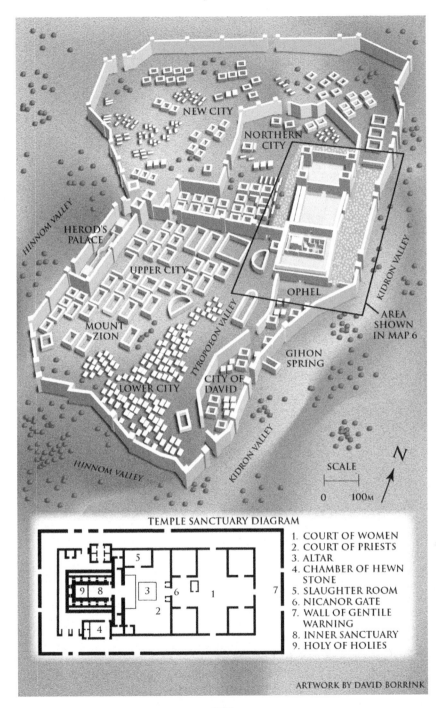

TEMPLE SANCTUARY DIAGRAM

1. COURT OF WOMEN
2. COURT OF PRIESTS
3. ALTAR
4. CHAMBER OF HEWN STONE
5. SLAUGHTER ROOM
6. NICANOR GATE
7. WALL OF GENTILE WARNING
8. INNER SANCTUARY
9. HOLY OF HOLIES

ARTWORK BY DAVID BORRINK

MAP 6 – THE TEMPLE COMPLEX

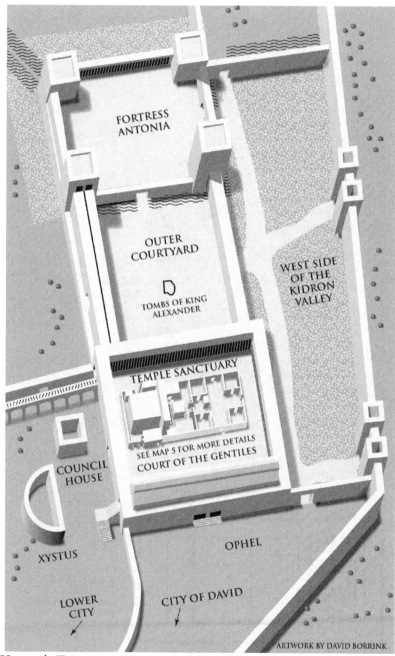

HEROD'S TEMPLE COMPLEX AS ENVISIONED BY JOSEPHUS SCHOLAR
THOMAS LEWIN

Map 7 – The Seven Hills of Rome and Its Fourteen Regions

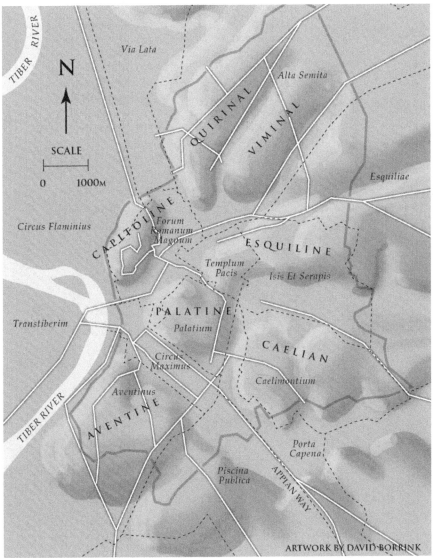

Via Lata

Alta Semita

N

SCALE

0   1000m

QUIRINAL

VIMINAL

Esquiliae

Circus Flaminius

CAPITOLINE

Forum Romanum Magnum

ESQUILINE

Templum Pacis

Isis Et Serapis

Transtiberim

PALATINE

Palatium

CAELIAN

Circus Maximus

Caelimontium

Aventinus

AVENTINE

Porta Capena

Piscina Publica

APPIAN WAY

TIBER RIVER

TIBER RIVER

ARTWORK BY DAVID BORRINK

THE WALLS (SOLID LINE) AND ROADS (OPEN LINES) OF FIRST CENTURY ROME

MAP 8 –THE CENTER OF ROME

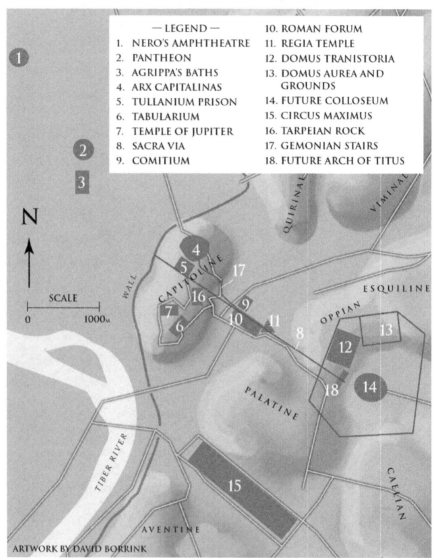

— LEGEND —
1. NERO'S AMPHTHEATRE
2. PANTHEON
3. AGRIPPA'S BATHS
4. ARX CAPITALINAS
5. TULLANIUM PRISON
6. TABULARIUM
7. TEMPLE OF JUPITER
8. SACRA VIA
9. COMITIUM
10. ROMAN FORUM
11. REGIA TEMPLE
12. DOMUS TRANISTORIA
13. DOMUS AUREA AND
    GROUNDS
14. FUTURE COLLOSEUM
15. CIRCUS MAXIMUS
16. TARPEIAN ROCK
17. GEMONIAN STAIRS
18. FUTURE ARCH OF TITUS

ARTWORK BY DAVID BORRINK

MAJOR FEATURES IN THE FIRST CENTURY CE

"A STAR WILL ARISE OUT OF JACOB,
AND A SCEPTOR OUT OF ISRAEL. HE
WILL CRUSH THE HEADS OF MOAB,
AND CONQUER ALL THE
DESCENDANTS OF SETH."

BALAAM BEN BEOR, CIRCA 1300 BCE

ACT I

I

ANTIPATRIS

Cestius Gallus looked up from the blank sheet of vellum before him. His aide, who was carrying a field water-clock, hesitated at the entrance to his tent.

"Lord, shall I?"—he motioned toward the small table beside the desk of the commander of the 12th Legion, a spot where the commander could see the *clepsydra* at a glance.

Gallus understood that the clerk needed instruction whether to set it up. How long would the legion be camped in Antipatris after such a... defeat? That word still hurt to conceive, much less speak or write—the task he faced now. The aftermath of the disgrace reeked and resonated around him. With not a breath of wind to carry it away, the coppery smell of blood from the newly dead, wounded and dying still smothered the camp as cries of men and screams of horses cut through the air.

"Go ahead," he nodded, not sure himself how long the legion could hold at Antipatris. Before the clerk bowed his head to comply, Gallus saw uncertainty in the young man's eyes. Defeats such as the one they had just suffered—the likes of which they had never known before—did not end with the battle. Gallus knew what his ultimate fate would be. But others on his staff did not know theirs. Meanwhile, he must still command and do his duty as best he could.

"Anything else, my lord?"

Gallus shook his head but asked, "Has my messenger returned from Caesarea?"

"Yes, lord, a short while ago, and confirmed that he personally gave your message to the Lady Cleo."

Gallus nodded. Sending that letter had been a necessary risk. Overland couriers were at increased danger of death or capture by the emboldened rebel forces patrolling the region. The farther they traveled from the legion's reach, the greater the jeopardy their messages would fall into someone else's hands. But now Cleo would forward the letter on a Roman coastal trading ship to Antioch, to his wife, Octavia. Cleo was smart enough to read into that message and be forewarned herself.

"Anything else, my lord?" the clerk asked again before turning to leave.

"Tell the quartermaster I said to go ahead—he can proceed." The clerk did not need to know that in a rush from Beth Horon, they had lost most of their remaining supplies. The quartermaster had asked permission to butcher the bodies of the dead horses and those severely injured animals that would have to be put down. Knowing many—himself included—had an aversion to eating horse meat, Gallus had told him to wait. But scouts had just reported the massing of rebel forces around them—that meant every attempt to forage and raid for supplies would result in a skirmish or battle. More men lost for little gain. Food would not be easy to come by to feed so many men. "After you see the quartermaster, return and see that I'm not disturbed." The clerk left, and Gallus pulled the sheet of parchment closer. After adding the proper imperial salutation, he began:

Sire, bad news—like lies—travels fastest, and there are those— unfortunately—who will hasten it further. So, you likely already know what I now tell you, which is the truth. What I report is terrible to write about, but I must. For reasons I believe justified, I halted our attack on Jerusalem. As we pulled back to reposition, so I could reassess the situation, a large force of well-commanded rebels—yes, sire... some of them are competent—trapped the 12th Legion and our allies in the pass of Beth Horon.

There we lost thousands of men, and most of what equipment and supplies remained to support the legion in the field. You have no doubt seen my previous dispatches concerning the loss of men and material because of the surprising ferocity and tenaciousness of the rebel attacks. I admit my failures as commander of the legion also contributed to our downfall.

Despite the defeat, there was much heroism, chief of which was in a centurion by the name of Nicanor. I believe you met him briefly in Rome, as he played a role in saving the Lady Cleo, a friend of the late empress, in the wreck of the *Salacia* on its way to Rome. Nicanor served bravely in Jerusalem and even more so at Beth Horon. Sensing I could count on him, I had him promoted to First Centurion. He commanded the men we left in the pass as decoys to fool the Jewish rebels into believing we remained in camp intending to meet them in battle the next morning. But with the rebels in far higher numbers than we expected, and secure above us with that advantage, and armed with arrows, spears, and slings—they turned the valley floor into their killing field. I could not commit more men to death by remaining there at such a disadvantage. The bulk of the legion escaped in the night, and the next day we entered Antipatris, where I write this.

The evening of the following day, two severely wounded men—from among those we had left in the pass—staggered into camp. Reporting that all other Romans at Beth Horon had died, they both soon afterward joined them. Were Nicanor still alive, I would recommend him for any honor that could be given. I know at one time he had been awarded a position within your Praetorian Guard, because of his previous bravery and the saving of a Roman noble's life, but circumstances changed that. His death was not in vain, but it is deeply regretted that Rome has lost such a soldier.

Though we may be forced to move, for now, we have secured our encampment to regroup, and here I will plan what to do next as I await a response with further orders.

Gallus rubbed his eyes—the words had formed and rattled around inside his head during the retreat from Beth Horon; even the stumbling of his exhausted mount had not jostled them from his thoughts. But they were still painful, almost too hard to write. His tired eyes shifted to the stack of several pieces of folded parchment set to one side. He lifted them and tied them together, strapped tightly with a wide leather cord. He then wrapped them in a larger sheet of vellum, folding the four corners to the center, and dropped a blob of molten red wax onto the opening from the handless brass cup set in a holder over a sputtering lantern. Slipping the ring with his personal crest from his hand, he blew three times on the wax to cool it and then pressed the ring into the congealing glob. Then he slid the packet into a pouch made of animal hide, open only along the end he would personally sew shut and seal before it left his hands. He had spent some time creating that packet of letters to include with what he had to write next. He straightened a kink in his back and bent again to continue:

I mentioned above there are other factors regarding this defeat, and I report them not to lessen my responsibility but to make you aware of them, as they will inevitably also affect the man you choose to replace me. Accompanying this report are my notes concerning my suspicion of the man who, during this campaign, rose to become Camp-Prefect, Tyrannius Priseus. And that he and Galerius Senna, a senior military tribune, conspired to intentionally misadvise me, and that resulted in our earlier losses of men, equipment, and supplies before our attack on Jerusalem. I take responsibility for listening to them, and for not realizing until too late that I should not have heeded their advice.

The question of why they did this and at whose request or order they would do such a treasonous thing is—I believe—answered in the copies of several letters that accompany my report to you. I have the originals for safekeeping and attest that what I've given you is authentically recreated and accurate to match the documents that I received during our assault on Jerusalem. Their contents were then and still are shocking to me. But I believe they tell the truth. What they contain—along with what had happened with the loss of supplies and siege equipment—led me to cease the attack on Jerusalem, disengage, and pull my force back to consider alternatives. I cannot change that decision, and I know that judgment awaits me.

There was nothing more to be said, at least to the emperor. He signed it—*Gaius Cestius Gallus, Legate of Syria, Commander of the 12th Legion*—sanded the parchment to dry the ink, and blew the grains free. He folded it, sealed it with another glob of wax, and added it to the outer pouch, wondering if he could get the package safely to Rome.

II

"You're sure the man traveling with the new Procurator is what he says he is and can do as he claims?"

"Yes, lord," Capito replied, tugging his cloak around him. A brisk draught swirled around them, as there was no windbreak on the terrace facing the sea. Why had Florus had him led here to talk? "I knew him from my time in Alexandria."

"I don't need more foreign mercenaries that will draw even more attention now—I want someone who seems to belong in the city."

"He's a Jerusalem Jew, born and raised in the city for years, and he—"

Florus cut him off—"Will he be known there for what he is?"

"No, lord, not for what he truly is. His family is dead. The father, a stonecutter, died in an earth shake in that city over thirty years ago when the man was a babe. The mother died of a wasting disease ten years later, giving him to an Alexandrian tradesman who promised to make the boy his apprentice. He took the boy back to Alexandria and abused him for years until the boy could stand no more and slit the man's throat. Afterward, Hananiah bar Dodalos grew up on the streets and alleys of Alexandria—and became a capable cutthroat."

"That name sounds Greek—you're sure he has the look and sound of city-born Jerusalem?"

"Yes, lord. If Hananiah hasn't changed in the nearly two years since I saw him last, I doubt I could tell him from those I've seen in that city. He even holds to what Jews can and can't eat."

"So, he's religious? He's loyal to the Jewish faith?"

"He is faithful and loyal only to gold and silver, one thing that tradesman did instill in him... and love of blades."

"Murena was a hardened mercenary and skilled weapons master, and this Sicarri 'Hand' in Jerusalem bested him—among others of my men. He slaughtered my spy in the Sanhedrin, one of their own priests. I need a man who can hunt down and kill this Jewish assassin, so they do not discover and interfere with another who now helps me. He shall not take my money and fail."

"Hananiah is a *castratus*—one of the Alexandrian's torments of him as a boy. Though he is no longer a man, I've witnessed that he grew up to become a cruel being who enjoys killing men. Unlike

5

Murena, he knows only one weapon, but he is the best with it I've ever seen or heard stories of."

"How did you manage things to have him travel with the new Procurator?" Florus asked, gazing at the sea.

"I had him request protected travel to Caesarea as a commercial venture of benefit to the garrison there. Then your contact on the Prefect's staff in Alexandria approved it. The tradesman that took Hananiah was a knife-maker and a blade sharpener who also sold metal stock for swords, javelin, and arrow tips. He brought Hananiah with him to sell to armorers and blacksmiths in Caesarea and Jerusalem. So Hananiah became a well-known dealer in metal and blades, too. Who better to have a reason for travel to where a new war has started... and to profit from it?" Capito could not help the flush of avarice that came over him, but it quickly lessened when he saw the cold, appraising look in Gessius Florus's eyes.

"Let me know when they arrive, then quietly bring him here from wherever he is in town. I'll meet with him after I speak with Marcus Antonius Julianus about his assumption of my duties." Florus turned from looking at the sea and walked toward what would soon be his former residence—now to be inhabited by the new Procurator. "I won't spend much time with Julianus, once he's gone, I want to talk to this cruel man of yours." He studied the building and surrounding grounds, nothing in Ptolemais would match it, but that was only a minor inconvenience to contend with on his journey to a far greater reward.

As they approached the main house, Capito saw the large blotch of a bruise on Lady Cleo's face. She stood in the sun, wrapped to her throat in a sky-blue cloak as she watched men carry furnishings and their belongings to load on wagons that would deliver them to the ship Gallus had arranged to take them up the coast to Ptolemais. Her eyes flashed toward him, and though he doubted he would see her ever again, he looked away.

* * *

As her husband and his dog—Capito—passed, Cleo moved aside and walked to the edge of the portico to where she could see the area where she had always practiced her archery—her target had been flattened and kicked to pieces. A question flickered—*Who did that?*—likely Glaucio, her husband's chief spy and household *major domus*, or Florus himself. But the flicker came and went because two other recent shocks fully occupied her thoughts.

6

First, she had never imagined a Roman legion could be beaten by what she thought were meager forces of the Jews. The abrupt end of the assault on Jerusalem and the Roman retreat had emboldened the rebels far beyond what she had thought possible. She likely had some responsibility for Cestius Gallus's decision to pull back the 12th Legion and its allied forces.

And then the messenger from Cestius Gallus had brought the second shock.

Cleo touched her jaw and the swelling. Gallus's letter had been worded carefully to tell Octavia he was alive but that she should be prepared for what was to come for them all. There had been a distinct space between *them* and *all*. And the very next sentence had urged her: "Lady Cleo, please send this to my wife as soon as possible, and I hope you, too, plan to be prepared and remain safe." Not wanting to hold the message too long, she had immediately resealed it and taken it to the port. There she found the olive-wood trader Sayid had connected her with and paid him with all the silver she wore that he might board a ship and carry the letter to Octavia in Antioch.

Florus—Glaucio smirking beside him—had met her on her return, demanding to see the message. When she told him she did not have it, that's when he had struck her for the first time. Now she feared that was just a beginning. Not long ago, she had known too much of what her husband was up to, suspecting things he had done in Rome and in Judea. She had struggled with what to do—how could she use what she had learned to prevent a war. Then she had put her friend Sayid in danger to pass on that suspicion and that information.

Now she had to bear not knowing his fate... or her own.

III

The cloak he wore was stiff with dried blood, but at least it was whole, though unwieldy at first until the crust broke, and most of it flaked away. His own mantle had been equally stained but slashed and torn so it could not be gathered more closely to him. His clothing beneath was in almost as poor condition. He ignored the smell of the cloth soiled by more than blood, as was common on battlefields. The bodies piled on and around him had proven that death often takes a man with emptied bowels.

Lightheaded and chilled, he had lost a lot of blood, had not eaten in days, and had drunk little from the sparse offshoots of the creeks that seemed to be lined with rebels. He had staggered across over 20 miles of rebel-held territory. But their jubilation at defeating the Romans had made them careless and weak and fuzzy-headed as he was, he had slipped past them. Years of marching had given him an innate sense of pace and distance traveled—and of the crucial need for knowledge of the terrain, important locations, and where he was relative to them. Those details often made the difference between living and dying when things went wrong in battle.

Things had gone very, very wrong. But then he was alive, and he had not expected that.

As he neared his destination, the rise in elevation wore him down and slowed his pace. The town and its tower—Aphek—had been a strategic fortress for centuries because of its location at the headwaters of the Yarkon River, in terrain that formed a narrow funnel between the river and the mountains. It made sense as a point to pull back to and regroup. Above him, the steep slopes rose to the remnants of old defensive ramparts, eight feet wide. Though worn down by years of rain and wind, their crumbling walls were still near the shoulder height of an average man.

The injured leg gave way, and he fell at the bank of the river he had to cross. Though thirst taunted him, demanding he plunge his head in the water to slake it, he scanned the area first. To his right were sounds... like the scrape of digging and labored breathing. As soon as he noticed, the noise ended. Then he heard crying. But he had to drink, so he leaned forward to cup the water to his lips and then wash some of the blood and dirt from his face. He got to his knees and levered himself up to stand. Above, higher on the slopes, he heard the familiar noises of men bearing arms as they moved about. The easiest path uphill carried him toward the crying sound to where it wound around. At the bend was a section of ground that ran straight and level to the riverbank. Halfway toward the water was a slumped figure, back toward him, that sat on haunches facing a mound of dirt. He recognized the mass of dark hair and the set of the young man's shoulders.

Sayid looked up when the shadow fell over him. "He saved me," he said, as if unsurprised to see his friend. "... got me here even though badly hurt. I found Aulus, your medic friend... who tended to him. Aulus told me he had done all he could, and"—Sayid gestured at the mound—"he lasted until this morning. With a cry that shook me awake, he struggled to stand but could only get to his knees. Then he reared his head up, looked around... I think hoping to see you. His head dropped to his chest again... and he died." He shook his head sadly, gazing down at the mound again. "I couldn't leave him there... in the camp. They're going around butchering the dead horses, and I thought he deserved better. I found Aulus again, and he got two mules... and we dragged him here. Where he can rest."

Nicanor knelt by the mound where Sayid had placed the harness, one Nicanor had fashioned himself for the large, broad head. He picked up the leather in a thick-tendoned hand, fresh blood seeping as the clots and newly formed scabs broke free from a slash that across the knuckles. He lowered his head, "I'll miss you, Abigieus." A swirl of wind twisted dust and dirt from the grave to spiral into the sky.

"Farewell, my friend—run with the gods." He laid the harness at the head of the horse's grave. As he stood, he reached down to Sayid, who gripped his hand and pulled himself up to stand beside him.

"I'm glad you're alive, Nicanor."

"Me, too. Are there any others... from Beth Horon?" Nicanor grunted, gripping his right leg, bright blood now showing through on a crude bandage at mid-thigh.

"There were two men—I didn't see them—that came in a day or day-and-a-half after we got here. They were astride a mule they must have found along the way. But they died that night. I heard they believed everyone else was dead."

Nicanor lurched—it was getting harder to lift the injured leg—and Sayid steadied him. "Nearly"—the centurion shook his head—"Thought I was for a while... I came to when the *canum fera* tugged the bodies of two dead rebels off me. Those carrion-eaters scared the Hades out of me, but I startled the dogs when I lunged up. Then I fell flat on my face, hit my head"—he touched a blood-crusted gash over his right eye—"That knocked me out again. How many days has it been?"

"Three since we got here, nearly five since escaping Beth Horon."

Minutes later, they passed through the wall's northern gate and the encampment entry, and the sentries gave them both a hard look until Nicanor pulled his cloak away to show his centurion's harness.

"Stop staring and return to your posts." He blinked as they moved farther into the camp to where the centurions, officers, and command tents would be located. The noise he had heard from below was louder, but something was missing. He could not quite figure out what as he looked around the camp and worked the aching muscles in his neck and cursed the painful stiffness in his hands.

Sayid shook his head as they passed more men as they moved deeper into the encampment. "I've never seen"—he turned to Nicanor, who also slowed to a stop.

"Seen what?"

"I mean... I've never seen men in camp and not heard cursing. At their work, at each other... at the food... at... at the army."

Nicanor nodded now. That was it—he never had in his soldier's life encountered that strange silence.

"The spirit is gone from the men's faces. They move and perform their duties, but since we got here, I see them drink and eat... but..." Sayid's voice faded.

"I understand them. Losing has a bitter taste and this—what happened at Beth Horon—more than most. Have you heard of any orders or plans?"

"Lord Gallus has not called a council of his staff, but surely he must soon. We can defend here, can't we?" Sayid asked.

Nicanor knew they could—they had the men—but for the first time looking at his fellow Roman soldiers, knew they needed to find the will. "We can hold... but not for long, not against an entire country. We cannot wait for them to pin us here to bleed us dry. The walls will not keep out a determined assault, and they might starve us into desperation. Lord Gallus will have to decide where we go... and soon."

IV

The legate has aged a decade, Nicanor thought as he studied Cestius Gallus's haggard face. "Sorry for the delay, Lord Gallus," he said. "I didn't want to come to you as I was when I entered the camp." He blinked and nudged higher the new bandage that held a thick square of cloth over the deep gash in his brow. Sayid had fetched Aulus, and the medic had sewn up his deepest wounds—head and thigh. But those were not the worst of his hurts... inside something had been torn from him as the rebels in the battle of Beth Horon had ripped away the 12th Legion's *aquila* and butchered his men. He had lost the part of him that wanted to remain a soldier. It had died with his men at Beth Horon. The centurion scrutinized Gallus and knew they understood one another. Gallus respected Nicanor as a man and a soldier and appreciated that the centurion measured those he served under and served with by those standards. They both knew that the men under them bore the burden of their decisions.

"Centurion, I did not know how badly hurt you were. I would have come to you or had a litter bring you to me."

"I'm fine, Lord Gallus. As long as I can stand... I can walk. And if I can walk, I can report to my commanding officer."

"I understand and appreciate the determination; please sit." Gallus gestured at his aide to help the centurion, who, with a grimace, lowered himself into a seat in front of the legate's camp desk and, with another clench of his jaw, stretched the injured leg out angled to one side. "I won't ask about Beth Horon," Gallus said, "about what happened after my leaving you and your men."

"You had no choice, lord. The rebels would have slaughtered thousands more."

"So, I sacrificed hundreds..."

"It was the only way to save the legion, Lord Gallus. Though it was a hard decision to make, you did what any good field commander must do."

Gallus's expression sagged, then tightened. "The two men that survived—at least survived the battle—reported the loss of our *aquila.*"

"That was my fault, lord." The pain in Nicanor's tone betrayed him. "Never has a legion lost its standard—that haunts me and will until I die... and then I hope the gods will forgive me."

"No, it's my fault, centurion. You had 400 men to fight against five times that number, and they held the heights above the pass.

"Still, lord... I was in command." Nicanor closed his eyes. The cries of anger from the Jews had echoed down on him and his men at daybreak when the rebels could see how small a Roman force remained. Their angry shouts were soon replaced with the screams of his men as the rebels poured from the heights onto the valley floor. That red tide of men and flashing blades washed over them, leaving heaps of dead Romans behind. He shook his head and opened his eyes to find Gallus leaning toward him, watching what passed over his face.

"And you were acting on my orders, centurion. Let's leave it at that... what's done is done and in the past. Now, we must face today—and what comes with the tomorrows the gods grant us."

"What are your orders for the legion, lord?" asked Nicanor. "Will you call staff to counsel and discuss options before you decide?" On his way to the commander's tent, he had passed Galerius Senna, the legion's senior military tribune, and Tyrannius Priseus, the Camp-Prefect. Senna had given him a hesitant, curt nod, and Priseus had given a cold glare that Nicanor had returned until the man looked away. They—Priseus, especially—were responsible for decisions that resulted in the legion's supply and equipment losses. That, he felt, ultimately led to the defeat at Beth Horon.

"After what's happened, things you too have seen and spoken of," Gallus said, "I think you realize I have no one I'm sure I can trust—except for you." He shifted a stack of parchment to the center of his desk and, reaching behind him, took a stiff new courier pouch of leather, sealed, and set it on top of the pile. "Learning that you live has been the only brightness in many dark days since I left Jerusalem." His eyes moved from the centurion to what was before him on the desk. "King Agrippa has taken his men and his allies' troops to return home and secure their lands against the rebels. We, for now, stand alone. I plan to hold here at Antipatris until I receive orders to do otherwise. We will defend ourselves and limit our aggression to raids for supplies."

He looked up at Nicanor. "But we will respond to any threats to Romans in Caesarea and Ptolemais. Those two seaports must remain open to us, as must the road to Alexandria. It's from those points that reinforcements—and my replacement—will probably come."

Nicanor doubted it would happen, but felt he must say it: "I hope the orders are for you to remain commander of the legion."

"We both know that it is improbable, centurion. But I'll do my duty—at least as I see it—until I'm relieved and lay this burden down for others to carry. Fate is fate, and mine is sealed. Which brings me to this"—he put a hand atop the courier pouch and documents, lifting the leather bag—"This contains my official report to Emperor Nero and includes copies of the original letters your Syrian friend brought to me at Mount Scopus outside of Jerusalem. Those, along with my report of what has happened since bringing the 12th Legion south from Antioch—which includes my suspicions some of my officers have sabotaged our efforts—must reach the emperor. But unless this is carried by the hand of someone I trust, I fear he will never see it"— he patted the pouch—"and know the truth."

Nicanor feared what was coming next and wanted no part in it. "Lord Gallus—"

The legate's raised hand stopped him.

"I have no one else I can depend on, centurion. In my report to the emperor, I also tell him a true account of your bravery... and request that you finally receive the reward long promised you."

"Lord, I..." What Nicanor was about to say faded at the expression on the man's face. Here was a man who had little left in him but the desire to do something right before he no longer could.

"Centurion, you have served and sacrificed much for Rome. I know I'm asking more from you, but there is not another man I can turn to. While I expect not to hold this influence much longer, I now have the power to ask the emperor to reward you and to expect he will grant it. And that is the only reasonable excuse to use you as a courier. You will protect this"—he touched the leather bag—"and see that it's put in the emperor's hands." Gallus paused to focus Nicanor's attention. "But you must not—and I know you hate lying as much as I, but if you're asked—and you will be asked directly or slyly... For your own safety, you must let no one know that you know what's in the report and letters."

Nicanor's head dipped, and Gallus stood. "Now go rest... think about my request and know that's what it is... a request and not an order. But I must have your answer tomorrow. If you do this, then maybe in Rome you can find a place to rest and heal... and leave this gods-forsaken war behind."

* * *

"What will you tell him?" Sayid asked.

Nicanor's slow, painful return to where Sayid had arranged a tent for him had also been a journey through his thoughts. Once before, he had felt it was time to step away from the fighting... from the land he was familiar with, but that would never be at rest. He had been drawn back. And now if he remained—even if there was not a war—among those that strained and bit at the Roman leash... how could he ever truly heal and be happy? He could do as Cestius Gallus asked—do his bidding this last time and see that the emperor had what the legate wanted him to have. Then it was up to Nero to look into it and to punish Tyrannius Priseus, Galerius Senna, and even Gessius Florus, who Nicanor knew must be at the root of it all. He could go to Rome and finish out his time in the army in a city with good beer, where he could find an equally good woman. *Is that what I still want?* He wondered.

"Nicanor?" Sayid touched the centurion's shoulder. "If you go, what will happen to me?"

"What's that?" Nicanor blinked his thoughts away and rubbed his eyes. "I don't know what I'll tell Lord Gallus... I have to think..." He shook his head, realized what the boy had just asked him, and almost answered with what he always had—until now—told himself when he questioned what was next for him: *Serve the legion.* He paused and focused on Sayid and not his own quandary. "What do you want to do?"

Sayid bowed his head, as if with his own memory or inner longing. "I would go to see my mother.... before they send far more than the 12th Legion into Judea. When that happens, I may never make it home to see her again."

* * *

The next morning Nicanor awoke and felt worse than the day before. The sunrise brightening the horizon had none of the cheer of past dawns. His head pounded, and his leg throbbed, shooting jolts of stinging pain with each step as he made his way to see Cestius Gallus to give him an answer. The sentry outside the legate's tent had him wait while he got the commander's aide to announce him.

"I'm not surprised to see you this early, centurion," Cestius Gallus said with a glance at the water-clock that drew Nicanor's eyes there, too. *Just half-past hora sexta...* The question of the day before still hung heavy in the tent. The silence grew as the legate waited. Then it was broken by the centurion's deep sigh.

"I'll do it, Lord Gallus... and to recover from my lingering injuries will explain my acting as your courier, but" Nicanor hesitated. He was not good at asking for favors, especially when it would seem the favor was the price for doing the legate's bidding.

"What is it, centurion?

"I'll do this... not for the reward... but for you, lord. Even if you can't or won't do this one other thing for me.... well, not me... for someone else."

"What is it that you wish?"

"Lord, I ask that you discharge Sayid the Syrian auxiliary from service, so he can travel to see his mother before the real war that's coming tears this region apart."

Gallus nodded. "We need every man, but I can do that. Are you sure? You know that traveling alone across the country could mean his death if the rebels capture him."

"Lord, if the boy—no, he's no longer a boy. If this young man... is anything... he's a survivor. He, too, has served Rome, and he deserves this."

V

Nero gazed at the verdant expanse before him set into the vast city that was still fire-scarred and smoke-blackened for much of its breadth. That return of foliage—brought from the countryside to replace what had been lost and to hasten new growth—came at great expense. But it was well worth it to make again the lush setting, the perfect location for the Domus Aurea being built over the bones of his former palace. Over 300 acres would include the structures, groves of trees, pastures with flocks, and his private vineyards. It would cover parts of the slopes of the Palatine, Esquiline, Oppian, and Caelian hills. Below were the mule-drawn carts and wagons—a steady antlike stream of them—hauling dredged earth away from the excavation of what would become an emperor-made private lake in the marshy valley between those hills.

With his private quarters remaining on Quirinal Hill, his golden house had been designed as a place of entertainment... of theater where he could revel. The three hundred rooms, to be sheathed in dazzling polished white marble, had been designed with richly varied floor plans. Niches and exedras—semicircular recesses, many crowned by a semi-dome, set into the exterior and interior facade and ringed with curved, high-backed stone benches. There would be pools inset in the floors and fountains splashing in the corridors. Mosaics, previously used only on floors, would inlay and line the many vaulted ceilings. The lower ceilings of stucco would be covered with ivory veneers and semi-precious stones. The frescoes, which would cover every surface not more richly finished, would be done by Famulus. That artist and the assistants from his studio would become responsible for adorning a spectacular amount of wall area with scenes of deep blue, green, indigo, purple, and cinnabar red in Famulus's fashion that would give motion to each scene. The coordinated frescoes were to carry different themes in each major group of rooms.

Many parts of the buildings were being constructed using newly developed concrete materials and architectural forms that reduced the need for quarried stone, lowering that cost—that more could be spent elsewhere.

His engineer-architects had, Nero thought, captured his imagination and desire to have finally a dwelling where he could live as a human being. Celer and Severus had designed two of the principal dining rooms to flank an octagonal court surmounted by a dome with a giant central oculus to let in light. They had also created an ingenious mechanism, cranked by slaves, that would make the ceiling underneath the dome revolve like the heavens. At the same time, perfume sprayed, and rose petals dropped on his guests.

In the main hall, another artist he had retained, Amulius, would paint upon the chamber's highest and broadest wall, a towering figure of Minerva. It would be made in such a way that wherever her spectators viewed her, she would watch them in return. Nero had seen the man's smaller works in that style, and the odd feeling of being studied by a work of art should prove even more powerful when the painting bore the eyes of a goddess.

The day before, he had visited the Greek sculptor and craftsman Zenodorus, who was at work on his imperial commission. The architects and engineers would place the colossal 100-foot high bronze statue of Nero just outside the main palace entrance, at the terminus of the via Appia, within a large atrium of porticoes that divided the city from his private villa. How appropriate to have the empire's main southern route, the regina varum, or queen of roads, start and end at his feet. An excellent place to lay the treasure to come from the southern provinces, he thought.

Nero turned from the view of his surroundings and inner vision to scrutinize the actual construction work... and it displeased him. That displeasure radiated from the emperor as had the heat from the great fire that had nearly destroyed the city a year and a half before. The workers—even the architects, being paid large sums to erect a building more edifice than a residence—hurried away from the sight of the scowling young emperor.

"Half-done only"—he muttered and darted dark looks at the nearby men—"and at such cost." To complete the work as planned required even more investment, and would the money come in time to quicken the pace? He tapped two fingers against his pursed lips. But what the workmen had done so far met what his mind had envisioned and followed the design drawings he had ordered. His thoughts went back to filling in what was to come and thinking of his joy at its completion.

The sounds of hooves striking stone and of the clatter of loose rock, the blowing of winded horses, and the rattle of armed men dismounting interfered with that return to his vision. The interruption bothered but did not alarm him. Two dozen Praetorian Guards surrounded him, at a close distance, at all times. Confident in his safety, he waited with back turned to the approaching footsteps that rustled and crunched on the gravel of the path used by the workmen's carts loaded with materials and trundled away empty to return with more.

"Sire." The steps stopped at the mandatory ten-foot distance from the emperor of Rome.

Nero continued to watch the men working and did not turn to the owner of the voice he recognized. "What is it, Tigellinus?"

"What we suspected is true."

Gathering his cloak about him, Nero faced his chief advisor and the Prefect of the Praetorian Guard. He motioned for him to come closer and then continued the gesture to wave away his four personal guards, the only ones allowed within arm's reach. Nero took three steps more from them, and Tigellinus followed.

"Gaius Piso's supporters have stirred trouble, sire, and I feel they plan more in the Senate. I don't have proof yet, but I trust my spies' report."

"I had nineteen of them executed—Gaius Calpurnius Piso included," Nero said with disgust. "Is it the 13 I agreed to merely exile? Are they back?" The emperor's eyes flashed at his advisor. "I knew I should have ordered their deaths, too!"

"No, sire"—Tigellinus rushed to placate him. An agitated and angry Nero was prone to rashness, and the two guards now had hands on the hilt of their gladii. Tigellinus paused as if to call down calm. "Remember, sire, there were nine others believed to be conspiring with Piso—his family's wealth swayed many to his side who were never revealed. I believe some of them were powerful men, intent on wresting power from you. They still pretend fealty—but have remained in the shadows. Puppet masters were out of sight, pulling the cords of those you punished, including Gaius Piso."

Nero stalked back and forth on the path and cursed, knowing that Piso and his ilk felt his decisions and overspending had diminished the empire's power, leading to the current unrest in some provinces. "I will rebuild Rome," Nero said, "and I'll still not be rid of them and my other troubles." He stopped, bringing the Prefect to a halt, too. "Gessius Florus has confirmed his new orders"—he cast a sideways glance at Tigellinus, who nodded—"and once the new Judean Procurator replacing him assumes his duties, Florus is to focus on one thing only... to squeeze more taxes out of any source in my southern provinces. But his main aim must be to acquire the Jews' treasury. He's proven so far that he can manipulate Cestius Gallus through the men he has co-opted, to set the stage... and now it's time for his intrigues to reward me. Jerusalem must fall, and its treasury becomes mine. But have your man in Caesarea keep a close watch on

Gessius Florus... I do not trust that man until the treasure is in my hands."

Nero began to turn away to dismiss the Prefect.

"Sire," Ofonius Tigellinus said nervously, glancing at the emperor's four personal bodyguards to gauge how far away they were and then at his own men who had remained far from him. "There's other news that I must give you."

Nero stopped at a half-turn, said nothing, his cold eyes looking over his shoulder and locking on the Prefect, a hand coming up with two fingers to tap his lips.

Tigellinus swallowed. "My spy rode several horses to death from Caesarea to Alexandria to catch a war galley to Ostia in time to carry a message to arrive as soon as possible. And... and that news is bad, sire." He took a step back, though Nero had not moved. "Cestius Gallus halted his attack on Jerusalem... and in their retreat from the city, the troops were ambushed and beaten. He lost several thousand men... and the Jewish rebels took the 12th Legion's aquila. Jerusalem has not fallen."

VI

Mathias looked with pride at his youngest son beside him at table... and then felt the draining of that warm spirit, his satisfaction diminished by his growing dread for Yosef... for them all. He felt pride because of the Sanhedrin's meeting at the Temple the afternoon before, how the leaders of Jerusalem acknowledged Yosef's intelligence and experience with the Romans as the main reasons for choosing him to become the military commander of Galilee. He was not selected for his lineage, though Mathias realized that partly had some influence.

All of Judea was now considered in rebellion, though some cities either remained pro-Roman or had taken recent events as an opportunity to break away and demand autonomy. But every citizen across the country knew that the Roman spear—the might of the empire's military—was soon to be hurled at its heart, Jerusalem. And that was where Mathias's fear—and that of so many others—had taken root and spread.

It had been decided that Eleasar ben Ananias, the current Temple Guard captain, would command in the south and in Jerusalem itself. Roman legions and their auxiliaries would come from Alexandria, Egypt, and possibly Caesarea and Ptolemais, near where Mathias now sat. Yosef believed those two ports were vulnerable and geographically suited for Jewish forces to pin the Romans against the sea, denying them the means to get a large number of men ashore and push them inland. Yosef thought—and he had said as much to the Sanhedrin at the meeting—the Romans would probably not bring their legions into those parts. More likely and almost certainly they would come through the north—Galilee—with the bulk of the Roman army to crush them from there. Galilee was abundant in the resources need to sustain Roman legions, and the Romans would plunder it at will.

That short statement had been what determined the decision that his son would command the defense of the northern region through which the Romans would move their forces south from Syria to attack the largest city in Judea. Yosef would lead the men—hold the Galilean towns and towns—that would initially bear the brunt of Rome's wrath in the path of the Roman juggernaut headed to Jerusalem.

Mathias glanced at his wife. Rebecca's fear for their sons overrode any remaining vestige of pride in him that their family now held an important role in defending their country and city. She lifted and draped her heavy braid of gray-shot hair over her right shoulder as she raised a pitcher of fresh well water from the table. She had not looked at him during the recitation of prayers, as she usually did at least once. That single glance signified their decades-long bond, their faith, and love for their children—that was something he counted on, especially in times of worry and trouble. He felt its absence from Shabbat keenly.

Rebecca must have felt her husband's eyes on her as she had so many times over the decades, but she did not respond. She would not blame the Sanhedrin's decision on him, but she knew that he had not objected to it. She drew in a deep breath and held it as she studied the faces of her three children. Mathias knew her thoughts: to keep them here... in this place and moment where they were safe and with their parents... as long as she could—that was all she wanted. With everything that had happened to them over the last three years... the future beyond today was far darker-looking than the past. She let the breath go as her eyes lifted to catch his.

Mathias, relieved, said mostly for her comfort, but directed to his son, "Yosef, I've spoken with Yohanan ben Zaccai, and he will travel with you to Galilee. He was raised there and has long been a religious leader and teacher for those who live in Galilee. His counsel and presence should help you."

"—But only with some people." Matthew ignored the expression of irritation from his father in return for the retort. "Almost all the leaders ignore ben Zaccai because of Yohanan ben Levi in Gischala. That man will be trouble for you, Yosef. Most of the other Galilean leaders follow him and do his bidding. And Sepphoris has always favored the Romans because the Greek aristocrats there made their fortunes in Roman trade. You'll find them difficult, too."

Rebecca spoke for the first time since the recitations: "You"—she shifted in her seat to face her husband—"you said last evening that Yosef will have two co-commanders accompany him. Is that so?"

Mathias nodded. "Yoazar and Yehoshua—two priests from the Temple."

"A couple of tithe-collectors, you mean." Matthew's laugh held no humor in it. "They have no military experience."

Rebecca looked puzzled. "Then why would they make them Yosef's co-commanders?"

"We need money to buy materials and arms to fight Rome," Mathias replied. "Yoazar and Yehoshua are to ensure Galilee contributes to that effort. The Galileans must not hoard their silver nor the crops and food they produce. We must have access to their fishing and processing capability—they must send Jerusalem its share of *opsarion*, to feed us in war as they did in peace. And the fees, the tolls for distribution and fishing licenses they used to pay to the Romans—those must go now to help fund the new Judean government and development of our army."

"Still, it makes no sense if they are to really help Yosef." Rebecca turned to look at her youngest son.

Yosef, who had been quiet, reached across the table to take her hand. "Mother, I'm needed to collect weapons to assess what we have to fight with to form and equip a defensive force and to get the northern cities to fight together and not against each other. They—we—must work together to fortify their towns and create plans to fight the Romans while we have time."

"Why do the Romans remain in Antipatris?" Miriam had been silent for weeks, rarely leaving her room. "Has the Roman legion's commander lost his will to fight us?"

Mathias blinked at her tone, almost as if she regretted that Cestius Gallus had halted the attack on Jerusalem. Yosef, too, drew back a bit and shook his head. "No, Miriam. But I think he had doubts—and still does—about the reasons and events that led to the assault... to all the distrust and fighting. The first time he showed this by sending an emissary, a Roman centurion I know and trust, Nicanor who you've met. Matthew and I met with him to discuss a stop to the fighting and to attempt again to resolve the issues between Rome and Judea. Then again—when Gallus pulled his men out of Jerusalem when they were about to breach our inner walls. Both events—those gestures on his part—could have been a path to peace. But"—he shook his head again—"our stupidity and inability to come together have ended that avenue." He paused and lowered his head for a moment before continuing.

"What happened during our"—Yosef looked up at his brother and then at his father—"our meeting with Nicanor at the Gennath gate was bad faith. A violation of the trust we had and our intention to talk peace. Then there was the decision to ambush the Romans as they pulled back from Jerusalem. That attack and the slaughter at Beth Horon and the taking of the legion's eagle, their standard... that will never be forgotten. Not even when"—Yosef shook his head at what they all knew was an inevitable outcome—"they return in force, overrun us, and devastate Judea."

Miriam's eyes flared and Mathias wondered again why she acted so, not in worry but in defiance. Of them all, she had changed the most, and he worried more for her than he did for his sons.

VII

Between Jerusalem and Sepphoris

"Tomorrow morning, we'll reach Sebaste, and from there, you say the road is better?" Yosef asked as he handed a goatskin of water to Yohanan ben Zaccai. The man was much older than Yosef and the other two men in their party but seemed the least tired of them all.

"I've used it many times," Yohanan answered. "It's a well-maintained Roman road from Sebaste to Megiddo, and from there on to Sepphoris. But you still believe we won't meet any Romans?" He looked at the two priests Yoazar and Yehoshua. "We're not exactly fighting men." He glanced at the sword sheathed at Yosef's waist, then took a deep drink and hung the water skin from the jutting stub of a limb on the fallen tree that served them as a seat.

Yosef laughed, following his eyes. "They're not much for walking fast for very far." He had more than once had to slow down for the two city priests. It was roughly 90 miles to Sepphoris from Jerusalem, and at their pace, it would take two days longer than he had thought. He had considered riding, but horses and mules caught the eye of brigands much quicker than did men on foot, and he worried as much about them as he did about the Romans. "Reports still say that Cestius Gallus and the 12th Legion remain in Antipatris. And you mentioned that the road was clear last week around the Roman encampment at Legio. The three of us ought to be able to pass by them without attracting attention."

I hope, anyway, Yosef thought, because there's no way to talk our way out of being taken captive. Since he was the only one armed, they would never stand a chance against a real Roman legionary.

* * *

Sepphoris

The mid-morning sun filled the valley on their left and below them, shining on the pools of standing water that dappled the ground as far as he could see. Yosef had heard of Beit Natofa, this fertile valley that began near Shikmona. This small harbor town produced the traditional *tekhelet* dye, the blue used for Jewish priests' Temple clothing. The valley ran southeast and then split northeast to where he now stood, on the range of steep limestone hills atop which

24

Sepphoris sat, overlooking that long and narrow valley. Every year it flooded with the winter rains, and the fertile soil and the abundant crops grown there contributed to the prosperity of Sepphoris.

Yosef had breathed easier that morning as they neared the road that climbed to the city. The dangerous area surrounding Legio was behind them; they had passed it with not a Roman to be seen. A trader on a mule cart barreling down the same path—nearly running over Yosef, and not stopping until he recognized Yohanan ben Zaccai—had confirmed why. The camp at Legio was empty. The Romans had been seen moving equipment and supplies to Ptolemais—*reinforcing their base there*, Yosef thought. Without secure supply lines, any Roman camp inland was at risk of being cut off. Until more legions could arrive, the Romans would focus on holding their coastal cities.

But his most crucial hope was not to get here without encountering Romans—most of all, he wanted to find countrymen who would stand in solidarity and face the Romans.

* * *

Yosef lifted his head to watch the bunched clouds, heavy and gray gathering above. His hope for help from Sepphoris now seemed doomed. Sepphoris had a distinctly Roman feel and look in the road leading to the city, the theater they had passed, and in the architectural features of several of the buildings. It was the wealthiest city in Galilee and the most distinctive. Unique, too, were the city leaders he had just left. They had told him, "We have no interest in your issues with Rome... or in your rebellion. You're welcome here, but we will not help or hinder your efforts. We ask you to leave us alone and leave us out of your rebellion."

Yosef met Yohanan ben Zaccai as he walked down the steps of the meeting hall to the main street.

Yohanan studied him. "I see by your expression your talk with them turned out as I told you to expect."

"Where are Yoazar and Yehoshua?"

"I left them with a man eager to talk about the great sums of money Yohanan ben Levi of Gischala is making with his exorbitant prices for corn and oil."

"That's who the city leaders suggested I speak to next," Yosef said. "They want me to rein him in from interfering with their trade. It appears they don't mind my help but won't give me theirs. They say people in nearby towns are complaining of ben Levi's attempts to extend his interests into their cities and villages."

"Is Gischala where we go next?"

"Yes, but not until I advise Jerusalem about what I've heard here—and of these rumors of profiteering. I need to know what they want me to do next."

"I've arranged a place to stay," said Yohanan, "a *pandocheion* owned by a man I know. With the rooms, he also provides food for guests, and his son can ride to Jerusalem with your message and question."

* * *

Four days later...

The innkeeper's son returned from Jerusalem just as Yosef dipped the last of his breakfast loaf into a small bowl of wine vinegar. Paying the exhausted boy, he opened the messenger pouch, took out the folded sheet of parchment, and read. His father had warned him, and what he just read had confirmed it. Minutes later, he found his companions.

"Take care of Galilee'... is that all they had to say? No advice on how?" Yohanan ben Zaccai shook his head. "Yosef, answers like that are why I've stayed far from Jerusalem... and its leadership—or lack thereof." That comment drew frowns from Yoazar and Yehoshua, and they moved away from him as he asked, "What now?"

"I must come up with that on my own, Yohanan. My father told me that Galilee has long been a problem for the Sanhedrin. A problem they can't seem to figure out."

"—Because they don't understand the common people," Yohanan raised his voice, then he shook his head and lowered it. "When Herod's construction work ended after hundreds of projects, steady pay ended too. Many thousands of the newly idle from Galilee now had no means of income—and Jerusalem had no answers for them... and no help either. So"—he motioned for Yoazar and Yehoshua to rejoin them—"now we go to Gischala?"

"No," Yosef answered. "Shimon ben Gamliel, speaking for the Sanhedrin did instruct me—us—to go to Tiberias first. The council has ordered that Herod's temple there be stripped of its pagan animal decorations. I've sent word ahead to Justus ben Pistus, leader of that city. We'll stop to be sure it's been done. Then to Gischala, where I'll arrange to meet with Yohanan ben Levi."

26

VIII

Yosef had purchased mules from the innkeeper in Sepphoris, sturdy, sure-footed animals that were used to climbing the hills of Galilee. We must move faster, Yosef thought, and with the Romans choosing to remain close to the coast, travel on four legs was better than on two. He caught the distant smudge of smoke and heeled the mule to quicken their pace.

"Something burns... in the town," Yoazar pointed ahead of them.

"Yes, that's usually what smoke means," Yohanan ben Zaccai observed with a glance at the man and slight shake of his head.

Thirty minutes later, they could better see the still-smoldering building.

"That looks like their temple," said Yoazar, slowing to fall farther behind.

Yohanan ben Zaccai nudged his mule forward alongside Yosef and leaned toward him as they approached a group of men standing close to the temple, but upwind of the billowing smoke. "The two in front that seem to argue are Justus ben Pistus, and the one with the shorn beard is a Greek named Capellus. He's a wealthy trader, loyal to King Agrippa... unless he's changed allegiance—and I doubt that."

They stopped their mules near the men. The Greek, Capellus, was shouting: "You know it was Yeshua ben Sapphias and his low-born men—and you know where to find them! You bow to Jerusalem and strip away what Jerusalem calls idols—and that has emboldened them. This"—he gestured at the nearly destroyed temple—"is your responsibility."

Justus ben Pistus's beard jutted with indignation. "Capellus, I could not stop them—"

"But you have men to go after them, right?" Cappellus's dark eyes swept toward a cluster of armed men near a copse of trees, standing among tethered horses, watching them and temple. "Order them to do so!"

"Yes, but they're not my—"

"Please,"—Yosef interjected as he dismounted and walked toward the two men—"pardon me, but if you have fighting men, you should be after those who did this."

27

"Who are you?" Justus ben Pistus demanded, his glare shifting beyond Yosef to the men with him. "Yohanan... who is this man?"— he gestured at Yosef.

"He and these two priests"—Yohanan indicated Yoazar and Yehoshua—"are appointed by the Judean government to command Galilee against the Romans."

"You're the Yosef ben Mathias who wrote me—at Jerusalem's orders—about stripping the pagan decorations from this temple?"

"Yes, and you agreed to do so." Yosef looked at Capellus, "You also said the other leaders would support such an order. It looks as though the unfortunate result has been this destruction. Greedy men, thinking they were suddenly entitled to such brigandry, stole from the temple. I think you'll agree that Jerusalem would want those looters caught and punished. As do we"—he waved a hand at his fellow commanders.

Yosef looked from the city's leader to the Greek and asked him, "Do you agree with Jerusalem on this, too?"

The Greek, nonplussed, paused, and then nodded. "Yes..."

"Then"—Yosef turned back to Justus ben Pistus—"please gather those men, have them mount, and I'll lead them."

* * *

Within a day they had cornered the looters, most of whom scattered and ran, leaving handcarts loaded with the temple's silver and gold. The men Yosef had commandeered had been quiet, not friendly nor much for conversation, but they knew how to track the looters. It had not taken long to run them down. Yosef worried at the men's hesitation to turn the laden carts back toward Tiberias—their expressions seemed to mask thoughts Yosef might not wish to know. But they had finally hitched the horses to the wagons and followed him back to the town. Now he sat at the single inn Tiberias offered travelers with Yohanan ben Zaccai, Yoazar, and Yehoshua. The latter two had stern—almost angry—expressions they cast at Yosef and at the Greek who sat across from him.

What Yosef had just told the Greek had alarmed the two priests and confused Capellus. "You're giving me the recovered silver and gold... to hold?"

"Yes, for King Agrippa,... it is his, isn't it?"

"Yes, but I thought..." The Greek trader still did not understand.

"You thought we would keep the looted treasure? Not all from Jerusalem, nor all Judeans, including Galileans... are thieves or dishonest. Our war is with Rome... not our countrymen. And not with

28

Agrippa—unless he remains allied with Rome and continues to fight us. I understand you are one of ten councilors aligned with him. I ask you to hold this treasure for Agrippa and consider my words and actions this day... repeat them for him."

Cappellus sat and blinked for several moments, then he nodded and got up from the table to leave.

"Jerusalem needs that money," Yoazar growled but kept his voice down, as there were many slaking their thirst in the inn's public room, but the words still cut through the air. Yehoshua beside him nodded grimly.

"Yes, but we need every one of our countrymen and sojourners to stand with us and not with Rome thousands of miles away," Yosef replied. "If we don't unify, we stand no chance against the Romans. If that silver and a little bit of gold 'buy' us some goodwill... then it's well worth the cost."

"And what if it doesn't?" The voice rang out and silenced the room. Yosef turned toward the speaker, the man standing next to Justus ben Pistus, who continued, all ears listening. "Then, you've given back money we could use to fight the Romans, and Agrippa has more money to help fight alongside the Romans against us."

Yosef asked the man, knowing the answer, "And who are you?"

"Yohanan ben Levi of Gischala. It was my men you took to chase the looters to retrieve the money they stole from the temple. Now you give it back to the Greeks. It makes me wonder—yet again—which is the greater enemy... Rome or Jerusalem. And now because of your decision, Yeshua ben Sapphias and his men are killing the Greeks who live here and in the nearby villages. The poor ones, those not protected by money, power, and position." He shook his head and scanned the room, eyes lingering on each man. "Is that the wisdom we should expect from Jerusalem," his glare swung to focus on Yosef, "and its leaders?"

IX

AT SEA, TO ROME

This is not the season to be where I have no wish to be, thought Nicanor as he spat over the ship's side. And I can still taste the sea here. But so far, no storms... no wreck... no swimming with sharks. The bireme *Mercurius* was three days from Ostia, and the passage, despite the stormy time of year, had been uneventful. Nicanor missed the company of Sayid and Yosef... and Lady Cleo... Those friendships he would never have imagined before his previous voyage to Rome from the southern provinces.

Cestius Gallus had fulfilled his request and given Sayid permission to leave the legion to see his mother. Sayid had been alight with joy at the news, but that joy had dimmed when Nicanor had told him he had accepted orders to Rome. Nicanor had left Judea wondering what would happen to Sayid, and to Yosef and Lady Cleo. The pitch and yaw of a ship at sea had aggravated his injured leg, turning its twinges into a steady throb of pain. That and the ache of his damaged shoulder had reaffirmed his belief he had made the right choice. The Jewish rebels at Beth Horon had nearly killed him, and it was time to put fighting behind him. It had long been part of his life. To be out of the fighting, he must go where there was peace, finish his time, and retire. Yet, he regretted he would never see his friends again.

The previous sea leg of his journey on the *triconter* from Caesarea to Alexandria had been more entertaining. The centurion leading his escort—a novelty, as Nicanor had never been 'escorted' anywhere—had held his interest for the short transit. Nicanor had asked about the new Procurator they had accompanied on the trip from Rome. It seemed he was a better man than Gessius Florus. Would that Lady Cleo could have Florus replaced as her husband, too. After that conversation ran its course, the centurion had told stories of a man who had joined them in Alexandria, a metals trader with authorization from the Egyptian Prefect himself to travel with them to Caesarea. The man had spent most of the time below deck in the cargo hold with his stores, and that had piqued the centurion's interest.

"The man did not seem to like daylight, Nicanor... or other people. I might have heard him speak only a dozen words the whole time. But he had a lover's touch when he sharpened a blade. One of the men saw him honing the two daggers he always wore at his waist and asked him to put a good edge on his new pugio... you know how a new dagger's metal takes a bit of work to sharpen? Well, the man—he had some Greek name—returned the dagger later, and the man said he could shave with it. When I heard that and ran my thumb over his blade, and sure enough, it was razor-sharp. I took my faithful pugio and gladius to him, too, hoping he could smooth out their nicks and notches. After years with me, the haft and hilt of both were worn to fit my hand comfortably, and I did not want to replace my weapons. Without a word, he took them and got to work. I watched him, sunlight shafting down from the open hatch with more light on his face from a lantern at his side that also caught the sheen of the metal in his hands. His touch was like that of a man in bed with a lover, but not some *taberna* serving wench earning a coin. He had the look of a smitten man devoted to his wife. It was the only time I saw any flicker of a change to his expression. I think his name was Hananiah... something like that."

Nicanor had then inspected the centurion's weapons. Both dagger and short sword smoothly shaved hair from his forearm. Holding their blades under the light, he turned and rotated them to study them carefully, and he could not find a single flawed stroke, not one cross-grained scratch. The metal was unblemished. "The man is a craftsman," he had said as he handed the knife back to the centurion.

"Smooth. Like a young virgin's thigh, right?" the centurion had quipped with a grin, "and almost as deadly." I'll remember that one... a skilled man but strange."

The stories ran out as they arrived in Alexandria.

On this second leg of his journey, Nicanor had spent most of his time within his own thoughts. Gallus's orders had not been that he just join the escorts for their return to Alexandria. He also had the authority, once in Alexandria, to order a ship to take him immediately to Rome. As soon as he stepped off the coastal vessel at Alexandria, he had gone straight to the port master. His orders were, as usual, for a centurion, folded and tucked into the stiff *balteus*, the sword belt at his waist. But the sealed pouch with Cestus Gallus's private report and copied letters for Nero was strapped flat across his midriff, giving him the portly appearance of a veteran beer-drinker. He looked forward to losing that weight in Rome.

31

X

Rome

The roads that led into Rome seemed less maintained than before, Nicanor thought, as he jolted along in the carriage with others coming from Ostia. The approach to the city was dotted with almost as many enclaves as when he had left Rome three years ago. But the temporary dwellings for the poor had taken on a permanent appearance.

The sun was setting as he stepped down from the carriage at the inn, he recalled Yosef had used before. He touched the purse full of coins Cestius Gallus had given him and remembered his detailed instructions: "Centurion, you travel on my personal directive, not the Roman army's orders. So, you will not be expected, and you must not report in nor arrange barracking. Take this money and, when you arrive in Rome, stay somewhere modest. The next early morning, go to the Comitium—it's part of the *forum romanum*—located between the Capitoline and Palatine hills. The office of the Prefect of the Praetorian Guard is near the Tabularium, located in the western area. And you must go through the Prefect, Ofonius Tigellinus, both to get a private meeting with the emperor and to secure your placement in the guard. That should not be an issue, as you're qualified and deserve it... and the emperor had approved you previously. Take only my personal orders, not my report nor the copied letters. I am not sure of Tigellinus, so tell him you'll deliver the documents to the emperor yourself. I do not know if I'll hear of what happens with this, Nicanor, or to you, but I pray the gods will favor you."

* * *

The night before, Nicanor had been surprised by the gossip and rumors that usually made a taberna lively at the dinner hour and drinking that followed. That night's interchanges lacked the usual jollity. There were complaints about the slow reconstruction of parts of the city even with the tax increases, and hints of anger and spite at the resources and manpower the emperor was putting into his "magnificent" Domus Aurea. The provinces had the usual dissent, but little was mentioned about the Jewish revolt in Judea. And nothing about the 12th Legion's defeat.

That still puzzled him as he ate his breakfast of barley gruel and fruit, thankful for Gallus's coin that enabled that purchase. Prices had gone much higher since the fire. Wiping his mouth with a cloth, he stood dropping a coin on the table. It was time to find Tigellinus.

* * *

"Please send word to Prefect Tigellinus that I wish to see him." Nicanor, in full regalia, was imposing, especially with his scarred face and the bearing of command he wore as easily as his centurion's cloak.

"On what matter, centurion?" The clerk looked up from his worktable centered like a sentry gate just within the office building.

"A matter to be discussed only with the Prefect."

"Do you have orders to see him?"

"I have this"—Nicanor handed him an authenticated copy of Cestius Gallus's travel orders and the legate's order for him to request—through the Praetorian Guard Prefect—a private audience with Emperor Nero. He had arrived at the Comitium, found the Tabularium, and gone inside this headquarters of the empire's extensive records to ask someone to point out the guard's offices. There a man at a table just inside the entry stopped him to ask, "Do you need copies of any documents, centurion?" The man had lifted a wooden-handled stamp on a leather cord around his neck. "I can do them quickly for you." It had seemed a good idea to have a legally authenticated copy of Gallus's orders, so he had handed the man the document and minutes later paid him and tucked the originals into his sword belt.

The Prefect's clerk checked the scribe's seal, verifying that the copy he held matched the original, and nodded. "He's not here, centurion, but"—the clerk motioned a young slave toward him—"I will get your request to him." He scribbled a note to put with Nicanor's copy of the orders. Then he wrapped it all with a strap and slipped it into a leather pouch with a fold-over flap that he sealed with a blob of wax and stamped with a seal he took from a drawer. "Please check back this afternoon, and you should have a word about meeting with the Prefect."

* * *

Three days later...

The emperor had changed since Lady Cleo's welcome-home party, Nicanor thought. Dark bags under his eyes, puffy face.... a layer of fat beginning to obscure the line of the young emperor's jaw. His ruler seemed merely curious about meeting at the request of a lowly centurion... even one he had met once before. The Prefect, however, looked displeased, and Nicanor understood why. Their meeting had been awkward—Cestius Gallus had been right. Tigellinus had his own idea of who should and should not see the emperor. He wanted Gallus's report and letters before considering asking the emperor for a private meeting. Nicanor had respectfully refused, telling the Prefect they were safe and in good hands, and he would bring them with him to the meeting with the emperor. The responding expression on Tigellinus's face was worrisome.

After that morning at the Prefect's office, Nicanor had recalled the night of the fire and gone to the site of the Lady Cleo's destroyed domus. He smiled at the memory of Sayid fighting with the singed bird and remembered carrying Cleo's major domus, Graius, from the fire, saving the man's life. He scanned the area, noting again the contrast between the green of the hills where the affluent were rebuilding and the still-devastated grayish-black parts of the city where the lower classes of Rome had lived.

What should I do? He wondered. Lord Gallus had his original letters and report, but Nicanor knew the man's fate was determined— he would not survive his defeat. But if Tigellinus took the copies Nicanor had and did nothing, his delivering the information would have served no purpose. How could he ensure that somehow someone other than he knew what Lord Gallus wanted the emperor to know? Graius—that's it! He recalled Cleo had retired the man as she planned her move to Judea, and Graius had then gone to Cleo's father's household. And there Nicanor had found him. Graius had recognized him. Of course, he would hold the package of information for the man who had saved him—his lady's friend—and keep it safe until he heard from Nicanor.

"Sire, and Lord Tigellinus"—Nicanor focused on the present and handed the packet to the Prefect—"this is the information Lord Gallus wished me to give to you personally."

"But why, centurion?" Nero asked.

"I believe he had concerns, sire, that it might not reach you through normal means."

"Do you know the contents?" Tigellinus raised the packet and gave it a shake.

34

Nicanor dug a thumb into his still healing thigh, pain shot through the wound, and that helped mask the lie he found so distasteful to speak. "No, lord... sire..."

"Are you hurt, centurion?" Nero's eyes narrowed as he studied Nicanor.

"I'm recovering, sire. A wound... the leg still pains me." Nicanor straightened. "I'll soon be fully healed, sire, and fit for duty."

"I hear that you told the Prefect you fought at Beth Horon." The emperor nodded toward Tigellinus, who had opened the pouch. The legion's report was on top, and he was reading it.

"Yes, sire... I believe Lord Gallus has details in his report."

"The legate lauds and commends your bravery, centurion"— Tigellinus looked up—"and says you should be rewarded... with a position in the Praetorian Guard."

"I did my duty for Rome, lord... I seek no reward."

Tigellinus passed Gallus's report to Nero, who scanned it and said, "But Lord Gallus, the 12th Legion's commander feels you should receive one.... a reward you had been offered before. But then you asked for something else. Why accept it now?"

Nicanor let the pain show again, and some of his weariness. "I've served Rome for many years, sire... all in what have become unforgiving lands for Romans. I'd like to finish my service to the empire here at its heart, and then retire in comfort."

Nero pulled at his lower lip, rings flashing as they reflected the light streaming into the room from the bank of westward-facing windows. "Why did the 12th Legion fail in its mission, centurion?"

"Sire, I'm sure Lord Gallus has information on that in his report."

"I'm asking you, centurion. You were there. You have thoughts... you've served a long time in the army and fought in many campaigns. Surely you have an opinion."

Tigellinus had shuffled through all the letters. "And Lord Gallus has the originals of these?" he held a handful of parchment up and rattled the sheets.

"I don't know about that, lord. In this, I'm only my commander's courier."

"Was it your commander's failures and mistakes that led to this embarrassing defeat?" Nero leaned toward Nicanor.

He was not going to dishonor Cestius Gallus. "I believe—and I witnessed it, sire—Lord Gallus received bad advice, sire." Nicanor did not flinch from the emperor's glare.

"Perhaps." Nero leaned back and flicked a hand at Tigellinus. "We'll read this information, centurion, and consider this request. Check with the Prefect in three days to learn my decision."

35

* * *

After the centurion left, Nero stood and paced the room. "Have him followed, Tigellinus."

"Yes, sire, I've already planned that... a man awaits him in the street. I don't trust that he tells the truth."

Nero nodded. "I think it best to give him his reward... and keep him close. See to it... assign him to where he can be watched."

"As you wish, sire." Tigellinus bowed to leave.

"And find me a general—a competent one but not ambitious—to replace that fool, Gallus."

XI

"You should rest, my friend; I know you plan to leave early tomorrow morning." Mathias put a hand on Yohanan ben Zaccai's shoulder. "Stay with us here—you can sleep in Yosef's room."

"Yes, Yohanan," Rebecca said as she cleared the dinner dishes from the table in the courtyard. "Miriam, take these away, please"— she handed her daughter the empty bowls—"and bring some fruit and more water." She turned back to the priest. "Please stay, and if you can take a few more minutes before you sleep, tell me more of what my youngest son is doing"—she waved a hand at the sheaf of pages on the table, letters he had brought from Yosef—"More than what's in those."

Yohanan's eyes had followed Miriam. "Your daughter, —he glanced at Mathias—"is so much thinner than when I saw her last. But she doesn't seem ill—not happy... but not sick, which is good. But...." He shrugged and smoothed a tangle in his beard, then shifted in his chair to smile at Rebecca. "Yosef is a fine young man, intelligent and a studier—and questioner—of all around him, mostly the people. I have known that since he sojourned with the Essenes years ago, and now his experience in Rome has matured him even more. But he's a deep thinker who tries to find a single solution to satisfy all."

"Isn't that good... the right thing for him to do and what he should do?" Rebecca asked, looking from the priest to her husband.

"Yes, but it's not a simple thing to accomplish." Mathias nodded to his wife.

"It's impossible," Matthew said, his first words at the dinner. Matthew had effectively become the Temple Guard captain, with Eleasar ben Ananias now in command of southern Judea, and all were stretched thin, maintaining night and day watches and helping to supervise a dozen crews working to strengthen the city's defenses. "Eleasar has it much easier than Yosef, whose letters confirm what we feared. All—well, most here"—his arm swept out to include the city and beyond, to the west and south—"most listen to and obey him." Matthew shook his head. "That's not what my brother has to deal with."

"Galilee is complex," Yohanan agreed, "as Yosef says,"—he tapped the letters. "So many pieces—the towns and villages whose leaders have their own demands—they may never come together."

37

"Then the Romans will cut through them—chop them down—one by one." Miriam set the tray of dried figs, apples, and dates and the water pitcher next to her father, who slid them closer to their guest.

Yohanan was surprised at the aggressive tone of the words, accurate as they might be, coming from a young lady he had watched grow from birth. He looked at Rebecca, who was studying her daughter, a flash of concern passing over the mother's face. "Yes, Rebecca, that's what your brother fears, as do many." He turned to Mathias. "And that's what he hopes to prevent from happening—and we must prevent it." He poured water into his cup and took a fat fig from the tray.

"Will he... can we"—Miriam's eyes swept those at the table—"bring the Galileans together?"

"I don't know," Yohanan said, shaking his head wearily and wiping his lips with a cloth, "but Yosef's working on that... and I'm trying to help him as best I can. While I'm gone, serving as a courier and speaker of sorts for him, Yosef is getting together with Yohanan at Gischala for talks. As the northernmost large town in Galilee, Gischala is important to its defense. Yosef needs a town like that to serve as his headquarters in the region, a location he can secure against the Romans when they come. He believes they will not bypass such a stronghold and hopes to hold them up, delay them as far north as possible, and give you and Jerusalem as much time to prepare as he can." He nodded toward Mathias, "And he hopes to hear a positive response to the Sanhedrin's call for allies."

"All who aren't with us against the Romans are our enemies as much as Rome is." Miriam's tone was flat and cold. "Perhaps that is a message that Yosef—and you—can give those in Galilee, or give any who refuse to help fight the Romans. That's something for them to think about." She turned from them, and seconds later, they heard her climbing the steps to her room.

Yohanan ben Zaccai looked around the table at the others, lingering at Rebecca and Mathias. "I remember the fullness of her smile as a child... where has it gone?"

"She is still young," Mathias sighed.

"—But not stupid." Rebecca shot a sharp look at her husband. "Mathias, she is a grown woman who thinks and feels as many do... as an adult with a strong belief does."

"And she's not wrong, Father"—Matthew stood and stretched, covering a yawn with one hand—"Yohanan, tonight I must write Yosef about his contacts with the Essenes. When you return to Galilee, will you deliver my letter to him for me and ask him to reply as quickly as he can?"

"Of course. Please... all of you write to him," said the old priest. "I know he feels alone with this burden he bears... hearing from you will help him carry it."

XII

Miriam took the soft-leather-wrapped bundle from beneath her bedding and listened for any steps, especially her mother's soft tread, outside her door. Reassured that no one might walk in on her, she carried the packet to the table by the window, setting it beside the lamp Zechariah had given her. That lamp was her only possession she prized more than the blades he had also given her. Tilting it, she traced with a fingertip the lines on the bottom of the lamp, Zechariah's carving of a *hamsa*, the Hand of Miriam, for her protection. She set it down to one side, lighted it, then sat to undo the cord securing the bundle. Unrolled on the table, it revealed the two blades in their sheaths, and a small bladder of the oil Zechariah had shown her was best to use with the rectangular sharpening stone that lay between the daggers.

It had become a nightly ritual, the honing of her blades. Only lightly—a few strokes more out of reverence than need—if the blades had not been used. She would make more strokes when the daggers had served their purpose. A dull knife does no good, Zechariah had drilled into her, and his meaning had been as much for her training as it had been about the sharpness of her knives. Lately, she had not had a reason to wield them. It disturbed the part of her that remained from who she had been before Zechariah had helped her, but she increasingly wished she did have a reason.

The scuffle of steps was a second ahead of the knock on her door. Already moving, she flipped the ends and corners of the leather piece over her weapons and stepped to the door carrying the lamp, leaving the table darkened. "Yes?"

"Miriam, you should write Yosef... I'm going to write to him now, and Yohanan will take our letters with him when he leaves tomorrow."

"I will, Matthew... goodnight."

"Goodnight."

She waited until she heard him enter his room and settle down. At the table, she finished her routine and re-wrapped the blades, the oil and stone, and put them back under her bed. Returning to sit by the lamp, she took out a parchment, pen, and ink. Thankful her father had insisted she learn how to read and write unlike most women in Jerusalem, she dipped her pen and then set it down.

40

What can I tell him? she wondered. *Can I say that as often as I can I sneak to the Lower City... to an old blind potter's shop, the home of the man who was killed protecting me because I'm a female Sicarii assassin who has killed Romans or Roman agents? One of them had tracked her... to kill her. But the old blind man was also a deadly fighter who had trained her to fight. He taught her well, and she killed his killer. And now, she still practiced at the shop, where he taught her how to handle a dagger, how to creep up on a target, how to disappear quickly after she struck. Every time she trained, she worried she would be caught there. But I have nowhere else to go. I want to tell someone who cares for me about what happened to me. Talk about how I feel about what I've done... though I have had good reasons.* She rubbed her eyes with the palms of her hands. *But I won't tell him that I want to keep doing it and that when the Romans come, I will.*

She picked up the pen, and instead of writing what she wanted to say, she wrote what she could:

Yossi, we all miss you, but I do most of all. You have always listened to me and respected my thoughts; I always felt better after talking with you. Mother and Father, these past few years, do not understand how I think about the things that have happened, and I know I'm not good at talking about it with them. They grow older and more tired every day... but parents must all feel a terrible weight when their children live in a time like ours and face events as we do now. Before you left, we talked of Leah and Rachel.

She paused—bringing those two up could deflect Yosef's questions that made her uncomfortable. Someone else's troubles diverted attention from her secrets.

Leah's situation is the same; married to a brute she detests. Rachel—I see her in the market sometimes—helps her sister cope as best she can. Leah's predicament saddens all of us, but when Rachel asks about you, which is every time I see her, it seems to cheer her up to talk of you. She has such a generous heart and only wants to help others. I hope she finds a man who will love and care for her.

She wrote for a few minutes more on mindless things, then ended and sealed the letter, leaving it on the table. Picking up a small, bronze, cone-shaped cap by its stub of a handle, she snuffed out the lamp. As she lay down, the uncertainty she felt so often crept over her, there was so much unknown for so many she knew. What would come in the days and nights ahead?

* * *

Unlike his brother, who could just sit down and write effortlessly and sometimes seemingly endlessly, Matthew had to drag the words from his head to put them on paper. He tapped the pen's blunt end against his forehead before dipping its copper nib into the small jar of ink. His mother had cured him of that head tap after he loaded his pen with ink and splattered it on his clothing—she made him practice his writing without a tunic on. It had taken only two winter mornings at their courtyard table to stop that bad habit. He sighed and loaded the nib:

Yosef, from your letters, that Yohanan delivered, you sound well but frustrated. I know you expected that at first but also that you hoped to make progress. I pray you soon get past the difficult part of establishing trust with the Galileans. We need them in the coming days. Here, the Zealots and others still resist trying to work together for the common good. Some think the Romans showed by their retreat and defeat they do not wish to fight us. They are only a small voice; those with any sense knows the Romans will retaliate. So, tension is high in the city. I worry that the leaders of the city will not unite until the Romans are at our gates. And that it will prove too late. So, we must now do what we talked about some time ago. To protect the Temple treasure, we must continue with our plans to move and hide it. I will only send messages regarding this with Yohanan ben Zaccai. He is respected and revered by many, especially outside of Jerusalem, and will not be interfered with as a messenger.

The nib scratched dry, and he lifted to rap the pen's other end against his head. *Should I bother him about the other things that worry me? He has so much on his mind. No*—Matthew set the pen down—*I'll talk to her.* He blew on the parchment, folded it, folded it again, and sealed it with a wax stick he had warmed over the table lamp. *And if she won't tell me... I'll follow her and find out where she goes.*

XIII

The sunset behind the stable had lined its frame in reddish-orange and ochre as Yosef approached the corral behind the inn. His mule saw him near the fence and, familiar with the routine set since they'd left Sepphoris, lifted his head to drape it over the top rail. Yosef fed him two handfuls of salted wheat and barley from the small bag he carried.

He felt even more alone since he had watched Yohanan ben Zaccai, astride his own mule, head to Jerusalem. He had asked the old priest and teacher to deliver his report to the Sanhedrin about the Tiberias temple destruction, the capture of the looters, and his return to the Greeks what treasure belonged to Agrippa and why he did it. He knew that action would stir anger with many in Jerusalem, just as it had with Yoazar and Yehoshua.

Yohanan of Gischala, the man in the region he most needed to talk to, had disappeared, leaving Tiberias shortly after his barbed parting shot to Yosef at the inn.

Yosef had told Yohanan ben Zaccai that while he was in Jerusalem, he planned to seek out the Gischalan leader and have what would be a difficult conversation, but a necessary one. Yet he had stalled, and he now regretted sending the old priest to Jerusalem. Although ben Zaccai was the courier least likely to be accosted or attacked, Yosef would rather have him at his side when meeting Yohanan of Gischala. But now he could wait no longer. With a last stroke of the mule's muzzle, he went to find Yoazar and Yehoshua to tell them they would leave for Gischala in the morning.

Entering the inn, he heard his companions' voices in the eating area and spotted them at a table in the far corner facing the entry. Across from them sat a man whose broad back was toward Yosef. As he approached, he saw it was Yohanan of Gischala. Sitting before them on the table was a basket made of plaited date palm leaves and covered by a square of cloth.

Yoazar and Yehoshua stood when they saw Yosef. The Gischalan leader glanced over his shoulder, then pushed the basket toward them. It seemed heavier than it looked as Yehoshua lifted it, both arms wrapped around it, from the table. The two walked past Yosef with barely a nod and without a word.

Yosef half-turned to watch them go. Then he took a seat across from the Gischalan. There was an awkward silence at first, and then Yosef said, "May I ask Yohanan, what were you talking about with them?"

"Gischala has no need of you... nor of Jerusalem. Nor does Galilee."

"You don't speak for all of Galilee, though, do you?"

"I will soon enough." The Gischalan crossed his arms and locked eyes with Yosef.

"Why did your men help me get back the gold and silver stolen from the Tiberian temple?" Yosef asked.

"I had heard you were in Galilee and told my men to watch for you. When they heard you wished to go after the looters, they knew I would want to see what you would do with it—who you would support with these funds." Yohanan's beard bristled with the jut of his chin. "And as I thought, you have your own interests."

"Only to sway Agrippa or some of his men to our side."

Yohanan snorted. "There is no 'our.' We—my people—we don't need them. We can fight the Romans."

"Not alone, you can't, Yohanan. All Jews in Judea and Galilee must band together."

"There are many I can gather to my side... to fight for Galilee. You Judeans care only for Jerusalem." He stood and strode from the room.

Yosef rubbed his brow with the palm of a hand and accepted the cup of wine the innkeeper had thoughtfully foreseen might be needed. Considering going after the Gischalan, he decided to wait until he had seen the many other Galilean leaders he must meet in dozens of the surrounding towns. He trusted—or hoped—that honesty and proof of integrity would convince them and draw men to fight with him for greater Judea, not just for Galilee. He emptied the cup and went to look instead for Yoazar and Yehoshua.

They were in their rooms, counting coins from the plaited basket set on the table between them. The cloth had been removed to reveal a pile of silver.

"What's this?" Yosef pointed at the stacks.

"The leader of Gischala has paid us its tithes—what was owed and enough against the future." Yoazar's eyes flashed at Yosef, and he had a slight curl to his lip. "We will return to Jerusalem with it and leave Galilee yours to command. This was our job here... to collect taxes."

Yosef disheartened that all it took was bribes to weaken the effort to unite Galilee, left them sweeping the coins from the table into two leather bags.

XIV

PTOLEMAIS

The domicile of the imperial collector of revenues and tribute for the empire's southern and eastern provinces was not as elaborate as that of the Procurator of Judea in Caesarea, and Cleo hated it just as much for who she shared it with. In the middle of the atrium was the *impluvium*, a shallow pool sunk into the floor to catch rainwater from the roof. Cleo sat beside it and wept. She had never cried much—not as a child, not even during the aftermath of the *Salacia's* shipwreck when death was so near—until the past year. But even in these miserable months, she had never cried in front of her husband Gessius Florus—only when she thought she was alone.

Cicero shuddered, preening and strutting upon his perch, rattling the cage beside Cleo. The bird's unrest, which always preceded testing his voice and the words he knew, shook her from the worry and fear that had increasingly gripped her. Her husband's anger always teetered on an edge that had grown thinner every day, and it did not take much for him to lash out at her. But his dislike of her only companion had broadened and deepened, so she always kept Cicero at her side. To leave him alone for too long could tempt Glaucio to extend his cruelties and feel his master's approval in doing so.

She heard a rattle and clatter from the portico grow louder as it neared, and she quickly stood, grabbing the cage's carrying handle. From the corner of her eye, she saw her husband had returned. He was followed as always by the centurion he had brought from Alexandria, the man who had been his blunt instrument, the enforcer of things Gessius Florus would not dirty his hands with since their arrival in Judea.

The last two days without her husband had been peaceful, though full of worry. Cleo still did not know whether Sayid had died in the fighting or what would happen to her if Florus found out about her secret letters to Octavia and what they contained. Her mind had turned and turned to think of some way of escape, but how could she... in a foreign land now aflame with war? She turned toward her rooms at the other end of the residence and regretted it was not as large as the

Procurator's palace in Caesarea. Here in Ptolemais, she could not get as far away from the man she loathed and feared.

* * *

Entering his office, Gessius Florus detached his heavy cloak and swung it from his shoulders. Hanging it from the peg on the wall behind his desk, he turned to Capito. "You spoke directly with Galerius Senna and Tyrannius Priseus?"

"Yes, lord, just outside Antipatris, and they confirmed that the legate Cestius Gallus has agreed to the request of the new Procurator, Marcus Antonius Julianus."

"So, he'll move the 12th Legion—what's left of it—north, and leave half in Caesarea under Tribune Senna's command, and bring the rest here," Florus repeated. "Good… if they are remaining in the area, they can still serve a purpose."

"—To convince the legate to regain his honor, and that of the legion, by assaulting Jerusalem again?"

Florus gave the man a withering stare. "Would Gallus agree to split his legion if he had considered doing that?"

Capito had learned enough to be quiet after saying something ill-thought-out that irritated Gessius Florus.

"That won't happen until Gallus's replacement arrives." Florus wondered yet again who Nero would send—likely someone in political favor or who could provide the emperor with some advantage. Whoever it was, he must sway him or at least ensure he did not interfere with his plans. "And with him will come more men and equipment to turn Jerusalem's walls into rubble and to crush the rebels." He took the scroll of parchment tucked inside his tunic and rolled it between his palms. "Senna and Priseus can still help counter or refute any excuses or explanations Gallus has offered the emperor for his embarrassing defeat."

Through the office doorway, he heard the squawking of his wife's pet echoing through the halls. "That damn bird," he muttered as he unrolled the message, he had received that morning.

"What's that?" The centurion took a step closer to the desk.

"None of your concern"—Florus waved the man away—"Go find Glaucio—I'm sure he has things to tell me." He waited for the centurion to go, then bent over the scroll to re-read it. This man—an

48

Idumean—had hidden well his festering hatred for Jews. And that hate seemed surmounted only by his greed. The death of Yehudah ish Krioth, his spy in Jerusalem's Sanhedrin, had led him to discover a man even better suited to help him from within the Jews' leadership. This man could trace his lineage to the Kings of Edom, whose country had been taken by the Jews long ago and his people forced to assimilate—to accept the Jewish faith or be banned from the land of their birth. To bring that ethnic hatred to the fore had taken only the Jewish rebel leader Simon bar Giora's recent attacks on the Jewish converts of Upper Idumea, plundering the surrounding villages and countryside in that region. Florus shook his head and folded the parchment. These Jews seemed bound to continue to destroy their own country... and he would pick up the valuable pieces from its ruin.

XV

ROME

Nicanor followed Ophonius Tigellinus, and his Praetorian Guard escort up the Gemonian Stairs that climbed from the Roman Forum to the Arx Capitolina, the fortress atop the spur of the Capitoline Hill overlooking Rome. On the left slope was the Tabularium he had visited previously and the Temple of Concordia, a series of shrines to the goddess. On the right was the Tullianum, the prison he had visited with Yosef so that he could speak with the imprisoned Jewish priests a lifetime ago.

After a steep climb, they reached the top, and Tigellinus stopped as the steps leveled into a raised landing that farther descended onto a gravel path. Nicanor kept the stoic expression he had assumed within the first dozen steps of the climb as he followed the Praetorian Prefect and his two men. Other than gripping his leg where the thigh joined at his hip, he ignored the darts of pain shooting through his leg and forced his breathing to steady. He looked around as clouds parted, and shafts of sunlight slanted down to brighten the hill.

That day long ago, Yosef had pointed out the array of buildings on the southwestern part of the hill. The Jew from Judea, who had never been to Rome, had known much of the Temple of Jupiter Optimus Maximus as the center of Rome's religious system and its great political importance, and that had irritated him at first. Then he realized Yosef's study of Rome and the empire was part of the young man's desire for knowledge, and since he knew Nicanor had never served in the city, he had shared that with him because of his interest in that symbol of the sovereignty and power of Rome.

Rising over the irregular retaining walls that followed the hillside contours, Nicanor could see where the temple was being repaired and reconstructed after the great fire. The scorched and smoke-scarred colonnade that stretched down the sides of the hill had been mostly replaced, and only a few remaining new Corinthian columns to be set in place as the old damaged ones were removed. The roofline frieze had been re-plastered and shone a brilliant white under the sun. He heard the barking of dogs, an ululating bay that carried across the hill, and his eyes followed that sound to two small buildings surrounded by a low fence near the northernmost back corner of the temple. Yosef had told him that trained dogs guarded and patrolled the area.

He shifted his feet to take the weight off his bad leg and turned to the Prefect. "Where do we go now, Lord Tigellinus?"

The Prefect studied him for a moment, then his eyes flashed and shifted from the centurion to scan the hilltop, coming in a full arc back to Nicanor. The Prefect waved a hand at the citadel that sat far back from the path leading to the steps. "This is where the condemned—those of a certain rank or position, or those malcontents that must become examples—where they are brought after their judgment. They are strangled in this fortress or in the Tullianum below and brought here for their bodies to be cast down the steps to rot within view of the forum and citizens of Rome. Such punishment—upon these stairs of mourning—serves as a reminder of the consequences for those who consider opposing the emperor or those who conspire against the empire. What the wild dogs leave is then thrown into the Tiber for the fish and other carrion eaters that frequent the river banks at night."

Tigellinus strode across the crest of the hill to a large rock on the southern summit, an overhang that brooded over the sheer cliff. The boulder's upper surface had been flattened, forming the landing he now stepped onto and stood upon. "This is the *Saxum Tarpeium*, the rock named for the man who betrayed Rome to the Sabines. It is the spot from which the most traitorous are thrown."

Tigellinus looked down upon the city and then back at Nicanor as he stepped off the stone to walk toward the fortress, waving for the centurion to follow him. "The emperor has decided that there"—he motioned ahead—"and Tullianum is to be your post. You are now a *trecenarius*, a senior centurion assigned as one of the watch captains, and your 100 men serve as guards. And there"—his hand flicked toward the steps down to the prison—"and here"—he pointed at the citadel—"we have several interesting men." He looked at Nicanor with a mocking smile. "These men await execution. One is a follower of the Jewish prophet you likely heard of in your service in the southern provinces. A citizen of Rome and a Christian and former citizen of Tarsus, he now rejects his birth name of Saul for what the Jewish Christ apparently called him—Paul. Perhaps you know that city from your service in Antioch?" He looked over his shoulder again. "Well, you may see him meet his fate... like others of his faith have done."

Tigellinus stopped and turned fully toward Nicanor, his eyes a dark flint whose hardness matched his stern tone. "Centurion, the emperor felt this a rewarding post for a loyal soldier after such hard service. Continue on"—he pointed up the path—"and report to the citadel commander. He expects you and will give you more details of your responsibilities and arrange your quarters."

"Yes, Lord Tigellinus." Nicanor moved past the two men beside the Prefect toward the fortress. Once he had passed the Prefect, he released the pain to flicker across his face. He wasn't sure what hurt worse—his leg or the realization that duty and honor—his loyalty to Cestius Gallus—had led to his becoming a jailor and party in the execution of criminals. He stopped at the Prefect's call behind him.

"Centurion, perform well at your new duties for the empire... and then when the time comes... retire with honor. There is a saying here in Rome that I'll leave you with. Remember this... *arx tarpeia capitoli proxima*. The Tarpeian Rock is not far... and one's fall from grace can come swiftly."

XVI

ROME

The emperor's gaze swept the modest amphitheater of wood he had constructed to replace the original unimpressive Statilius Taurus, named for the dull statesman who had built it—*He had no artistic imagination*. The great fire had consumed that structure, the intense heat cracking its stone foundation and burning its wooden frame down to cinders. Were it not for the cost of his majestic Domus Aurea and its priority, he would have reconstructed this arena using far more elaborate stonework, but wood must serve until enough treasure has been taken from the provincial temples, he thought, including from the rebels in Judea, and then he would build the expansive Amphitheater Neronis he had dreamed about.

Nero turned his attention to Marcus Attilus of Capua, the gladiator trainer he had recently brought to Rome as his imperial *lanista*. The man stood before him a level below on the stadium ground. Nero leaned forward and called to him: "Bring them out well-oiled and, after the testing of the dogs, put them through a series of trial combat with wooden swords. I want them rehearsed and ready to perform well for King Tiridates of Armenia. The new client-ruler must be impressed and thus eager to pay tribute to his emperor."

"Yes, sire, I have prepared them as you command," the scarred former gladiator said, acknowledging the requirement. "But sire, they are less experienced than even the *novicius*, for the new recruits I normally get to work with know something of fighting. These"—he gestured at the tunnel where fighters entered the arena—"know nothing of handling weapons, and I have never trained wom—"

"Enough!" Nero cut him off. "Bring them out. How well these women handle weapons does not matter. I'm told they will fight well enough—even if only barehanded—when forced to protect their children. And they're a novelty, and I'm told I'll find them delightful. With time, any that survive should become capable fighters."

"Yes, sire." Marcus Attilus gestured to someone unseen in the arena underneath the raised center section where the emperor sat. Soon the rattle of chain and clank of iron shackles cut through the silence of the empty amphitheater and grew louder as a dozen figures came into the sunlight. Naked, their ebon skin glinted, but the sun held little warmth and most shivered with each gust of cold wind that whirled around them. The oldest had flattened, pendulous breasts, but others were younger, and their breasts firmer and higher. Some women were as slender as young boys. Almost every one of them had a child tethered to her, attached leg to leg. Some glared up at the emperor who dictated their fate—he sat above them with his personal guard. They betrayed no fear for themselves but wrapped protective arms around the child beside each of them.

Nero's eyes narrowed as he shaded his eyes with one jeweled hand. "Bring out the dogs, but don't give them slack or turn them loose until I give the order."

The lanista turned again toward the ground-level entrance and barked a command. From deep within the opening came the grinding sound of a heavy *cataracta* being raised, the latticed grille of wood and iron that slid in grooves inset within each jamb of the gateway between the animal pens and the amphitheater. Marcus Attilus moved farther away from the opening as the growling and snarls grew louder.

As they left the darkness, the animals—starved for days—snapped at their handlers and at each other. They were six massive *molossuses*, dogs bred for fighting, with heavy square heads, leonine muzzles that bared wicked teeth, thick corded necks, and barrel torsos with muscle-bunched hindquarters, their weight fully that of a grown man. They lunged and dragged the men, restraining them to within reach of the Ethiopian women and their children.

"Back them off and hold them there!" Attilus commanded and looked up at the emperor for his next orders. Then his eyes shifted to the right.

Nero followed the lanista's look to glance over a shoulder at whoever had been allowed to pass through his outer personal guards. "What is it, Tigellinus?"

"Sire, I've seen to the duty posting of the centurion Nicanor, as you wished. I left him with orders to report to the commander of Arx Capitolina."

"Good. How did he react to his new assignment?"

"No response at all, sire—he seemed to accept it well."

"Your idea of testing him with this duty was a good one, Tigellinus." Nero had been intrigued by the Prefect's observation that field soldiers rarely do well as prison guards or executioners. This duty should rankle such a one, perhaps lead him into imprudent actions if he were so inclined. If he wished to just finish his time and retire, he would accept that role for the time he had left to serve. If not, he could have an eye kept on him and then be disposed of if he proves false. Nero turned back to study the occupants of the arena floor. "What do you think of my gladiatrices?"

Tigellinus glanced at the shivering women and children. The women had gathered in a huddle, children in the center, with their backs to the bitter wind. "I'm sure they'll do fine for you, sire." They would die quickly and provide little entertainment, but that was no matter. "Sire..."

Nero tapped his lips and moved in his chair to face the Praetorian Prefect. "What else...?"

"I've found a general to crush the Jewish rebels in Judea for you."

"Who?" The wind had picked up, and Nero gestured for the Prefect to come closer.

"Titus Flavius Vespasianus, sire."

"Vespasian!" Isn't he the one I banished for rudely falling asleep during my performance? Nero's eyes narrowed and drilled into the Prefect's, the displeasure at recalling that moment drawing down the corners of his mouth in disgust. "I should have had him executed."

"That's him, sire. That disrespect happened in Achaea, but he has the experience you need. Twenty years ago, he helped conquer Britannia for Claudius and received the *ornamenta triumphalia* and victory procession through Rome. He also subdued a revolt in Germania, and he has a reputation as a good—honest— administrator. And most importantly, sire, he has no ambition. At least there is no account of it I have been able to find. When you sent him from Rome, he retired quietly to his family's home, far from Rome and from its intrigues."

"Does he come from wealth, then?"

"No, sire. During his governorship of Africa a few years, ago unlike most in that position, he did little to gain any and became virtually bankrupt. He apparently does not have political connections—though those who have served with him speak highly of him and say he has a calm head and a sharp military mind and is never rash."

"What has he done since I exiled him from Rome, and he left the army?"

"I found that he has mortgaged his family home for capital and has turned to the breeding and selling of mules for his livelihood, sire. Now those who know him call him the 'Mule Driver.'"

A smile played on Nero's face as he leaned toward the arena and rested his forearms on his knees. He raised a hand to rub the fringe of beard that lined a jaw, softening with plump flesh. A thumb and forefinger tugged at his lower lip. "The Mule Driver... Yes, Tigellinus, send for him. He sounds like a good choice to crush the Jews."

The thumb and finger released the lip and were replaced with two drumming fingers. "And he might be just the man to provide a check for Gessius Florus. Yes. Better yet, go to him and present the opportunity for him to serve Rome again. Do not fail to bring him back with you."

Nero dismissed the Praetorian Prefect and called down to the trainer, "Attilus, free one woman and a child. Separate them... and make the child run. Then turn loose one of your animals.... let's see how she fights."

XVII

FALACRINE, NORTHEAST OF ROME

Two days' ride northeast of Rome, Ophonius Tigellinus led a unit of thirty men from the *equites singulares augusti* through the mountains and rolling hills of the Sabina region. The *turmae* standard was emblazoned with a scorpion—the birth sign of Emperor Tiberius, the second founder of the Praetorian Guard—and caught dappled sunlight through the trees that lined the road like sentinels. That quick-striking creature was also displayed fourfold on the shields the cavalry carried on one arm, their reins in the other hand.

Local woodsmen had informed them that morning that the winding valley road would soon straighten, and there they would find Falacrine. The surroundings had become steadily less wild, and as the trees thinned, and the road leveled into a broad plain between the mountains, they began to see signs of cultivation. Beyond the extensive areas of worked land, a village took shape as the sun burned through the morning mist to climb above the valley.

That must be the villa, Tigellinus thought as they got closer to the structure nestled in the foothills. It had that air of country nobility, though it had been built during a time of rare good fortune by an otherwise undistinguished family. Tigellinus smiled at the leverage it gave him—it was no doubt the collateral for Vespasian's debt.

* * *

In the courtyard that spanned the rear of the villa, Titus Flavius Vespasianus turned from his view of the newly planted, well-ordered olive orchard.

"What is it, Gaheris?" he asked the military aide who had followed him into retirement to continue serving him in private life.

"There's someone... a messenger... from Rome..." Gaheris Clineas had an unsure, puzzled look on his well-lined face.

"Is there a problem?" Vespasian asked, "some issue with the mule supply to the northern legions?" He prayed not. Unlike many, he had not left his service to the empire with a full purse, and he needed means to increase his wealth. That supply contract could become an essential source of income.

"I don't know"—Gaheris rubbed his chin—"he asks to speak with you, general."

"About what? What message does he bring?"

"He is not your usual courier. He says he is Ophonius Tigellinus, Prefect of the Praetorian Guard. And he's accompanied by a unit of the emperor's personal cavalry."

It had been a year or more, and Vespasian had assumed Nero had forgotten his inadvertent disrespect. Music recitals bored him, and he had been tired that night. Such an inconsequential thing as falling asleep as the emperor played his instrument had led to his ouster from Rome. He braced himself with the usual stoicism needed. "Bring him to me, then find my Antonia and ask her to join us in the tablinum."

Antonia had been a slave and secretary to the mother of Emperor Claudius, but her remarkable memory and intellect had given her considerable influence with the emperor's administration, and her advice had many times proven beneficial. When she was freed as her reward, he was fortunate to have met and developed a relationship with her. Her knowledge had proven invaluable, and she was a shrewd listener, thinker, and advisor. Though not a wife in name, since his wife's death, she had been his companion and lover. He trusted her. His older son, Titus, had accepted her—he wished his younger son Domitian would do the same.

It had been Antonia's idea to plant the olive orchards and expand Sabina's production to a higher level. The fertile soil yielded an abundant harvest of the green-gold fruit, and as Rome grew, so did the demand for olives as both food and fuel that burned without smoke or soot. He hoped the investment would become a stable, recurring cash crop for his own family, for his son's children, and for theirs on and on. The arrival of a messenger from Rome did not bode well for that future.

* * *

"Your family has done well to hold so much land." Tigellinus had made a show of admiring the villa, with its peristyle that wrapped continuously around the exterior. The modest interior had no columns for the atrium—a *tuscanicum*—and the openness was unexpected. But he knew how close the retired general was to losing it all. Tigellinus now stood in a square chamber off the atrium, and the retired general moved behind a writing table and sat gesturing at one of the chairs before it. Along the wall to his right was a lower table holding two large, sturdy boxes, and above were wall shelves holding what looked like mementos of Vespasian's military service.

Vespasian rested his thick forearms on the table and nodded, but he did not seem moved by the Prefect's honeyed voice. "Long ago," Vespasian explained, "we received this land as a grant from the tribune Spurius Carvilius when he crushed the Sabines and confiscated much of the region to give to Roman settlers. My grandfather then brought my family to distinction serving as a centurion under Pompey. After that, he retired as a debt collector."

"And his son, your father, had some accomplishment as a moneylender, did he not?"

"Yes... some small success. He married well, which helped him to build this"—Vespasian spread his hands to encompass the villa—"It is my birthplace and our family home."

A half-smile curled the Prefect's lips, though he tried to tame it. "Has it become difficult to keep all of it in your grasp... for your family?"

Vespasian blinked once at that question and asked, "Why are you here, Lord Tigellinus? Has the emperor finally decided I merit a sterner punishment?"

"Not at all, general." Tigellinus shook his head, carefully giving it a down-angled quarter turn twice, and then looked at Vespasian through the tangle of his eyebrows.

"Then, does it have to do with my bid to provide mules to the nearby legions in Pannonia, Illyricum, and Moesia?" Vespasian asked and continued without waiting for an answer: "I have not attempted to sell to any legions near Rome. And my pricing is fair... I do not ask for favors..."

"No, general. In fact, depending on this meeting,"—Tigellinus stopped at the sound of approaching steps and raised his head.

A woman as tall as the stocky general entered the office, a servant with her bearing a tray holding an amphora and three goblets.

"I bring you mulled wine to welcome and warm you, Lord Tigellinus," the woman said as she half-bowed and motioned the serving girl forward. "We make it here from our own grapes, with cloves, cinnamon, and dates. I hope it is to your liking."

"Lord Tigellinus, this is my companion since my wife's death... Antonia Caenis."

The Praetorian Prefect knew of her but became alarmed as he considered the implications. While the general had little acumen or interest in politics, Antonia Caenis did. Tigellinus had not considered how close she might have become to Vespasian when he assured Nero that the retired general had no connections. That was still true of the general, but Antonia Caenis, without a doubt, had hers.

59

He inclined his head to acknowledge the introduction and accepted the spiced wine, his mind racing, and his senses on high alert. The serving girl quickly left, but the woman casually sat in the chair beside the writing desk and nearer to Vespasian than himself. She half-turned toward Tigellinus and brought the wine to her lips, studying him over the brim of the cup.

Vespasian smiled at Antonia, turned back to the Prefect, and prompted him to continue. "You were saying, Lord Tigellinus..."

The Prefect darted a look at Antonia, then at Vespasian, who gave no inclination he would ask her to leave them. So he changed what he had planned to say. "General, you had much success as the legate in command of the 2nd Legion in Britannia. You captured twenty *appida* hill forts... and that was after your success under Aulus Plautius in the initial invasion. In Germania, your legion also put down a revolt for Emperor Claudius."

"Yes... I did." Vespasian noted how closely Antonia was listening to the Prefect. He had met the man before but knew him most by his reputation as a talker whose meaning and intention was often in the words, he left unsaid. "If you're not here regarding my offense to the emperor or my current business circumstances... why should my past be important to you?"

"I'm here because the empire"—he knew not to express it as the emperor's interest—"needs your military experience." Tigellinus's eyes flicked to Antonia Caenis, who still gave no hint she would leave them to talk alone. "And as governor of Africa, you had a reputation as a fair and honest administrator. But you were tough and able to collect tax and tribute without issues often met by others who have held that responsibility."

Vespasian nodded and held his eyes steady on the Prefect. "Again... why are you here, Lord Tigellinus?"

"Emperor Nero is offering you a chance to serve the empire again."

"I'm retired... and my interests and focus are here with my family and business ventures."

"I understand, but one never knows what the future holds for such ventures... does one?"

"What do you mean, lord?" Antonia leaned forward with a smile on her lips but not in her eyes.

"What if you could be sure your interests prospered? What if you knew that should you succeed in doing what the empire needs to be done—after serving it one more time—you could retire again, here"—he mimicked Vespasian's earlier gesture to encompass his surroundings—"to enjoy that reward? You could build upon what you already have. And it would come at no cost or harm to Roman citizens."

XVIII

The Praetorian Prefect had left instructions with his clerk for Vespasian to be admitted into his private office at the Tabularium and to await him. The general—wearing full military regalia he had not worn in a year—released the clasp and shrugged off his cloak to hang it from a peg at the entrance. Tugging his tunic to straighten it beneath the breastplate, he scanned the room and sat in a broad chair next to billowing curtains and looked out to the balcony over the Capitoline Hill and Rome. Riding through the city the day before, for the first time in more than a year, he had confirmed his feeling that he had not missed it.

A gameboard beside the chair caught his eye. Its square grid was carved into an inch-thick stone slab and two rows of markers—one set black, the other white—ranged on opposite sides of the board. All were made of much finer materials than in his own set in Falacrine. He and Antonia played *latrunculi* each evening after they dined. Three evenings ago, after that meeting with Tigellinus, knowing it might be a long time before they had these private moments again, she had made him a little speech:

"You play this game well"—her hand had waved over the board—"and just as you win on the field of war. You win much more than you lose. Before you leave for Rome, I want you to remember something and always keep it in mind... to help you focus on who you are and put this prospect in perspective. It may be that coming battles will not be fought on fields of dirt, grass, and stone." She went to the shelf over the hearth and took down a leather cylinder, loosened its circular cap, then reached in and withdrew a scroll. She came back to sit beside him and read it aloud:

When you are weary with the weight you bear, if perhaps you are pleased not to be inactive but to start games of skill, in a more clever way you vary the moves of your counters on the open board, and wars are fought out by a soldiery of glass, so that at one time a white counter traps blacks, and at another a black traps whites. Yet what counter has not fled from you? What counter gave way when you were its leader? What counter of yours, though doomed to die, has not destroyed its foe? Your battle line joins combat in a thousand ways: that counter, flying from a pursuer, itself makes a capture; another, which stood at a vantage point, comes from a position far retired; this one dares to trust itself to the struggle and deceives an enemy advancing on its prey; that one risks dangerous traps, and, apparently entrapped itself, counter traps two opponents; this one is advanced to greater things, so that when the formation is broken, it may quickly burst into the columns, and so that, when the rampart is overthrown, it may devastate the closed walls. Meanwhile, however keenly the battle rages with cut-up soldiers, you conquer with a formation that is full, or bereft of only a few soldiers, and each of your hands rattles with its band of captives.

Antonia had rolled the parchment and rose to slide it back into the container. "I know how you tired of Rome and the emperor's court... and its never-ending game that everyone around you there played. And you do not wish to return there. But what has been offered is an opportunity to spend but a little time in Rome and then go to where you can do what suits you best.

"I know you still find battle appealing and perhaps even miss it. You love to fight and win. I hear news and tales from those I still know in Rome, and I sense there is more to this war you have been asked to become part of. It could lead to a time that will unsettle the order of things. Do not become drawn into the disorder. Do your duty. Win the battles before you... and should a storm sweep through Rome... let it all pass you by. Then return here to your family and fortune... and to me."

The sound of heavy steps and the rustle of a heavy cloak loosened him from memory, and he turned toward the room's entrance.

"Do you play, general?" Tigellinus had hung his cloak up, too, and pointed at the table, his eyes going to the game piece Vespasian held in his hand.

"From time to time, lord." Vespasian rubbed the smoothness of the counter, the white marble surely from the quarries in Luna. He set it back in place on the board and stood. "You have given my answer and request to the emperor, lord?"

"Yes. The emperor is pleased and agrees that you can choose your own staff, including your son Titus as one of your field commanders. You have full command and will receive all you need to break the rebels. You and I will dine with the emperor tonight to talk more."

* * *

As the sun sank below the horizon, Vespasian watched the fires being set in large shallow bronze bowls, casting a ruddy glow around them. A dozen of the lights encircled the massive, elaborate tent they had dined in, its rolled-up sides overlooking the construction. Vespasian had heard of Nero's plans for his new palace, but having seen it in full in the late-afternoon light, his breath had caught at the magnificence that mere words and second-hand descriptions could not convey. Still, it was an unjust contrast to so much of the rest of Rome that still had yet to be rebuilt.

Recalling Antonia's advice had returned his focus to the present and to what he must take into his own hands. The city of Rome was not his responsibility. Though the Praetorian Prefect had said that morning that the emperor had agreed to his requests and that this chance could secure his family's financial future, it could all change with any moment of inattention or a misspoken word to Nero.

"So, general, you must prepare and move quickly." The emperor drained another goblet of wine. The nearby attendant filled it as soon as it had been placed on the table beside the ruler.

"I will, sire." Throughout the evening's conversation, it had become increasingly clear the pressure Nero was under to stop the growing unrest in the empire and to bring in all the tax revenue owed. Crushing the Judean rebels would send a message to those in Samaria and other provinces where trouble had stirred: Test Rome, and you will be destroyed. Pay your taxes or suffer the consequences of not paying.

"My trust in you, general, is inspired by your humble origins... and by your past service. And the confidence inspired because"—Nero's eyes flickered to Tigellinus, who sat next to Vespasian, "because you seem to have not taken the path taken by many who have served the empire."

Vespasian was ready for any allusion to his present circumstances. Antonia had warned him that such a question would arise, and it was a question he had asked himself until he had realized the answer. He gave that answer to the emperor: "Sire, I enjoy fine things as many do." He cast his own sideways glance at Tigellinus, and said, "And you know my family, and that I have worked for what we have. I wish more for my family. But I want that more only through my efforts and not unfairly... I want no favors for myself over others."

The emperor's rings flashed in the firelight as he reached for the brimming goblet. "Does your loyalty lie with... these others? Or with Rome?" Nero drank deeply and shifted forward in his chair, waving at the attendant to take the empty goblet from him.

"With Rome, sire. I serve the empire now, as I always have... and always will." Vespasian sensed the emperor wanted to end their conversation on that, but he still had a question not yet asked. "Sire, I've thought more about what I need to help me prepare for this campaign. Can you arrange for me to speak to any who have served recently in Judea?" He saw the emperor's eyes go directly to the Praetorian Prefect and felt Tigellinus stir in his seat—a flicker of wonder grew in him as that exchange came and went, and the emperor stood. He rose quickly with him.

"Lord Tigellinus will see if any are in Rome and available to meet with you."

XIX

GALILEE

YOTAPTA

"You look tired, Yosef," remarked Yohanan ben Zaccai as he pulled a chair out to join his friend at the table he used as a desk.

Yosef folded and sealed the sheet of parchment he had just filled with his elegant script and set it atop two others to his right. With the back of his left hand, he nudged to one side the small jar of ink and set his pen beside it, then stretched the fingers of his hand and rotated his wrist to loosen it. He pulled to him a sheaf of messages just in from some of the men in the surrounding towns—leaders he had placed or who had volunteered to work with him. "The administration of command is more tiring than traveling to establish it."

"But you are having some success. Yotapta has welcomed you." The priest and teacher looked around the room. "For now, this is a good place they've given you for an office and to sleep in. And much of the area, many of the small towns of Galilee, have joined us."

Yosef leafed through the pages before him, pausing at three: "Bersabe, Selamin, and Tarichaea announce here that they are with us and agree to send men"—he looked up at Yohanan—"But many others have not—will not—and we need them all. We need them now." Yosef rubbed his eyes and then raised the first report to read from the leader of Chabolo that they had strengthened their defenses, but more was needed, and asking when Yosef could provide additional men and resources to further reinforce the town. It was close to Ptolemais and would likely bear the brunt of early attacks from that Roman stronghold. Yosef rubbed his brow and swept a hand over his hair to rest it at the base of his neck, squeezing to try to relax the muscles. Chabolo was directly between the Romans at Ptolemais and the Yotapta headquarters. Once Yotapta was as fortified as possible, he must further buttress Chabolo.

"The Romans remain quiet even when their 12th Legion has left Antipatris, divided, and moved into Caesarea and Ptolemais," Yohanan remarked. "Since then, they've yet to strike back. So maybe we'll have time to convince more here in Galilee that we must unite for the defense of all."

"That Roman 'quiet' won't last much longer," Yosef said with a shake of his head. "And we cannot assume we have time to do what should have already been done. If only those who still hesitate had acted as they should have—and when.

"But why do the Romans wait... and what for?" Yohanan asked.

"Maybe whatever made Cestius Gallus pull back from the attack on Jerusalem still stays his hand. I am sure Rome is choosing his replacement, someone who will not hesitate as Gallus has. The man they send will not question his orders nor his purpose. He will come with more men... far more men—two or three legions at least. Supported by auxiliaries and allies like King Agrippa. The Romans will attack when they are ready... and once they do, they will not stop.

"Can we withstand them?" asked Yohanan.

"I've met with dozens of leaders going from town to town, consolidating support and gathering men. I have the leaders promises"—he rustled the pages in his hand—"real commitments. A thousand are now encamped just outside Yotapta, and I hope for thousands more. I just need them to get here, so we have some chance to prepare them and plan. And I must persuade more to join us."

"Yohanan of Gischala works against that... and against us." Yohanan pulled at the tangle of beard that lay upon his chest. "Those who shout loudest for the longest always intend their words to be taken as fact and truth... as what is right. But the twisted words they spew are only to serve their interests."

"I've learned there is much of that in our land," Yosef answered, "and even in Rome. Probably everywhere, men live." Yosef was glad the old priest did not press him to answer that question he had asked. In his heart, he knew the answer was that there was no way they could survive the Roman onslaught surely coming their way. "I don't know if I can reach Yohanan of Gischala through all his noise. He believes that if he does not align with Jerusalem, the Romans will leave him alone. And his persuasion to the towns who will join him is to offer them that they, too. They will be left alone. I have told him I know the Romans, and that is foolish thinking. The Roman army will not discriminate. But he will not listen to me. And likely he will not exchange his support for our help—he won't join us until a Roman has a sword at his throat."

"He resents that many towns have allied with you," Yohana observed. "I've heard he feels they betray him by following you."

"He is driven by ego, Yohanan. I have tried to show him and others that we must fight together or risk dying alone. The Romans will crush each city, town, and village... killing its people, slaughtering each outlying family as they strip the crops and livestock to feed their men." Yosef's tone lowered as his head dipped over the desk, recalling tales of Rome's conquests. "Their Galilean bones will enrich the gravel of a road the Romans will build to stab deeper into Judea."

"Into its heart..." Yohanan shook his head sadly. "But even there in Jerusalem are some who resist standing united."

Yosef nodded. "For most of us it is the heart, and ours is flawed and risks being torn asunder. But what happens to our people... to our faith... if Jerusalem falls?"

Yohanan gestured at the stack of letters beside Yosef. "Are these for me to take to Jerusalem?"

"Yes." Yosef slid the stack of three to him. "When will you leave?"

"In the morn—"

"—Excuse me..." A tall boy, layered in dust, stood in the doorway, casting a shadow into the room. "I have an urgent message for Yosef from Silas in Tiberias. I was told I could find him here."

"Is Silas the commander you put in place there?" Yohanan asked.

Yosef nodded. "Though it's perched on the water and seems a good place to live, the Tiberians have been difficult. But Silas seemed capable." He looked at the boy and said, "I'm Yosef" and held out his hand. The boy gave him the message, and he broke the seal and unfolded the sheet. "Silas reports that Yohanan of Gischala has been there several days... supposedly to 'take the baths.'"

"Their hot springs do have a healing quality... perhaps he will come from them a better man..." The priest smiled, but the quip failed as Yosef continued grimly:

"It seems he is really there to incite the Tiberians to break from any loyalty to Jerusalem... and give allegiance solely to him. Silas reports he has been seen with Justus ben Pistus and his father, who both speak strongly against Jerusalem, and they draw crowds of men to them."

"Sirs..." the two men turned to the boy who still stood wide-eyed and waiting. "Do you have a reply? I have ridden one of Silas's mules and was told to ask for a response and then return immediately."

"Yes"—Yosef reached for pen and parchment, wrote quickly, blew on it to dry, folded the parchment into a square, and sealed it. "Take this to Silas as quickly as you can." He handed the message and a coin from his purse to the boy.

When he left, Yohanan ben Zaccai leaned toward Yosef. "What did you tell him?"

"Silas's message also said that the men with Justus are now openly carrying weapons—swords and bows, likely provided by Yohanan of Gischala. He fears they intend to take the town by force and asks for help." Yosef gathered the pages and scrolls of parchment upon the table and swept them into a large leather document case that he secured with a broad strap. He rose from the table and took from the wall behind it the belted sword that hung alongside his cloak. Fixing the sword and scabbard around his waist and settling it at his hip, he spun the robe on and secured its clasp at his right shoulder.

"What are you going to do, Yosef?"

"Prepare our men to go to Tiberias. I told Silas I will march tonight with two hundred, and we'll be there at daybreak."

"I will go with you."

"No, my friend. I know you are sturdy, but a night march is not easy, and we must move quickly. I want you to get those letters to my family... and report to my father and the Sanhedrin that I may have to raise arms against Yohanan of Gischala."

"So, we have to fight against ourselves before we fight the Romans."

"I hope not... I pray it will not come to a confrontation with him or his men. But if it does, I will do what I must." Yosef clapped the priest on the shoulder and stepped out into the late-afternoon sun. The boy was just mounting his mule and turned its head toward the easterly road. Yosef scanned the rolling hills to the west and the bunching of clouds behind and above them and thought again, *it should have never come to this.*

XX

Yosef sensed as much as smelled the moisture on the wind blowing from the east and off the great lake whose western shore Tiberias sat upon. He relished the freshness in the coming dawn as much as he disliked his purpose for entering the town on such a beautiful morning. Just outside Tiberias, he halted the long train of men behind him and sent one ahead to find and bring Silas to him.

The sun had climbed only a little higher by the time the man arrived.

"What do you plan, Yosef?" Silas asked without greeting, out of breath, and clearly worried.

"I've brought men to show I am serious about maintaining order in Galilee—we have a much larger enemy to prepare for and face—and this morning, I'll speak to the people."

"The boats are already out... none of the fishermen will hear you."

"Send a crier through town to bring the others here—all that can come—to the stadium. What I tell them will spread to the fishermen on their return."

* * *

"They're calling for the town's people to come to the stadium," Justus ben Pistus said as he entered the room with a tall boy at his side. "Yosef will speak to them. Just as my nephew's friend here said was in the message to Silas." He clapped a heavy hand on the boy's shoulder. "He also overhead Yosef and Yohanan ben Zaccai when he delivered the message and when Silas read Yosef's reply and told his men."

"Yosef ben Mathias does just as I hoped," replied Yohanan of Gischala with a broad smile. "All of his kind from Jerusalem love to talk and talk. Tell our men to not appear there. I have many of mine in waiting that are not known here. Let Yosef and his dog Silas think he speaks to a responsive audience. But few who hear him will be friendly."

* * *

70

Yosef stood before the parapet that formed a narrow balcony perimeter around the mid-level of the town's small stadium, and the number of people who had gathered there surprised him. They shaped two wings around the arc of the stadium, and many took seats below him, filling the two rows. When he talked, he would need to bend and turn to include them. He wanted all there to know he was speaking directly with them.

As he stood to face the townspeople who had gathered, he went over all the words that had spun through his head during the night's march from Yotapta. Tired and with aching legs as they neared Tiberias and dawn approached, he was nevertheless energized by the words and his belief in them. He knew what he wanted to say... what he must say. He straightened to stand tall before them, to convince them to stand with him and Jerusalem.

"Tiberians"—suddenly, he realized most of what he planned to say had been said before... by King Agrippa... in Jerusalem. He remembered the king's speech that day, for he had written much of it down afterward. It had not changed the minds of those already decided in their thinking. He stuttered to a stop. He blinked into the sun that had risen over the low buildings of the town. Taking a deep breath that had just a hint of a breeze and the smell of the lake, he forgot all the words he had planned—the words borrowed from Agrippa. Instead, he spoke his own words:

"You might think I will speak to you of Romans and the threat they pose to all of us. And I had planned to do so because the danger is real and inescapable. But..." His voice trailed off, and the men below him stirred. After a moment, he continued—"Your town... Tiberias... is about five decades old and named for a Roman emperor. That has mattered a great deal to many of you as you consider how you feel about your town's identity. And maybe many here and elsewhere nearby are not loyal to Rome, but they also believe they are not part of a Jewish nation under the leaders in Jerusalem.

"But beneath you... beneath us—below this stadium—are the earth and stone of the ancient village, Rakkath, the village that Tiberias was built upon. The *Sefer Yehoshua* records this land we stand upon as the home of the Tribe of Naphtali, the northernmost of the Twelve Tribes, of the Bnei Yisra'el. We stand upon our history as Joshua tells it, and as Jews, we should stand together so that what and who we are... do not cease to exist. And that is what will happen if we do not put aside our differences and petty disagreements. All towns and villages... all people within Galilee must join in fighting against the Romans."

Yosef's eyes swept left to right. He had split his men into groups. Fifty of them sat above him with Silas, to one side where the curve of the stadium seating allowed them to look up at him at an angle. Fifty more had taken positions at the stadium entrance with some of Silas's men to watch for Justus ben Pistus, Yohanan of Gischala, or any men known to follow them. Yosef wanted no trouble as he spoke to as many of the people of Tiberias as possible. One hundred more men were at the waterfront should Yohanan's men be lurking nearby to come by boat and create a disturbance. Silas had told him they had dropped from sight after he sent the message to Yotapta.

He started to speak again, turning to include the men arrayed on the rows below him. "Think of our common heritage and what threatens it... not about what you are told you should fear from Jerusal--"

The arrow slanted up but had been aimed too high, or perhaps his turn had spoiled the shot. It slashed through the top of his shoulder, gouging flesh and tearing his cloak. The force of the heavy shaft half spun him around, and he stumbled and fell, one hand grabbing at the edge of the parapet to halt his fall. Below him, as he stumbled to one knee, he saw the men shrug off their robes and bring out the smaller composite bows used by Romans.

An incongruous flash of memory—Nicanor showing him one of the bows on the Field of Mars in Rome as they trained one morning—came and went. Made from layers of wood, bone, horn, and sinew, that bow was firm and springy, powerful for its size but accurate only for short distances. The man who shot him, among the other men below, was not over twenty feet away. A dozen of them nocked, pulled, and rereleased to fire, this time into the cluster of his men just above him.

Yosef shot a glance over his shoulder. Many of his men had gone down, arrows protruding from high on their chests or into their stomachs. The men below fired again, and more of his men clambering toward him fell. Silas and five of the other men almost made it to him. Yosef got to his feet to be slammed down as a thrown club struck his head. As he fell to stare into Silas's dead eyes, all went dark.

XXI

Miriam no longer thought of it consciously. The simple clothes and rough cloak that most of the women in the Lower City wore now seemed more natural than the more elegant garb she wore with her privileged family. As she passed through the agora, she would be taken as a shop-girl. And once down the steps at the southwest corner of the Temple enclosure and into the working-class area of Jerusalem, she fit in with all the women of the Lower City going about their daily lives.

There was something, though, that occupied her thoughts: The moment she gave it focus, it filled her with grief. The only two people she had ever been able to easily talk to were gone. Zechariah, her mentor, was dead, and Yosef was now off in Galilee. She felt terrible that she was both sad and glad at Yosef's absence. Despite all the events since his return from Rome and the threat of what was to come, he had grown more curious about how she had changed from the happy girl she had been before he left for Rome.

A sweet, talkative girl who was to be married had transformed into a withdrawn, sullen young woman who now seemed dark and secretive. Those were his words in their last conversation before he left. She had deflected that line of thought at the time by shifting to a topic that she realized afterward hurt Yosef deeply. And she still regretted that she had brought up Leah and Rachel and then done so again in the letter she had last written to him. The morning he had left, when she mentioned Leah, Yosef's hand had unconsciously toyed with the cord around his neck from which dangled a small coin, the kinyan given him by Leah years ago as a remembrance of her when he left to study with the Essenes. She had taken Yosef's hand, stopping him from twining the cord around a finger, and told him she was fine—and not to worry about her. Then it was time for him to leave.

But she was not fine and felt she never would be again.

In the crispness of a late winter's morning that hinted of early spring, she smelled what now always signaled to her that she was near Zechariah's—the sharp tang on the air that came from the leatherworker's shop across the alley from Zechariah's shop. Pottery was the craft he had turned to after his blindness meant he could no longer work as a stonemason, quarrier, and miner. He had joked to her he had spent so much time underground as a young man that he must have been fated to live his later years in the dark, too. Then the bitterness of memory had taken away his smile. The darkness had begun even before his eyes became too cloudy to see when his wife and daughter were killed by a Roman. She knew, though he did not talk of it, that that had been when the light went out of his life.

As she made the turn onto the street where most tradesmen had stalls and shops, the sound of clayware crashing to the ground came from behind her. She turned, and no more than twenty feet away was the broad back of a cloaked Temple Guard officer as he stooped and tried to pick up pieces of a shattered jar that dripped oil. An angry woman glared down at him, shaking a finger in the face she could not see. When he began making apologies, Miriam recognized his voice. Matthew! He rose, the woman still shaking head and finger at him, and started to turn in Miriam's direction, and she stepped inside the nearest shop, one she remembered being vacant.

"May I help you?"

Miriam whirled to see a young man holding a long knife in one hand and turning the wheel of a sharpening stone with the other. In the glow of the large lamp next to him, he had a grim expression, almost if the interruption were more irritation than the opportunity of a customer. "May I help you?" he asked again. This time he stood and came forward into the light cast from the morning sun through the open door behind her.

"N-no"—Miriam sputtered, darting a glance over her shoulder at the street as Matthew moved past and away—"I mean yes..." She looked around at the tables stacked with flat tongues of metal she knew would become blades and another table where the shaped metal was being fitted to an array of hafts and handles. "Do you sharpen household knives?"

The man came fully into the sunlight, and she saw that his thin face was pale, yet handsome. His unblinking gaze locked on her. "Yes. Do you want to wait, or will you pick them up later?"

"Oh... I don't have them with me..." She had never had a man stare at her so and thought quickly. "The lady... the lady I serve wished me to find someone who..."

"Yes. Someone to sharpen them... next time bring the knives with you." He turned and went back to his sharpening. As he focused again on the metal he held, the material becoming a blade, his expression softened.

She stepped outside, wondering if Matthew had been following her. Why else would he be in the Lower City at this hour? Had he ever been there before? No. He could not have. If he had and had seen her enter Zechariah's, he would have confronted her there or would surely have told their mother and father to question her when she returned home.

She scanned the street up and down, then continued to Zechariah's. She wondered that no one had taken it as their own and moved into the shop. Each time she had stood before this door, she had worried that as she stepped inside and began her series of exercises—the attacks and feints that Zechariah had made her practice over and over—someone would discover her. And then it would be over, but that purpose that consumed her had been the only thing that had brought her from back from considering killing herself.

She would no longer be what she had become—an executioner of those who had hurt her and who threatened other Jews, especially those she loved. She was a deliverer of retribution and an avenger of Zechariah. She stepped inside, and it felt like she was in her real home.

* * *

As Miriam spun, with a twist of the right-hand wrist, the blade came free from the man-sized practice targets Zechariah had made her from straw, targets she had now strengthened with fabric and a coating of clay to bear her now-far-more-powerful strikes. Continuing the arc, pivoting on the toes of her left foot, she brought the blade in her left hand around to stab to the hilt into the base of its neck. A solid *thunk* told her she had struck deep enough to hit the ten-inch thick log Zechariah had used as the core skeleton and frame for the cladding that gave the target shape. Chunks and large patches of that covering were coming loose, and she would need to repair before using it again.

"You move and strike as quickly as Menahem told me," said a voice from the darkness, startling her. A stocky man came from the shadows in what had been Zechariah's sleeping area, a place she had never entered. "You must be Miriam," he said.

"Who are you? And what do you"—Miriam stood beside the target, breathing heavily.

"Do not be alarmed," the man said, pressing both hands, palm down, toward the floor. "Please lower your blades." He moved along the wall but got no closer to her. "I am Elazar ben Yair... I'm a Sicarii... as was Zechariah. As I was told, it seems that so are you—the only woman Sicarii and as impressive as Menahem ben Judah claimed. I was one of his men—a co-leader of the Sicarii—and he told me he had plans for you."

"So, you're the one who has kept Zechariah's place here?" Miriam rubbed the sweat from her eyes with her right forearm, still gripping her daggers in both hands.

"Yes, and I have seen you enter and leave here before. I suspected but did not know until now that you were the one he was so proud of—and Zechariah has trained dozens."

"I thought all the Sicarii had left Jerusalem..."

"We have. I have taken them and their families to Masada. From there, we will fight the Romans."

"Why not here in Jerusalem?"

"There is a rot in the leadership here... within these walls. Too many see things differently, and that is a weakness. In Masada, we are all strong. No longer is it a place for King Herod's ten-hour banquets and orgiastic feasts and dancers to entertain his debauched guests. It is now a Jewish fortress."

"Why are you here, then?" Miriam asked, watching his eyes as Zechariah had taught her to.

"To find something Zechariah had. Should others find it, especially those who still sympathize with or will yield to the Romans when they get here, it could jeopardize Masada's security."

"What?"

Elazar did not answer but stepped closer as Miriam's hands dropped to her sides. "I know Zechariah trusted you," he said, "and Menahem trusted and even planned to use you. But can I?"

"And I don't know you. How can I trust you to not speak of this?" Miriam spun and thrust the knife into the melon that formed the target's head.

"I think we can work out how to trust each other," Elazar said with a smile, "and in the days to come, we can help each other do what we must—kill Romans and those who work with or for them."

"What are you looking for?"

"Zechariah created maps of the tunnels under Masada, secret routes that few knew about. Zechariah and his father and grandfather before him worked on them. He knew more about them than did anyone. But his maps remain hidden... somewhere."

76

XXII

Vespasian had the servants take out the small-but-ornate pedestal-legged slab of stone intended to serve as his desk and had his aide Gaheris Clineas find a larger wooden-topped table to replace it. It had folding bronze legs like his desk at home in Falacrine and was much more practical. He could move it closer to the window for natural light, and it was wide enough to unroll maps on it and still have ample room to write.

He had put away the charts and plots that Lord Tigellinus had provided him from the 12th Legion's actions in Judea. Some of them were annotated by the commander or a staff member to detail the legion's movements and engagements with the rebels. The notes were straightforward but could tell him only so much without more context. The reports the Praetorian Prefect had also given him gave more of a picture, but something seemed lacking. Part of the depiction was absent—the part that would allow him to understand what had happened to the 12th Legion that resulted in its abrupt withdrawal from Jerusalem. The general refolded the two dozen sheets of vellum containing the reports and slid them with the maps into his loculus, a goat-hide satchel he had carried as a soldier for over 20 years. He hoisted the strap over his shoulder as he rose from the desk. He must speak again with the Praetorian Prefect and ask him—or someone else—to fill in the missing pieces.

* * *

"Why is the man here?" Nero asked Tigellinus with the expression of a petulant child whose play had been interrupted. He held the kithara lowered in his left hand, the fingers and thumb of his right lightly plucking its strings to make soft, disjointed sounds. "My architects have studied Pollio's *De Architectura* to replicate the acoustics of Greek theaters here... I will perform in this room for my guests."

"The general came to see me, and my office told him I was here, sire. Instead of waiting there, he came here. He has questions about the reports and information from Cestius Gallus that I provided him."

"Not the real reports showing Gallus's suspicions!"

"No, sire, the excerpted versions I had prepared, along with the 12th Legion battle maps and diagrams of their march from Antioch into Judea, then to Jerusalem, and then their retreat from Beth Horon to Antipatris."

"What else does he need, then?" Nero began to strum, cocking an ear toward the instrument.

"General Vespasian has questions about what seems to be missing," Tigellinus replied.

"Well, answer him, then." The petulance had hardened into a frown.

"Sire, I told him I would. But I said that right now I was with you discussing your upcoming tour of Greece. So, he asked to speak to you. He is most direct."

Nero's fingers stopped their plucking. "Perhaps I should punish him for his impertinence. Who is he to be so forward?!"

"I understand, sire. It affronts me too. But I believe he is the man you need to deal with the Judean rebels. I have yet to find another with his combination of experience and reputation. We can offer him enough enticement acceptable to his own code of honor to make it all rewarding for him. He is the man who can bring Gessius Florus to heel, too, if that is ever called for... as you wanted."

Nero's glower eased. "It is important that we get him on his way before I leave for Greece. Bring him to me here, then"—he raised the kithara and began to play. The sound had an eerie tone in the emptiness of the vast room.

* * *

Vespasian stood waiting, escorted, outside the chamber at the end of a lengthy, broad hallway that led to an open gallery still under construction, partially capped to support the framing of that section of the domus's second floor. The workers must have been sent elsewhere, and all was still. Threads of music flowed from the hall toward him like mist creeping along the hollow between the hills around his home. He recognized the instrument... one that never failed to lull him to sleep when he was tired. Surely that wasn't the emperor playing. But who else would dare to play music at the emperor's construction site? Echoing steps accompanied the chords of the melody, and the Praetorian Prefect approached with a nod at the two Praetorian Guards to move aside.

"The emperor will see you. Come with me, general." As they neared the chamber, a discordant, plaintive twang resonated, and the emperor reattempted the combination with the same result.

78

"Say nothing about the music—don't even acknowledge it," Tigellinus admonished in a low voice as they stepped into the chamber.

"Sire, General Vespasian, thanks you for a few minutes of your time." He waved the old soldier forward.

Vespasian passed through the Praetorian Guards stationed at the entrance and stepped into the chamber. His unfailing sense of direction told him he faced west, and looking back at him was a perfect rendition painted on the far wall of something he had not seen since Egypt—the resting figure of a fabulous creature with the body of a lion and the head of a man. A sphinx. The perspective of its foreshortened arms ended in paws that seemed to reach to either side of Emperor Nero, who was standing in front of it. The walls of the rest of the high-domed chamber were flickeringly alight from the bronze wall sconces burning smokeless olive-oil and the large pedestal-mounted corner lanterns of the same. The walls were covered with richly painted murals of both real and fabled creatures. His eyes went next to a centaur, and another figure he thought was Faunus, one of the oldest Roman deities, but as had become the norm, it was presented as the Greek god Pan with hindquarters, legs, and horns of a goat. On another wall was a man with his sword held high in a jungle, defending himself from the attack of a fierce panther. The scenes pulsed in vivid reds, greens, and yellows, with a flutter of shadow across them when the lamp's flame caught a stray thread of wind or one the guards shifted his stance. Vespasian had never seen anything like this room, not in any of the palaces he had visited in his career.

Nero stopped playing but kept the instrument tucked under his left arm. "What questions do you have, general?" He glanced at Tigellinus. "The Prefect says you wish to speak to me about them."

"Yes, sire." Vespasian resettled the satchel's shoulder strap and patted its side. "The 12th Legion's reports seem to lack an analysis of how the Judean rebels could force the legion to halt its attack on Jerusalem and then pull back. The ambush afterward at Beth Horon—their defeat there—is easily explained. The rebels had the tactical advantage, and relentlessly used it. It was all because the legion did not secure that route, specifically the heights of the valley pass. And that is inexcusable. For that alone, you are right, sire, to remove Cestius Gallus from command. But why did he retreat from Jerusalem?" Vespasian asked.

"It was a failure of the man, general, of Lord Gallus... who will soon face judgment for those failures." Nero's tone was brusque, and his eyes slid to Tigellinus and back to Vespasian. "The Prefect could have answered that for you."

"Sire, I read that the former Judean Procurator, Gessius Florus, was replaced... but not seemingly as his punishment. He was reassigned to remain in the area as an imperial tax collector at your command. As I understand it, he is the reason for some unrest that led to this revolt. Should he have not been recalled to help lessen tensions with the Judeans?"

"It is more important for the empire to collect what is due than to appease a conquered-yet-restive province under our domain. They have been given several opportunities to turn from the path they have chosen. To revolt is foolish, and they must know the consequences. Cestus Gallus was not the man to crush these rebels and make them bow to Rome... or die. Lord Florus is there to collect what is owed to the empire. Your job is to subdue the rebels and defeat the rebellion, to punish any of its leaders that live... and to ensure that Lord Florus has your support to do his job. Can you do that, General Vespasian? Can you do this job the empire requires of you?"

"Yes, sire..." Vespasian confirmed. But he still did not understand Gallus's decision to stop his attack on Jerusalem. This focus on tax and tribute collection was understandable with the pressing need to rebuild Rome. He looked around and could not help wondering what the cost of just this room alone was. Its purpose seemed only to suit the emperor's ego.

Nero turned to dismiss him and walked to the center of the room, raising the kithara to his chest. Right hand at the ready over the strings, he stopped to stare at the general as he followed him. "What?"

"Sire, the reports mention a centurion named Nicanor who was commended for his bravery at Beth Horon. Lord Gallus recommended you reward him. Is he—this Nicanor—here in Rome? How can I speak with him?"

XXIII

GALILEE

ON THE GALILEAN SEA

The sea seeping through the bottom of the boat, where he lay, brought Yosef awake. Dazed, the right side of his face wet with that cold-water sting just beginning to clear his head, he noticed the differences in the planks beneath him. Their rough—uneven—joining had gouged his cheek. Planting his hands, Yosef pushed himself upright. There were fifteen other men in a typical Galilean fishing boat, such as he had seen many times offshore or on the beaches of the towns that dotted the edge of the largest body of water in the region.

The men and a tangle of nets and ropes and a small water barrel, he presumed, filled the boat's nearly eight-foot width and 26-foot length. The boat rode low in the water, and the occasional larger white cap, kicked up by the brisk wind, cascaded over the side. Yosef blinked, looked up at the single mast holding a billowing sail of patched canvas framed by a bright, cerulean sky, shook his head, and raised a hand to the back of it, wincing from a stab of pain on his shoulder. His hand came away, palm coated with blood, and he looked around. They were well out on the great lake of Gennesaret, and behind them to the west must be Tiberias. That answered his question of where he was. He looked at the surrounding men to learn with whom.

Levi of Yotapta? Yosef thought as the man nearest him reached a hand to touch his shoulder.

"Yosef! I'm glad you are okay... I was worried," said Levi ben Alpheus, eyes alight." You did not move after you went down, and then we found you still breathing and got you out of the stadium and onto this boat. You're safe now, thanks to Nathan and his two sons,"— he gestured to the tall, thin, gray-bearded man at the tiller, who nodded back. "He was working on his boat and not out with the others."

Yosef bowed his head toward the Galilean fisherman and looked back up at Levi. "Thanks also to you and the others. Where are we headed?"

"Tarichaea, south from Tiberias. Nathan knows people there who can tend to your wound."

"What of the rest of our men?" Yosef asked, wiping more blood from the back of his neck, a trickle of it fresh.

"Another dozen, maybe more, escaped. After the battle inside the stadium, we met at the water. They fled over land and will join us there." He pointed ahead to the right toward a smaller town on the shore, one not allied with Yohanan of Gischala. "Silas is dead."

"I know..." Yosef closed his eyes, remembering that Silas's body was the last thing he had seen at the Tiberian stadium.

"We must bring more men from Yotapta, return to Tiberias, and avenge him," declared Levi, "and the other men who died. We must make the Tiberians pay for their attack on you."

"No, Levi, that will lead to a civil war here in Galilee... and we cannot have that." He shook his head but stopped at the shooting pain. "That only aids the Romans." He lowered his head to hold it between his hands. His eyes went again to the planks beneath him, following their joints and then up the strakes that formed the hull. Some wood was Lebanese cedar, but much was low-quality lumber: pine, jujube, or willow... he wasn't sure. No experienced boatwright would consider using that kind of wood.

On his arrival in Galilee, he had visited with many fishermen, as their craft was a crucial part of the economy and the means of livelihood for many. He had met with a master craftsman who constructed, repaired, and maintained the fishing boats used on the great lake. Over the days spent with the man, he watched as he worked and a well-built boat hull of cedar strakes and planks joined with mortise-and-tenon joints, pegged together with oak and then sealed with pine resin to render the hull mostly watertight, then the boat's underside was coated with pitch. This boat's owner could not afford better or had fallen on hard times, and his repairs and maintenance were makeshift. Some of the tenons were loose, sprung open by the warping of poorer materials. Nathan and his sons must work as hard to keep it afloat as they did to fish.

That thought struck Yosef. The different lumber, the working with mismatched materials... trying to make them form a single unity. So much effort Nathan and his boys must put in every day. There was a similarity in what he faced—trying to join the towns and people of Galilee and not sink. It was a daily effort to keep hopes afloat and not drown. Just to have a chance at life, and all so they could face the Romans.

* * *

GISCHALA

Yohanan of Gischala believed in his right to lead his people... and not just those of his home, though they welcomed him with joy even if he had only been gone a few days. He and they were as one. He had been born to lead, and the people of Galilee needed him to lead them all, to keep them separate and distinct from Jerusalem and its interference. Those thoughts filled his mind and guided his plans. It galled him that he had failed at becoming the sole leader needed to unify Galilee, and he raged at his men: "How could you not kill Yosef ben Mathias? That interloper from Jerusalem was right there... in front of you... and unconscious!"

"His men fought ferociously, Yohanan... and there weren't supposed to be any boats at the docks. We thought even if they escaped the stadium, we had them trapped and could run them down. Some of Yosef's men got to him and carried him out. We slew most of them in the stadium... and nearly all of Yosef's men at the waterfront. But most of ours fell, too.

"But they still got him into a boat and away." The man shook his head. "We needed more men." He looked at his leader, who had calmed down.

"What's the name of that man in Sepphoris?" Yohanan of Gischala asked his lieutenant. "The brigand who wouldn't join us unless he was paid... he has 800 men."

"His name was Ezekias," the man replied. "But Yohanan, I thought you did not want to use someone so mercenary..."

"I'll use who and what I must to run that Jerusalemite out of Galilee—or to kill him." Yohanan turned from him. "Gather the men and tell them we leave for Sepphoris in the morning."

XXIV

Galilee

Tarichaea

Yosef rose from the cot and walked to the window, opening the shutters onto a view of a small dock jutting into the water from a reed-choked bank. Two boats were tied up, and the man Nathan and his two slender sons worked on the more dilapidated one while two men unloaded a haul of fish from the boat in better shape into a cart hitched to a mule.

"You're feeling better?"

It was Nathan's wife, Imma, standing in the doorway with a bowl of porridge in her hands. She had tended to him since her brother had brought him here.

"That's a good sign—that you're up," she said with a nod to him. "I have six brothers, a dozen nephews, and four sons of my own... I have cared for many cracked heads before, and sometimes the dizziness does not go away for a week or more. I do not think whatever hit you landed squarely. The swelling is down, but it tore a nice gash in the back of your head." Imma brought the bowl to him.

Yosef's fingers gingerly touched where she had stitched the wound... he vaguely remembered her comment that it was "just like repairing a sail that must hold even in a stout wind" as her fingers had deftly closed the wound. Despite his dizziness, her words had registered, and he had smiled. He would surely need her handiwork to hold and to keep his wits about him. He was still shocked that Yohanan of Gischala had so brazenly attacked him—intending to kill. He wasn't sure how to deal with the Gischalan if so much of Galilee was against him. That was indeed a stout wind to sail against.

"Your friend Levi ben Altheus is here... outside"—she gestured toward the common area of the house—"if you feel up to talking." Imma watched him empty the bowl as he stood at the window. "Another good sign," she said as she took the empty bowl from him. "So, I'll tell him you're doing much better and will speak with him."

She left, and Yosef returned to the window to see the sky filling with scudding gray clouds that looked heavy with rain. A minute later, he heard Levi enter.

"On your feet, too... I'm glad to see that!" Levi was a few years older than Yosef and stockier but not as tall. This sturdy man had been one of the first to volunteer for the militia for not just his own town but all of Galilee.

"The first morning after we got here," Yosef mused, "I remember you telling me our other men had arrived from the battle in Tiberias. Any other news? Has Yohanan of Gischala brought more men, and does he now come after us here?"

"No," Levi said with a grin. "His men retreated toward Gischala instead. I'm not sure why—maybe they had to report to him of their failure—but I'm glad they did."

"So now we might have enough time to bring more men from Yotapta." Yosef knew it was not over with Yohanan of Gischala until they stood face to face, to settle who would lead Galilee.

Levi still smiled. "Yosef, word has spread of Yohanan's attack, and it has upset many people. A dozen villages—the farmers and fishermen he has overlooked—have sent men—here—to join you. Still more, I'm told, are going to Yotapta... to join our men there."

"How many are here now?" As he had recovered, the thought had grown on Yosef that Levi had become a capable lieutenant. *But could he trust him?*

"Hundreds, Yosef... just in the past few days."

Yosef blinked and rubbed his eyes; thankful they no longer were blurred. "Why... why do they come now?"

"Like I said, many dislike what the Gischalan did... and is doing. Even more, have heard your words and believed them. As have I."

* * *

SEPPHORIS

This time it was late in the day and nearing sunset as Yosef approached the city. The valley of Beit Natofa on their left and below them no longer held shining pools of standing water; large swaths of the valley floor were in shadow. In contrast was the brightness of the limestone as waning sunlight slanted down on the hills upon which Sepphoris sat, now in sight just ahead and farther up their climbing and winding road.

The view was much the same as it had been not long before, but much had changed for Yosef. This time he led a thousand men, and he wasn't there to convince the Sepphoran leaders to join him and stand with Galilee against the Romans. He now knew they would not, but he hoped they would not intercede on the side of Yohanan of Gischala, who was in the city. One man who had joined him in Tiberias was a defector from the Gischalan leader's camp, and he had told Levi ben Altheus of the plans to hire a brigand leader from Sepphoris to attack Yosef with his 800 men... no matter where he was.

The men swelling his ranks and the news of exactly where Yohanan of Gischala was and what he was doing had given Yosef an answer to his question since the attack in Tiberias: "What do I do next?" The issue had been even further clarified by the news from Jerusalem brought him by the old priest who now rode next to him.

Yohanan ben Zaccai's arrival in Tiberias had been the only positive development in many days. He needed his counsel and needed someone he could talk to that would listen to him. He nudged his mount closer to his friend and leaned toward him. "Do you think my father can counter Shimon ben Gamliel's efforts to undermine me?" Yosef had been surprised at the revelation from Yohanan, but his father's letter had confirmed it.

"Shimon has always believed he deserves more power since he is a direct descendant of King David."

"He's president of the Sanhedrin. He has power."

"Not as much as that position once held—there are too many factions now."

"Then why doesn't he support me? I want to unify our country."

"But you were against rebelling, at least early on," Yohanan reminded him. "You advocated talking to resolve the issues with Roman rule and the actions of the last two procurators. In the private Sanhedrin discussions, Shimon opposed assigning you as commander in Galilee—he feels you are reluctant to fight the Romans."

"I was against starting a war we cannot win... that was why we needed to attempt to settle our problems peacefully first." Yosef shook his head, his eyes tightening he looked at the priest. "I will fight the Romans as best I can with what and who I have."

"I know. And now,"—the priest waved a fly from his face—"you convince others to fight with you." He flicked the fly away again as he leaned so close to Yosef he almost fell from his mule. "I trust in you, Yosef, and in what we must do. But do you still believe we cannot win?"

"We're nearing the gates," Yosef said, ignoring the question. "Levi!" he called over his shoulder, "I'll take fifty men with me to call upon the Sepphoran leaders. You take the rest and split them to cover the city gates. If you catch Yohanan of Gischala leaving... hold him for me."

* * *

"You seem uneasy, Ezekias," said Yohanan of Gischala, studying the man he had come to meet. Yohanan glanced around the market, at the few people eating and drinking around them in the open-air tavern beneath its sky-blue canopy. "Only a few of my men came with me into the city... and I come to speak fairly with you. I will pay your price if you attack the Jerusalemite, Yosef, and his men in Tiberias."

"That price and willingness... were then. This is now." The brigand leader shook his head, ignoring the Gischalan's offer of a goblet of wine. "And now I cannot help you."

"Why not? Do you want more money?"

"While money, more of it, is very important to me, my life is more valuable than coin. My grandfather"—Ezekias laughed—"and my father, too—don't you consider us all bandits? My grandfather, who detested those who would force rule on us, taught me that."

"What do you mean? Yosef poses no threat to you... he does not have enough men—"

"—The Romans do," Ezekias retorted. "My people watching them tell me the legion in Ptolemais begins to stir. The hammer they wield is coming, and I cannot commit men to kill others that some see as future allies. They will be allies when we all—very soon—have thousands of Romans to face." Ezekias caught the signal sent by one of his men on watch in the crowd and rose to leave. Then he paused, to lean down and whisper in the Gischalan's ear: "And your Jerusalemite... this Yosef... he now has more men than you think."

As the brigand chief quickly walked away toward the eastern end of the market, a commotion at the western end made the Gischalan turn in his chair to see its cause. Yosef ben Mathias—the milling crowd of market-goers parting before him—led two dozen armed men straight toward him. That rustling sound of many people moving behind him drew his look in that direction. More armed men... many more... were closing on him. He sat back and crossed his arms to stare at Yosef, who was now close enough to hear him.

"So, what will you do?" Yohanan of Gischela asked. "Will you kill me here or take me outside the city for that?"

Yosef pulled out the chair that Ezekias had just left, rested his forearms on the table, and folded his hands. "You'll be coming with me, but you will come as a prisoner awaiting punishment if you fail to see reason. We will talk about how we can put what you've done behind us and work together for the good of Galilee. Your answer decides your fate."

* * *

The Sepphoran leaders—not willing to hinder nor aid Yosef with the Gischalan—had graciously offered lodging for the night. The bed was far more comfortable than the cot he had slept on lately, but he did not think he would ever be able to sleep easily again. Yohanan of Gischala, after a lengthy discussion with Yosef and Yohanan ben Zaccai, had agreed to join forces with them. Yosef knew that alliance would be unsteady and would likely last only as long as it served the Gischalan. But it was a truce of sorts and allowed Yosef to focus on returning to Yotapta and using the men who had joined him and the new support to do more to secure Galilee. Perhaps that would put at ease those in Jerusalem who doubted him. He worried about that until he accepted it as where things stood—then he had fallen asleep with his last thoughts on what Yohanan ben Zaccai had asked him before entering Sepphoris. The question he had not answered, because what he truly believed frightened him. His eyes finally closed, and he slept.

Yosef tossed and turned as voices around him echoed—softly—off the stone, and within his dream, he sensed that he was surrounded. Through that faint murmur, one voice grew louder. It came not off the rock but through it. He felt the chill of a damp floor and stiffness from sleeping on stone. He half-stumbled over others sitting in the shadows and made his way toward the wall where that distinct voice seemed strongest. A voice he recognized but could not quite place called to him: "Yosef... you must surrender... come out... you must... you will be safe."

XXV

ROME

Even as a *trecenarius*, Nicanor was still junior to two of the other watch captains and thus had the next-to-most onerous watch assigned: from *diluculum*, the end of the daytime watch at twilight, up to *media noctis*, midnight. It had not taken long, but he now disliked the Tullianum even more than when he had first visited it with Yosef nearly three years before. The lower portion that held the prisoner's cells was rank and damp, and he understood the grumbling of the watch guard who had to walk the post in the poorly lit dankness below. But since he had arrived, it had grown to more than the usual soldier's complaints.

One benefit and appeal of duty in the Praetorian Guards were the bonuses—relatively easy duties and better food. But the most important had been that the pay three times a soldier's equivalent rank in the legions. Nicanor had agreed to what Cestius Gallus had asked him to do because of a sense of duty and loyalty he felt he owed the man, but the higher pay had mattered too.

But now the pay had been cut in half and twice delayed. The rumors were quiet for now but spreading with the men's unrest. That feeling of uncertainty about their pay bothered the men more than anything, though, for Nicanor, the money had never been a priority until now when he was on the verge of retiring. He lived frugally, cared little for gambling... and other than indulging a fondness for beer, he had spent little other than on necessities. He had hoped the unaccustomed surplus pay could be saved to grow and ease his retirement years.

"What is it, Darius?" Nicanor watched as the guard came onto the central administrative level of the prison. The legionary, his large frame wracked by a series of harsh rattling coughs, tried to stand straight before him.

"Centurion... I'm sick..." He coughed again, and his pale face was slick with sweat. He shivered, his teeth chattering, "I'm sorry, but I don't think I can fini—" The man tottered and fell to the floor, the chills and cough wracking him yet again as he lay on the stones.

It looked like the ague, *febris acuta*, that Nicanor had seen in some men who had served in Africa. He turned to the auxiliary clerk-courier, always on duty. "Florin, go to Arx Capitolina and bring back a medic." He bent and hauled the man toward a bench. With a grunt—

the legionary was almost as big as he was—Nicanor got him onto the bench where he lay insensible. As he waited on the medic, he checked the guard roster. Darius had been charged with watching the next-to-lowest level and was a little more than halfway through his watch.

Nicanor peered closer, trying to make out a scribbled name of who was on that level. Oddly, it was only one man. "Paul, a Christian," he muttered and went to the watch desk and pulled out the prisoner manifest. He flipped the sheets open and ran a thick finger down the lines until he found him. "Moved to the Tullianum after two years of house arrest as he awaited trial. Then condemned as a heretic for impiety against the gods because of his conversion to Christianity and an enemy of the empire because of his preaching and spreading of those seditious beliefs. By order of the emperor, he now awaits execution." According to the entry, the prisoner had come here nearly five years before.

This Paul, originally a Roman citizen from Antioch, was the man Lord Tigellinus had mentioned to him that day as they climbed to Arx Capitolina for Nicanor to report for duty. He had heard some guards talk about the man. Some spoke in tones that seemed to show what the prisoner had said to them had made sense or had touched them emotionally.

A few minutes later, the clerk scurried in, breathing heavily, with two men behind him. "Take care of this man," Nicanor directed the medics, pointing at the guard prone on the bench. "Carry him to the barracks where you can treat him."

"Florin"—he looked at the clerk—"I'll be below and will stand the rest of Darius's watch." He pointed at the sick man and rechecked the roster for his watch post level. "Come get me if I'm needed up here, and when the next watch-captain and guard relief reports."

* * *

Nicanor had been told that only in the driest months did it cease—the faint *drip drip drip* of water from the stone overhead that ran down the walls. The farther and deeper one went, the more dripping and the louder the sound. And the deeper and farther back one went, the more serious the occupant's transgressions against Rome. Paul was in the next-to-last level, and Nicanor had heard that he was slated for beheading, unlike the more common sentence of execution by strangulation. After five years, only the emperor knew when. He reached the next lowest level, stepped down, and followed the corridor to the cells, his steps loud on the stone.

"Hello... is that you, Darius? Are you okay?"

The thin, reedy voice echoed around Nicanor as the puddles of light from torches, and an occasional oil lantern were mounted farther apart, and it became harder to see. He cursed at not thinking to bring a lamp.

"Is that you, Darius?"

Just then, Nicanor came into the arc of light from the lantern hung from a hook beside the cell. The man inside stood in front of a pile of damp straw and a roll of tattered blankets. The man seemed old—but possibly not as old as he looked. This place, a domain only Pluto would enjoy, would age any man if he could live very long in such conditions. And all while awaiting the release of the imprisonment by a single stroke of the executioner's ax.

"Oh... you're not Darius... he seemed terribly ill... is he okay?" The tall, thin man gripped the bars of his cell and peered at him.

Nicanor wondered at the man's concern for his jailor. "He is sick, but I've called medics to care for him."

"Good... good..." The ragged man swept back a lank length of unkempt hair—only a top tuft like a scraggly bush grown in a bare patch of dirt. He studied Nicanor. "You're not a guard, are you, centurion?"

"No, I'm the watch-captain."

The man stooped to drag a wooden stool clear of the damp straw and closer to the cell door. He sat and looked up. In the lantern's glow, Nicanor recognized him. His first day, when the prison commander had toured him through parts of the prison, he would prefer not to have seen. In the lowest chamber—the level beneath his feet now—they had come upon a scene with four guards and four prisoners. He had watched as this man had performed some Jewish or Christian ritual for his fellow prisoners. He dipped them in a shallow pool of water that had gathered in a cavity in the natural stone floor and spoke some prayer or intonation over them. Then he proclaimed them "reborn" as he helped them rise. The men had looked the same to him—only wetter—though they'd lost some dirt and grime on their faces.

"Why do you let him do this?" he had asked the commander.

"All the lower cells have plenty of water during rains—it is no loss to accommodate their ritual... I think it is called a baptism. It puts them at peace, so they cause no trouble. What does it matter? They will all sooner or later die here or"—the commander had jabbed a thumb up at the ceiling and what lay beyond it far above—"be thrown from the rock." The Tullianum's commander had then turned away, beckoning Nicanor to follow, and he had not seen the man since that day.

"Why are you here?" Paul asked.

Nicanor looked down at Paul and hesitated... he did not have an answer for him. He commanded a hundred men with duties that covered both guard duty here at the Tullianum and several posts at the fortress above and could have called for a replacement. But for this one prisoner—an old, relatively frail man—locked in a cell underground with only a single exit, there was little risk in that guard's absence. And he was curious. "I saw you... doing... what is it called... a baptism on some of the other prisoners."

"I baptized them, yes... a baptism."

"Why?" Before meeting and developing an unexpected friendship with Yosef, Nicanor had seldom talked with Jews, or those he knew were Jewish. And he was sure he had never spoken with any that were Christians. The conversations with Yosef had intrigued him but never inclined him to convert as he had heard some Romans were secretly doing. He was just curious at what some saw as a reason to abandon their Roman gods.

"Why not, centurion?" Paul straightened his clothing, such as it was, being too long worn, ragged, and soiled. He sat there calmly as if under a tree and talking with a student or friend. "Why wouldn't I provide them what they seek? To be cleansed by the Spirit of God, to gain His forgiveness and feel not just redeemed and reborn, but unburdened"—he smiled up at Nicanor— "and to have the promise of eternal life awaiting them beyond this place."

* * *

It had been days, and Nicanor had not replaced Darius on the watch list. Florin, the clerk, had more than once looked questioningly at the centurion as Nicanor said, "Call me if I'm needed up here," and readied to descend to the prisoner levels. The watch-captain who relieved him—a younger man without the too-thick crust of experience that jades many men—had asked, "Why stand that watch, Nicanor?"

He liked the young man whose assignment to the Praetorian Guard came from his father's connections and not from having served in a legion in the provinces—and he had told him a half-truth: "I won't do this for long. It helps me to understand what the men— the regular guards—go through on their posts. That way, when I command, they know I have done what they have done. I have not always just sat on my ass far above them... warm and dry among bright lights."

The whole truth was that he found his conversations with Paul interesting. Duty in Rome was proving more tedious than in the provinces, even for a man of simple taste.

With a last nod to Florin, he headed down. Tucked beneath his arm was the folding stool he had purchased so he would have a place to sit. Standing was tiresome, and looking down at the old man gave him a crick in his neck by time the watch ended.

"*Bonum vesper*—good evening, Nicanor." Paul had stopped calling him "centurion" the second night, at Nicanor's request.

Nicanor nodded, unfolded the stool, and set it a step from the cell's bars, swept his cloak back with one arm, and sat down to relax. "I was here once before"—he waved a hand at their surroundings— "years ago, with a Judean who had come to Rome to free some priests being held here."

"I was glad when I heard of their release," Paul said with a smile.

"After the fire." Nicanor tugged the tail of his cloak back from a thread of water winding through the cell floor.

Paul's smile faded. "That was a terrible tragedy... so many died and even more lost all they owned. All they had."

"Did the Christians really start it?" He and Yosef had often wondered about that, and this man would surely know.

"No... but in some ways, the accusation has made more people come to the Lord Yeshua, the Divine One."

"How is that?"

"Yeshua brings a message of hope... and of love and peace. Many seek that"—Paul scratched an eyebrow tangled like a thicket—"and I tell everyone this—his is a message of nonviolence."

"The emperor and others in the Senate believe the Christians did it to destroy Rome." Nicanor watched Paul's expression closely. The man's sardonic smile had matched Nicanor's own thoughts when he had talked with Yosef about the empire's claim.

"How could they?"—Paul touched his chest—"How could such as we... destroy vast and powerful Rome even by burning one city?" He shook his head. "Our Lord Yeshua would never call for inflicting such terror. We seek peaceful resolutions. Why do something so horrible that the consequences would only make things harder on us?"

"My Jewish friend is from Jerusalem... he is the Judean I mentioned that was here in Rome with me, before and after the fire, and he believes the same way."

Paul was quiet, but the arch of one eyebrow showed his surprise at a Roman claiming a Jewish friend. "Would that be Yosef ben Mathias?"

"Yes, I believe so. His father is one of the ruling council in Jerusalem."

"Yes, we heard that he had been the one who had helped to free the priests. I knew of his father in my early years in Jerusalem."

Nicanor continued, "He had a vision... a dream that foretold the fire...."

"Where is your friend Yosef now?"

"I would have assumed in Jerusalem.... but now... I don't know," Nicanor said with a shrug.

The splat of a fat drop of water landed, and Saul bent his head and wiped it and his face with a sleeve. "I've heard the guards' talk of the rebellion there, and the fighting... is Yosef also a fighter? Good with the sword, like you?"

"No," Nicanor grinned, "not like me at all... not a soldier, although I trained him on some basics."

Paul blinked. "It seems odd that you should have met and become friends."

Nicanor silently agreed with him and could tell he was curious. But that was a story for another time.

"You say Yosef had a vision... of the fire here?" Paul asked.

Nicanor nodded. "Yes... he has had more than one such dream come to pass."

"Our Lord Yeshua also can see into the future. He has foretold that Jerusalem would also fall... and burn, most likely, as did Rome. And our Lord has never been wrong. I fear for Yosef's safety, as for all in Judea these days. I will pray that your friend remains safe." Paul folded his hands on his chest and closed his eyes.

"I now fear for him too, and for others, I know in Judea and Jerusalem," Nicanor said as the man bowed his head. He knew that soon—if not already—the legions would converge in Judea, and there would be little hope left for that city, or his friend and his family.

"But"—Paul looked up at the ceiling of his cell and then into Nicanor's eyes—"as your Roman writer Seneca the Elder said in his writings, 'Every new beginning comes from some other beginning's end.'"

A shout rang down the corridor. "Centurion... centurion... you are needed!" He stood and folded the stool, tucking it under one arm. "I must go and see"—he nodded at Paul, who bowed his head.

"Take care, centurion."

The clerk was at the end of the corridor at the foot of the ladder from the levels above. "What is it, Florin?"

"A visitor has asked for you."

"What does he need?"

"I don't know centurion... and did not ask,"—Florin looked shocked—"He's a general!"

XXVI

Laodicea ad Mare, Syria (Roman Eastern Province)

Sayid checked on his mother before washing the blood from his hand to see how bad the gash was. The swath of cloth cut from the tail of his tunic and wrapped around it would do for a while longer, though it was so soaked it now dripped with each step. He peeked into her bedroom. His aunt, Yara, who helped watch her sister during the day, was nodding in a chair. She opened her eyes as he stepped in and went to his mother's bedside.

"She is the same, Sayid. The fever comes and goes... and she is still weak."

"Thanks, Yara... I'll watch her now."

His aunt rose and gathered her robe around her, "I will see you in the morning, then. I made the *yakhanit batata*, but I had no lamb for the stew, so it has slices of braised goat meat spiced with *bharat* instead." Yara pointed at his hand—"You've hurt yourself again?"

Sayid looked up from smoothing the damp hair from his mother's sweating brow and shrugged off how often he brought home the nicks and cuts of hard manual labor. When he had first arrived home, he had been shocked to find his mother so sick. She had gone entirely gray in just a few years—four since he had seen her last—and that had frightened him. She had always been a slender woman, but now she was so frail.

"Let me clean that wound and put a fresh bandage on it before I go"—Yara gestured toward the doorway.

He nodded and, with a last caress of his mother's brow, followed his aunt to the washroom. His mother and aunt were all the family he had until he found his father. And then—if he did—he wondered if he would ask him the questions he had held deep inside for so long.

* * *

It was a tiny house of only three rooms, with a small back porch away from the street, screened by a wall, with a large bowl on a low bench and a water barrel for washing. The house felt even smaller when his father, a large man, had been around. That had been a rare occasion when Sayid was young, and he had not seen him for a long time. On the kitchen table was bowl covered by a cloth, and a cup and a clay pitcher Sayid knew held fresh well water. Yara, not wishing to use the brackish water from the storage barrel, would have drawn it for him just before she expected him home from work.

In the common area of the house—a combination of cooking, eating, and living space—was a Roman-style couch his father had brought home long ago. Sayid slept there, close enough to see into his mother's room, and to hear her if she should call for him. His aunt had tied his bedding into a neat roll that now sat in a corner. He sat on the end closest to his mother and stretched his legs out, resting his throbbing hand on his lap, grateful the rest of his body did not ache as much as it had for his first two months working at the seaport.

As a soldier—an auxiliary—he was used to hard work and long days. But loading and unloading boats and ships on the busy docks used different muscles, and the man he worked for was meaner and more demanding than any legionary *tesserarius*. And for the last few years, his duties as part of Lady Cleo's escort had been easy, but for the adventures of the shipwreck of the *Salacia* and his serving as a courier for Lady Cleo and Lord Gallus's wife, Octavia. All of that had led to a race to get to the 12th Legion's commander before the attack on Jerusalem with information that could stop the attack. Sayid had been delayed and was too late, but what was in those letters must have mattered—Lord Gallus had halted the attack and pulled back. After that, many men had been killed at Beth Horon, himself nearly included. Poor Abigieus—though dying, he carried me to safety—such a noble horse, he sighed.

Thinking of Lady Cleo made him sad.... and he felt the pressure building, the urgency that he needed to be doing what Lady Octavia had asked him just before he left her in Antioch. Sayid was to tell her husband she was well but missed him sorely, and when he returned to Ptolemais, would he please also check on Cleo and make sure she was safe and well. Sayid cared for Lady Cleo and wanted to do as Lady Octavia asked, and he would. But he had needed to see his mother. It had been so long, and he had been so near before but could not go to visit her in Laodicea ad Mare. And it would have been even longer without Lord Gallus's grace to give him permission.

Back in Antipatris, before he departed for his new duty in Rome, Nicanor had told Sayid Lord Gallus had granted him leave to visit his mother. The next morning, as Nicanor had instructed him, Sayid had reported to the 12th Legion's commander to receive the document he must carry at all times that granted him leave from the legion and proved he was not a deserter. Without the document, he could be detained by Roman patrols between Antipatris and Antioch, and then with all Romans on edge and wary, he would likely be summarily executed. The legate had handed him the paperwork bearing two stamped seals and explained:

"This—your leave authorization—is for an undetermined and indefinite time, which is why I've also attested to it with both the official seal and my personal seal." Sayid had not understood what he meant, but Lord Gallus went on: "I ask you to do something for me, and I don't know how much time it will take. I ask this of you not for the Roman army, but for me personally. Will you do it?"

He had almost asked the commander what he wanted him to do; he must know before he could answer. But couldn't seem so discourteous and instead had replied, "If I can, my lord."

Lord Gallus had then turned to take a broad belt of supple leather from the table behind him that had an empty coin purse tied to it. Flipping it over, beneath a plain flap that ran the length of the belt, he revealed a hidden slit in its backside that formed a pouch. Sayid had never seen a belt with something like that. The legate had then laid the belt on his desk and taken a long, flattened, thin rectangular packet that looked as if it had been coated in wax to protect it, and he slid it into the belt's pouch and folded over the flap to cover it. He flipped it over again. "These are important documents for my wife. She—and only she—must receive them. Antioch will be hard to get into now, so this will help you"—he held up another sheet of parchment that he then folded and sealed—"Along with the orders granting you leave; this is my personal authorization that will get you into the city and to my wife."

He had reached again to the table behind him and, with the clink of metal, turned back with a small sack in his hands. He transferred its contents—silver coins—into the belt's coin purse and cinched it closed with its pull cord. "Use this as you need, if you're stopped or robbed... let them have the money but not the belt. Keep it on you always. Can you—will you—do this for me, Sayid?"

The young man had felt the pressure of the commander's request—his grim expression, the thrust of his gaze—upon him. Nicanor had told him Lord Gallus was a good man who had been wrongly advised, and that was part of why Nicanor had accepted orders to go to Rome and take the commander's message to Nero. Now, how could he not do what Lord Gallus had requested of him, especially since the man had just given him the freedom to see his mother? So, he had told his commander. "I will do this for you, lord."

From that day, it had taken him more than a month of walking, running, and hiding to get to Antioch. His home, Laodicea, was only three days walk, south and along the coast, from Antioch. But Lord Gallus had stressed the importance of Sayid delivering the contents of the belt to Lady Octavia first. So, that is what he had done. In Antioch, he had given her the packet Lord Gallus had secreted away, and though he had told her that he had said he would join her soon, Lady Octavia had been distraught and feared for her husband.

Arriving in Antioch with much of the money Lord Gallus had given him, Sayid had, despite her protests, given it to Lady Octavia. She had made him accept five silver coins, and that, along with almost all the money he made laboring at the port, he was saving to help his mother once he returned to the legion.

Sayid got up and moved to the small kitchen table he had pulled to where he could sit, eat, and still see and hear his mother. He could not leave her until she could care for herself.

He lifted the cloth from the bowl, and the aroma wafting from it lifted his spirits. The *bharat* perfumed the surrounding air, its blend of black pepper, cinnamon, ginger, nutmeg, cloves, and cardamom, always making him think of his mother. The neighborhood had always praised her and his Aunt Yara for their preparation of the spice. Until he returned to it, he had not realized how much he missed the food of his childhood.

Sayid looked at his hands, holding the cloth. They had taken such a beating in his labor. Laodicea was a trade center, and his supervisor—the wharf master—worked the men hard. But along with earning money for his mother, Sayid found it useful for another reason—it was an excellent place to hear the news and rumors of the empire and the surrounding region. He had listened to the tales coming from Galilee, of a new military commander that had come from Jerusalem. He seemed to have brought some people and towns together to unite in their coming war with Rome. Sayid knew from his capture and then release by Yohanan of Gischala how stubborn Galileans could be, and that getting them to come together was quite an accomplishment. He had asked the man with the news what this commander from Jerusalem's name was and had been shocked to hear it. Could it really be the Yosef ben Mathias that he knew! The same sailor—from a Roman trading vessel that worked the coast from Alexandria to Antioch—had told him the gossip in Alexandria was that a Roman general would soon come to lead the legions against the Jewish rebels. This time it would be a real battle-tested general, not like the one before who had disgraced Rome with his failures. The new one would show those rebels how foolish it was to stand against Rome.

Sayid sighed and began to eat, wondering at Lord Gallus's fate. In Antioch, he had seen the forces massing there in readiness to march. He prayed his mother would be well soon. He must check on Lady

Cleo and let Lord Gallus know he had made the delivery to his wife—before new fighting turned all of Galilee into a battlefield.

XXVII

The promise of spring was in the air on this sunny day, a welcome sign that winter's grip had loosened. Though the morning coolness lingered, the wind was not the only thing that chilled Cleo's heart and soul. Ptolemais was securely Roman, but still, she felt the occasional sharp looks and shifting squints of the locals who were uneasy or unhappy with her presence on their streets and in their market. Some of them left her with the sensation that they, too, dreaded what was to come. That feeling was even stronger within the confines of her home—well, where she lived now was not home. She had not had a home since marrying Gessius Florus and leaving Rome. Now she felt always adrift and alone in a way she had not experienced even after the shipwreck of the *Salacia*.

Over her shoulder, she saw the boy a few steps behind, a new servant she had selected to attend her. Not allowing Glaucio, her husband's household manager, to make the choice. "Are you doing well, Elian?" She almost smiled as she asked, seeing him so carefully carrying Cicero's cage. Around them, the people in the crowd seemed to stare at the bird and boy as much as at her. Maybe they gawked because Cicero sat so regally on his perch, bobbing his head with each step and enjoying the movement and the freshness of the breeze. A large green parrot in a golden cage was not something often seen on the streets. But she could not bear to stay inside that residence with the weather so lovely. Nor would she leave Cicero alone there—not when her husband was pacing its halls and grounds. Not with Glaucio's constant spying and leering grin when in her presence. So, for the scarce hours possible, every day she could, she escaped to the market. She went ostensibly to shop for decor to match what her husband admired at Herod's Palace in Caesarea, their residence when Gessius Florus had been the Judean Procurator. Many of the fittings and objects he liked were part of the palace's furnishings and had remained there. She cared little if she found any of it for her husband, as long as she could use its pursuit as an excuse to create even a momentary sense of freedom from him.

"Stay close to me, Elian,"—she beckoned with a hand to draw him nearer. The two men her husband insisted accompany her—watchers and spies in their own right, no doubt—tried to serve as a buffer, but the press of people thickened as they neared the port. The people in the market strolling about and shopping frequently got between them, and she worried she might get separated from the boy and the bird.

"Lady Cleo!" a voice called out, and before she could locate the direction from whence it came, she felt a slight tug of her sleeve from behind. She turned as the hand released her to behold a man with the chapped and wind-burned face that spoke of his having been many days at sea and under the sun. His broad smile broke through the thicket of his black beard and shone against his darkened skin. It was Costas, the olive-wood trader who had carried letters and messages from her to Lady Octavia in Antioch. She had not seen him since November in Caesarea, and she had received no word from Octavia in return—that had become another of her fears.

"In Caesarea," Costas said, "I heard that you were now in Ptolemais, and I just arrived in port here. The harbormaster knew of your husband's location in the city, and while the men unload, I was heading to see if you were home. How fortunate to find you here!" The trader bowed toward her and then straightened, still grinning.

Cleo's eyes immediately went to her escorts, who were unaware she had stopped and had moved several steps away from her. Afraid to move farther from them and catch their attention, but fearful not to—she must escape their eyes and ears—she hesitated.

It was too late to do either, as the man too loudly declared, "I have letters for you from Lady Octavia!" Costas's eyes had shifted with Cleo's, puzzled at who she looked toward, and then back to her.

Cleo darted another look at her husband's men—a handful of men and women were now between them and her—and hoped the buzz of marketplace conversation and noise smothered his voice. She held a palm out toward the trader, who did not realize her need to be discreet. "Please, Costas... speak quietly"—she half-turned as if studying the wares of the shop before her and gestured for the trader to stand on her left away from the two escorts. "What do you have for me?"

The men, she saw from the corner of her eye, had noted she was looking at something and waited patiently. Not moving toward her, they turned their scrutiny returned to the throng of shoppers that milled about them amid the vendors brazenly hawking their goods at every passerby.

The trader reached into a fold of his robe and, with a little twisting to free it, withdrew two squares of parchment, one larger than the other, banded together with a leather strap. "These are from Lady Octavia. I... I mean with my new ship, my own that I just picked up in Alexandria"—the man's proud smile flashed again—"I have many stops up the coast to offload cargo and must wait at Tyre and then Sidon to load shipments destined for Antioch." He handed the bundle to her. "So, it will be some time before I reach Antioch, but do you have any messages you wish me to take to her?"

Cleo quickly tucked the letters into the drape of her robe and out of sight. Thinking fast, she saw to her left, in front of a stall that sold parchment and vellum, an old man at a small table offering letter writing services. Checking that the two men were not watching her closely, Cleo stepped over to the table and dropped a coin in the bowl beside his left elbow. "Pardon me..." she took the piece of parchment that listed the items to look for in the market and flipped it over to its blank side. She picked up the reed pen of Egyptian bamboo the letter writer had just set down and dipped it into his inkpot, writing hurriedly:

Octavia, I hope you are well, but I know you must be full of concern for your husband. I worry too and fear for our future. Have you seen or heard anything of Sayid, the Syrian who brought you my letters? I have not. But know he must have reached your husband in time. Has Lord Gallus mentioned anything of him? I have yet to read what Costas, the trader who has carried our letters, brought me from you this day. But if the letters do not answer what I ask in this message, please let me know as soon as you can. I fear that I have put Sayid in danger—he, despite his misgivings, carried those letters to you as a favor to me. I hope you remain safe, and please take care!

Blowing on the jotted message to dry the ink, Cleo folded it in quarters then dropped a blob of wax from the letter writer's bronze bowl of sealant kept warm by a small brazier of charcoal embers. She reached into her robe for her *lunula*, the pendant she had begun wearing again after Gessius Florus struck her the first time. Its crescent-shaped moon—meant to ward off evil for the wearer and to provide protection—had been added to by her friend Poppaea, who was then married to her brother and had given it to her as a gift when she was a young girl. The talisman's original design now included a golden arrow that crossed the moon. Poppaea had jokingly called

Cleo her private Diana... goddess of the hunt and the moon—for her interest in archery. Octavia would recognize the seal as hers. Cleo pressed it into the cooling wax, leaving its distinct impression, and turned back to the trader, moving closer to hand the message to him.

"Please get his to Lady Octavia as soon as you can." She emptied her purse of its several coins, and just as she gave them to the trader, Cicero squawked his annoyance at the too-long halt. The two men escorting Cleo turned at the parrot's distinctive call that cut through the noise and spotted the trader too close to their charge, nearly touching and holding out a hand toward her.

"What's this?!" one called, and they pushed toward her, the fast-moving bulk of their thick bodies parting the way as they shoved men and women aside.

"Go quickly," she whispered to the trader whose eyes widened and slid sideways toward the two very large Romans closing on him. He nodded at Cleo, then spun around and swiftly slipped into the crowd and was soon lost to sight.

"He was just a beggar man seeking alms... no harm at all"—she pacified the men and noticed—with some concern—the wide-eyed expression on Elian's face. She would have to later caution the boy to never speak of what was seen or heard when he was with her. "I'm done for the day and ready to return now." She turned from the two men and walked in the direction opposite of the one Costas had taken. With an elbow, she pressed Octavia's letters to her side, before they slipped farther down inside her robe.

Cleo did not notice the old woman following who had blended so well with all the other local woman shopping. The woman that had witnessed everything said between her and the trader. She no longer trailed Cleo, but then she did not need to know where the lady went— they had the same destination.

XXVIII

Miriam held Yosef's letter in her hand but still thought about what she had just overheard from down in the courtyard beneath her window. She picked up her pen dipped in ink, flattened the sheet of parchment on the table, and began to write:

> Yossi, I just heard Matthew ask our father if there had been any response to the government's request to our neighboring rulers and those leaders with a significant Jewish population... He's asking them to join us against the Romans, thinking they will stand with Jerusalem. Our father—and oh Yossi, I have never heard him sound so tired and sad—he told Matthew that most of them have not answered, though they have been asked repeatedly. Some had replied that they cannot or will not help, nor even vocally support our rebellion. It seems no one will come to aid Jerusalem.
>
> Purim approaches, and I have thought Rome is our Haman, and they will destroy us because, as Haman claimed, "The Jews are a scattered and divided nation." But our story will not be the Megillat Esther... no one will write our Book of Esther with a joyous ending at our survival. Midah ke-neged midah... measure for measure... we shall reap what we sow. I do not mean to distress you with my words. You have so many burdens to bear of your own, and I pray for your safety.
>
> You mentioned in your last letter that Matthew was concerned about me and that you are, too. I thank both of

you, my older brothers, and will tell this to Matthew in person as I wish I could say it to you. I love you and pray for our salvation that will release you from your duty so you can return home. So many miss you. But do not worry about me... we all must be strong and do what we can to defend our faith and city against the Romans and any who assist them.

If survival is not our fate, then I wish that this part of the Megillat Esther should come true: "And the Jews struck down all their enemies with the sword, killing them, and they did what they pleased to those who hated them."

* * *

Miriam re-read what she had written the night before to her brother far from home and away from those who loved him. He was among people who distrusted him, according to their parents' conversations with Matthew, and according to the concerns Yosef shared in his letters. She walked to the window and opened the shutter. A bracing night breeze lifted tendrils of her unbound hair. It was still dark out, and the gray promise of dawn was yet to come, so she moved Zechariah's lamp closer as she sat at the table. She should not alarm Yosef further—he might encourage Matthew's intervention—so she re-wrote the letter to leave out the last part. Once that was done, with dawn lightening the sky, she dressed and left for Zechariah's.

* * *

In Zechariah's shop, Miriam stood before a tall mirror of highly polished brass, framed in olive-wood mounted over a connected shallow bronze basin. She had found it—the bowl filled with what looked like dry, brittle stems and dead petals of some flower—in a dark corner of Zechariah's home. She had come upon the mirror as she and Elzar ben Yair searched again for Zechariah's tunnel maps, in his sleeping room covered by a large dusty canvas. Flipping the sheet away, she had been surprised to see such an object in the home of a blind man.

106

Elazar ben Yair had looked so somber when she mentioned that, and then she wished she had not commented about it that way. With a sigh, he had told her, "It was his wife's... he made the mirror for her when he still had his sight." The Sicarii leader had put his hand on the frame as if patting the shoulder of his old friend. "Zechariah was a skilled craftsman in many things." He stepped away from the mirror to the shuttered window and partially opened it to scan outside. "And he was surprising in even more ways."

Miriam wondered what he meant by that, but she knew his wife and daughter had been killed by the Romans. Zechariah had shared that much of his past with her, and now she knew why the mirror had been covered. That was a tradition in Jewish families who have lost a loved one. Covering the mirror for a time after the death meant that you should think of the one you could no longer see. *Do not focus on your image... instead, remember theirs—though they're gone.*

Her words questioning a blind man's need for a mirror would have hurt Zechariah if he had heard them, and that had made Miriam sick to her stomach. That thoughtless remark disrespected a man she cared for a great deal, a man who had given her a great gift—the ability and will to fight back against those who had hurt her.

She stood before that mirror now and thought of what the rabbis said about mirrors and the grieving. Those who have lost someone or something dear to them can become so vulnerable that they see visions within the mirror in the days and nights following that loss. The emotions reflected within it—of how things once were, before—can eat away at the bereaved and empty the soul. Then the images can fill the mourner with anger, remorse... and maybe the most bitter of all—any fault one feels at the loved one's death. In the mirror, the burning rage and accusation stare back.

Looking at herself in the mirror, Miriam felt all those emotions, especially the fury. And she thought, with a fading sense of regret, that she—the old Miriam—was the one who had died. The new Miriam in the mirror was the fault of the Romans, and they would pay for her creation. Letting those judgments pass, she examined what she wore. The padding around her midriff, along with the cloth strapped around her chest to flatten her breasts, gave Miriam the appearance of a short, portly man once she put on a man's tunic and *ezor*, the apron worn around the hips and loins. But even with her face shrouded by a *keffiyeh*, bound with a cord circlet around her head, that covered her forehead to drape across her shoulders... she thought her features still too feminine.

Miriam tested her movement, twisting her torso, feeling the padding settle lower beneath her chest. There was something

Zechariah had said during a training session before he was killed. He suggested that perhaps a false beard would help the disguise. Then a few days later, he had shown one to her. Where he got it, she had no idea. A wiry, spade-shaped full-brush of real hair, he had said. Then he had put it away somewhere, and three days afterward, he was dead. Where did he keep it? She and Elazar ben Yair had hunted everywhere for Zechariah's maps. That search would surely have revealed where Zechariah kept the false beard.

She straightened and faced the mirror again. The sun's angle through the partially open shutter had changed, and light waned in the room. An arc of dimness had grown larger at the high point of the mirror, even with the lighted lantern she had placed on a table nearby. She shifted the mirror closer and angled it toward the window, carefully, as it caught on something and almost tottered. Opening the shutter wider—just long enough for a quick look—cast more light into the room and illuminated the mirror and the space it had occupied. In the spot where it had stood, in the sun, she saw what the mirror had snagged on. A small square of stone rode higher than the rest. She knelt and tried to press it down with her hands, and it felt like a box lid that would not lie flat. Curious, she took the old utility knife from her belt sheath and dug the tip into that corner. Pushing down to pry up the slab, she discovered it was only an inch thick and came free. Holding it up with one hand, she tugged it to the side with the other to reveal a dark square hole only slightly smaller than the stone covering it. A rock chip was lodged on the ledge, where the piece should have rested evenly. She spun on her knees to reach the lantern on the table and set it beside the opening. There, sitting atop a square of thick wood fitted into the hole was the beard; it was dusty but just as she remembered it. Why it was so well-hidden, she did not know, but she was glad she had found it.

* * *

The glue once watered down, worked well to hold the beard in place. She knew Zechariah, who had gotten the glue from the leatherworker's shop across the alley, had used that concoction to hold broken shards from large pots in place as he re-clayed and then fired them. He could make a fractured piece whole and just as good as one that had never been broken. More than once—as she watched him deftly make such repairs—she had thought he had done the same for her. He had given her something to hold her together as she healed. She still hoped one day she would feel complete, but she knew what the Romans had broken inside her would never mend.

With a last look in the mirror, she left Zechariah's, finding the day had grown overcast. The clouds had clotted into a single mass over Jerusalem and were laden with rain that would surely break soon and pour down on the city. That was good for her. People sensing the coming storm moved quickly with heads down, and only a few even looked her way. More people were streaming into Jerusalem, and perhaps she seemed to others as just another new arrival in Jerusalem seeking protection behind its walls. Or—as Matthew and Eleasar ben Ananias had discussed—many were likely coming into the city now to make money with products and services demanded by a citizenry desperately focused on war preparations.

A stray gust of wind caught her *keffiyeh*, lifting its tail from the nape of her neck and off her shoulders. She felt the beard slip and pressed it back in place. Just ahead of her—ten feet away—a man stepped out of a shop. He looked right at her and then turned up the street. It was the knife-sharpener she had seen... Miriam observed the cast looks over his shoulder as if watching for someone following him. The mannerism was familiar; she had done the same ever since Matthew had followed her the day she had hidden inside the knife-sharpener's shop. She followed him—as another test—using all the tricks Zechariah had taught her to avoid notice, especially that of the target.

He went through the Lower City almost to the steps leading to the Upper City near the Temple enclosure and stopped at a series of large limestone support columns. He knelt before the center pillar and scanned left, right, and behind him. Knowing—from Zechariah's constant admonishments—to watch for such a sweep made by a cautious or nervous target, Miriam quickly ducked behind a column toward the end of the row. She heard something... a mournful sigh like a soft cry... or was it a trick of the wind as it swirled around the columns? She leaned to peer around the pillar that shielded her, flattening and holding the beard in place so she could see. The knife-sharpener traced something on the column with a long thin finger and then bowed as if in thought or prayer. After a moment, his head whipped up, and he looked to his left as a street vendor clattered by trying to beat the rain, running with his pushcart through an alley crossing. Miriam pulled back behind the column. There was a lull, and she heard the scrape of sandals that faded in the dying wind's silence. She leaned from behind the pillar. He was gone. She went to where he had stooped and did the same. Her fingers touched the chiseled inscription on the shaft of that stone column: '*Hananiah bar Dodalos mi-Yerushalayim*'—Hananiah, the son of Dodalos from Jerusalem.

The man's actions on the street had made Miriam suspicious, and why he would stop and read something he knew was there puzzled her. The raindrops beginning to fall seemed as large as quail eggs. She felt the weight of them tumbling through the rising wind, striking her as she hurried for the closest shelter. The beard had held in place until it became soaked, which fortunately was just as she reached Zechariah's again. She opened the door and entered. She stripped the *keffiyeh* from her head and walked to Zechariah's sleeping area. Moving the mirror, she had replaced to cover Zechariah's hidden storage compartment, she lifted the slab and started to put the beard in, then dried it with a cloth and combed it out. As she laid it in the hole and smoothed it flat, she noticed a small cut-out in one corner of the wood lining the bottom of the hole. Inserting a finger, she lifted, and it came loose, revealing a larger area underneath. She reached in and lifted out a thick stack of parchment and several flattened scrolls strapped with bands of cloth or leather cords. A scroll fell to one side, and she picked it up. Slipping its cord free, she unrolled and held up to the lamp. She caught her name mentioned several times. Someone had written about her!

XXIX

The sun shone down on Yosef as he viewed the mass of men grouped on the broadest piece of level ground near Yotapta. The sun's warmth was welcome, but the thoughts of how he missed his friend Nicanor right now were not. He had spent many days with the Roman centurion on the fields of Mars just outside Rome in an earlier year, viewing and then training among a mass of men doing the same under the hot sun upon such a martial plain. But there were two—no, three important differences. The Romans had far, far more men... and far, far better weapons and equipment than did the Jews. And though this did not shame Yosef, it added to his sleepless nights. Rome had officers and leaders like Nicanor. But Yotapta and Galilee... had only him. Yosef was a far cry from a military man and had no experience in battle. "How many blacksmiths and metal workers do we have in Yotapta?" Yosef asked Levi ben Altheus, the newly appointed lieutenant who stood at his side.

"Two, Yosef... but one is old," Levi replied.

"Then we must find apprentices and helpers for them... or enlist the help of craftsmen and skilled metalworkers from other towns and villages. Now we must do the opposite of what Isaiah says in the Tanakh." Yosef gazed on the men who must lead but that were so poorly armed... and he quoted, "And they shall beat their swords into plowshares, and their spears into pruning hooks: nation shall not lift up sword against nation, neither shall they learn war anymore."

Squinting, Yosef shaded his eyes with one hand and continued. "Instead, we must beat our plowshares into swords and our pruning hooks... and boat hooks"—he almost smiled—"into spears. So the weak will say, I am strong." He lowered his hand and turned toward Levi.

"Still, the youngest men embrace learning some Roman training and the tactics you've shared." Levi pointed at a cluster of them practicing with some success, the making of a testudo, though most did not have shields and held their arms crossed over their heads. The Roman turtle formation was a simple defense maneuver to shelter men from attack but also, with coordinated movement, enabled them to advance under protection.

"I know, but I can show them only uncomplicated things, Levi... there's so much I don't know, and some that I saw while in Rome, I cannot explain, so we can replicate it here." Yosef continued to gaze at the men on the field. "On to other things... any news from Yohanan of Gischala? He promised to recruit more men from the towns I've not yet reached."

Levi scowled. "No, Yosef... he remains in his city."

"Is he doing anything to interfere with our work... has he returned to undermining me?" Yosef nodded as if expecting it.

"No. He sits in Gischala quietly, though I hear he has a steady flow of visitors."

"Well, at least he's quiet, and that is good news. I'll deal with him later. First, we must find or make more weapons for our men. As long as Yohanan continues to stay in Gischala and does not cause trouble for us..."

"But he might, Yosef..." Levi's grimace deepened.

"What do you mean?"

"You asked about the rumors that have now become complaints about someone charging exorbitant prices for scarce commodities: corn and olive-oil that follows our dietary laws. And that is causing an outcry among the people."

"It's a terrible sign that we still do not stand together. When someone uses circumstances and the hardship of others to profit, it perpetuates the belief that we Jews will always be fragmented... that every man is out for himself at the expense of others." Yosef looked at Levi. "What did you find out?"

"I worked through two layers of sellers that were being used merely as deception and got to the real seller. I found the root of all the profiteering in the region." The frown hardened on Levi's face, and his eyes narrowed, drawing deep lines that ran parallel on either side of his nose.

Yosef made the connection: "Yohanan of Gischala..."

"Exactly."

Long before being assigned its command, Yosef knew Galilee to be an agricultural region with an important fishing industry. The people depended on selling their crops and catches mostly to those who lived in the larger cities like Sepphoris, Tiberias, and to as far as Jerusalem. There were few storage facilities for surplus food in Galilee except those of King Agrippa had established in the neighboring land he claimed. And recently those stores had been raided by bandits. Galileans consumed what they did not sell, but without food storage, they literally lived hand to mouth. When a harvest or fishing catch was bad—or the pursuit of those industries was disrupted as they had been intermittently for a year—many went hungry. They would spend what money they had to feed their children and themselves. Yohanan of Gischala was taking advantage of them, and they were not happy.

"I will deal with him," Yosef said, turning from the overlook to mount his mule. "Stay here with the men and finish out the day. I must reach out to someone I had rather not." Yosef pulled on the reins and headed toward Yotapta.

* * *

"Yosef, the Sepphoran you sent for is here," announced Levi ben Altheus from the doorway.

"Please bring him in and join us, Levi." Yosef had seen the man only briefly in Sepphoris, as he left his meeting with Yohanan of Gischala, but knew more of him from the tales told throughout Galilee. Ezekias was a brigand and led hundreds of bandits. But Yosef had heard the man was not without a measure of principle. That personal honor was what Yosef hoped to reach by meeting with him.

"Sit, please"—Yosef gestured to the two chairs in front of his desk. "I'm told you once offered your 800 men to Yohanan of Gischala, and he turned you down. Then when he came to you and asked for your help to kill me, you turned him down. Why?"

Ezekias settled comfortably into the chair as Levi took the other. "Circumstances have much changed," he said. "As I told Yohanan of Gischala, the Romans are moving, already making small strikes in northern Galilee. I thought it better that we focus on killing them and not each other. Attacking you would be short-sighted and not worth what the Gischalan would pay me."

Yosef studied the Sepphoran, "Do you still feel that way?"

"I would not have come if I did not."

"Will you join me, then?" Yosef asked. "You know I need more men to face the Romans... and to deal with some things that now it seems I must."

"I know your need and what you face," Ezekias said as he leaned forward, "but my men are fighters, not farmers growing crops nor merchants plying their trade. My men have to be fed, as do their families." He sat back and crossed his arms.

"So, you still want to be paid?" Yosef asked, raising a palm at Levi ben Altheus, who had started to stand with indignance.

Ezekias ignored Levi's reaction and kept his eyes on Yosef. "Of course. Fighting is our trade, and it is all we offer. We must be paid, or we must raid wherever we can to earn what we can."

113

"And if we pay for your 800 men," Levi asked through gritted teeth, "will you and they be loyal?"

"My men and I will fight for you"—Ezekias uncrossed his arms and placed his palms flat on his thighs, still looking at Yosef—"I keep my word."

"You mean you will fight for Galilee and all Jews... against the Romans." Yosef stood and held out his hand.

"Yes, but it's not just 800 men anymore," Ezekias said with a smile. "I have raised an army of nearly 2,000 men, and all are equipped with good weapons."

"Can you help us with Yohanan of Gischala?" Levi asked what was also on Yosef's mind.

"As I told him in Sepphoris, I choose not to kill my fellow Jews—I save the fighting for the Romans." Ezekias shook his head and added, "The Gischalan is your problem to deal with."

XXX

When Nicanor emerged from the dimness of the prisoner levels below, the brightness of a man's *paludamentum* dazzled him. Obviously new, the cloak contrasted with the rest of the sturdy man's attire, making the clerk-courier Florin, next to him, seem slender as a reed. The man had not taken off his galea. Made of orichalcum or some alloy instead of the usual iron, it was well-worn and suited the man, as if the head it sat upon had grown into it. Beneath the embossed eyebrows and circular brass bosses, the helmet's only ornamentation, the eyes that peered at Nicanor were more determined than severe, and they held no tinge of the disdain evident in most of the generals he had seen up close.

The well-kept highly polished breastplate and backplate of *lorica musculata* were not for show. The armor had seen years of use attested to by its many scratches and smoothed-out dents. In the moments he took it all in, Nicanor recognized arrow creases or the glancing shots of a slinger's lead projectiles. The chest plate was unadorned, while other high-ranking officers wore their medals, especially in Rome.

The *caligae*, heavy-soled military sandals he wore were equally plain, the same type any legionary or unassuming centurion would wear. The hilt of the gladius appeared worn and smooth; its sheen created only by years of handling. But the short sword's leather *balteus* and sheath worn over the shoulder was stiff and seemed as new as the cloak. Also, under the cloak, across his shoulder opposite the *balteus* draped a loculus, a legionary's personal satchel.

Before Nicanor could salute or speak, but after his instincts had taken in the measure of the man, the general stepped toward him. In his left hand was a stout old wooden cudgel. He tapped its tapered end—tipped with a bronze ferrule—in the palm of his right hand.

"Are you the *tesserarius*, Nicanor," he asked, "who recently served under Cestius Gallus's 12th Legion in Antioch and Judea?"

A hollowness formed in Nicanor's stomach with his first thought that his subterfuge with the copies of Lord Gallus's letters and reports had somehow been discovered. But no... if that were so, he would not be confronted by a general. A squad of Praetorian Guard would have come for him, and they would know who he was, and there would be no questioning.

"Yes, lord...." Nicanor had no idea who this senior officer was.

"Titus Flavius Vespianus... Vespasian," the general announced, his cudgel tapping stopped, and he nodded at Nicanor, half-smile curling his lips. "Well met, centurion." He glanced toward the clerk-courier. "Can we talk privately here?"

"Lord Vespasian, I'm standing a watch...."

Vespasian's right eyebrow arched. "You're the watch-captain, are you not? Not a sentry nor a guard."

"One of my men is ill, lord... it's a simple matter to stand the watch for him. But I'll now call for a replacement." Nicanor turned to Florin. "Go to the fortress and bring the first man from the reserve list."

Vespasian watched the auxiliary hurry from the room and out toward the steps leading up to Arx Capitolina.

"So, you are willing to stand the watch of an ordinary legionary?" The cudgel rotated in the general's large hands while he held a bemused expression.

"Lord, only to make a point or set an example... and it's sometimes better than sitting among administrative work and watching Florin yawn. There is only so much I can have him do at this hour." Nicanor saw the general's slight nod and knew he had judged his visitor correctly by dress, manner, and reputation. He had heard of Vespasian from men who had served under him that the general was a soldier's soldier—more action than words—and not one who stayed in his tent and loitered comfortably in camp. "Lord, how may I be of service to you?"

Vespasian shrewdly studied Nicanor. "Mostly I think you wonder why would I come to you at this hour and not just send a request through your commander to have you report to me when off duty?"

"Well, yes, lord, this is unusual."

"The emperor has asked me to replace Lord Gallus and to take command of not just the 12th Legion but a much larger force being gathered—likely at least three legions plus allies and auxiliaries—to break the rebellion in Judea and return order to the region. It took me a while to get some of the details of Cestius Gallus's and the 12th Legion's defeat. You were there and are mentioned prominently in Lord Gallus's reports. I wanted to see the man he commended for bravery, but also prefer that he be unprepared for meeting me. I get a better reading—and understanding—of the man in that circumstance." The cudgel tapping began again. "I want to hear from you what happened, at least to the extent you were involved or observed."

"But the reports should tell you what happened, lord"—Nicanor shook his head—"There's little that I can add...." That pit-of-the-stomach sick feeling had returned, but he kept the roiling, churning sensation from showing.

"I believe reports don't always tell all that should be known, centurion. I have learned it's far better to listen to what the men say who fought in the battles." Vespasian's face tightened, and his visage grew stern—"Especially when the commander of the Roman legion they served has suffered such an embarrassing defeat."

Nicanor had obliged generals and senior officers for over two decades. Most of the senior officers had that patrician air of those born to command, that they deserved it. Many did not, and some were ineffectual fools who got their men killed needlessly. But the army veterans like Nicanor—the backbone of Rome's military might—made those men a success despite their foolishness. The legionaries that bled and died were what made the Roman army the most powerful force in the world.

Cestius Gallus had been an example of a patrician who had been led astray by the men who should have made up for his shortcomings and lack of combat experience. Gallus was a good man in a position he was not suited for.

Nicanor met Vespasian's steady look and knew that before him stood another good man, and a better general and commander of men than was Lord Gallus. If he were to lead a successful campaign in Judea, there were things he should know. But if Nicanor told him—and the copies he had made of Gallus's letters and reports discovered—it could mean Nicanor's immediate death sentence for lying to the emperor. No trial for him—and he had no desire to test the fall from the Tarpeian Rock.

A clatter of steps on stone announced Florin, followed by a legionary who had not erased his look of displeasure at the unexpected call to stand watch. That countenance vanished when he saw Nicanor standing next to a general in full regalia. The man stopped and came to attention.

Nicanor nodded at the legionary, then turned back to Vespasian. "Lord, by your leave, I must tend to my duties. May we meet tomorrow and talk then... in private?"

Vespasian again scrutinized Nicanor for a handful of heartbeats before replying: "I have a temporary office in the Tabularium. Call on me there early in the morning, the first hour after daybreak."

XXXI

The kalends of *Aprilis* approached, and the first day of the month promised to be fair and sunny. Nicanor enjoyed the quiet of the morning and the Comitium being empty, save for a few servants or clerks that crossed to and from the nearby Tabularium. When last in Rome, he had learned more from Yosef about this administrative area of not only the city but also of the empire. This stranger from a faraway land had more knowledge than did he, a citizen of Rome.

At the northwest part of the Forum, Rome's early leaders had first built the Comitium as a temple, and its sides faced the rise and fall of the sun. Now it was a public meeting space, open toward the Forum and the surrounding monuments and sculptures—famous Romans and memorialized political events. Originally the area had been a circular site defined by Romulus during a sacred rite at the founding of Rome. A trench had been dug and placed inside the circle were ceremonial offerings from each man's native lands. Everything within this expanse was revered and consecrated, and from that point, the location for a wall was marked, the footings excavated, and the barrier constructed to encircle and protect the city.

Nicanor raised his face to the dawn sky, turned from east to north, then west and south, offering a prayer to the gods to reconcile the turmoil he felt within. The night before, he had dreamed of his experiences so far away—across the sparkling Mare Nostrum to a land where he had made and left friends and lost so many men. Once the dream awakened him, he spent the night full of more thought than sleep, and within him grew a gnawing concern over what he would tell General Vespasian.

The remnants of the dream still troubled him as he followed the arc of the amphitheater and came upon a lone figure who stood near the steps of the *curia* that led toward one of the original Senate houses. The gray-haired man—his body as thick as Nicanor's but slightly shorter—stood before a fig tree with his broad back toward him. Something in his stance and the set of his shoulders made Nicanor picture an old horse at a moment of rest before called upon to the day's work. Not a sleek or shiny-coated younger, faster horse, but stolid, a plodder, and unwavering. The man, dressed in a civilian tunic and robe, looked up at the tree and scanned the sunrise over the hills. Nicanor then recognized the square block of the head and the

118

face of the man who had called on him at the Tullianum the night before—General Vespasian.

Nicanor approached him, glad to meet out here and not within the offices near the Praetorian Prefect, "Good morning, general."

"Centurion! This is one of the few spots in Rome I miss"—he gestured toward the tree. Seeing the question on Nicanor's face, he asked, "You know of it, right?"

"I think so, lord. A friend once told me of four sacred fig trees in the city, three of which were within the Forum. This must be one of them."

"Your friend knows something about Rome; many do not. Have you heard its story?"

"No, lord. Other than one season a few years ago, I've never served or even been in Rome."

"Hmmm..." Vespasian considered that for a moment and turned to the tree. "This is the *ficus navia*, named for Attus Navius, a priest and an augur who experienced a miracle on this site. There's a bronze statue of him nearby and a commemorative wellhead"—the general waved a hand—"close to the *curia hostilia*. This fig tree is at the very spot where, according to legend, the tree gave shade to the she-wolf that suckled Romulus and Remus. The tree was struck by lightning and died"—he hitched his satchel higher on his shoulder—"It's a sign of death and rebirth."

Nicanor studied the tree. "This one seems to wither."

"Yes." Vespasian nodded, a sad expression flashing across his face. "It withered before but revived and put forth new shoots. That it droops now is a sign—say many—of the current predicaments that sap Rome's strength." He shook his head. "We must pray for its resilience, that it be reinvigorated."

Nicanor had heard the mutter of such concerns from the Praetorian Guards sworn to the emperor's service and loyal above all to the empire, but now stirred to unrest. His own doubts had shaken long-held beliefs and disturbed his sleep and the prayers to the gods.

"You've seen some of those troubles, haven't you, centurion?" Vespasian patted the satchel with Cestius Gallus's reports.

"Yes, lord, I have," said Nicanor, the dream still shadowing his thoughts.

"Centurion, I read in Lord Gallus's reports about your bravery at the Beth Horon pass. I was surprised to read that before that battle, he chose you to speak for him in Jerusalem—a final attempt for a peaceful resolution with the rebels—because of your connection to a prominent Jew associated with the city's leadership. So, not only are you brave, as Lord Gallus claims... but also a diplomat."

Nicanor shook his head. "I'm no hero, lord. Just a survivor... who lost all his men in that pass. That's not heroic, and I am no proper envoy. The Jew I met with asked for me because of our friendship."

"Perhaps the gods favored you."

"Maybe so, lord... I don't know... I was doing my duty."

"Why did Cestius Gallus halt the 12th Legion's attack on Jerusalem?" The nonchalance of the conversation changed at that moment. "It puzzles me."

"Lord, I'm sure it's in the commander's report."

Vespasian shifted to face the centurion squarely, his stance widened, with hands on his hips. "Perhaps, but I want to hear what you think."

Nicanor realized he could not evade the question. "We'd lost most of our supplies and siege equipment to the rebel raids on our formation."

"So, you could not press the assault with what remained?" The fingers of Vespasian's right hand drummed on the satchel.

Nicanor told him the truth, "The commander doubted we could."

"Did you doubt?" Vespasian was unrelenting.

Nicanor squirmed, "Lord, I'm a soldier—I follow orders."

"Even if they are bad or ill-conceived commands?"

"It's not for me to say, lord. Orders are orders, and I obey them." Nicanor knew Vespasian in his decades of service had witnessed the punishment for disobedient soldiers and wondered why the general pressed him so hard.

"Let's talk like a soldier to a soldier... set rank aside." Despite what he said, the full force of a commander used to clear and direct answers to his questions was in Vespasian's voice—"Did you agree with your orders, centurion?"

Nicanor was increasingly uncomfortable. "I think circumstances and concerns led to the 12th Legion commander's decision, Lord Vespasian."

The instant held both men's unflinching stares as more people entered the area and moved around them as the workday started. Vespasian accepted the impasse for the moment and Nicanor's reply. "Come with me, centurion... we will go over the 12th Legion's maps, and you will help me try to understand more of what I face in Judea." Vespasian flashed a sharp look at the centurion—"And later we must talk about this Jewish friend of yours." He headed toward the Tabularium.

Nicanor followed. As they neared the door, a man came out, moving quickly, his arms full of scrolls of parchment and elbows stuck out. As he passed, one scroll struck Nicanor, and the armload tumbled to the ground.

"Please excuse me, centur—" the scribe looked up from gathering the scrolls—"Centurion!" The man had earned good coin from Nicanor and, in his eyes, was the recognition of an excellent customer. "Do you have more documents that need copying?"

Nicanor knelt to help the scribe and darted a look to see if Vespasian waited for him—then he shot up straight. The general was talking to Lord Tigellinus, who had come through the door following the scribe, and the Praetorian Prefect stared intently at him.

XXXII

Yosef had spent the day checking the progress of the new fortifications for the city and the strengthening of the old walls. He welcomed the new men that flooded in to swell the ranks of the force he was gathering to defend Galilee. They would not be just fighters but badly needed manpower for the wall work. The new and improved man-made defenses enhanced the natural obstacles of the terrain surrounding Yotapta to make the town one of the most secure in Galilee.

Yosef had inspected nearly every building and wall over the previous two days. Positioned on an isolated hill, the city was well-hidden between high peaks and surrounded on three sides by deep ravines. Yoptapta was easily accessible only through a pass to the north where a casemate, a solid wall reinforced with towers, was now under construction to protect the city's northern side. The wall closely followed the topography of the hill and in sections abutted or combined with existing buildings to enclose the city center, which was further defended by a massive central tower. An additional two parallel walls encompassed both the summit and the land south of it for an area of roughly 12 acres.

"You look tired, Yosef," commented Yohanan ben Zaccai as he removed the leather pouch from where it hung over his shoulder and set it on the desk. With a sigh of relief, he sat and rubbed his face with both hands, then turned a friendly gaze toward Yosef, who returned it from where he stood, shoulders slumped, by a window.

"As do you, my friend," Yosef gazed again at the view from the summit of the hill toward the southern plateau. A spread of camp fires and light from lanterns bloomed in the dusk, dotting the slopes, and clustered along the ravines below, then climbed the neighboring hills. Once the walls were strengthened, the new sections completed, and the gates reinforced, most of the men camped outside could be brought within the city's series of walls.

"I'm not young, so sometimes the road feels longer"—Yohanan straightened in the chair—"but each time I return, I see how many more have joined us. Your stance on treating everyone as members of one people—and not by city allegiance—has swayed many to your side."

"I've officially made seventy men local Galilean authorities, and now nineteen of the largest and most vital towns are being fortified. I think the people respond to seeing action taken—that it is not all just words from us. And that draws men to join the fight." Yosef squared his shoulders and sat to face the old priest.

"Now, I must somehow feed them all, and since we lack a natural spring of water and the wells go dry in the late summer, we must also build more cisterns." Yosef kept his even more pressing concern to himself—despite Levi ben Altheus's optimism about the basic training he had gleaned from the Romans to implement for their men, Yosef knew that they could not stand in open combat against the Romans. Even with more men... few were experienced in warfare. He did not believe they could become a real field army and go head to head against Roman legions, even if they had more time. There was no way to match Roman military experience and seasoned leadership if it came to clashes other than raids or sorties to protect cities from behind whatever defenses they could hastily erect. The Romans could project power—one thing that Nicanor had stressed to him often—and the truth was, that was something Judeans could not match.

"Do you have messages from Jerusalem for me?" He glanced at the pouch.

"One from the Sanhedrin." A smile added to the creases of the old priest's face—"and letters from your family." He reached into the courier bag and took out a bundle and slid it toward Yosef. "Those are the ones on top."

Yohanan stood and yawned. "I'm going to wash up and then rest, Yosef"—he nodded his goodnight—"I'll see you in the morning."

Yosef watched him leave, wondering again if he asked too much of the older man to be his principal courier to and from Jerusalem. Yohanan had suggested that as a way, he could help him, and Yosef did not have another he trusted so much. No one else could also pick up the nuances of what was going on in Jerusalem—things not in the messages or letters—and share that with him. He picked up the bundle, slipped free the cord, and separated the letters. He began with his mother's.

* * *

The lamp sputtered, and the wick's flame burned low as Yosef set aside the dispatch from the Sanhedrin president, Shimon ben

Gamliel. It contained yet more demands, buried within seemingly polite comments and questions that implied the body's doubt about the decision to pay mercenaries and take on the other expenses that lessened the flow of money to Jerusalem. More and more, that was the nature of the Sanhedrin president's and the government leadership's correspondence, demands, questions, and almost no direction nor reliable advice.

It was late, but he picked up Matthew's letter and began to re-read the part with his brother's concern about Miriam. The next day Yosef planned to go with Ezekias to his encampment near Sepphoris and would not have time to reply before Yohanan ben Zaccai left Yotapta early in the morning. He pulled a sheet of parchment to him and picked up his pen:

Matthew, I know you have many responsibilities, but I share your concerns about Miriam and ask you to spend time with her. Our sister has—I believe—a great heartache, and we must find out how to help her either carry it or find a way to heal. I know she resists talking about it, but at some point, she must. I knew Miriam had taken to walking the city alone, and you were right to follow her to make sure she stays safe. But do not bring mother into it unless you feel Miriam is truly in danger. As much as she is still our little sister... she is also becoming a grown woman—

Yosef looked up at the sound of someone approaching, the stillness amplifying the steps on stone.

"Yosef..." Levi ben Altheus stood in the doorway, the lamp in his hand casting half his features in shadow.

"Yes, Levi?"

"Two men—deserters—from King Agrippa were just brought in by the night guard. They showed up at the northern gate asking for you."

* * *

The next morning...

124

"We must not circumcise these men," Yosef said for the third time. The night before, he had welcomed the two deserters from King Agrippa, both nobles, and had given them a meal and lodging, promising to hear them out. By the time he arose that morning, he had found that dozens of his men protesting their arrival had called for them to prove they were trustworthy by embracing Judaism and accepting circumcision to show it. He looked at the group of men facing him. Off to one side stood his lieutenant, Levi, and Yohanan ben Zaccai with the two deserters.

"We now reject and stand against a foreign ruler that many believe interferes with our way of life. We cannot be free as long as we are forced to obey those who hold sway over us... who have harmed us. So, how can we force these men"—Yosef pointed at the two deserters—"to do anything without free choice? They deserve religious freedom and the right to live a law-abiding life as much I do... as much as any of you."

His eyes swept the group of men. "We have much work to do and little time for this talk of forcing our ways on others. Set that aside, put it away, and let us get busy doing what we must for all our sakes."

Yosef watched as they left; some still muttered and cast dark looks at the two men. Yohanan followed them, and Yosef knew he would try to smooth away their anger.

"Thank you, Yosef," said the younger of the two nobles beside Levi. "We come to you in good faith. We wish to help you." The man's eyes darted to his companion. "Because of your defense of us to your people, I feel bound to tell you that Agrippa is livid at the attacks on his people—east and south of the Galilean sea, down to salt works at Lake Asphaltitis—and the looting of food stores. He plans to retaliate."

Despite King Agrippa having brought much of his army into positions along the eastern Galilean border, Yosef had counted on him waiting for the Romans to arrive in force before attacking the rebels. That would have given Yosef and his men more time to prepare. "What will he do?"

"He is already doing it. As we speak, his most vicious pro-Roman officer, Aequus Modius, leads a force against Gamala to destroy it."

* * *

Yosef could tell the bandit leader was not bothered by the scowl on Levi ben Altheus's face. Though Levi disliked him, the brigand leader had the only organized and well-equipped force that could be quickly

125

deployed without halting work on Yotapta's defense. "I've not been to Gamala yet. What do you think, Ezekias?" Yosef studied it on the rough chart he had made of Galilee, listing the towns, villages, and their locations.

"It sits on a ridge between steep hills," Ezekias began, "surrounded by deep gorges formed by the creeks Gamala and Daliot, so the city is well protected, and they have good water. The only road approach to the city is from the east, and a massive fortress and wall of thick stone protect it. Along that wall, they have recently built towers, and on the hill at the northern end is an older watchtower. In the lower part of the wall, two more towers buttress and protect the entrance to the city, which sits on the lower slope. I would not want to raid it."

Levi nodded, seemingly reluctant to agree with the brigand. "I've been there, Yosef. Gamala will not be taken easily nor quickly. The defenders will hold the heights, and if they are forced to fall back, they will make a stand at the fortress atop the highest hill. That—like Yotapta—has a sharp climb, and that makes it difficult to move troops quickly."

"Then, with Agrippa's force focused on the city," declared Yosef, "we might strike their rear or flanks and quickly withdraw. Maybe we can pull them away from Gamala or at least cut down some of Agrippa's men." Yosef rolled the chart as he stood. "Levi, I leave you in charge here. Ezekias and I go to gather his men and then on to Gamala."

XXXIII

"Lord Gallus, this dispatch just came in with a rider from the decurion Aebutius." Galerius Senna held out the message. Since the retreat at Antipatris, the senior military tribune had steadily lost his currying-the-favor-of-a-superior-officer tone when speaking to the 12th Legion's commander. Now that word had come of Gallus's replacement within the next two months, that trace of respect had faded entirely, and he spoke flatly, almost indifferent to the man who sat behind the campaign desk.

Cestius Gallus took his eyes from the letter he was writing to his wife and sat back. "Leave us"—he nodded at the clerk, who ducked his head away from the commander's frown for not announcing his caller—"Sit, tribune." He held out a hand for the message, took it, and read quickly.

Aebutius was leading the unit to make their deepest thrust yet since the bitter defeat at Beth Horon. Gallus had sent the decurion into the Plains of Esdraelon because it offered a broad expanse of level travel east-to-west from the coast to the river. It provided a narrower but still-easy movement north and south. On the plain, there were no heights for the rebels to control; they would have to fight without that advantage and without stout walls to protect them. Or they could flee and be run down. Aebutius's orders were to strike and raid any villages on and along the plain, but most importantly to gather information and scout for rebel forces—their encampments or their movements.

His command of the 12th Legion, Gallus thought, would end with bearing the disgrace of what happed at Beth Horon and questions about the pull-back from Jerusalem. But until the legion was no longer his, it would do the work that could benefit the new commander.

"Aebutius reports his scouts have spotted a large force of rebels encamped between Sepphoris and Simonias."

Cestius Gallus's eyes narrowed at the tribune's presumption... as if he could not read the message for himself. He glared over the square of parchment at Senna. "And that the rebels number almost 2,000 men. The decurion doesn't have what... even half that?"

"One hundred cavalry, 200 infantry, and we recruited men from Gaba as an auxiliary force." replied the tribune.

"So, less than 1,000 men," *and most of them from Gaba and likely not recruited but conscripted.* Gallus was sure of this but left it unsaid. Yet he could not dismiss the report or avoid taking action against the rebels. There were many men in the legion who muttered among themselves—increasingly loudly—about what had happened at Beth Horon. The defeat and retreat to Antipatris soured in their stomachs more every day. He could not ignore such a sizable rebel target out in the open and vulnerable. He must attack without exposing the force to defeat and must draw the rebels closer to Ptolemais, where he could wield more of the legion's power. "Did you hold the messenger for my orders in reply?"

"Of course, commander."

Gallus took a blank sheet of vellum, wrote on it quickly, and sealed it. "Give this to the messenger, tell him to ride fast to give it decurion Aebutius, get an update on the rebels from him, and report back here directly to me." He stressed the last three words.

Galerius Senna nodded, stood with the message in his hand then looked from it to the legion commander. "What are your orders, Lord Gallus?"

"To attack, tribune"—he locked eyes with Senna—"to strike, to inflict casualties and damage... then to withdraw."

"Withdraw!" the tribune scoffed, shaking his head.

"Yes." Cestius Gallus smiled at the man's expression—"To incite and tempt the rebels to pursue a smaller force they feel they can defeat, and thus for them to come nearer to Ptolemais where we can encircle and destroy them." *It won't come close to making up for Beth Horon*, the legion commander thought, *and it seems my report and suspicions sent to Nero have not made it to the emperor. Or*, he considered as shifted back in his chair, *the reports did not matter to him*. Regardless, when he stood before the emperor, he would accept—again—the blame for Beth Horon.

But before his punishment, he would tell Nero why he had halted the attack on Jerusalem and who he believed had precipitated events and could not be trusted. First, he would deliver what small victories he could to the new commander... and warn him.

* * *

BETWEEN SEPPHORIS AND SIMONIAS

An outrider patrolling the perimeter raised the alarm almost at the same time as the sole survivor from the wood-gathering party staggered into camp, his dying words, "The Romans..." As the man breathed his last, a lathered blood-streaked horse raced into camp, shuddering to a halt in front of Yosef and Ezekias.

"Cavalry, Ezekias..." the patrol captain gasped, dismounting awkwardly and favoring a slashed leg that glistened red—with a flash of exposed white bone. "The Romans are sweeping all four quarters"—he pointed in the direction he had come from and then west, north and east. "My men had the area east of the camp, and we had to circle—the Roman horsemen and infantry were between us and camp—before we could find a clear path to return. As we did, we found the bodies of the other patrols—eight dead horses and fifteen dead men."

Ezekias waved a man over to tend to the wounded patrol captain.

"How many Romans?" Yosef asked.

The man winced as a swath of cloth was wrapped tight around the long gash in his thigh. "Too many—they tore through us as we moved, a dozen or more each time until they killed all but me. The foot soldiers I saw were grouped astride the main trails... there had to be hundreds of them."

Yosef turned to Ezekias. "But if they had enough men, they'd be on us right now." He thought of what Simon bar Giora had done to the Romans on their marches to and from Jerusalem. "Move the animals inside the perimeter now. They'll try to put us all on foot, so we lose mobility and have to face their infantry in the open. Then their cavalry will do as they did with the patrols... rapid strikes to cut us down man by man."

He studied the camp's temporary barrier thrown together from the natural materials at hand. The fortification followed the terrain and used fledgling acacia thorn trees as pickets for the row of thick tangles of brush stacked waist-high. If they grew close enough together and formed a line, the trees served well to anchor a defensible barrier. The wood gatherers always left the youngest and nearest acacia for that purpose and cut down the larger trees even if they were further away.

"I'll see to it," agreed the brigand leader, "but we must send men after them before nightfall." Ezekias glanced at the sun, now low on the horizon, and then at Yosef.

Yosef considered it, noted the deepening twilight, and shook his head. "No, that's too risky. But we need to post watches beyond the perimeter. Have four or five men with a runner for each post secure a spot far enough out to give us the warning to prepare for an attack. And they should check-in every two hours."

* * *

Sunrise...

Yosef watched as Ezekias issued orders to break camp and prepare to move out. A chorus of sharp nickers came from horses glad to be unhobbled, and donkeys and mules brayed and snorted while being loaded the dawn's stillness. "All quiet..." he murmured. He had not slept and had heard the encouraging check-in from each outpost through the long night. The last and final one had been a little over two hours before. The sentries should come in now to join the formation. He had filled the waking hours with deciding what to do—continue as planned to aid Gamala and attack Agrippa's force assaulting that city, or pursue the Romans? Ezekias and his lieutenants were enraged at the slaughter of their men. They wanted to kill the Romans. So did he... but....

"My men are dead..."

Yosef heard the brigand commander before he turned to see him marching toward him. "What?!"

"Dead, Yosef... every man of the night posts." White-faced and bristling, Ezekias gripped Yosef's arm. "We must go after them."

"What about Gamala?" Yosef asked.

"Gamala will stand," Ezekias replied. "King Agrippa's soldiers are not Romans... but here we have some within our reach and can make them pay."

Yosef felt the man's anger flare through the firm grip on his arm, and the stab of his stare. He shook his arm free.

"The men on this morning's water detail found the men of the night posts and then farther out a dead Roman—a horseman, judging by his equipment. They followed his tracks to a dead horse with a cracked right fetlock—the ankle shattered, dug into a deep hole—and a broken neck. It had stumbled into a bush-filled hole and pitched forward, its muzzle pulled in tight and head bent at an odd angle. The Roman must have been a courier, for he carried this"—Ezekias shook a crumpled, soiled sheet of parchment.

Yosef took it from him and smoothed it to flatten it and read. "This is their commander's reply to confirm being recalled to Besera... and there to guard a delivery of grain to be stored for King Agrippa's sister, Queen Berenice." He looked up at the brigand. "We'll follow and kill them and take the grain."

Ezekias smiled fiercely.

XXXIV

Cleo had waited days to read her brother Otho's letter. As soon as she returned to the residence that day, she had hurried alone to her room. Costa—the olive-wood trader—had delivered the message to her in the market, and she slipped it immediately into the hollow base of Cicero's cage. A better keeper than Cicero she could not find, for he protected her secret items, especially from Glaucio and Florus—the bird did not let near without squawking.

Cicero preened and bobbed his head as she reached in and withdrew the letter at last. She quickly read it... then slowly re-read. There was much from her brother to read between the lines, within its retelling of third-hand gossip and rumor. Otho seemed to know the risk of having the letter fall into other hands, so he couched what he wrote as what he "heard" from unknown "others." The message heavily hinted at the anger and unrest caused by Nero's focus on his own whims and desires, which he put above the rebuilding of common areas of the city and the property of lesser Romans. Otho had begun the letter:

> *"Dear sister, I am concerned for your safety... that you now live where there is so much risk and danger. I hope that any who are near that threaten you fail and that they know they will be punished should they harm you. Rome and these who care for it, will not stand still. They will act and punish those who sow fear and create the chaos that troubles us all. I wish you safely out of harm's way and that you know a just Roman judgment will be delivered against those who oppose Rome."*

He continued with more about the unrest in other provinces and within Rome itself. He said that soon choices would be put before the people and payment demanded for ill decisions made in the past. This, too, had a double meaning. Otho had protested her betrothal and marriage to Gessius Florus and even argued with their father.

But that had not mattered—their father was ambitious but not aggressively so. Her father saw that having a son-in-law such as Gessius Florus could serve his purpose. The price for that was only a daughter she knew he had worried would never find a suitor given her independent streak. So, the marriage accomplished two things to her father's benefit.

Cleo was glad she had hidden Otho's letter quickly because shortly after her return from that close call in the market with Costas, her husband had walked in on her. After hiding Otho's message, she read Octavia's and had planned to put it in the carved olive-wood box where she kept her pen, ink, and parchment. With Octavia's letter still in hand, she had turned at the sound of someone entering her room.

"So, my wife, what did you bring from the market?" Gessius Florus asked, and the pleasant tone had not matched the hard glint in his eyes as he stared at the sheets of parchment in her hand. In the doorway behind them, she glimpsed Glaucio and the new woman— Eris, she thought was her name—he had brought in to manage the kitchen. The two slid to one side out of sight, and their footsteps receded down the hall.

Florus had taken two quick steps forward and snatched the sheets from her hand: "Hmmm... so, Lady Octavia fears for her husband... Well"—he read, then let the pages fall from his grasp—"she should. Cestius Gallus's replacement will be in Antioch before long, and the disgraced fallen commander of the 12th Legion will be taken to Rome to face the emperor."

Cleo had said nothing as she stooped to pick up Octavia's letter, thankful it mentioned nothing to alarm her husband. Gessius Florus seemed disappointed at not finding anything he could take exception to... or strike her for. Then he had given her some good news.

"I'll be gone for several days and have asked Glaucio to be attentive to your needs while I'm away."

He had paused, and then a flicker of anger flashed when she did not ask him where he was going or why. Inside, she smiled, despite knowing that Glaucio no doubt looked forward to her being alone with him. In reality, she was always under his thumb. Without a word, Florus had spun and stomped toward his office, calling for Capito.

* * *

The second day after Gessius Florus's departure, Cleo awoke, still happy in knowing she would not see him that day. She wished to never see him again. An hour later, after a scared girl served breakfast under the baleful supervision of Eris, who made the servants tremble even more than did Glaucio, she thought about going to the market but knew she could only do so with an escort. She chafed at that thought. But the walls—and the ever-watching eyes—pressed in on her—she must be free of them even if for a short while.

This *domus* was not as imposing as Herod's palace they'd had in Caesarea. The sweep of the ocean vista here was not as dramatic as the palace's view of the man-made harbor and port and the terraces dotted with beautifully placed gardens and sitting areas that stretched down to the sea. But behind this building, after an expanse of well-tended grounds, there was a winding path that led to—and she assumed through—a jumble of building stones, some as tall as the columns of the portico. And those stones trailed down to the sea below, probably rejected and cast off when the beautiful home was constructed. Perhaps that path also led to a quiet stretch of beach where she could find peace. She headed toward it.

"Lady!"

The call of her name was more "at" her than "to" her... its shrill sound an accusation, not a question. Cleo stopped and turned to see Eris standing at the edge of the back portico off the kitchen and dining areas. The woman increasingly seemed a female Glaucio.

Cleo did not wait for her to say anything else and tested a dismissal: "I do not need you further this morning... I'm going to walk the grounds." Without waiting for an answer or acknowledgment, she walked faster, not looking back at the woman. She had gone around the first bank of hewn stones that screened her from the view of the house when she heard another cry.

"Lady Cleo... Lady Cleo..." the boy—Elian—came to a stumbling stop at the turn of the path leading down the slope. "Lady Cleo... may I come with you?"

She smiled for the boy. "Yes, but stay with me." They walked in silence for several minutes as scattered building stones gave way to dunes. The path was half-choked with the brush grown between the dunes but still afforded them sound footing, though it began to soften as they neared the beach. Cleo soon heard the crash of waves, and her nose wrinkled at the sharp salt-water tang that filled the air. As they passed through sand hills formed by tempest-swirled wind and erosion, they came upon what seemed more discarded building stones in the water that formed a small man-made cove, an embrace of two arms of slick rocks that stretched out into the water. The narrow, secluded beach was a bed of clean, smooth sand glinting in the morning sun.

"Lady Cleo... may I play...?" The boy gestured at the surf.

"Yes, but don't go in too far—just wade in the water."

The boy flashed a smile that eclipsed the sunshine that filled this hidden cove and ran to the water's edge as Cleo found a flat rock to sit upon. Arms around her knees, she tilted her face to the sky, feeling the warm sun and the freshness of the breeze off the water, closed her eyes, and let her mind drift. The heavy moisture with its taste of the sea spray on her lips made her think of the shipwreck of the *Salacia* and all that had happened since.

What if she had still survived, but been washed ashore somewhere she could start a new life? And what if Yosef had been castaway with her? They could be together instead of her marrying Gessius Florus, and Yosef would not be at the very center of a bloody war to come. Together they could be what they wanted to be. Happy. She could be accepted for who she was—a woman of strength and desire to be more than what Roman society dictated for her. And Yosef could be free of doing what everyone asked—no, expected of him. He could be free to find a love to replace what he had lost. They could have a life together.

The smile that she had unknowingly formed faded with the threads of that sweet daydream as she opened her eyes to check on the boy... and did not see him. She stood, walked to the water's edge, turned left and right, and called his name.

"Elian... Elian..." She whirled to scan the surf, looking farther out for a struggling boy caught in the tide... "Elian!" The wind dropped, and she caught a faint call and saw tracks leading into the water near the jumble of half-submerged stones.

Cleo gathered her robe, pulled it up above her knees, and stepped into the water, following the rocks that formed the base of that arm projecting into the sea. Feeling her way step by step more than seeing what was beneath a froth of sea, she reached a low area of the stone and clambered over it, getting soaked by the spray as it struck the rocks, showered, and cascaded around her. Once over the stones that ran what seemed even farther and deeper under the water, she found herself in a trough bound by the rocks that formed a pool that rose and fell with the tide.

"Lady Cleo... here!" Elian's voice was louder, nearer. She pushed toward the sound through the knee-deep water, shielding her eyes from the spray with a forearm. A minute later, she had cleared another low bank of stones to see the boy stood on the beach in the wash of surf that churned through an opening in the rocks.

Slipping on the smooth stones beneath a foot of water, she moved toward him. "Elian... I told you..."

"I'm sorry, lady... I saw a gull land and followed it here... come see what I found." He turned and pointed behind him, beckoning her.

Cleo followed him to a structure almost completely buried within the dunes, hidden from sight until she was right upon it.

* * *

Leaving the sand-buried building, Cleo and Elian followed the sloped path that brought them back to the crest of the dunes at a point along the side of the domus containing the private area and sleeping chambers. She saw the shutters to her room just on the other side of Gessius's office and the sleeping chamber her husband had taken for his own. She knelt below the outcrop of rock that hid the path and the steps down to the secret cove and motioned to the boy to do the same.

"Elian, you must tell no one of this, of what we found... and tell nothing of what you see or hear when you're with me."

The boy nodded. "I know Lord Florus hurts you, Lady Cleo, and how mean Glaucio is to you. I won't tell anyone..."

A loud cry—a man's—made her raise her head. It was Glaucio, angrily calling her name.

ACT II

XXXV

Sycaminum (port)

Gessius Florus had boarded the cargo vessel well before dawn when the Ptolemais port was quiet. A scant three hours later, he was dockside at the smaller port of Sycaminum. Though the boat carried other shipments it would deliver along the coast, its primary cargo was sand, one of the first significant loads of that commodity destined for the *vitriarii,* the glass manufacturers in Alexandria, Egypt. As Procurator, he had been surprised to learn that near Ptolemais, where the Belus, the Na-aman river joined the sea, was some of the finest for producing high-quality *vitrum* in volume. The glass was needed to meet the growing demand for containers such as cups, bowls, plates, and bottles, and for decorative use in mosaics and panels, requiring an abundant source of sand. Florus now controlled the sand and the means to get it to the manufacturers.

"Were they there, Capito?" Florus asked the centurion he had appropriated as his aide, a man who looked out-of-place wearing civilian clothing as he stepped from a narrow ladder descending from the main deck through a small hatch. Graceless, Capito, in his military attire and equipment, had never moved without an accompanying clatter. A centurion's uniform gave his bearing a legitimacy of sorts and a stern countenance he lacked in civilian tunic and robe. As a simple Roman citizen, the man looked merely brutish. But at least he did not clatter.

"Yes, Lord Florus, they were at the taberna waiting. They did not wish to be seen boarding with me, so they followed far behind. They should be here shortly."

"It's their ship... they should have no qualms about it."

"They did not seem pleased to meet with you, lord."

Gessius Florus did not care. The man he was about to see, Meshulam, the owner of the vessel who had not wanted that ownership to be known, had made a lot of money from trade with Rome and the empire's provinces before and during the recent events. The ship testified to the trader's burgeoning wealth. If Meshulam expected the business to continue after the rebels were crushed, and if he and his family wanted to live... he would comply. *All debts come due,* Florus thought, and after all, no matter the fancy title the emperor had given him, Florus was a debt collector.

The space where Florus and Capito stood below the main deck and a level above the larger cargo hold was furnished with lanterns that created pools of illumination, but the area brightened considerably as the central loading access hatch was pulled back and sunlight flooded in. Two men came down the broad steps of a not-quite vertical ladder with their shadows cast before them.

"Lord Florus," came the voice of the heavier, older man as he neared the two Roman., "Why did you insist we meet here, in Sycaminum?"

"Because that's what I wish, Meshulam, but if you like, I could meet you where the rebels—the Sicarii—can see you openly collaborate with a Roman and know of the wealth you've attained"—Florus waved a hand to encompass the ship they stood within—"and that it continues to grow."

The man shuddered. "The Sicarii have eyes everywhere..."

"—And knives, too... which you know."

"Why did I have to bring my son?" He glanced beside him at the younger, taller version of himself.

"Because I need him, Meshulam... in Jerusalem. As my eyes and ears."

The trader's eyes widened. "That's not possible, lord..."

"Is it known that your son has disagreed with you... about your business practices... and partners?"

"No, Ehud has quarreled with me only among family... I assure you, Lord Fl—"

"How did you get him to join you for this meeting?"

"Your message said that if he did not... something would happen to him or to others of my family," Meshulam replied flatly.

Hands clenched at his side, the trader's son, Ehud, moved a half-step toward the Romans.

Capito stepped closer and positioned himself between Florus and the younger man, his hand on the hilt of the dagger at his waist. Meshulam put a hand on his son's chest, pressing lightly for him to move back, then harder when Ehud did not budge.

"So, it is a convincing motive for you to do what I want. A real reason"—Florus turned to the young man—"which is why you came. Ehud... that's your name, right?" The young man nodded, and Florus continued: "Whether by Roman hands—or your own countrymen's if they find out about your father's alliance with their enemy—the threat of death hangs over you if you don't do what I want."

"I'm no threat to whatever arrangements my father has with you," said Ehud. "I will not be part of it... but I will remain silent and not jeopardize what you do."

Florus's laugh was brief, a derisive snort—"I want you to loudly condemn your father... voice your disagreement, and break openly with him."

"What?!" both father and son exclaimed at the same time.

"Your father and family can remain safe in Ptolemais if you do what I want. You are to return to your birthplace." Florus's eyes moved from father to son, then locked on the trader. "Meshulam, when I was Procurator, and you met with me in Caesarea, you told me of your hope for a mutually beneficial relationship despite any Roman issues with those in Jerusalem. It is the city your family is from and where your children were born and grew up. There are people in that city I want watched and reported on."

Florus's gaze shifted to the son. "Ehud, you will do that for me. You will not be suspected because you will be convincingly outspoken about separating yourself from your father, who many suspect of collaborating since he remains with his business interests intact in a Roman-held city." He waved a hand at Capito—"This man will instruct you on what to do, who to watch, and he will show you how to send messages to me. Know that if you do not do as I order... your father, mother, sisters, and brother will die."

Florus shifted to face the father again. "Meshulam, your son can die in Jerusalem just as easily as I can have him killed here. Go... and I expect your son to report that he is settled in Jerusalem within seven days."

Florus stepped back into the shadows, and as the father and son turned to leave, he added, "Meshulam, I'll travel on your ship to Caesarea and Azzah... tell your captain." Florus nodded at the centurion, "Capito, go with them and see that it is done."

* * *

CAESAREA (PORT)

Even with waiting for tides and daylight, with good winds, it took a half-day for the heavily laden vessel to reach Caesarea. Then Gessius Florus had to wait for nightfall for his meeting. He filled the time with sifting through his thoughts. Most were centered on his wife... and a growing suspicion she had alerted or alarmed her friend Octavia, who then did the same with her husband, Cestius Gallus. And perhaps that had prompted the 12th Legion's commander to halt the attack on Jerusalem when he was only a wall breach away from the temple and all its treasure.

The man he was waiting for had helped to create the conditions within the legion, so in the chaos of battle, his hand-picked men could take the treasure and bring it out of the city to him. Then they would claim the rebels had counter-attacked and the treasure retrieved by the Jews. Such a defeat by the rebels was in keeping with what had already happened to the 12th Legion. The men who lost the treasure to the rebels cared little for the added stigma—the pittance he would have paid them from the treasure would still have made them wealthy men in their retirement.

The tremendous wealth of the Jewish cache would be then his to send partly to Emperor Nero—enough to sate the man's greed and need—but to keep mostly for himself. But all those plans had gone so well… and then failed quickly with Cestius Gallus's decision to retreat from Jerusalem. Maybe Cleo had something to do with it. But he needed proof to do more than knock her around. If he found it, she would be declared a traitor, and he could kill her with impunity. Or she could disappear as the war tore Judea apart.

"Lord, Tyrannius Priseus is here." The centurion stood in the cabin's doorway.

Florus nodded at Capito and studied the 12th Legion's Camp-Prefect as he entered the arc of light from the swaying lamp above the table he used as a desk. This won't take long, Priseus. Who is the emperor sending? Do you have a name for me?"

"It surprised me, but I do, lord."

Florus looked up at the man, noting the concerned look. Well, who is replacing Cestius Gallus?"

"Titus Flavius Vespasianus, lord… he is not anyone that was expected. He's not a political appointee."

"What do you mean?"

"Vespasian's a combat commander… a true military leader, lord… and a very successful general. He will not be manipulated like Lord Gallus."

"When does he arrive? asked Florus.

"A month from now. He's still organizing… maybe two months at the most, lord."

"Let me know as soon as you can find out precisely. That's all, Prefect…"

Florus waited until Tyrannius Priseus left, then turned to Capito. "Send a message to your contact on the staff of Tiberius Julius Alexander, in Alexandria, and have them find out everything they can about Vespasian and get to me as soon as possible." He watched as the centurion left and thought of his next stop—to deal with the man who could help him get his hands on the treasure once and for all.

* * *

AZZAH

Gessius Florus stood at the stern of the cargo ship, unconcerned about being seen, though he had been in Caesarea and Sycaminum. His eyes swept Gazaeorum Portus and the town above it on a low, round hill overlooking the port and harbor. He had made a point of learning about the city before agreeing to travel to meet the Idumean at a safe location closest to the man's native home. The town's name—Azzah—meant "the strong." Near the border of Egypt, it was a well-fortified Roman town adorned with many pagan temples, the foremost being that of Marnas, also known as Dagon. Other temples were dedicated to Zeus, Helios, Aphrodite, Apollo, Athene, and the local Tyche. It was a stable Roman outpost not likely to succumb to any appeals from the Jews. From his vantage point, Florus could see the length of the dock to where it became a broad street lined with warehouses. Then beyond them, it began its slight climb to the city proper and its marketplace. Coming down the road, passing the warehouses and seemingly at ease, was Capito in uniform as a centurion. A minute later, he boarded the ship and hurried to join his master.

"The Idumean, Esau ben Beor, expected to meet with you, Lord Florus."

"I've traveled—at his request—to come close enough to him to respond quickly to this urgent need he alluded to in his message to me, Capito. I want what he can find out for me but need not meet him. What does he say? He should be in Jerusalem, not down here."

"His people requested he come to see what's been done by Simon bar Giora... the Jewish rebel commander who led the forces at Beth Horon. He says you should know the man and his men remain in the region and parade around with the 12th Legion's aquila."

"Im sure that hardly matters to him. What does he want?" Florus asked with irritation.

"He demands you order Roman units to hunt down and kill Simon bar Giora for his attacks on the Idumean villages... and he rages that the leaders in Jerusalem will not punish Giora or hold him accountable."

"Does he wait for my reply as I told you to have him do?" At the centurion's nod, Florus continued: "Go now and tell him that if he delivers the information, I need about the Temple treasure... I will see he gets revenge on the Jerusalemites. And say to him that in the coming war Simon bar Giora will be killed or captured and receive the harshest Roman judgment and punishment.

"On your return," Florus continued, "tell the captain we leave his ship here. Then we'll board the *quinquereme* from Alexandria that just docked. I have spoken with its captain, and it's headed for Ptolemais, then on to Antioch."

XXXVI

The pack train of heavily loaded mules and carts stretched far behind Yosef as he approached the northern gate. It was not a considerable distance from Besara to Yotapta if travel were in a straight line. But the winding road, often only a rough trail barely wide enough for a one-mule cart, climbed and descended to rise again all the way to Yotapta's gate.

He wiped the dust from his face as a shift in the wind billowed and lifted the top layers of the dirt piles left from the recent wall reinforcement excavation. The welcome call of "Open the gate, it's Yosef" came from behind the wall, and he smiled. The men were doing as told—gates closed and secured... not to be opened unless those outside it were recognized as friendly, and the approach watched day and night. He heard the groan of the heavy timbers, some logs still carrying their original bark as the gate swung open, pushed from within by several stout men.

Levi ben Altheus greeted Yosef as he passed through the gate and moved to one side to watch tired men and mules trundle past with their loads. "I received your news of the attack on Ezekias's camp and that you were pursuing the attackers. So, there was grain at Besara"— he waved a hand at the laden carts. "What of the Romans that attacked you?"

Yosef swung down from his horse and handed the reins to one of the several boys who had poured out to tend to the animals and help unload the wagons. "We killed some, but after a brief skirmish, most of them retreated—"

"—Toward Ptolemais," Levi finished, "to the legion."

"No"—Yosef shook his head—"they fled east and south toward Nazareth."

"Are you sure they were Romans, not Agrippa's troops?"

"The dead men were Romans—they wore the markings of the 12th Legion. It was important to get the grain where we could secure it, so I ordered Ezekias to pursue them while these 200 men and all the pack mules and carts brought it here." Yosef watched as the steady stream of grain flowed into the buildings that housed massive stone storage vessels for grain. "I think we will need more containers"—he turned back and caught Levi smiling at a young woman walking by carrying a large jar full of grain. Her face lighted with a smile that matched Levi's, but she looked away when she spotted Yosef watching them. "A pretty girl... Is she a friend, Levi?"

His lieutenant's already-dark face tinged a deep red as he shook his head. "There are many new faces here, Yosef." He darted a last glance at the girl striding away, easily carrying the heavy stone jar that filled her arms. "I'll send more men with the empty wagons to the quarry at Cana for more of the chalkstone amphoras they make there—they should be back with them tomorrow."

* * *

"Where are we going, Levi?" Yosef asked, covering a yawn with the back of his hand. The man had woken him at dawn as usual, but instead of leaving, he had beckoned at Yosef to hurry, dress, and come with him. Yosef followed him to the steps that climbed to the new watch post at the center of the eastern section of the outer wall. The sky was awash with yellows, oranges, and a purple that seemed to change to blue as he climbed. They stopped at a platform atop the wall, where on a table were bowls of fruit and a stone pitcher with three cups.

"Breakfast," Levi announced and then swept his arm across the horizon before them, the dawn lighting the tops of the surrounding hills, leaving the valleys and ravines still in dark shadow. "And the beauty of the land... our land, Yosef... and my home."

"It's beautiful... the sun rising over the hills"—a female voice came from behind them. "It always makes me catch my breath and hold it, to make the colors stay that way a little longer."

Yosef turned to see the young woman from the day before, who carried a wooden tray with three bowls of gruel, steam rising from them in the coolness of the early spring morning.

"Good morning"—Yosef looked from the girl to his lieutenant, whose eyes were fixed on her.

"Yosef, this is Ariella bat Gidon—she has come to Yotapta to help," Levi said. "She thought of this"—he gestured at the table—"to introduce herself."

Ariella set the bowls on the table, picked up the stone pitcher, and poured water into the three cups. "Please sit, Yosef"—her smile flashed as bright as the sun peeking over the hills—"and Levi. Or are you not hungry?"

Yosef glanced again from Levi to the young woman. "Thank you for coming to help us... where are you from?"

"When you sent men to fortify my town—Sogane—near Gabara"— she peeped sideways at Levi and blinked, then came back to Yosef— "I heard you were seeking recruits to defend Galilee from the Romans."

"Yes, but that was meant for men who can help fight..." Yosef shrugged an apology, for man or woman, he was grateful for any support he found—he smiled to show he did not mean that to offend her. *Good women are often the strength behind the men who fight.* The grin remained on Ariella's face but tightened, and Yosef—for an instant—saw Miriam's face as it had been when they had talked before, he left Jerusalem.

"My father's father was a warrior... that is my family's heritage... so, I will do what I can to help in the fight against the Romans." Ariella's face relaxed. "Please eat."

* * *

Yosef and Levi stood at the gate. A runner had fetched them with news that the men from Cana had returned with a wounded man. As soon as the opening was wide enough, both slipped out. The six men and wagons, loaded with huge stone jars, were bunched close to the gate.

The first driver was lifting a blood-soaked man from the cart to lie upon the ground. "He came upon us, his horse dying under him, between Cana and here."

Yosef knew him as one of Ezekias's men. With a cry of pain, the man opened his eyes and, in turn, recognized him.

"Yosef, Romans—two or three times our number... cavalry and heavy infantry—hid in the forests north and south... They fell on us. They cut us down like barley to the scythe. Ezekias sent me to...." Blood bubbled and frothed at the man's lips as he choked and died.

"What should we do, Yosef... muster our men and march to help Ezekias?" Levi waved the wagons to get them moving through the gate, to the safety within the walls.

"Rider approaching!" was the shout from a sentry in the nearest tower, and they turned to face the road as a dozen men with bows joined Yosef and Levi outside the gate.

"Hold—do not fire!" Yosef commanded, and they lowered their bows as the single rider coming toward them at full gallop pounded up the road and slid to a stop before them. He dismounted, staggering to catch his balance and then straighten.

145

"I have an urgent message for the commander, Yosef ben Mathias"—the man gasped and stepped back at seeing the bloody man on the ground nearly at his feet.

"I'm Yosef... what's your message?"

"Tiberias is under attack from King Agrippa. A large force of men led by his commander, Neapolitanus, has killed dozens outside the town and driven hundreds more to take refuge within the city."

Neapolitanus had once been an emissary from King Agrippa to help resolve the differences between the Judeans and Rome—Yosef vividly recalled that day of Agrippa's speech in Jerusalem. He had pled that they do not resort to war and rebellion against Rome, that they not suffer the destruction it would bring. The warning had not been heeded. Yosef looked at the dead man on the ground before him and wondered how many more he would see before the war was over.

XXXVII

Jerusalem

Once the hall emptied, Mathias waved Matthew over to join him as he and two other men stepped over to one side of the antechamber. He caught Shimon ben Gamliel's curious expression as the man passed him at the passageway leading to the Inner Court of the priests around the Temple.

"Father"—Matthew greeted him and gave a nod to Eleasar ben Ananias, who stood on his father's right. He squinted at the burly man on his father's left.

Mathias noted the question in his son's eyes. "Matthew, this is Esau ben Beor, and he has been appointed the overseer of all sources of building materials needed to strengthen Jerusalem's defenses. That will ensure that Eleasar"—he nodded at the Temple Guard captain—"and his work crews have all they need when they need it."

"It will be so," Esau confirmed. "I'll coordinate with production supervisors at all sites to make sure all goes as planned."

"About the plans for Jerusalem's defense," said Matthew. "Father, I need to talk to you and Eleasar about something." He paused and darted a look at Eleasar, then slid his eyes toward the man he did not know.

"Thank you, Esau"—the guard captain clapped the man's thick shoulder—"I'll meet with you again later today and provide a list of immediate requirements for the most critical work."

"An interesting man and choice," Mathias murmured as they watched him amble from the antechamber.

"Why do you say that, Father?" Matthew asked once Beor was out of sight.

"Esau ben Beor can be a difficult man, but he is also resolute... he'll get what he wants. So, hopefully, we won't have any issues or shortages that keep the workmen waiting."

"There's too much to be done," agreed Eleasar and turned to Matthew. "I suspect you've heard of Elazar ben Yair's declaration? It was the talk of the Sanhedrin before the meeting... but not mentioned during..."

Matthew frowned. "So, Yair and his Sicarii—and they are truly his since Menahem ben Judah's death—will remain at Masada. They will not return to Jerusalem nor aid in its defense." The glower deepened. "Then he should not receive any resources from Jerusalem... no material nor food supplies... no men, no arms. We'll need all that Beor's prodding can provide to reinforce our defenses. Whatever arms we have on hand from the Antonia Fortress's former Roman garrison, and what our own armorers can manufacture. Plus all the siege equipment we captured from the Romans last year. And all the food we can gather from local farms and communities—for their people will take refuge here once the Romans arrive. We must focus on the city and the people here."

"Yair has been steadily laying in stores since the Romans fled Beth Horon, so Masada can withstand its own siege," said Mathias. "He refuses to come under Eleasar's command for the security of southern Judea, and he will not listen to the government nor the Sanhedrin." He swayed and brought a hand up to his head, touching his brow furrowed in discomfort.

"Father, are you still not well?" Matthew reached a hand out to steady him.

"I'm tired, son—it's just a moment of dizziness." Mathias straightened, shaking off whatever troubled him. "I'm afraid Yair has in his hands the fate of those who have remained in Masada, and there's nothing we can do." A rustle outside the antechamber made him pause. "Just before the Sanhedrin met, your mother sent Miriam to tell me Yohanan ben Zaccai has arrived from Yotapta. He reports the Romans are ranging farther from Ptolemais and in greater numbers. And he has news from Yosef and about his contact with the Essenes."

"We should discuss that at home, Father"—Matthew softly squeezed the arm he still gripped, feeling its faint tremble.

"Son, Eleasar can be trusted"—Mathias peered at the Temple Guard captain. "If not him, then who can we trust? We must have his help with planning to protect the Temple's treasure." He patted Matthew's hand and spoke to Eleasar: "Come with us to our home and hear what Yohanan has to tell us."

As they left the antechamber—each man deep in his own thoughts—the sound of hurried steps echoed ahead of them. They exited the Temple grounds and crossed the viaduct and descended into the Upper City, and the swirl of activity and chatter surrounded them, a buzzing sound of worried tones. Word had spread of the Romans' increased activity, and all understood that meant that what had been but a small sample of war would soon turn into a full-fledged invasion, culminating eventually with an unrelenting assault on Jerusalem.

XXXVIII

JERUSALEM

At the foot of the hill of Bezetha, a large man strode toward the broad path that led to Zedekiah's cave. Its naturally formed opening led to the entrance of his destination, a much greater and deeper man-made cavity, an underground quarry. Several minutes later, he passed a resting team of oxen and men sitting atop a dozen large logs de-barked and smoothed into wooden rollers. They would use these to bring up the massive cut blocks of stone from the depths of the quarry. And then they would use them again for controlled descent of the hill to transport the blocks into the city or to a work area where they would be cut into smaller chunks, slabs or columns.

Esau reached the cave, and the few men outside paid no attention to him. Over recent days, he had made a point of getting them familiar with seeing him there. Without acknowledgment of them or hesitation, he entered and passed through the cavern's immense 300-foot-long chamber that dripped water—Zedekiah's Tears—from its ceiling. The cavern gradually sloped down into a honeycombed series of galleries—a vast man-made grotto—hewn from the limestone over centuries by generations of stonecutters. The muddled maze of interconnected tunnels and hollowed-out chambers extended about 650 feet to the farthest point and, at its widest, spanned about 330 feet. The levels being mined were only thirty feet below the streets of the Northern City, although several lower levels and blocked shafts ran much deeper. Well-worn paths led to every corner of the quarry.

The Royal Quarries—or Solomon's Quarry—had for centuries yielded large quantities of *Melekeh*, a pure white limestone that often kept its color for many years but also had proven to transform into a light golden hue as it aged. Stoneworkers had long ago discovered that once the rock was cut and exposed, with time, it became even harder, resisting erosion, and its clear surface could take on a high polish. Builders had used it to construct much of the Temple and many of the most important buildings in Jerusalem. The quarry was almost as busy now as at its peak during Herod's building program decades earlier, but now, instead of monuments, palaces, and temples, the stone was used for fortifying existing defenses, and erecting new ones.

On his first visit to the cave and quarry, Esau had done precisely as the Roman had instructed—he entered the quarry area and located the polished section of wall where countless stone workers and quarrymen had etched their names, initials and sometimes crude insults. He had searched just beyond that for the stub of a rock above head height that pointed toward the opposite wall, where it angled away into the declivity of a long-ago abandoned shaft sealed by a cave-in. Between the spill of light from the entrance and the series of large lanterns affixed to the wall at intervals into the depths, the mouth of the shaft was hidden in shadow. Checking for any men loitering around him, as he crossed and entered the darkness, he took out a small hand-lamp, worked the lighting stones, and as the flame bloomed on the wick, shielded its glow with the bulk of his body. Several feet into the darkness, he found and knelt before a fissure that ran from the rock floor to knee height. He lifted a rock to reveal a stone jar. Its lid was wrapped and rimmed with a tarred cloth, and he removed that and put into the pot the message he had prepared—his first important news to share with the Roman. He replaced the lid and then the flat rock that concealed the pot, then stood and pinched the lamp's wick between thumb and forefinger to extinguish the flame. He left without being seen.

* * *

Next morning...

The man seemed too slender to handle the loaded cart but had pulled it up the slope without signs of strain and stopped just inside the entrance of the quarry. He called to a nearby worker heading deeper inside, "When you see Nachum ish Chaim or his brother Noam, tell them there's a delivery of tools: pick-axes, chisels, and wedges for him."

The worker came toward him, unslinging a leather bag from his shoulder. "Can I exchange these?" he reached into the pocket and brought out three large chisels, their cutting edges notched and dulled.

The man nodded and held out his hand for them, put them in a separate bag, and reaching into the cart, withdrew three new chisels with glinting edges.

"Thanks"—the worker put the new tools into his bag—"I'll go find one of the foremen for you."

The man watched as the worker descended far down the slope into the mine, then he trundled the cart farther in to leave it in the cave's largest natural cavity, at the edge of the excavated area. The Roman had asked him to come up with a good location for the exchange of messages. He had been a water-boy in this quarry years before, and he knew it as well as did those who toiled within. His father had been one of the many who had died there.

Moving quickly, he went farther in under the faint light of lanterns along the walls, the fingers of his left hand brushing the wall until it came to the section etched by hundreds of men. He lingered where he and his father had added their initials just before his father died, so long ago. He needed no light to see the rock pointing to where to cross to the far wall. Nor did he need help to find the opening of the closed shaft where his father's bones were buried hundreds of feet within, never to be recovered nor given a proper burial.

Maybe it was the years of working in dim light—sometimes none, but even as a boy he had known where he was in the labyrinth of galleries. Even the most experienced men would sometimes get lost in darkness. Not him. The pitch-black had never frightened him; he felt closest to his father when in the dark.

He sensed he was at the spot, felt for it, and knelt at the crevice. He retrieved the message within the jar, put it in the pouch at his waist, and re-secured the hiding place. It had taken only a few moments, and he was back at his cart. He waited for a manager to arrive and sign for the tool delivery.

* * *

Three hours from the city, the man halted his mule, dismounted, and led the beast off the road. Those who often traveled the busy trade road to Shechem or perhaps were going on to Damascus paid little attention to the Roman mile marker effaced with age. Those who traveled the road less did not realize it was there at all, hidden at the foot of the gnarled acacia trees grown close together and entwined to become almost one. On the other side of the trees, away from the road, was a dense tangle of thorn-bush, and behind it was a square of dirt the size of a man's spread-fingered hand. He brushed away the dirt and scrub weed to reveal a flat slab of rock. Digging his fingers beneath one edge, he lifted it and set aside. Beneath was a thick stone storage amphora with a lid that fitted securely over the lipped rim. He pulled the wax-sealed pouch from inside his tunic and set it inside the jar. Then he closed the vessel, replaced the slab over its hiding place, and his hand swept a thick layer of dirt over the capstone. He kicked loose two nearby clumps of dry brush to spread over it with a few hand-sized rocks to help anchor the brush against the wind.

Mounting the mule, he turned south, and he would be back in Jerusalem by sundown.

XXXIX

As Nicanor came in, the clerk-courier, an auxiliary, darted a warning glance from him to a visitor in the fine armor of a soldier on the Praetorian Prefect's personal staff—in stark contrast to the clerk's everyday garb of an auxiliary. The legionary had entered the prison during the last watch and disdainfully demanded to see the centurion and had waited for Nicanor, not wishing to leave the message with the previous watch-captain. The legionary was an *evocatus*, the highest non-officer rank. Lord Tigellinus had tempted many evocati back to service with high wages and exclusive rewards to form a cadre devoted to him. Nicanor wondered if they had had their pay cut, too, or how long they would be loyal once it was withheld.

"Centurion, Lord Tigellinus will see you in the morning, the first hour from sunrise." It was not a request but demand, and with a sharp dip of his head, not waiting for a reply, the soldier spun on a heel and left.

The clerk-courier muttered something under his breath and glared at the legionary's departing back.

"Back to your duties, Florin," Nicanor said with a nod to the clerk. The young auxiliary bowed his head over a desk cluttered by the day watch's disorder and sorted through scrolls and slips of parchment, filing them away. Not once had Florin asked Nicanor about the occasional nights he had stood the watch below for an hour or two of conversation with the Christian leader, the prisoner Paul.

But was it Florin who watched and reported on him to Lord Tigellinus? Nicanor had sensed eyes on him at the Tullianum and the fortress and sometimes even when off duty, as he walked the city. Or was it that chance meeting and the statement by the scribe that morning, when Tigellinus came upon him meeting with Vespasian? Had the Prefect overheard, and was he now worried something had been concealed from him?

Nicanor shook his head—the long watch would be even longer as he chased those thoughts around inside his head.

* * *

Nicanor stood to wait, not accepting the soldier's invitation to sit. After a while, the ache in his leg made him regret that decision. But he sensed the condescension emanating from the man that Florin had felt at the prison the day before. He would not sit now, no matter the discomfort.

Clerks came and went, going about the business of the empire and specifically the administration of the three cohorts of praetorians stationed in Rome itself. He thought about his meeting with General Vespasian that had likely prompted the Prefect's summons. He had followed the general to an office much less sumptuous than he had imagined it would be, entirely unlike the offices of other senior officers in the administrative buildings.

"What does it mean to serve, centurion?" Vespasian had asked him as he settled behind the plain desk with its well-ordered arrangement of what appeared to be reports on legion status, readiness, and provisioning. The general took the satchel from his shoulder, opened it, and slid its contents onto the open area of the desk. He looked up at Nicanor and placed his hands on either side of the stack.

Nicanor had known not to come up with some clever reply to this man, especially since he was not smart with that sort of interchange, so had been straightforward. "It's dictated by honor, lord. When you serve, you agree to the duties assigned, and you must do them to the best of your abilities?

"And have you, centurion?"

Nicanor raised his eyes from the drum roll of Vespasian's thick fingers on the folded square of what he knew must be the 12th Legion's campaign maps from Jerusalem and Beth Horon. He met the evaluating prod of the general's gaze. "I have, lord. Always."

"And do you serve Rome's needs or a man's—do you serve your commander... or your superior officer?"

"Aren't they the same, lord?"

"They should be." The fingers gave the charts a hard tap and stopped. "No need to call me lord, centurion—we're both soldiers." Vespasian rose and went to the antechamber entry and spoke to his aide: "Gaheris, have *calda* brought to us."

The silence that seemed too long was broken within minutes by a servant entering with a tray holding a steaming carafe and two cups. The man followed Vespasian's pointing finger and set it on the corner of the desk. The general reached for the carafe, poured to fill the cups, and pushed one toward Nicanor. "Are you content with your current duties, centurion?"

That was a question and concern that had grown to trouble Nicanor since he had come back to Rome. To create time to consider a reply, he took a sip of the warm water and wine laced with spices.

"Are you happy with where you serve?" Vespasian pressed.

The impulse to answer honestly was powerful, but Nicanor realized there were many ears in Rome—in the very building—listening for ill-thought words and noting the men who spoke them. He knew even simple words often had consequences and could not be unsaid—he hoped the general would let the question pass unanswered. His eyes swept the room, lingering on the doorway to the antechamber and the passageway beyond, then he returned his gaze to the general's face.

Vespasian's eyes followed Nicanor's and, with a slight nod, changed his query. "Centurion, I need someone with your recent experience and knowledge of the terrain in Judea and its inhabitants—I need such a man on my staff who will serve under my son, Titus, but have direct access to me. I will not order it or request you to be assigned to my command unless it is a duty that appeals to you. Will you consider it? I must have your answer soon."

Nicanor's memory of that meeting with Vespasian passed as the evocatus rose and left the room. The soldier returned moments later from the private inner offices to announce, "The Prefect will see you, now, centurion."

Nicanor followed him down a short hall that ended in an expansive, ornately furnished office with a balcony that looked out on the forum three floors below. He could not help but contrast this setting to the one in which he had spoken to Vespasian.

"You've met with General Vespasian...." The Prefect's tone was neutral, neither friendly nor hostile.

"Yes, I have, Lord Tigellinus."

The Prefect looked up expectantly, and a frown began to form, narrowing the man's features. "Well, what did you discuss with him?"

"Nothing, lord."

"He asked you no questions?"

"Lord, General Vespasian asked if I would serve on his staff—under his son—in the coming campaign in Judea." He did not trust the Prefect, but that not make him feel better about shading the truth, but he knew he must. "I told him I serve Rome how, when, and where I'm assigned."

"Do you want to accept his offer?"

"Lord, I will serve where ordered... as I have done for many years."

"Perhaps it would be good to have you in such a position..." the Prefect mused.

"I'm not sure I understand, lord." Nicanor had assumed the man did not want him to tell General Vespasian anything further about

Cestius Gallus's command of the 12th Legion, or to even be around the general and become tempted to do so.

"If you joined him and serve me well... I would guarantee your return to the Praetorian Guard... at a much higher rank... and much to the benefit of your coming retirement. Does that interest you?"

Nicanor heard the "serve me" emphasis—it implied that the Prefect presumed he had found another veteran soldier he could bring to his side. More importantly, he realized what was unsaid but would be expected of him in exchange for such a reward.

He gripped his tongue and temper and replied with what he hoped was open to interpretation, but still what the Prefect wanted to hear. "I will serve as ordered, Lord Tigellinus."

"Then let's see if General Vespasian requests you. That will be all... for now."

XL

ROME

When not on duty or in field drills or training, Nicanor had spent many of his hours walking the city. He had noted the beautiful and once-beautiful residences—many of them palatial—that dotted the hills above the town and just outside Rome. The homes of those who reaped the benefit of the empire's strength and wealth were being rebuilt after the great fire. And he had seen those who had been overlooked, as evidenced by the smoke-scarred rubble where the less-fortunate had once lived. Many of them now lived in hastily erected wooden structures never meant to be permanent.

The new routine of walking without a destination suited his mulling over what to do... or whether he should do anything at all. If he joined Vespasian, even in a staff position, it likely meant combat again. From what he had learned, the general did not lead from his desk in a tent far from where his men fought battles. Nicanor did not fear injury or even death; he had faced both too many times. But to see men who served under him wounded, maimed or killed... he had experienced enough of that to last a lifetime and was reluctant to voluntarily endure more, especially if he doubted the men giving the orders.

But a recent conversation with the prisoner Paul also had him thinking. If he returned to Judea, he would likely not have to fight his friend Yosef, and their friendship might be of help when the fighting ended. If the rebels were defeated, with insurmountable forces surrounding Jerusalem, maybe his presence on General Vespasian's staff would help. He could talk to Yosef and his father about presenting the rebel leader's terms of surrender to prevent the destruction of their city.

Finally, his conscience overrode his reluctance. But before he was sure, he had to first meet with Graius, Lady Cleo's former major domus, to whom he had given copies of Cestius Gallus's original report and the letters intended for Emperor Nero. As Nicanor had suspected and now fully believed, Nero either did not care about the truth or knew and had played a role in what had happened in Judea. The accurate report and the letters were a threat to Nicanor—Nero would do anything to protect himself from any damning revelations in them—but they might be useful.

Nicanor had thought long and deliberated before he had left the copies with Graius. But he knew Gessius Florus, once married to Cleo, had forced Graius out by replacing him with his own major domus in Judea. If Florus wanted Graius out of his way and Cleo loved Graius... then the man must be trustworthy. Nicanor just needed to determine what to have him do with the copies of the documents.

If someone were following or watching him, his random changes might throw them off or convince them his walks were without purpose. But still, instead of going to where Graius lived, Nicanor found a merchant with many food stalls around the city who also delivered letters within Rome. He sent a message to Graius, who lived in an *insula* near the Campus Martius. The apartment building's street-level floor was the taberna where he and Nicanor had met on his return to Rome, but that feeling of being watched had not faded, and the taberna was too close to the Tabularium. A location with more people was needed, one where a mixing of the classes was the rule and not the exception. In Nicanor's message, he asked Graius to meet him in two days at a prominent and popular public bath.

* * *

Nicanor, having served in so many years in dry regions or in the field where baths were often rudimentary at best and nonexistent at worst, loved the public baths of Rome. And the Baths of Agrippa were like nothing he had ever seen. Outside the main entrance stood Apoxyomenos, a sculpture of an athlete scraping sweat and dust from his body with a *strigil*, a small curved instrument used to clean the body after exercise or an athletic event. The area covered by decorated, glazed terra cotta tile was over 300 feet on each side and surrounded by gardens. The large rotunda on the north side of the building was over two hundred feet in diameter. He had been told it was the central gathering spot for the bathers, a place where members of the senatorial class encountered lower society, and the slaves there to attend to their masters.

Surrounding and among the buildings were food stands and attendants who offered every sort of service. Inside were the *thermae,* the actual baths, a series of heated rooms, and pools. Nicanor went to the baths strictly for cleansing, but he had seen most Romans would visit the different places in a specific order and to socialize. They would start at the *apodyterium,* or dressing room, where they would undress and leave their clothing, which would be watched over by a servant or slave. They would then visit the *palaestra*, or gymnasium, where they could exercise and have their body oiled before the baths themselves. Then the *frigidarium*, or cold room, contained a cold plunge bath for before they visited the *tepidarium*, or warm place, to recover. The final room was the *caldarium*, a steamy hot room that might also have a hot plunge bath or *labrum*. After all this, the oil would be scraped off their skin by a servant, and they would end up back where the afternoon's bathing had begun to get dressed and head home.

* * *

"Do you come here often, centurion?" Graius asked.

Nicanor had quickly recognized the man at the entrance to the rotunda and greeted him. "No, never this bath... I've used simpler ones and mostly the nearest to the Arx Capitolina... by the Praetorian barracks." Nicanor did not need to elaborate on the difference between those he frequented and where he now stood. He looked around and took in their surroundings. They had picked the busiest afternoon hour. Dozens of men thronged around them, though he saw a few women, all wearing the color, style, and quality of togas and robes that distinguished the wealthy and well-positioned citizens from the ordinary people. Once the clothes were off, it was harder to tell the men apart, though Nicanor thought the size and paleness of their paunch might betray social status. The working-class was not as well fed. "I've never seen one like this. Do you come here, Graius?"

"I have not been in a long time... I spent decades around men like them"—he waved a hand at a nearby cluster of heavy-set Romans, naked and sweaty from one of the steam rooms—"and I prefer a simpler setting." He motioned to Nicanor to follow him farther into the crowded rotunda and turned to the centurion. "Have you decided about what you left with me?"

"I wanted to speak with you first. I may soon get new orders to return to Judea but need to get the articles into the hands of someone who can put them to good use if necessary."

"Then perhaps Lord Otho, Lady Cleo's brother, the governor in Lusitania? He and Cleo are close, and I've known him most of his life—and they continue to stay in touch." Graius paused, and a pang of worry crossed his face. "Centurion, I'm concerned about Lady Cleo. If you go to Judea... could you, would you check on her, please? I fear for her and not just because of what we hear of the rebellion and brewing war. I detest Gessius Florus and fear she may come to harm at his hands. Lord Otho is also concerned and would welcome my telling him you will check on his sister's safety and well-being."

That resonated with Nicanor, and he felt the heaviness lift from him once his decision was clear. He would return to doing what he did well—soldiering—and get away from Rome and the scrutiny of Tigellinus, to return to an environment where he felt most at ease. He would do what he could to help Vespasian, check on Cleo's safety and on Sayid, too... and maybe help his friend Yosef, that the Jewish people not be wholly crushed by Rome. He had his answer for General Vespasian.

XLI

Jerusalem

Miriam suspected there were eyes on her from the leatherworker's shop across the alley from Zechariah's as she changed the glazed pottery hamsa to hang higher from a knotted cord, its longest finger now even with the top of the lintel. Quickly adjusted as she entered, it was the pre-arranged signal set with Elazar to let the Sicarii leader know she needed to meet with him. He should now show up at Zechariah's shop within three days.

With Purim over—her family obligations met and her personal *tzedakah* done—helping the wife and children of a man killed by the Romans during the attack on Jerusalem—she could come to Zechariah's that many days in a row with no complaints from her mother. That is if she was sure to return home by nightfall. She set the bundle of household knives she carried on the worktable. They were her excuse should Matthew follow her yet again, which she was sure would happen soon. Just as she sensed the leatherworker or one of his apprentices was connected with the Sicarii—as had been Zechariah—and watched her coming and going from Zechariah's, so did her brother watch her more closely. Thankfully, he had many demands that kept him busy and mostly away from her, except at night and at home. There she took refuge in her room, only coming out for meals and to help her mother.

Everything in the shop was precisely as Zechariah had left it, but she kept his workbench and tools dusted and used his sharpening stones and the practice targets he had made for her. She went to the back room, where Zechariah had slept, knelt at his hidden compartment, and took out the maps and letters she had found. The letters had made her cry—there was so much love and pain in them—and she put them back inside without re-reading. Sitting on the floor, she unfolded the maps to study them again. Masada's tunnels held no interest—she would give that chart to Elazar. But the Jerusalem maps were fascinating. Some of the underground passages shown—just a few—were those that she, Yosef, and Matthew had explored as children.

Her finger traced the one closest to the Temple—just outside the enclosure and courtyards—and started to tremble. That was where all the darkness in her life began, the place where nightmares and shadows were born that still threatened her no matter how bright the day. She looked up and away from the map, blinked tears away and wiped them with the back of her hand, then stood. Leaving the chart of tunnels spread on the floor, she walked to Zechariah's workbench and touched each of his tools, something that at all times settled her when the fear resurfaced. She missed him terribly, his gruff voice always advising... ever direct, firm, but compassionate. His presence, even when he grew quiet as he often had, made her feel safe.

In the corner was his staff, where it had been since she returned it to its usual spot after his death. She had used it to kill his killer, a Roman mercenary. That same staff was what he had used to save her from the two Romans that had raped her in that dark passage her wavering finger had just traced. Six feet long, made of acacia wood so old it was iron-hard, it was nicked and scarred from much use but remained a rich, dark brown with hints of red in the grain, and it was capped at the narrow end by a thick ferrule honed to a point. She carried it back and sat cross-legged on the floor with it across her knees as she studied the map.

Zechariah had shown her several tunnels; she had no idea existed beneath the city and told her about even more. She still wondered whether anyone even knew of them all or what else might lie just beneath the streets of the town. There were many underground passages, and Zechariah had shown her the entrances and the exits of only a few of them. She could see others marked on the chart that were not known to her—that he had not talked about—and questioned their purpose. One ran a considerable distance beneath Jerusalem at some depth, since it seemed to span the Lower City and the Upper City, and stretched into the area near the New City, the hill just north of the Temple enclosure and Fortress Antonia to the northern wall. Large shaded regions, at both ends of that tunnel, marked something, but what the marking meant she had no idea.

* * *

The third morning, Miriam knew Elazar would show that day, and might likely already be at Zechariah's. The problem was that she had spotted Matthew following her as she glanced over her shoulder at the steps that descended the southwest corner of the Temple enclosure into the Lower City. *Try to lose him?* Or should she do as Zechariah had told her when trapped... find a good spot to defend, then turn and fight. She slowed her pace to let Matthew catch up and see her clearly. Minutes later, she stepped into the knife-sharpener's shop.

"So, you brought them with you this time"—the young man raised his head as she came in.

Miriam half-turned from leaning out and peering down the street through the still-open door. Matthew was headed straight for the shop. The man behind the work table—she thought he must be closer to Yosef's or Matthew's age than her own—had the same unblinking stare, but it was not as fierce as it had been the first time she had come into his shop. She walked toward him just as she heard someone enter behind her.

"Miriam?" Matthew called to her.

She saw the shopkeeper's features tighten and narrow, dark, thick eyebrows formed an inverted triangle that pointed down toward his hawk-like blade of a nose. His deep-set eyes gazed beyond her at Matthew, but she did not turn from him to face her brother. "I have these for you"—she set the packet of knives on the table before the man—"I think some also need repair, but you decide." Miriam unwrapped the cloth covering an assortment of blades.

"Do you have guard duties that bring you to the Lower City, Matthew?" she asked, turning to look at him. He seemed flustered at the question, so she pressed, "What is the progress for the preparations to defend the city? Are you here checking on something for Eleasar ben Ananias?"

"Um... yes... and I saw you and wanted to see—" Matthew avoided her glare.

"—If I was fine?" She fixed a smile for Matthew, but seeing his discomfort, she felt the distaste of lying to him... and to her family. But if the truth came out, she would never get to do what she must do to make things right. She owed herself the righteousness and justice that was the literal meaning of tzedakah.

"Some of these handles need to be replaced or re-seated with a new binding... this will take more time," the man said as he picked up and inspected each knife.

"If you can work on them now, I don't mind waiting." Miriam glanced at Matthew, who had begun shifting from foot to foot. She looked back at the knife-sharpener and wondered again about the day she had followed him—in her bearded disguise—to that column with the carved name. "I am fine, Matthew... but you act as if you have much to do and other places to be. Do you?"

The knife-sharpener bent to his work, pulling a lamp closer, its arc of light on his hands, his face now in shadow. He rocked back and forth to the rhythm and sound of metal on stone.

"I will wait, but you should go," Miriam pressed.

"Sister"—Matthew shook his head—"We must talk soon." With a last look at the knife-sharpener and an uncertain squint at her, he turned and left.

Miriam watched to make sure he was well down the street toward the gate and steps that led up to the Temple enclosure and out of sight. She must hurry, because Elazar, the Sicarii leader, might not wait; he did not care to be in Jerusalem too often for too long.

The absence of sound brought her around from watching the street. The man had stopped working the blade against the grindstone and studied her with eyes that glinted in the lamplight. She knew he had watched her make sure Matthew was gone.

"I've remembered another errand I must take care of... I'll return later to pick them up," she told him and felt his stare even once she was on the street.

XLII

Miriam walked a good distance away from the knife-sharpener's shop before the sensation of being watched faded. She stopped at the weaver's stall across from Zechariah's to make sure. The weaver had a gathering of women around him as he extolled his wares, displaying a bolt of saffron yellow fabric that gleamed in the sunlight. She moved around the cluster of women to the far side and looked through the crowd while seeming to pay attention to the portly weaver. There was still no sign that Matthew had doubled back to watch her. In that direction, at the end of the distance up the street, she could see clearly; the knife-sharpener stood at the entrance to his shop. His head pivoted and swept up and down the street. *Is he looking for me?* Then he went back inside. She waited a few more minutes, waving away the weaver's offer to drape the cloth over her arm to feel its softness. With a curt bow of thanks to him, she crossed the street quickly and passed down the alley to the side entrance to Zechariah's shop and entered, closing the door quickly behind her.

"I thought I had missed you." The deep voice was followed by a streak of sparks that flashed in the dark interior. The sparks caught, the lamp's wick bloomed, and the flame's growing light showed Elazar ben Yair's face.

He looks tired and worried, Miriam thought. "My brother, Matthew, followed me this morning."

"Will that become a problem?" There was an edge to his voice that hinted at intervention.

"No, Elazar... it won't be... and I'll be careful."

"You must be, Miriam. Soon there will be work to do, and you need no distractions nor concerns. The Romans are stirring... no longer sitting and waiting. I've received word they've killed 2,000 men between Besara and Nazareth, a band of Sepphoran mercenaries... bandits who took grain from a Roman storage center south and east of Ptolemais." Elazar stopped as if he wanted to say more. "But that's not what's most important"—he shook his head—"What do you need to speak with me about?"

"What is more important than 2,000 of our countrymen losing their lives?" Miriam's voice pitched up, taking on its own harshness. No news had reached Jerusalem of such a defeat, and in Galilee, where Yosef was!

"Lives taken... by the Romans, Miriam, not lost. We will get vengeance for the dead, but now I have a report on new Roman collaborators in the area, maybe already here in Jerusalem. The new Roman commander will soon leave Rome if he has not already. He will come with more legions than we have ever seen." Elazar set the lamp on the worktable and rubbed his face with both hands. "Now, what is it you need of me?"

"Nothing. I wanted to let you know I found Zechariah's maps. It seemed urgent and important to you to help prepare Masada's defenses." She picked up the lamp from the table and beckoned him to follow. In the back room, she first opened the shutter to let in more light, then knelt to reveal the secret compartment Zechariah had built into the floor. "And with them, a bunch of letters." She took out the Masada map and handed it to him.

Elazar walked to the window and unfolded the chart in the sunlight. "Exactly what I was looking for. Now, we can close up—or be ready to seal and defend—any passageways the Romans might know of or discover that could allow them to get around our defenses at Masada." A bright smile broke the darkness of his face—weathered skin and the heavy black beard that framed it. "You say you also found Zechariah's letters?"

"Yes." Miriam carried the letters with her to stand beside Elazar, who folded the map and tucked it under an arm, then held out a hand. "These"—she gave them to him.

The Sicarii leader leafed through them, pausing at some to read a few lines and one or two he seemed to read entirely.

"I never saw him write... and didn't think he..." what Miriam was going to say trailed off as she thought of her mentor.

"You didn't think he could." Elazar nodded. "I knew Zechariah a very long time... his wife and daughter, too. He always wrote notes and messages to Bayla and Meira, leaving them around for them to find and enjoy." He held up the sheaf of letters—"And he didn't stop when they were killed, and he was blinded." He separated a sheet of parchment from the others. "Zechariah wrote to them about you, too"—he looked at her—"and he told me more than once how alike you and Meira were. His daughter's name means 'one who gives light,' and he felt that despite what brought you two together, you could overcome the darkness that took hold of you and again become someone who also gives light.

"There is a spark in you, Miriam. Even blind Zechariah could see more than most can with two good eyes. He made Menachem ben Judah—my leader—see that spark in you. too... and he told me of you before he was killed."

"I cried as I read them."

"Zechariah would not want you to be saddened by the letters. His writing, after Bayla and Meira died, was more to help him heal... than him expecting anyone would ever read them."

"Did he ever heal?" Miriam asked, and the empty tone reflected how hollow the hope was that she would one day heal.

"I don't know. Zechariah would not talk of Bayla and Meira after their deaths... but he kept talking to them... through these." Elazar handed the letters to her. "Keep them—keep the memory of him in your heart. The letters and our remembrance of him are proof that hate cannot quench love. A loved one's death does not mean our life is over, that it is purposeless." He gripped her shoulder. "I must go... but I will be in touch soon. Time is coming for you to continue your purpose."

* * *

The morning crowd of shoppers and workers had thinned out by early afternoon as Miriam waited after Elazar left. She had passed the workshop before remembering the knives. Turning back, she found its doors and front shutters closed. Opening the door, she stepped into pitch-black gloom.

"Hello..." Her whisper was eerie-sounding in her ears as she took a shuffling step toward where she recalled the knife-sharpener's worktable was. A few steps inside and in the far back corner, to the left, she saw a flickering glow and moved toward it. Carefully, making little noise, just as Zechariah had taught her, she could see a squatting figure near the wall, rocking on its heels, next to a small oil-lamp, and hunched over something held in its hands. Another silent step forward and she could see it was a man—the knife-sharpener—and he was dropping something, one piece at a time, into a hide bag.

With a hiss of sound, as he realized someone was there, he shot up, and his white face glared at her. She stopped before speaking, seeing that the man was crying. His stark, angry stare changed to the veil of a flat expression as if to hide what those eyes had revealed—something inside him no one should see.

"Your knives aren't ready... I told you it would take more time." He did not move, but that fierce look spread over his features, and she saw the cords in his neck stand out as if he strained to lift something heavy... or to contain himself. He moved faster than she realized he could—or would—and before she could react and step back... he was right in front of her.

"You must come back later."

167

The small lamp left behind on the floor cast the only light in the dark place; Miriam let him lead her to the door. Something in the man puzzled and almost frightened her—it would have scared her if not for worse things she had experienced. She stepped out into the street and turned to him.

"I'm sorry I bothered you—I'll come back another day." She hesitated, then said, "I don't even know your name."

"Hananiah...." and just before the door shut, she heard him add... "Miriam."

* * *

Full of thoughts about the strange knife-sharpener, *Hananiah*... the name she had found carved on that column he had visited—if "visit" was the right word to explain his actions the day she followed him. He had been so furtive, and that moment in his shop... the naked pain and rage in his eyes that vanished as he glared at her. Was there something other than pain he was hiding?

As she crossed the agora, she almost did not see Leah and Rachel. She called out before she thought about it, and they both seemed to wish she had not noticed them. But they paused and waited for her to join them. The afternoon sun was full on Leah's face before she turned away from it and stepped into the shadow of one of the market's street-side awnings. The bruise and swelling covered the left side of her face, and her eye was puffy and nearly closed; her scarf slipped to reveal a spit swollen lower lip. Leah's eyes welled with tears as Rachel took Miriam's arm and hugged it tightly. "Please do not tell Yosef or Matthew."

XLIII

Father, Yosef remembered, always said that having patience so things could become clearer was prudent more times than not. But it was hard to do with so many people around—and so many plausible reasonings or agendas—that demanded an immediate decision and action. Still, despite the frustration and anger he faced from them, he had followed his father's advice and waited on details before deciding what to do. "How does Gamala stand, Levi—what have you heard from our scouts?" Yosef asked his lieutenant.

"Agrippa's commander Aequus Modius has established his force and is prepared for a siege of the town," Levi replied. "But, Gamala is secure... for now."

Yosef heard the emphasis. Gamala was ready and could withstand whatever men and equipment King Agrippa had brought to lay siege. But if Agrippa was reinforced, especially by actual Roman legionaries and their siege engines, things would change. Quickly. "Should we send men there or to Tiberias?"

"Neapolitanus's cavalry is wreaking havoc around Tiberias," Levi replied, "with constant raids on anything moving to or from the city. But many there who ask for help now are the ones who tried to kill you. Maybe we should go after the Romans that killed Ezekias and his men."

"We need Tiberias and its people with us, Levi," Yosef said, understanding how he felt. Were it not for Levi, he would not have survived the assassination attempt in that city. "I think we must go to the aid of Tiberias. We can do nothing about what happened to Ezekias and his men." The scene of the bloody messenger outside the gates flashed into his mind and caused an involuntary shudder, but he pressed on: "The Roman commander Aebutius has returned to Ptolemais, our scouts claim, or at least his unit has repositioned too close for us to even think about engaging his men there. As you said, Gamala can hold for now.

"Muster the men," Yosef continued. "We'll go to Tiberias to deal with Agrippa's raiders, and then I must stop at Tarichaea."

* * *

TARICHAEA

After routing King Agrippa's field commander Ptolemy and his men, Yosef and his men had regrouped just outside of Tiberias, and a dozen men had arrived to report what had happened with the Dabaritthans, who had taken the temple gold and silver from Agrippa. The treasure was welcome and needed, Yosef thought, but he knew the people were watching, doubtful of Yosef's intentions.

"Yosef, what will you do with the treasure?" Levi asked, his tone suggesting again his doubt about why they had come to Tarichaea. "Yeshua ben Sapphias is claiming you will again take what was looted from their temple and return it to Agrippa. Many heed the chief magistrate and still do not trust you, despite the fact that we just drove Neapolitanus and his men away from the city. Ben Sapphias accuses you of intending to betray them and all the people of Galilee. He gathers crowds of Tiberians to him, holding a copy of the Law of Moses, and tells them you break that law."

"I've never shown by action or inaction that I care for anything or anyone more than our people and country," declared Yosef. "I will not return the treasure to Agrippa—I plan to use that gold and silver for the good of our people. It is meant to strengthen fortifications here in Tarichaea, in Tiberias, and in other towns that need help to prepare for the Romans. I want Yotapta's underlying and surrounding caves checked for passages into the city and then the exposed entrances hidden and defended or sealed."

Levi nodded. "I will see to that as soon as we return."

Yosef shook his head—"No, send a messenger to Yotapta now and have men start as soon as possible... I fear we're running out of time."

"The Dabaritthans say that several hundred men have gathered between Tiberias and here and are believed to follow Yohanan of Gischala. They move toward us."

"How far away are they?" asked Yosef.

"They could be here by nightfall if they pushed."

"Send that message now to Yotapta, and we'll follow at daybreak. Yohanan of Gischala has proved he cannot be trusted, but I have to counter his undermining of me and have asked Justus of Tiberias and his father Pistus to meet me here. At least here is an almost-neutral place away from their city. The council in Tiberias seems to listen to the Gischalan leader, and most of the citizens follow their lead, not thinking for themselves. I need to convince Justus and Pistus—who can sway some of them—that what I do is good. And that it's good not just for Jerusalem but for all of Galilee and our people."

* * *

"Thank you, Nathan and Imma, for all you have done for me and for sharing your home with me again." Yosef smiled at the fisherman who had saved him after the attack in Tiberias, and his wife, who had tended his wounds.

Levi had wanted Yosef to leave for Yotapta after his meeting with Justus and Pistus, and perhaps he should have. But he wanted to see Nathan and Imma and give them his thanks again, so he lingered in Tarichaea after the meeting. The two men had listened to him, but he could not tell if he had convinced them to stop sowing dissension as Yohanan of Gischala did, even if they would not become open allies.

Imma had insisted he eat dinner with them and spend the night. It was pleasant spending time with them and their family... but it made him homesick. At an early hour, he left them for the bed he had used while his wounds had healed—and sank into a deep sleep.

* * *

A scream awoke Yosef, and at first, he thought it was an echo from the shreds of the bad dream that began to fade as soon as his eyes opened. He smelled smoke. The shriek had been a woman's, he thought, though he was groggy. The shouts he heard now were of angry, cursing men who seemed to be moving away from the house. He had not undressed to sleep, but hurriedly slipped on his sandals, and grabbed his cloak and the sword he had leaned against the wall by the cot. He had to push hard to open the door of his room, and coming out into the family's central hall, he fell over a body that had blocked the door, someone whose clothing was on fire. On his knees, in the lurid light from flames still climbing the walls and that now licked the beams of the ceiling, he smelled the lamp oil that had been poured on the body. He used his cloak to smother the flames and carefully turned the head toward him and felt blood and bits of what must be bone smear his hands. Imma's hair and the left side of her face had been burned away, and she was dead.

He dragged her body toward the door that led toward the water. As he lifted and carried her through the door and onto the path that led to the dock, he heard more shouts, but these were coming toward him. Nathan and his sons rushed from the shadows along the bank.

"I'm sorry, Nathan," Yosef said, realizing he had brought a lifeless body from the fire.

"She told me to get the boys out and went to wake you," Nathan cried, falling to his knees beside her.

"Someone or something hit her from behind... she must have been unconscious...." Yosef prayed she had been before they set her aflame.

"There were men furious at our helping you... at her for caring for your wounds."

"I'm sorry, Nathan." Yosef wished he had left for Yotapta after all, as Levi had wanted.

"I don't blame you, Yosef, I blame them... the leaders of Tiberias who meddle here and tell people to seek retribution against anyone who helped you. I want them to pay."

Yosef saw in the light of the house burning and the sky brightening with the coming dawn the group of men approaching, and he soon saw they were led by Levi ben Altheus. He turned to Nathan. "I promise you they will pay."

The anger that burned in him was hotter than what had consumed Imma's home and her life. *We will make them pay.* Yosef did not know who he hated more for what had happened—the Romans that had pushed the situation in Judea to this point or his own people who, for selfish reasons, had killed the innocent or let them be killed. They were driving them all toward inevitable death and destruction.

XLIV

"They'll spread out as they run from here," Levi ben Altheus declared, his scorn and anger rang in the morning's quiet, "then they'll likely rejoin Yohanan of Gischala."

Levi followed Yosef, who circled the remnants of the home of Nathan, the fisherman. The men who had set the fire had not only drenched the outer walls in lamp oil but had also gone inside with the oil. The wood beams and thatched straw of the roof burned quickly, as had the interior framing of wood and straw—and the wood and fabric of the furnishings.

Yosef thought of poor Imma, Nathan's wife, who had come upon those men and died as she awakened Yosef with her screams. He approached the group of men near the still-smoldering rubble, some young boys in their late teens at most, and all surrounded Nathan. The fisherman had had little, to begin with... now even less.

But the loss of material things did not matter to Nathan, as Yosef knew from the time he had spent with family. But as the sun rose and revealed what had been the fisherman's home... as he watched Nathan cry over his wife's body, Yosef saw him change. Losing Imma, his most valued treasure, created an emptiness Nathan had replaced with rage.

Nathan turned to Yosef. "My brothers, my sons, Imma's brothers, and their sons... we must go after the men who did this... and kill them."

Yosef knew what Levi had just told him was right—those men were scattered by now. "The men who did this will be punished," he replied. "But like all who attack at night—who harm those who have done them no harm and then run in the light of day—they will be found, and justice delivered. Right now, there are others we must deal with first.

"They are men just as responsible as those who did this," Yosef continued, "and if you help me, I will punish them and give others notice of what to expect if they continue to fight against those who wish to stand together against the Romans. They must learn they cannot punish those who believe differently than they do.

"You know who I speak of and have told me as much"—Yosef looked from face to face—"Tiberias has been nothing but distress to its neighbors who wish to join me in unifying Galilee against the Romans. That city's leaders must understand the consequences of their choices. Whether they ally with Yohanan of Gischala or, as I just heard this morning"—he nodded at the messenger who stood next to Levi—"pursue their new interest in defecting to join with King Agrippa, they must no longer stir up trouble, support dissension... and cause harm.

"If they do," he said in a rising tone such as his father had used in all his years driving home the message of the Torah, "it will not be without reprisal." He paused, then became more familiar and gentler in his tone: "Nathan, I ask you and Imma's brothers to go to the leading families of Tarichaea... tell them I need their support in standing up for you and for others of this town. Ask them for boats and more men to join us."

He looked around again at all those gathered. "We will sail to Tiberias. We will find the city council and other leaders and see that justice is served."

* * *

Yosef loved the natural beauty of Lake Gennesaret and wished he could enjoy it under different circumstances. The lake was surrounded by the low mountains of the Decapolis, nearly 2,500 feet high on the eastern shore, with other steep slopes on all sides reaching 1,400 feet above the level of the sea and Mount Arbel on the west—which dropped sharply down to the sea. These hills were green in the spring and brown during the dry season, contrasting with the deep blue of the water. Gennesaret was also known for its violent storms, which could come up with life-threatening suddenness. Tempests formed quickly on the lake, created by the rift where cooler air masses from the surrounding mountains collided with the warm air in the lake's basin. The winds funneled through the east-west-oriented valleys in the hill country and rushed toward the lake.

And now those winds had turned vicious and developed into a squall that spanned the lake. The storm had given Yosef more than one fearful moment—nightmare flashes of the wreck of the *Salacia* on the far larger sea between Judea and Rome—but was now abating, and it had served a purpose. The fierce tempest had pushed them far faster than a gentler wind would have done, and their quick arrival at Tiberias, in a full gale, ensured they were unexpected. The Tarichaean fishermen were fearless, used to the storms, even as ten-foot waves slammed their boats against the docks of Tiberias, threatening to pitch them onto and over the tall pilings. Brave men with mooring lines and ropes around their waists leaped from wildly pitching boats to the slick pier and secured the ropes.

TIBERIAS

On the pier, huddled against a processing building for the salting, drying, and pickling of fish, Yosef squeezed water from his beard. He tugged at the cord and strap of the sword around his neck and pulled it over his head. "I'll take thirty men to the council house and secure that chamber. Do you have the list of council members Silas provided us?" Yosef omitted the detail that Silas had given that list to him before he was killed in the attack at the Tiberian stadium near this very building. Levi had been there too. Silas had been a good man, loyal to more than himself, concerned about his fellow Tiberians—he felt they were being led from what was best for the people of Galilee and more toward serving the pure self-interest of a handful of men.

"Yes," said Levi, "and two of Nathan's brothers have lived in Tiberias before and know them all... and where they live."

"Good. Find them and bring them to the council house." Yosef gripped his sword and shook the water from it as his other hand pulled out his undertunic to find a scrap of dry fabric to wipe the hilt. "Do not feel you must be courteous or diplomatic. Drag them if you have to."

* * *

YOTAPTA

Ariella greeted Levi ben Altheus as soon as they crossed through the gates. Yosef—not for the first time—concluded she had become his lieutenant's lieutenant. At Tiberias, he had received her urgent message that Yohanan ben Zaccai had arrived with important news for him from Jerusalem. So, he and Levi, with a dozen men, had ridden for Yotapta immediately, but news of what he had done in Tiberias arrived ahead of him.

"Yosef, Yohanan ben Zaccai must speak with you in private"— Ariella came closer and whispered—"but know that I and others think you did the right thing. You had to...." She turned and took Levi by the arm as Yosef entered his quarters.

When he saw Yohanan ben Zaccai, it was clear to Yosef the old priest's feelings did not match Ariella's. "It is good to see you,

Yosef"—he paused—"but the Tiberian council president, Cleitus, is merely a donkey that follows whoever pulls his lead rope the strongest. Did you have to cut off his hand as punishment? Is that the form of justice you wish to deliver?" There was as much disappointment as condemnation in Yohanan's stern expression. "How has that made things better?"

"Would you have me do nothing? Were it not for a good woman's warning, I would have died as she did"—Yosef ran a hand through his hair and shook his head—"Maybe I should have died. I wish it were me instead of her."

His friend shook his head sadly. "Galilee... no, we, all of us... need you, Yosef. But it seems some in Jerusalem still don't agree, and what you did in Tiberias likely will make them feel so even more strongly." The priest took a tight-wrapped scroll from within a fold of the sash of his robe. "Shimon ben Gamliel has demanded your removal from command of Galilee."

"What... why?" Yosef asked.

"Aside from his long friendship with Yohanan ben Levi of Gischala—who no doubt whispers poison against you in his ear— Shimon has never believed you were qualified," Yohanan answered. "He wanted someone more to his liking."

"You mean he wants someone who will do his—or the Sanhedrin's—bidding," said Yosef. "But that's not always best for all Galileans. That is exactly what the Galileans fear from Jerusalem... and that belief is what I've fought against since coming here."

"Yes, I agree with you," ben Zaccai replied and handed the scroll to Yosef. "His message says he is sending a delegation of representatives to meet with you—to demand you return with them to Jerusalem."

"Let them come... I'll listen and then send them back. I will remain here!" Part of Yosef questioned whether it was worth the continued effort—against such resistance—to do what should be done to prepare for the Romans. He still believed they could reach a resolution and not force a war. The doubts weighed heavily, and he was tired of the infighting before the Romans even brought their military might to bear against Galilee and Judea.

The priest took another message from his robe, and the stern look softened into regret. "I have another message... from your mother. Your father is sick, and she fears he may be dying."

XLV

Unlike the message from Ophonius Tigellinus, a Prefect's demand delivered by one of his cadre, Vespasian's message was a simple note left with Florin, who handed it to him when he arrived for the watch. Nicanor slid a thumb under the flap, broke the wax seal he did not recognize, and unfolded the square of parchment:

Centurion, it is time, and I must know if you have given what we discussed some thought. If your answer is "Yes," then meet me tomorrow morning at the Regia on the via Sacra near the Forum. It is fitting that this is the route of the Roman Triumph. If you join me, you will experience that firsthand when we return from Judea. —Vespasian

* * *

Nicanor had not thought about it during his last watch and had not gone below to talk with Paul. That would have made him think about not just what to tell General Vespasian but other matters, too. He had slept through the night dreamless, and much better than he had slept in a long time. He woke at dawn's light to a decision made and knew it was the right one.

Full of gruel and fruit an hour later, he stepped from the base of the Gemonian Stairs and crossed several smaller streets to reach the much broader via Sacra. Vendor stalls lined the avenue as far as he could see. He stopped at the first stand, a fruit-seller. "Do you know a building called the Regia, and how to get to it from here?" Nicanor pointed east—"I'm told it's near the Forum."

The young merchant, perhaps a Spaniard, shrugged his shoulders and shook his head, his attention shifting to a stocky man in a simple workman's tunic who had picked up a handful of dried figs and held out a coin.

Nicanor turned left along the broad avenue and had walked only a dozen steps when a gruff voice called to him. He turned.

"Centurion!" the workman called, still standing beside the fruit stall. "Some don't know of the Regia... but I've done work there, and it's just past the Forum. Keep going on this street until you pass through the new colonnades Emperor Nero has been good enough to erect"—he curled a lip with distaste—"to where the street continues between the Velian and Palatine hills." The man popped a fig into his mouth and then spoke around the chewing—"The Regia is old... and it will be on your right."

The building—actually two separate structures joined—was markedly older than the surrounding construction and set much farther back from the street. Nicanor recognized the large man in civilian garb who paced outside it.

Nicanor knew—and had expected—that General Vespasian would not say it, but also felt he would show it. Just as Nicanor dealt with his own subordinates who met a challenge or accomplished a task assigned them, Vespasian showed by his manner that he approved.

"You found it," Vespasian noted with a half-smile of. He gestured for Nicanor to follow him inside. "I never knew of the Regia until it was mentioned to me by someone you'll meet inside. It was the royal palace of Rome's second king, Numa Pompilius, and I'm told it has been rebuilt at least twice over the centuries."

Through the main entrance, they crossed into an irregularly formed, enclosed court paved in volcanic rock and bordered by a wooden portico. Passing through the courtyard, they entered a room with a set of wings that branched east and west off the large central room. The room on the right had two large wooden doors, closed, framed, and banded in bronze. "That's the sanctuary of Ops Consiva, a fertility deity... and only the Pontifex Maximus and Vestal Virgins are allowed within."

Vespasian turned left toward the western wing. "We're meeting here—it's appropriate."

At a large table in the room were two men. The gray-haired one standing wore a *toga picta*, richly embroidered, patterned and dyed in purple. The younger man sat at the table strewn with what looked like maps, ink pots, and drawing implements, and he wore a *toga pura*, plain white but of excellent quality. Behind them on the wall was the *ancilia* Nicanor recognized from stories about them—the twelve sacred shields believed to guarantee the continued imperium of Rome—and *hastae*, lances arrayed above and below the shields. The walls were decorated with terracotta friezes, and the one before him portrayed a minotaur.

The older man in purple followed his gaze. "Centurion, if, as we talk, the lances should vibrate, you may choose to leave. But by then, it may be too late,"—he laughed.

"Centurion—Nicanor—this is Gaius Licinius Mucianus"—Vespasian cast a stern look at the man—"who is to be the next governor of Syria... replacing Cestius Gallus."

Nicanor nodded his understanding and respect. "What is this room?"

"This is the *sacrarium martis* and these"—Mucianus pointed at the lances—"according to legend are the *hastae martiae,* consecrated to Mars in this, his shrine. If you believe the tales, if they vibrate, then something terrible will soon happen. Julius Caesar, the Pontifex Maximus at the time, on the night of 14 Martius, 123 years ago, witnessed that vibration here. Then he went to a Senate meeting afterward, and there he was assassinated."

The new Syrian governor sat down. "This building is where I and others meet as the Arval Brethren. Those who believe in the old ways, the *pignora imperii.* We of the *fratres arvales* hold to the pledges of rule and sacred objects that have made and keep Rome strong. It's a place few people frequent who are not among the priests. And this is how I found this young man, Sylvanus, who will help Lord Vespasian with updating a set of maps."

He invited Nicanor with a gesture to look more closely. "They depict where you have recently served. This is where the good general"—Mucianus inclined his head toward Vespasian—"will soon lead you and tens of thousands of Roman soldiers into battle against the Judean rebels. Sylvanus is the son of Pomponius Mela, now passed on but still thought of as Rome's finest mapmaker."

"Nicanor," Vespasian announced, "today I will request that you be transferred to my command, and I expect Lord Tigellinus will soon comply and make it official. I'll then have a staff meeting and want you to work with Sylvanus here to create updated maps that use what you recall of these lands. Soon we will deploy, and Lord Mucianus will travel with us to Antioch."

* * *

"Centurion—come here."

The honeyed yet barbed tone was one he could not mistake or choose to ignore. The Praetorian Prefect and his personal escort stood on the branch of the path that led to the steepest drop to the city center below.

"Yes, Lord Tigellinus... how may I serve you?" Nicanor stopped at attention before the Prefect.

"Lord Vespasian has asked for you on his personal staff, centurion, and I have agreed. The new orders will be in writing to you tomorrow morning. So this evening, you stand your last duty at the Tullianum." The Prefect walked to the edge of the Tarpeian Rock, gesturing for Nicanor to join him. "Remember this view, centurion. And the importance of loyalty..."

The Prefect did not say it, but the implication—a carryover from their last meeting—was clear. Nicanor's expected allegiance was not to Emperor Nero nor even to Rome, but to Tigellinus.

"One of my men will be in touch with you once you are settled in General Vespasian's circle of advisors." Tigellinus looked down from the rock and then back into Nicanor's eyes. "To fail me... is to face the fall." The Prefect spun on his heel and walked away.

* * *

"When will you leave for Judea?" Florin asked.

"When we sail, I don't know, but it will be soon." Nicanor paced the room. "This is my last watch."

"I wish I could serve with you... my next watch-captain will probably be slack, like the one I had before. On duty, but in his mind already retired."

"He'll likely make fewer demands of you." Nicanor glanced at the young auxiliary.

"I'll go back to not feeling like a soldier," Florin replied, shaking his head.

The young man's tone and feelings made Nicanor recall Sayid, who had told him much the same thing. Both desired the opportunity to be—or to become—a Roman soldier that others respect. He faced his watch-messenger and smiled. "You'll be fine, Florin. You'll not always serve here—you'll get other chances in other duty posts." Nicanor's eyes swept the room. "I'm going below and will send the guard up. I'll stand the watch there."

With a lantern in hand, he descended the steep steps into the prisoner levels below. On the next-to-last level, at the foot of the steps, the guard met him on his round of pacing the length of the passage. Without a word, Nicanor cocked his thumb up, and the guard nodded, then swiftly ascended to the main level.

"Your steps are lighter," Paul said as Nicanor came into the light of the larger lantern hung on the wall beside the cell. "I thought it might be your young messenger... not you." He pulled his stool closer to the bars and lantern light. "What has changed, centurion?"

"I'm at peace," Nicanor replied. "I will return to Judea."

"Good to hear," Paul responded. "As am I—also at peace. I have run a good race. My remaining days are few, but I will continue to pray for you and for Yosef and Jerusalem."

XLVI

General Vespasian—in full regalia—stood behind his massive campaign table and nodded as Nicanor came in and took his place at one side of the room. He stood next to Gaheris Clineas, the general's personal aide, who looked far more impressive in military harness and uniform than in the civilian tunic and robes Nicanor had seen him in before. Along the opposite wall were the other staff officers and functionaries necessary for a military campaign of this size and import. They ranged from the senior-rank *praefetus castrorum*, who would be the command coordinator with each legion's Camp-Prefect, to senior quartermasters in charge of weapons and supplies logistics, to the command senior *medicus* who would lead the dozen or more medics assigned to each legion, to the officer and senior *architecti*, who would lead the group of engineers and artillery in siege operations.

Nicanor had never served in a multi-legion campaign, and he wondered how they would all work together. General Vespasian's bearing showed complete confidence as his eyes ranged the assembled men.

On the table was spread a large map of the southern province seacoast from Alexandria in Egypt to Antioch in Syria, showing far enough inland to mark the location of Jerusalem, all of Galilee, then Damascus and up to the area east of Antioch. Vespasian lifted the helmet from his head and set it on the table to hold down one edge of the map that wanted to curl.

He picked up six blocks of wood—the size of his fist—and started to speak with no preamble: "The port masters and ship captains at Ostia and Alexandria report all supplies and equipment are nearly loaded on all support vessels and that they will sail in one week. The Ostia ships will go to Ptolemais, and the Alexandrian vessels will split between Gaza and Caesarea." He took four of the blocks—three with the carved symbols V, X, and XV, and a fourth with the simple letter A—and placed them on the map at Alexandria.

"My son, Titus, will be my field commander for this campaign. He is already underway for Alexandria and should arrive within the next two days. There he will take command of the 5th Legion Macedonia, the 10th Legion Fretensis, and the 15th Legion Apollinaris. They will form up and march overland to Gaza, where they will gather the equipment and supplies that will have been delivered there, then reassemble and move up the coast to a position near Caesarea where they will set up a fortified encampment. From there, the 15th Legion will continue to Ptolemais, where it will operate with the 12th Legion." He moved the respective blocks to those points on the map. "An Alexandrian auxiliary force will also deploy under his command and will support the 5th Legion," Vespasian put the A block near Caesarea. At the top of the map, near Antioch, he set the other A block, and the one marked XII.

"We will sail one week from today to Antioch. There, I will relieve Lord Cestius Gallus of military command—he will return to Rome on the ship we arrive on—and Lord Gaius Mucianus, who accompanies us, will assume the governorship of the region. Then I will take the holding force left in Antioch by the 12th Legion, with the large auxiliary and allied force now gathering there, and march to Ptolemais." He moved the two blocks from Antioch to that city. "I will set up a fortified encampment for my headquarters outside Ptolemais, and the forces will merge with the large balance of the 12th Legion already there.

"The units from that legion—which had been split off to encamp outside Caesarea to protect that vital port—will move up to Ptolemais and rejoin the 12th. We will then supply and equip for extended field operations."

He paused a moment to focus their attention. "Then we will crush the rebels step by step, town by town... all the way to Jerusalem. We bring an army of 60,000 men against the rebels, the power of which they have not yet witnessed nor endured, and we will inflict upon them a clear understanding that the Roman army will prevail. Through the fury of our intent, they will soon understand."

No retreat this time"—he picked up his cudgel and tapped—"no defeat this time"—it tapped again. Harder. "We will return that region to Roman rule." Vespasian's gaze swept the room, pausing at each man then moving to the next. "Are there any questions?"

"How could there be any other outcome, Lord Vespasian?"

Nicanor had not seen the Praetorian Prefect enter the room but recognized his voice and half-turned to locate him near the entrance to the antechamber.

"It seems you are well-prepared and have planned thoroughly," continued Tigellinus. "The emperor will be happy to hear that the empires... Judean problem... will be resolved through your capable efforts. I do not mean to interrupt"—he motioned to the assembled men—"I only stopped to tell you the emperor felt you needed another person with some experience in the region." His eyes slid sideways toward Nicanor. "When you reach Ptolemais, Galerius Senna—the 12th Legion's current senior military tribune—will join your staff. Please accept what help and insight he can provide you."

"Please give the emperor my thanks, Lord Tigellinus,"— Vespasian bowed, though he remained seated. Once the Prefect's footsteps receded, echoing down the corridor on its Carrara—pure white, *Statuario*—marble floor, he raised it, and with an arched eyebrow caught Nicanor's eye. He then studied the map for a moment before asking again: "So, are there any questions?"

Nicanor knew the questions would come from the general regarding about that last-minute addition to the staff. The uncertainty that Nicanor had dismissed with his decision to join Vespasian now crept back in. *What do I tell the general? Or should I just stay quiet but watch and question anything from Senna?* He would not let what happened to Cestius Gallus repeat itself. Something Yosef had mentioned to him once stirred more doubts in his mind—maybe he had said it at that last meeting in Jerusalem that had turned out so badly. Yosef had said how saddened he was that his own countrymen posed more of a risk to peace than did those they called enemies.

XLVII

LAODICEA AD MARE, SYRIA

"Have you ever seen the port this busy?" Sayid asked the man helping him lift another heavy bale to add to the handcart. Two more to go for a full load, and then they would trundle it down the broad pier, past ships large and small tied up on both sides, to the dock-front street lined with warehouses. There they would empty the cart, where the merchants designated, then come back and do it all again. Sayid and his work crew had three vessels to unload, and they had just started on the first. It had not taken long for the chill of an early spring morning to pass and the day to turn warm. Sayid used the tail of the cloth around his neck to wipe the sweat pouring from his brow.

"Not since about nine years ago," the older man replied, and Sayid knew he'd begin rehearsing his extensive knowledge of the Roman movements in this port. "That was when Gnaeus Domitius Corbulo led the 3rd Legion Gallica, 6th Ferrata—they shipped down from Germania—and the 10th Fretensis after Tridates the King of Armenia. War's good business for some, a backbreaker for others." The man stretched and massaged the small of his back.

Settling the bale evenly in the cart, Sayid squinted up at him and blinked the stinging sweat from his eyes. This work—cargo handling—had helped him earn the money he needed for his mother, but he did not want to reach this man's age and still work like this. *Mother is doing better... maybe I can soon get back to...*

"War, that's a thing you can plan business on," the man said with a laugh. "There's always one on, it seems. I'd hate to be a soldier, though... that's a poor choice. Taking orders... maybe get killed following them. That's not for me." The man grinned down at Sayid, showing his missing teeth. "How about you, Sayid?"

Being a Roman soldier is what I've always wanted, Sayid thought, neglecting to answer aloud. *But here I am. Not a soldier, but a human donkey only good for carrying, lifting, and shifting,* he wiped his eyes again and shook his head. *This work is only for right now. It is not who or what I'll always be.*

The man had barely paused—"I heard the master—or maybe the owner of these three ships we're working—say that at Ostia he had never seen so many ships loading supplies and equipment. All heading to only two destinations."

"Where to?" Sayid asked.

185

The man bent to grab another bale. "Ptolemais," he grunted as he lifted, got the load up past his waist, and tipped it into the cart. "And another bunch are loading for Gaza. That captain—he's a retired *navarch*—what they call a navy squadron commander, so he should know—he said the loads would support at least four legions... fighting for a year or more. They'll spend a year tearing up those Judean rebels. There might not be any Judea left after that," the man said with a chuckle. "Then, the ships will be busy carrying back to Rome all the treasure they take from there."

"Did he say anything about when they would sail?"

"He thought soon... that they could likely be at sea by the time he unloaded here and got loaded back for Puteoli."

"How many days does it take at sea... to get here from Ostia?"

The man shrugged. "Don't know, but this time of year... usually takes about 16- or 17-days' sailing."

They will be in Ptolemais by month's end, or first of Maius, Sayid thought. He did not have much time left.

* * *

The longest day he had worked at the port ended at last when it became too dark to work safely, even with the massive bronze bowls along the dock filled with wood and set afire to cast light upon the pier and waterfront. Sayid entered his home feeling as achingly old as the man he had worked with through the morning. Thankfully, by afternoon he had been replaced by a younger man who talked less and worked harder. That change, for a moment, had lightened the day.

Aunt Yara came from his mother's sleeping room. "How is she today?" he asked and set down the now-empty bag he carried water and food in.

"No fever today... so none since last night, and it is getting longer between her weak spells. She ate dinner—I have some for you, too"— she gestured at the table set with two cloth-covered bowls. "Tahir's been sleeping since she ate"—Yara gripped her nephew's shoulder and smiled—"Your mother is much better... stronger."

"Thank you, Aunt Yara... for all you've done to help us."

She patted his cheek. "Without the money for medicine... and the extra care you've given, she might not be recovering. So Tahir and I have you to thank for that... you're a good son."

* * *

186

The lamp sputtered and went out, but Sayid was too tired to move to refill and then re-light it. It was a clear night, and moonbeams spilled through the open shutter. His eyes adjusted, and he could see well enough from beside her that his mother's breathing remained deep and even. It was a relief after the shallow gasping that had scared him, so while she was racked with fever.

He checked her brow. Dry and cool. He leaned back in the chair and closed his eyes, but that did not stop the swirl of thoughts about what he had heard at the port. During a break that afternoon, he had talked with a man from one of the coastal ships who told him a story was being spread that a unit of the 12th Legion had wiped out a rebel force near Ptolemais. Two thousand rebels were killed, including a top Galilean military leader.

Sayid believed the rebellion was wrong... and Rome was right to not tolerate it. But he worried about his friend Yosef. The man also confirmed that a massive Roman army was forming and would be led by a real general, too. Vespasian, the man said, would soon arrive. "He is known as the Mule Driver... unlike Cestius Gallus," the man had scoffed. Vespasian was a real soldier who had no doubts and was relentless. If the Judeans were not already afraid, they would be soon.

Sayid listened to the man as he had all the port talk about the war against the Judeans. The men who talked loudest about what was coming had the bravery of spectators. Sayid, though he badly wanted to rejoin the 12th Legion, was afraid of what was to come. And Lady Octavia had been scared. If what she implied in her mention of Lady Cleo was real, then his friend Cleo was in danger too. Lord Gallus had not seemed frightened when he had talked to him but seemed resigned to his fate. Sayid knew what befell Roman military leaders who failed, especially as the 12th Legion had so miserably failed under Lord Gallus.

He shifted in the chair and wondered if he should wait to join the forces that would come south from Antioch, or leave as soon as possible—to reach Lord Gallus in Ptolemais before he was relieved of command. As he drifted, half-asleep, he was thankful Nicanor was in Rome and would be until he retired, and he remembered how sweet Lady Cleo had been to him. He prayed she was safe and well.

* * *

Sayid felt a hand stroke his head, opened his eyes, and sat straighter in the chair. The dim light— he thought from the moon at first but then realized was the rising dawn—showed his mother sitting up in bed and leaning toward him. She brushed back a tight-tangled curl that hung over one of his eyes. "I had forgotten how much you look like Marcus when you sleep."

He wondered again that she said his father's name with such affection, as she always sounded whenever she spoke of him. Marcus Sabinus was of African heritage, and Sayid had been teased mercilessly as a boy because of his mixed race. The insults and the stones thrown at him he could take. What had hurt most were the whisperings and snider remarks against his mother. They shouted and taunted, mocking her name—Tahir meant pure and chaste—saying that she had lost her honor by being with him. Sayid had been very young—not over four or five—when his father left them, and he barely remembered him other than how large a man he was and how strong he seemed.

Sayid still felt that old pit of anger burning in his stomach at his father for abandoning them. And then came the ache of needing to one day find him. He would prove he had become a strong man and a Roman soldier, just like his father.

* * *

Tahir sat on the back porch in the morning sunlight, robe pulled tightly around her, and studied her son. "Sayid, I understand what duty means... and love, too. Your father left us because of how strongly he felt about his duty as a Roman soldier—a legionary first, he said of himself. He thought he would lose what made him a man if they discovered he was married. The army was that important to him. And, despite what others thought, I married Marcus because I loved him. I still do. I know that that has always made it hard for you... even now. But I'm better, and I see you are restless... just as I saw in your father."

"I don't want to leave you..."

"If I were still sick, I know you'd never think of doing it. But I'm better—I can work soon. Yara is here to help me. You told me about your friend Lady Cleo you're concerned about. I've heard of what is happening... the legions that are coming, and the war. You must go now before it becomes even more dangerous for you to travel alone"— she took his hand and squeezed—"See to your friend, make sure she's safe, and then return to your duty."

XLVIII

Nicanor walked south across the Aventine Hill to the via Ostiensis and then followed the street as it bent southwesterly toward the *porta trigemina* that opened into the busy road to Ostia Antica, Rome's primary seaport and naval base. General Vespasian had arranged for him to pick up his mount at a stable just outside that gate. His pace was steady, and his leg ached less than it had even a month before. The extensive walking since arriving in Rome had strengthened it, and this would be his last long walk for nearly three weeks, given the gods granting good sailing weather and no delays. Once onboard the ship and headed to Antioch, he would have limited space to move about.

The rising sun cast long across the road, and right outside the gateway were a building and a large corralled field with a dozen grazing animals. He entered the stable, and one handler, seemingly the manager—a gray-haired, white-bearded man—greeted him.

"General Vespasian instructed us to expect you, centurion," the gray-haired, white-bearded man explained, "and I've got a good horse for you." The man's smile was missing a few teeth. "I served the general in Britannia."

"Just a steady one to get me to Ostia," Nicanor replied. He had not ridden in some time, not since Beth Horon. This horse would be just a horse, not Abigieus, who had died getting the wounded Syrian auxiliary Sayid to safety. *Now, that was a horse*, the best he ever had, and a four-legged legionary. Nicanor shook away the memories of the boy and the proud horse he had grown so unexpectedly fond of. "Just a steady one will do."

The roan the man brought out was as big as Abigieus, but when Nicanor looked closer, he could not find any fire in its eyes... no flaring of nostrils nor blowing of lips at his approach to mount. He swung up, almost expecting the horse to give that impatient half-side-step Abigieus always had. But this horse was stolid as he settled into the saddle with a twinge from his bad leg. He carried only his weapons and a large cured goatskin bladder of water, which he hung around one pommel of the saddle. His other belongings and equipment were traveling in a cart with Vespasian's carriage leaving later that morning.

* * *

OSTIA

Six and a half hours later, Nicanor turned the nameless horse into the port's stable and asked, "Where is the *Minervus* tied up?"

The man took the horse's reins and looped them around a fence rail, then walked to a table along an inside wall near the entrance to pick up a rolled sheet of parchment. His finger followed the lines to halfway down and then pointed over Nicanor's shoulder—"That way... down that street, straight to the marina gate. At the waterfront, take the left boardwalk past five ships. The *Minervus* should be the sixth one, the quinquereme on the left."

* * *

AT SEA, TO ANTIOCH

Three days at sea was enough for routine to set in, and Nicanor had spent it considering what he must tell General Vespasian. He approached the stout solitary figure and again appreciated the general's sensibility. Vespasian wore a military tunic like his own and stood at the midship rail. His feet were shod in hobnailed *caliga* and planted shoulder-width apart, and he moved easily with the pitch and roll of the ship. Nicanor had learned the general preferred to stand at that spot amidships—not in the bow, looking ahead, nor at the stern, studying the ship's wake trailing and fading into the distance behind them. Vespasian was squarely in the present, and at midship was where the pitch and roll were less severe. Over the past three years, Nicanor had seen more sea than in his first 17 years of service and still did not care for it. Choosing that spot on a ship's deck made good sense to him.

"Centurion"—Vespasian turned from the rail, his hearing sharp enough to hear the hobnails of Nicanor's own boots scraping on the deck close behind him—"is it better to talk out here than in Rome?"

Nicanor thought the general might have perceived him as too cautious, but he expected Vespasian understood why and did not consider him disrespectful in his reluctance to speak. With all the final preparations and the surrounding scurry in Rome, there were always too many people around for him to speak freely. "A sea wind— beneath billowing sails and on an open deck—takes away my concern, general." Nicanor stopped next to him.

"Tell me what you know of this Galerius Senna, whom Lord Tigellinus has given me," Vespasian said.

"Before that staff meeting"—Nicanor needed to explain before answering him—"Lord Tigellinus met me near the Arx Capitolina, and he took me over to the Tarpeian Rock. You know of it, sir?" Vespasian nodded, and he continued: "He used that moment to emphasize the importance of loyalty. Mine."

"To Rome?" Vespasian asked.

"Yes... but indirectly, well, maybe not so indirectly... he was pretty blunt about meaning allegiance to him, general. He had previously mentioned the many others who have pledged to him as the Praetorian Prefect."

"Is Galerius Senna one of them... someone who really works for Tigellinus?"

"I'm not sure, general, but Tribune Senna—and I have only my opinion to offer you—did not serve Lord Gallus well. The tribune's loyalty was not to the legion, to my mind. He and the Camp-Prefect, Tyrannius Priseus, gave Lord Gallus bad advice at critical points."

"Perhaps they're just fools... and did not know better..." Vespasian paused, seeing Nicanor's vehement shake of the head. "Do you think that's what led to Lord Gallus pulling back from Jerusalem and then to the defeat at Beth Horon?"

Nicanor knew the letters Sayid had delivered contained something that had made Cestius Gallus re-think the attack on Jerusalem. And he still was not sure that the contents of the messages should be mentioned to Vespasian by anyone other than Lord Gallus. "Their advice or decisions that Lord Gallus did not question led to the loss of men, supplies and equipment, general. I'm sure that when you meet with Lord Gallus, he'll discuss with you his decisions and what he based them on."

"So, Lord Tigellinus—or the emperor through him—expects Galerius Senna to sway or persuade me in some way?"

"I think he'll try, general... and Lord Tigellinus also expects me to report directly—secretly— to him."

"About what... and to what purpose?"

"About you, general... what you're doing, what you're thinking, and what's taking place."

"Did Lord Tigellinus say or order that exactly... and does he think your purpose is also to influence me?"

Nicanor shook his head. "My impression, general, is that you may listen to your staff... but you'll make your own decisions." He studied the general as Vespasian's eyes narrowed; the lines of his face became drawn deep on either side of his nose—the mere expression confirmed his perception.

"Report honestly to Lord Tigellinus then, centurion... as may Galerius Senna... if that's his purpose. Nothing I do or decide will be done is to be hidden"—Vespasian's features hardened—"but any that test me will learn I'm not someone to toy with." He moved from the rail toward the cabin he had secured as a working office. "Come with me—I want to go over the maps you worked on with Sylvanus Mela. Just before leaving, I received word from Titus. He is in Alexandria and sent me his order of battle and planned disposition as he moves into southern Judea. I want to get your thoughts on the terrain they will cross and then add that to our maps with your notes."

XLIX

AT SEA, THE MINERVUS

One of the bad things about being at sea for so many days, Nicanor thought, was the time he had to spend thinking. He met with Vespasian for any specific tasks he could work on aboard the *Minervus* and had annotated the campaign plan maps to show Titus's plan for marching into southern Judea. But most of his work on the maps had been in the sessions with Sylvanus Mela at the Regia in Rome. Those mornings with the mapmaker bent over the charts—the bald crown of his head beading with sweat—Nicanor could not help but give an occasional glance to the lances mounted on the wall. They never quivered even a bit, yet something told him a change was coming. It was not the clear visions or vivid dreams his friend Yosef experienced; his foreboding was just a vague sense that things he merely suspected were growing to become events that would affect countless lives, including his own.

Perhaps the feeling came from going back to what had made him such a good soldier. His instincts and awareness had kept him alive when others died. In battle, he recognized without consciously focusing on it how best to use the terrain and how to move troops to take the best advantage. He knew which of his men he could count on and which would break and fail him. He felt again the unconscious impulses he wielded during the dance of combat—the swing and thrust of a sword... the punch and slam of shield. He willed his arms, no matter how tired, to hold his weapons high, and to wield them as his opponent's arms weakened, and he dropped his guard. Then in the blink of an eye, he would strike or counter-strike.

Since Beth Horon, Nicanor had increasingly ignored those instincts. As a glorified messenger for Cestius Gallus, a prison watch-captain, he had the goal of enduring the days of guard duty until he reached retirement. Vespasian and Tigellinus had shaken him from that complacency, and—good or bad—that would lead to an outcome he could not foresee but was compelled to see through. What was happening in Rome—with those who should lead the empire—was on a different battlefield, but a potentially deadly one just the same.

His conversations with Paul the Christian had sparked him into new ideas, an unexpected self-review, and he had heard the muttering of unrest in Rome grow almost daily. But the muttering was not just among civilians and citizens, who always had issues to complain about, no matter whether they lived at the heart of the empire or in the most remote province. More dangerously, a growing undercurrent of resentment and dissatisfaction was reaching a level of open dissension among the Praetorian Guard units around and quartered outside the city. In a taberna near the Circus Maximus, he had come upon two officers he recognized, and he overheard them speak the name Gaius Piso, after their mention of Marcus Otho. Were it not for their including Otho, he would not have paid any attention, nor recognized them as officers dressed in civilian tunics.

At the Regia the next morning, he had mentioned Gaius Piso to the mapmaker. Sylvanus had commented that his father had known some of the men who had been executed with Piso as traitors to the empire and emperor, while others were never caught and punished. *Is Otho one of the uncaught conspirators?*

So Nicanor's decision to trust Gaius with delivering the Cestius Gallus letters and original report to Otho in Lusitania was a combat instinct. He now had a weapon ready to strike back with or at least to use as retribution if something happened. Gallus was doomed—as was he if he ran afoul of Tigellinus—but Gallus would have his say with Vespasian and give an honest accounting of what had happened in Judea. What Nicanor had sent to Otho might save Cestius Gallus, should he come before the emperor or the Senate. Or at least the record might set right the wrong opinion of the man that might harden into permanence after his death, should that be his punishment. Nicanor getting those documents to Otho, could employ a counter-strike on behalf of his former commander.

He turned his face up toward the sky. Yet another day was dawning, and shafts of sunlight cutting through the low clouds colored the sea in a wash of orange-yellow that turned into sea green with deeper swaths of ocean blue. Still more days ahead was Antioch... a place he had thought he would never see again. And from there, he would march into a land that had bloodied and crippled him. When he had left Judea for the second time, he had put behind him fighting Rome's enemies and regretted that his unexpected new friends there would be surrounded by it. But he had resolved that regret by rationalizing they were a part of his past life, and he would never see them again. That rationalization still bothered him.

The present moment became still, the wind-distended sails frozen, no longer billowing and breathing above him. The wind no longer feathered the water, but the waves seemed carved of stone and posed no danger because the *Minervus* no longer moved. Nicanor stood rooted in that moment as what was ahead—everything unknown—rushed toward him.

Cleo, he was sure to see again. Honor bound—not just by Graius's request—he would check on her and see she was safe, and if she was not, he would get her to safety. There was a chance he could find Sayid, and if he did, he would ask Vespasian to let him bring his young friend on as an orderly. And Yosef was surely safe behind Jerusalem's massive walls. For now. He hoped the Judeans would surrender before he had to persuade his friend to convince his people to surrender unconditionally. That was his task from Vespasian—to deliver the message that if they held, the Judeans would not be punished but destroyed. That was the final resolution to their rebellion if they chose not to bow to the Romans.

He blinked, and his world moved again. For a handful of heartbeats, the crests of the waves the *Minervus's* bow sliced through were tinted a froth of red until the sun climbed, the light shifted, and the sky brightened and blued to cerulean.

L

PTOLEMAIS

Word had spread that Titus Flavius Vespasianus was the new commander of the campaign to crush the Judean rebellion, and he would soon arrive in Antioch. Vespasian's reputation preceded him, and as Cestius Gallus walked through the encampment in the evenings, he came upon clusters of legionaries telling stories of the general. The news had lifted their spirits, and much of their conversation was of redeeming the legion's honor. At first, they had hushed at the outgoing commander's approach, but this past evening the men had kept talking, noticeably ignoring him. Before Jerusalem and Beth Horon, they had greeted or acknowledged Cestius Gallus, but not now. They all knew that a fast, oar-driven coastal galley had arrived late that afternoon from Alexandria. It was rumored to have brought orders relieving him of the legion's command now, not waiting for Vespasian's arrival.

The rumors were partially right. Orders had come in—his night had been sleepless, even more than usual, pondering them—and at daybreak, he had sent for Galerius Senna. He awaited his arrival to act upon those orders.

The clerk, who had learned it was best to not displease even a disgraced commander, contritely announced the legion's senior military tribune.

Galerius Senna entered wearing a full-dress uniform. His burnished chest plate glinted in the lamps that were still needed to light the command tent at that early hour. A pristine robe glowed dark crimson in the flickering light, and he held his gleaming helmet under one arm. That was not what was usually worn in camp, Gallus observed—so Senna already knew what orders were in the scroll of parchment, its imperial seal just broken.

"I've received orders—three—from Emperor Nero," Gallus said. "The first to be executed by my order as commander of the 12th Legion is to send one cohort to secure the town and port of Joppa and to increase patrols of the coast from Caesarea to Sidon." The order made no sense to him—it had puzzled him through the night. The coast and that city were already relatively secure. He knew of no threat, nor had he received any reports of one brewing.

"The second—also by my command—is for the legion to begin a series of raids to burn all the villages and settlements near

196

Ptolemais." This made sense. Vespasian would likely continue to use Ptolemais as his command headquarters and wanted to establish a firm hold of the surrounding area and not have to fight his way into it. "We—the units assigned this objective—will reach as far out as possible to clear and secure the area. But we are to leave any significant rebel positions as they are—to be dealt with by the forces under the new regional and campaign commander."

Gallus lifted his eyes from the parchment and caught the expression of expectation on the tribune's face before the man blinked it away. "Third—and last—the emperor orders that senior military tribune Galerius Senna is to take immediate command of the 12th Legion." He rolled the parchment and set it aside. "I am to go to Antioch and await Lord Vespasian's arrival." He knew not to expect any question or concern about what would happen to him after that meeting. Senna did not care. "Summon the Camp-Prefect and First Centurion so I can inform them... and they can tell their men."

"Will you leave for Antioch immediately?" Senna finally spoke.

"No, but very soon, tribune... First, execute my final orders, and once I see they are being followed... the legion is yours."

Senna left, and Cestius Gallus stored the emperor's orders and his own signed commands for the legion to obey them. His desk was clear—a rare thing—and he sat and continued the thoughts that had kept him awake through the night. Why had the orders from the emperor made such a point that the first two orders must come from him before he was relieved? Why not appoint Senna the new commander and have him comply with the emperor's orders and issue the commands for the legion? He took a rolled map from the table behind his desk and flattened it. And why was Joppa important?

LI

"Will Nathan do as you ask?" Levi asked Yosef as they rode into the gate into Yotapta. "And will his brothers and Imma's?"

"He told me they would... They are all well-respected around Tarichaea. They have earned the esteem with good character and hard work. None of them is wealthy if counted by coin... but they are rich in honesty. That can draw others to them, and they will need more men. Agrippa has increased his forces in Neronius and Scythopolis—easy striking distance against all the Galilean towns and villages surrounding the sea."

"Your reputation has drawn men to you here"—Levi gestured at the throng of people and the bustle of Yotapta preparing for the Romans—"They see how you treat people, and they know your decisions—which will affect them—are based on deliberation and not on blind whim or self-interest."

Yosef shrugged. "There are many good people in Galilee who recognize truthfulness... Nathan can help find more of them from around Tarichaea to give us more men near Tiberias, should that town remain a problem. I'm trying to do the right things for all in Galilee, not just for my people in Jerusalem. Galilee and Jerusalem must become one to face the Romans." He looked around, then, puzzled, leaned forward to grab Levi's arm before he dismounted. "Wait—there is something wrong here!"

Levi straightened, remained astride the horse, and scanned the broad courtyard just inside the gate. "What... I don't see—"

"—That's it"—Yosef cut him off—"I see no beautiful young lady hurrying to greet you!" Yosef smiled. "Where is Ariella?"

Levi's brown face reddened, then his grin matched Yosef's, and he laughed. "She planned to visit her father and uncle in Sogane and must still be there." His smile dimmed, and he shook his head. "Am I that obvious?"

Down from his mount, Yosef stretched, hands pressing the small of his back. "Obvious that you are in love... and that she loves you in return? Yes, and you, my friend, deserve such a blessing." Yosef tugged at the cord around his neck from which dangled the *kinyan* given him by Leah years ago, and that always hung on his chest, near his heart. He tried not to think of love he had lost: Leah to another man. Ruth, his wife, who had died. And—Cleo suddenly appeared in his mind, and he shook his head to clear it. There had been something between them too dangerous to allow to bloom. Both Leah and Cleo were now wed to men who did not deserve nor appreciate them. But though he was still alone himself, Yosef was pleased with his lieutenant's happiness and love for Ariella.

"What's that?" he asked, realizing only with the echo of the words that Levi had asked something.

"Are you well, Yosef?" Levi's eyes were on his friend's chest.

Yosef glanced down and released the fist that had gripped Leah's gift beneath the fabric of his tunic. "Yes... I'm fine, Levi. Please see to the men. I'm going to meet with Yohanan ben Zaccai. I'll see you in the morning, and we'll plan how to deal with Yohanan of Gischala and the dissent he continues to sow."

* * *

"I saw Yohanan ben Zaccai as he was leaving," Levi said as he entered Yosef's room. "He rides early—and you look as if you did not sleep."

"He and I talked until late"—Yosef covered a yawn with the back of his left hand—"He had much to share... and say."

"How is your father?" Levi asked.

"He's very ill, Yohanan says. But he hopes that if Father just rests... he might recover." Yosef sat at the table and poured water from a clay pitcher into a cup. "My mother and Matthew are trying to get him to remain in bed. The only one who has some success doing that, Mother tells me in her letter, is Miriam—when she sits with him."

The expression of concern on Levi's face turned into distaste. "And what of the Sanhedrin's demand you step down as commander of Galilee?"

"I'm tired of the posturing and positioning of men like Shimon ben Gamliel—he has shown he epitomizes what Galileans despise— and Yohanan of Gischala, who is just as bad for Galilee. I want to go home and see my father and mother... They grow old, and I was away from them for years. I want to see my brother and sister, for I worry about them, too." Yosef sighed and straightened his shoulders. "I think I must soon go ho—"

A knock at the room doorway made Yosef shift in his seat. "Yes?"

"There's a man at the gate to see you," said a young woman he recognized as one of Ariella's friends who helped tend to a herd of goats penned just outside the city walls. He must remember to ask

Levi to find room to bring them within the walls as soon as he could arrange a place.

"What does he want, Dalit?"

"He came upon me as I spread morning fodder for my goats—he says he delivers a message to you from a deputation of envoys from Jerusalem. I brought him to the gate and left him to wait there."

Dalit's Galilean dislike of strangers from Jerusalem—though Yosef had been able to overcome it somewhat—made him smile before it faded with concern about what message the man carried.

Yosef stood and turned to Levi. "Bring him here, and let's see what he has."

The girl turned to go with Levi, and Yosef heard her whisper: "Ariella will return by noon. She missed you and was worried."

* * *

"So, they—the so-called leaders in Jerusalem—did not wait to hear from you." Levi snorted with disgust. "Do they listen to anyone... or decide everything without knowing anything?"

"No, they didn't wait, but ben Zaccai will do as I asked him...he will look into what's making Gamliel demand I return to Jerusalem. I feel I must return, regardless of his or anyone else's reason to have me removed."

"What did the message say—from these envoys?" Levi spat the word with contempt.

Yosef unfolded it again and reported, "They 'request' I come to Gabara alone to meet with them."

"Meet... about what?" Levi questioned, "and why alone?"

"I assume about me turning command over to one of them. Or to all. One thing I've learned... sometimes the foolish find refuge in numbers. That way, no one person shoulders blame. And if there is a success... whether, from ambition or manipulation, they will separately claim they were responsible for it."

"Why send a message to meet in Gabara—why not just show up here?"

Levi's confusion matched Yosef's puzzlement. "It makes no sense."

"I know why!"

Both Yosef and Levi turned toward the voice at the doorway.

"In Sogane, I saw my cousin—she lives nearby, in Gabara. She works at the inn there, and men from Jerusalem—thirty of them—have filled it. She told me of one who drunkenly boasted they will 'take care' of Yosef ben Mathias." Ariella came farther in and took Levi's hand but spoke to Yosef.

"Take care of me?" Yosef shook his head. "What does that mean?"

"They are angry"—Ariella's face grew tight with her own anger—"They made several stops along the way to incite people against you. Apparently, they were ignored and asked to leave Sepphoris... And in Japha and Asochis, they were denounced. Some in those towns wanted to beat them for claims they made against you, Yosef. The drunken man called you an upstart that needed to be reined in. I think they plan to kill you... that's why they want you to come alone."

"Are you sure they're not Gischalan?" Yosef looked from Ariella to Levi.

"I'll go get the man they sent here and demand he answers us—he told me as he told you, the envoys are from Jerusalem." Ariella nodded, confirming the information. "He delivers their message."

Levi hesitated. "Would... could... a Sanhedrin president really be part of a plan to kill you, Yosef?"

"I pray not.... but"—Yosef rubbed his face—"I feel I must go... not to them in Gabara, but to Jerusalem, to face Shimon ben Gamliel. The Sanhedrin will either support me and formally confront Yohanan of Gischala, or I cannot command here. It can no longer be between him and me. It must be one or the other."

Levi's shoulders slumped, and Ariella gripped his hand and gave it an encouraging shake. "When will you go?"

"Bring the envoy's messenger to me, and I'll give him an answer to take to them in Gabara."

Levi nodded and left, hand-in-hand with Ariella. He was back soon with the envoy's messenger—the surly expression still on his face—and a sweat-drenched man Yosef recognized as the leader of one of the three-man scout units assigned to patrol the area around Yotapta. The man had ridden hard in the heat of a warm spring day and reeked of a lathered horse. Levi prodded the scout captain—"Give your report."

"Two cohorts of Roman heavy infantry, Yosef, and one of cavalry—12th Legion units—have plundered and destroyed three towns west of Yotapta—"

"—I need your answer now, Yosef," the envoy's messenger curtly interrupted. "I wish to leave before nightfall. Will you come with me to Gabara as requested?"

"Be quiet"—Yosef pointed at the messenger and beckoned the scout captain to follow him—"Levi, get our chart...." Yosef walked to the large campaign table as Levi unrolled the map to lay it flat. "What is the next town in their path?" Yosef asked.

The scout's finger traced a line from Ptolemais to each of the towns already raided and destroyed. "The next of any size is Chabolo in the foothills... so it is likely they'll strike there."

"We have how many men nearby, Levi?"

"Almost 5,000 camped around Yotapta. If we act now, we can mobilize them—get them formed up in two or three hours and move out before sundown. These men know the terrain—they've maneuvered through these hills and walked the land all their lives. So if we carry only weapons and water, we can reach Chabolo in three hours, maybe four at most, from when we start."

"Tell your envoys they can meet me in Chabolo tomorrow... if they wish to," said Yosef to the messenger. "That is the only way they get to see me with whatever demand they have or to deliver any message from Jerusalem they carry."

LII

Ptolemais (Port)

Gessius Florus had for some time suspected Cleo was hiding something from him, but his temper-fueled confrontations had done nothing but show him her fear was beginning to peak. But now her dread was not as great as her disgust for him. He could—and would—change that.

There were many ways to inflict punishment... ways that she did not know he was capable of, and soon he would give his perverse inclinations free rein. The letters between Octavia and Cleo through a means beyond his control had gone from bothersome to a nagging worry that he must put an end to. But Glaucio had found nothing incriminating.

And Cleo had let him read letters that showed she had no claims against him—he was doing nothing beyond acting as the emperor's tax collector. Glaucio reported she had taken to long walks daily down the strand of beach and among the dunes, and Florus had told him to let her wander. There was nowhere for her to go—no refuge in this remote stretch of the coast outside Ptolemais. That was one reason he had chosen this residence and its location.

The town and port were watched by a dozen men under Capito's direction; should she show up there, he would quickly know. A women's petulant gossiping with a friend against her husband was an easy matter to deal with, and when the time was right, he would teach Cleo how to behave. *No,* he thought, *right now, I will not get anything out of her, not without damaging her to a point where some might question it.* But with Vespasian soon to arrive, he planned to meet the general in Antioch the minute he set foot on land—and that meant he had an opportunity to talk to her correspondent, Octavia.

That woman had much to worry about, and her husband's precarious situation could make her vulnerable and willing to disclose anything he should be concerned about. That was the case, especially if he lied to her with a promise to intercede with the emperor on Cestius Gallus's behalf.

He lifted his goblet and drained it. The wine's bitterness brought a grimace to his face, but it was the best this shabby dockside taberna offered. "Capito, where is your galley captain?"

"I see Quintus now, Lord Florus."

A tall Alexandrian wearing a *sagulum*, a short cloak that reached only to his hips, strode inside, spotted Capito, and in four steps was standing before Gessius Florus. The man waited a fraction of a second for an invitation, then sat with his back to the entrance. His face was mostly in the shadow cast by the sunlight streaming through the door, but when he half-turned to glance over his shoulder—something that proved habitual—he displayed the long scar that bisected his right eye, a wound that left the orb a milky-white. According to Capito that had shortened the man's career as an imperial navy trierarch, and added to his avarice to make money as a civilian ship's captain.

"I know the orders you carried from Alexandria have been delivered to the 12th Legion," Florus said. "I require a fast galley to get me to Antioch. Since you are still here, I will pay extra for speed and wish to leave tonight if your ship is ready."

"I always keep my ship ready, lord," the captain replied. "I've been paid to transport the legion's former commander, Cestius Gallus, to Antioch. You could travel with him... only, as I understand it, he will remain here a few more days."

Florus shook his head as much at the thought of traveling with Gallus as at the delay, which was unacceptable. "I must leave sooner than that... do you know of another ship?"

"A trireme is just now sailing for Antioch, casting off as I walked to meet you. I thought it would be here longer, but its captain made his turn quicker. I guess he wanted to catch these steady winds we've been fortunate with." The galley captain scratched the scar where it left a hairless rift in his eyebrow, "I know of one other vessel that is replacing a mainmast and could sail in the next day or two. But if you want speed, you'd have to pay him to sail empty to Antioch or wait for him to load a paying cargo."

Florus had to get to Antioch ahead of Cestius Gallus. "Arrange that one then"—he stood to leave, and the two men followed him out. The waterfront entry of the taberna had a broad flange of decking that projected over the lip of the pier and created more room for those passing along the quay to step around the people entering and leaving. Florus waved Capito and the captain from the entry and onto the decking and took a purse of coins from his belt to pass to Capito. "Go with him and make sure the ship captain understands the commitment to haste." Florus did not miss the scarred captain's gauging inspection of the bag's weight.

* * *

Further down the wharf, a man wearing a gray hooded cloak approached the three men. The man slowed, head bowed but eyes up beneath the hood to study them in the bright sun, and then he moved quickly past. Minutes later, the cowl still pulled over his head, though now he was in the shadows of a series of market stall awnings, Cestius Gallus stopped to think. He had—with some relief—just seen his trireme captain friend, one of the few who had not abandoned him, do a final favor by leaving port early to get his urgent message to Octavia. The man would then carry her onto Puteoli, where she could reach her family home in Rome. Now he wondered what business Gessius Florus had at the port—he was not a man to be seen in the working-class areas. But it did not matter. Once he had given his messenger to Octavia enough of a lead, he would sail to face a more challenging—probably fatal—question from the man replacing him.

LIII

JERUSALEM

"Yosef is fine, Rebecca," said Yohanan ben Zaccai as he patted her arm where she sat at Mathias's bedside. *How to comfort her but fortify her, too, for what is needed?* "He carries a lot of responsibility but has borne it well... but many of the people he is trying to help have proven difficult."

"Yohanan"—she pressed the old priest with an intense gaze—"I know you do as Yossi asks you. I know you do not tell us all that has happened since he went to Galilee, but we have heard stories." Rebecca's tone had sharpened and grown louder, then she glanced at Mathias, whose eyes were closed, and lowered her voice to a whisper, but still with an edge. "The Galileans have tried to kill him... many times!"

She leaned forward to adjust the damp cloth on Mathias's forehead. His breathing remained raspy, and he wheezed as he fitfully slept. Straightening, she beckoned ben Zaccai to follow her. In the family room, still close enough to hear Mathias if he should need her, Rebecca stopped and faced ben Zaccai. "Yohanan, you must convince Yossi to come home to Jerusalem... he cannot trust those people."

"I'm a Galilean, too, Rebecca, and I've known Mathias since before you and he married. He would not want his son to abandon his duty to our people." Yohanan hoped to make her see the circumstances—and some of those in Galilee—differently.

"Mathias does not want his son to die! Not by the hand of those he is trying to help. Not for those who don't care that he does is necessary to stand against the Romans. He risks his life for their good!"

"Rebecca," Yohanan replied, "the only chance we have against Rome is to come together for the good of all. Young men like your son are the only ones who have a hope to make it happen. The Galileans do not have any confidence in Jerusalemites, especially those who have been in leadership for a long time. But some—many—trust Yosef because he has shown he is trying to do the right thing.

"You know he still believes rebelling against Rome was a foolish and probably fatal mistake for all in Judea and Galilee. But Yosef is taking the next step to salvage the situation." Yohanan glanced back at the room where his friend of 40 years lay gasping. "Mathias would want you to release your son to be a man and, despite the consequences, make his own decisions, Rebecca—without your censure or undue fretting.

"Yosef has done well, Rebecca," he said with the tone of an old friend. "He has not done it all perfectly, but he has brought unity to much of Galilee. Many have faith in him and will continue thus if some here refrain from undermining Yosef and ruining that trust."

"What do you mean?" Rebecca asked alarmed. "Who here means him harm?"

Oh, Mathias, he thought as he shook his head sadly, could you not have at least said something to her about Shimon ben Gamliel's order that Yosef be removed? But she might have supported that decision any way she could—even against Mathias's will—just to bring Yosef home. Mathias had probably considered that and kept it quiet.

"I don't know that any here mean to actually harm Yosef," he reassured her, "but we must find out why there is increasing opposition to Yosef as commander in Galilee. Do you know where Matthew is today? With Mathias so ill, I must speak with him about it all."

"He is with Eleasar ben Ananias... at Antonia Fortress or along the northern walls with the work crews. They are delivering new stone today, for strengthening the walls, and a new gate."

* * *

At Yohanan's shout of his name, Matthew looked down from the platform that allowed him to see the work underway along the wall. Two hundred men with mules and hoists sweated the blocks and slabs of stone into place for the stoneworkers and masons to anchor in place.

"Matthew, I must speak with you," Yohanan said once he had his attention, "but I'd rather not climb up." He was comfortable walking all the many miles and up and down the hills between Jerusalem and Galilee but did not like the risk of taking his old bones up and down the latticework of scaffolding the younger men climbed with ease.

"I'll be back shortly"—Matthew addressed the brawny man next to him—"Esau... you've done well. The materials are getting to the workmen just as they need them... and we have no more delays from the quarries." He nodded to Eleasar ben Ananias—"I must see what ben Zaccai wants."

* * *

The two men watched as Matthew clambered down from the platform. "Who is that?" Esau ben Beor asked the Temple Guard captain.

"Yohanan ben Zaccai," replied Eleasar, "a teacher and priest from Galilee. He is an old friend of Matthew's family. He probably has letters from Matthew's brother, Yosef, who commands in Galilee."

"Yohanan travels back and forth often?" Esau kept his tone casual.

"Fairly regularly, though Matthew has mentioned that from here he goes next to Qumran."

"Why, Qumran?" asked Esau.

"Yosef knows the Essenes well and has friends there. Yohanan likely has a message for them."

So much to be rooted out—but patiently, Esau reminded himself.

"Eleasar!" In a lull between cursing men and braying animals, they heard the shout and looked down to see Matthew, hands cupped around his mouth, standing next to the old priest. "I must go with ben Zaccai."

"Is it your father?" called Eleasar.

Matthew hesitated a half-second—"Yes... but I will find you later."

* * *

"Is that Miriam?" Yohanan ben Zaccai asked as they entered and heard a voice.

Matthew nodded. "When Mother must go out, Miriam reads to him."

"Do you think your father is strong enough to talk with us?" the priest asked. "It would be best if he could. There are things I must ask and that he must hear."

Mathias, haggard and pale, wrapped in a blanket, reclined on a low couch near the entrance to the inner courtyard. A warm breeze swirled in, bringing the scent of fruit trees and tugged at the fringe of Miriam's long tunic as she stood when they came in.

"Yohanan, how is Yossi?" she asked.

"He is well, and I have letters from him for you all... I left yours with your mother earlier."

"I have it to read later—and I will write a reply for you to take when you return to him."

Yohanan nodded to her and then studied his friend, hating to tire him when he was so weak, but it was a necessity. "Mathias, do you mind if we sit with you and talk?" He smiled at his old friend, who nodded.

"If you are staying here, I will go out for a while, but will return in an hour or two... no more." Miriam spoke to Matthew, who shot a look at his father and hesitated.

"I'm better, Matthew," Mathias wheezed. "She can go."

Miriam flashed a concerned look at her father. "Father, maybe I should stay with you, too."

"You've grown into a young woman who cares little for staying home," Mathias replied. "Your walks have strengthened you. But lately, you spend so much time with me, I know you want to go out again. So, go. Matthew and Yohanan will be here with me until you return, or your mother does."

Miriam swiftly left the room, and Yohanan wondered if he would see her again soon—she was so often out.

"Mathias," Yohanan began right away, "why would Shimon ben Gamliel demand Yosef's removal from command of Galilee? It has gone beyond his initial misgivings at the Sanhedrin vote—I know then he pointed Yosef lacked experience for such responsibility. But your son has done a good job even with the difficulties he has faced. And no one here in Jerusalem still rationally argues against him."

"Shimon and others in the Sanhedrin are almost as scared of change, Yohanan," replied Mathias, "of new thinking... as they are of the Romans." Mathias held up a hand, coughed, then covered his mouth with the cloth he held. "When I'm better, I will confront him and the Sanhedrin and get it resolved."

"Should I do that... before Yosef acts on his own?"

"You know there are many in the Sanhedrin who will not listen to you, Yohanan. They see you as Galilean... different from those of us here in Jerusalem. They are the ones who stir trouble for Yosef. You cannot change them." Mathias coughed again and pressed one hand against his chest as if that would stop the rattling.

"What does Yosef want to do?" Matthew asked.

"He's tired," Yohanan replied, "and he is torn between doing what he was assigned and ordered to do... and wanting to let someone else deal with it. If that is Yohanan of Gischala instead of him, then so be it. And he's worried about you, Mathias." Yohanan touched the arm of Mathias's chair. "It would be easy for him to choose to come home."

"The easy or selfish decisions have led us to what we face now," Mathias said with determination. "Different factions want what they want—at the expense of others." Mathias coughed again, a wracking shudder that bent him over.

"Father, let me help you back to bed." Matthew took his arm and helped him stand, taking most of his weight.

"Yohanan"—Mathias gasped—"tell Yosef—help him—to find the strength to do the right thing... not the convenient. Tell him if he does that for me... I have the will to be here to see him again when his duty is done. I will not die before."

Yohanan mulled these things while father and son crossed to Mathias's bedroom. Matthew returned minutes later to speak to the priest: "I must stay with him, but you should go. From here, do you plan to go to Qumran, as Yosef mentioned in his last letter? To see about... the treasure?"

"Yes, I'll be quick about it. Then I will go to Yosef in Yotapta, and as your father asked, I will help him make the right decision." Yohanan shook his head—"I fear it will be a hard one for your brother—that decision."

LIV

PTOLEMAIS

"Are you leaving?" Cleo stood in the doorway to her husband's private office, thankful Glaucio had not intercepted and steered her away; otherwise, she might not have realized Gessius Florus's plan. Her husband seemed to enjoy how his presence unsettled her, how life was uncomfortable for her when she was uncertain when he would appear to scrutinize and query her. His parting was a relief.

"Did Glaucio not find and tell you?" Florus bent over his desk, darted a quick look up at her, then went back to the sheaves of parchment he was putting into his large leather loculus. He would not chance leaving behind any traces of the spider's web he had woven to trap the Jews and secure their treasure. "He was to tell you I was leaving and would be gone for a while."

"I have not seen him"—Cleo gave him a lie for a lie. She had caught Glaucio not long ago coming from her bedchamber. His excuse had been that he had heard Cicero squawking and wanted to make sure her pet was well. She knew better—Glaucio despised the parrot. It upset Cicero that the man had entered her private quarters, and the bird had let him—and the household—know. Cicero's squawks had brought her from the atrium as she had been about to go outside. She knew immediately it was the major domus snooping—it had happened before.

"My lady"—and it was always a sneer from him—"I thought you were on one of your walks."

"I was leaving when I heard Cicero... and came back," she had told him. Cicero shook his wings and ruffled his neck feathers, then, seeing Cleo, with a bob of his head, settled onto his perch to stare at Glaucio, who scowled back at the parrot. "I'll take him with me"—she had walked to Cicero, expecting the major domus to leave the room. But Glaucio had seemed ready to say something else. His elbow, so close, was a temptation Cicero could not resist. The bird slowly leaned, stretched, and got his beak just inches away. But Cicero snapped air as Glaucio, realizing the bird's plan, yanked his arm out of reach with a murderous glower at the parrot as he stomped out.

"Cicero," she had warned the parrot as she gave him a reward of bits of dried barley bread from a small pouch in her robe, "you must behave." The bird looked up at her, head canted slightly—he

211

preferred the hard nuts he loved to crack so loudly—then accepted his treat.

Several minutes later, his cage in one hand and making sure Glaucio saw her leave, she went down to the shore. Hidden by a dense cluster of thick-stalked sea oats, she had peered over a dune to see Glaucio, and one of the kitchen girls walk to an outside storage room just off the kitchen portico. This happened almost every day, she knew he would dally there with the girl for some time. After a moment, Cleo stole back into the residence, returned Cicero to her room, and went to check Gessius Florus's office—and that's where she had unexpectedly found him packing.

"Lord Florus"—a gruff voice called behind Cleo.

She did not need to turn to see who spoke—Capito's heavy tread accompanied the voice, and the resulting clatter confirmed it was her husband's military aide. This time he brought not just noise but also a pungent reek of exertion as he brushed past her when she did not move from the doorway. Cleo saw runnels of sweat from under his helmet had left trails in the dust and dirt that caked his tired face.

"Capito"—Florus waved him in as Cleo moved back to let him pass.

Florus stepped to the doorway and addressed her: "I will speak with you later," he said as he shut the door between them.

* * *

"I'm glad I caught you before you left," said Capito, between heavy breaths. "There are messages from the Idumean and from Hananiah." He took from his shoulder bag two flat packets wrapped in soft hide and sealed along their edges in wax, handing them to Gessius Florus.

"So, anything from Meshulam's son Ehud? He should be in Jerusalem by now."

"Yes. Hananiah reports the sand trader's son has arrived in the city and has begun setting up a small glasswork."

"While I'm gone," instructed Florus, "if you do not hear from Ehud, send a message to him—and his father in Alexandria—that he is being watched. He must reinsert himself in Jerusalem's upper-class. His family was once close to some of the prominent families, and I must know any plans regarding the Jews' treasure. Between him and the Idumean, they should be able to learn what I need to know."

"But we cannot reach it—the treasure—lord. And the Jews have no reason to move it."

"They will soon, I suspect, and they will attempt to do so. Lord Vespasian is coming to crush these rebels and teach them and others a lesson about how foolish it is to rise against Rome. Though these Jews are foolish... many are not stupid. They realize—as do I—that Vespasian will make a priority of his attack on Jerusalem. The rest of the region does not matter. When Jerusalem falls, so does the rebellion. Those who know this will—no, I'm sure they *must*—make plans to protect their treasure. They have hinted as much before.

"They hoard the treasure for their god... and will not risk its loss. They know, too, that their city cannot survive a siege... not one of the scale and severity our army will inflict. Their walls will protect them for a time, but eventually, their city will fall. So, they must plan to save the treasure elsewhere, likely. I must know their plans for that, so in the chaos of what's coming, we can capture it." Gessius Florus slid the packets from the Idumean and his killer in Jerusalem into his own bag, hoisted it over his shoulder, and draped a light cloak over his arm. "Come with me to the port, but return here after my ship sails. And you must check with Glaucio each evening and each morning."

"Do you expect a problem with Lady Cleo?"

"No. She lacks the spirit to create real trouble. But mischief and aggravation? Yes, she provides those. So keep a close watch, and if anything happens, keep her here... Keep her unharmed, but let no one see her."

* * *

Cleo heard them depart, and she knew her husband would not take leave of her. Nor would Gessius Florus tell her where he went or for how long. Not that it mattered—his absence was her reprieve, though she would still be under Glaucio's scrutiny.

"My lady..." The boy was still timid, though he had shown signs of becoming more relaxed within the residence... as he was when outside with her and away from Glaucio and her husband, who both scared him.

"Yes, Elian?"

"May we go for a walk? I can carry Cicero!" He ran to the pedestal, and the parrot bounced its head, cocked it to one side, and watched the boy, eyes shifting to Elian's hands to see if he held anything to eat.

Elian was her one bright spot—with Cicero. "We can," she said with a smile. "Let's go now."

Twenty minutes later, they passed through the break in the series of high dunes formed partially by two half-buried columns, and they entered the mostly buried, abandoned building Elian had found. Cleo had no idea how long it had been there, but the sea was taking it year by year, bit by bit. The surf lapped against the seaward wall of the remnants of the structure, and at the next high tide, in a couple of hours, it would wash around and through its cracks to fill the lower level. The inches-deep sand that coated the stone floor beneath was still damp from the morning's tide, and dregs of seaweed littered the room and had collected in its corners.

Cleo followed Elian up a set of stone steps to the second level. The dunes—over decades of wind and water—had surrounded the building and piled high enough to reach that height. But a handful of windows facing the sea aligned with the creases of the dunes and let in sufficient afternoon sunlight that they could see without lighting the lantern she had stored there on a previous visit. A spill of sand from the largest opening formed a flat area between two low benches. Elian set Cicero's cage on a nearby broken column—one that had snapped off cleanly where the stone segments joined—about waist-high on Cleo. Elian sat on the bench, and from beside it, he drew the long slender rod of wood he kept for drawing lines and shapes in the sand.

Cleo unslung the goatskin of water and set it next to her on the bench. For several minutes she watched the clouds through an opening that was growing more extensive each year as the wall fractured, the fissure spreading with the settling and shifting of the sand beneath and around the building. A warm breeze laden with the tang of salt feathered her hair, and cooled her brow.

Elian had smoothed the sand twice to begin new assortments of drawings and looked up at her. "Will you show me how to draw a map? Last time you promised...."

"I can, Elian. But a map of what? Here, where we are now? Or bigger—this country... or the empire?"

"Where is Antioch?"

"Why do you ask that?" asked Cleo.

"Just before I came to see you when the smelly man and Lord Florus... I hid nearby. I don't think they like me, lady... not like you do. I heard Lord Florus say something about spying on some woman in Antioch. He sounded mean like when he shouts, but not as loud." Elian shrugged. "Anyway, where is Antioch... is it a town close to us?"

Distracted with thoughts of Octavia and the danger they were both in, Cleo did not hear Elian ask the second time.

LV

Jerusalem

Miriam had returned home after about two hours, judging by the late-afternoon sun, to find her mother preparing for the evening meal. "How is Father?" she asked.

"He's resting. I bought hyssop and brewed tea for him... and made a paste with it to coat his chest. It seems to help his breathing. The frankincense and myrrh help him, too... especially with the fever."

Miriam nodded and turned to go upstairs.

"Miriam, wait...."

"What is it, Mother?"

"Matthew asked me to ask you when you got home—to meet him in the agora."

"Why?"

"He didn't say." Rebecca would not ask more, and Miriam was both relieved and pained at that. Ever since she had broken off her betrothal to Yakov, her mother had not understood, and Miriam had never told her mother the reason, and even the brothers she was so close to did not fully understand her pain.

Miriam felt very alone but would not reach out to her mother, who surely needed no further worries and would not begin to understand her daughter's. Miriam and her brothers were adults now and needed to work out their own problems and their relationships with one another. That was how Miriam hoped her mother was thinking of it all.

"I sent him to Nachum's to pick up some fabric," Rebecca said. "I'm making a new robe for you"—she reached a hand out to touch Miriam's sleeve. "I hope you like it... and will stop wearing clothing like this"—she tugged at the rough cloth.

Miriam knew a look must have flashed and settled in her expression, and her mother released her sleeve and said, "I know—you feel more comfortable wearing this in the Lower City." Miriam did not respond to the unasked question.

Miriam had not expressed curiosity in the social and civic activities Rebecca had attempted to interest her in, that would provide her a means to be out more and engaged socially—in proper ways. Miriam had not even been willing to try—*Why, when it matters so little with all that our people face?*

After a too-long moment of mother and daughter staring at each other, Miriam turned toward the front entrance. "I'll meet with Matthew"—she began to walk away.

"Wait!"

"What, Mother?" Miriam knew her countenance could not be pleasing.

"Will-will you please change into something nicer?" Rebecca asked, salvaging some shred of motherly authority. "You are not in the Lower City now."

* * *

Miriam did not realize until she was nearly at Nachum's shop that it was the same one King Agrippa had visited before fleeing Jerusalem. If she had not killed the Roman mercenary sent to assassinate him, he would have died... right here. She paused outside the shop and stared at the alley just off the entrance—empty now, in the later afternoon. There, in its shadows, she had killed the man.

"Miriam." Matthew was standing beside her.

She blinked, worried that he was able to get so close without her hearing. *I must keep my wits about me, always.*

"What are you looking at? Is there something wrong?"

"Nothing"—Miriam shook her head—"nothing. Why did you need me to meet you here?"

Matthew tucked the bundle of cloth under his arm. "Let's sit over here"—he walked to a canopied area on the opposite side of the street, with a food and drink stall and several tables.

Miriam followed him to a table within sight of that alley. A heavy-set man greeted them as he filled with oil the several hanging lanterns beneath the canopy—twilight would come soon. She tried to ignore the alley and pushed the memory of the Roman mercenary from her mind to focus on her brother.

"What do you want, Matthew?"

"You know what I want to know... And don't tell me nothing is wrong—I'm not stupid."

"I never said you were."

Matthew leaned toward her. "But you act like you believe I am stupid... and that mother is, too."

Miriam crossed her arms and sat silently, meeting his gaze until he broke eye contact.

"Going to the Lower City so often and spending so much time there. Why? It's not about getting knives sharpened—that story works only once. What is it, Miriam?"

She had to give him something that would—hopefully—satisfy him and their mother. Miriam drew in a deep breath.

"Hananiah—that's the name of the knife-sharpener—is a metalsmith and armorer too. I have watched you and Yosef spar with weapons... and seen for myself what it means and feels like to use a blade to defend yourself. I will never forget the Roman soldiers slaughtering our people after Passover, here in this market"—she swung her head around, up and down the street—"The blood everywhere... right here... and they came into our homes to rape, rob, and kill. That we could be attacked in our own home, Matthew..." Her voice trailed off, then picked up, weakly: "Such power to kill a man to... to stop him... from...."

She released the held breath with a shudder that shook her. "I see the blades Hananiah makes and think of how safe I felt holding one... the knife that saved me. Hananiah—who is shy, but passionate about his work—is showing me how to make knives. It helps take my mind off the worry about what is to come with the Romans. I worry for Yossi, for Father. There is no harm in watching and learning from Hananiah if it helps ease my mind. And I need something that gives that solace to me."

"I didn't know you still dealt with that, Miriam... You have never talked of it, and I did not understand." Matthew gripped her hand.

Miriam's eyes moved—something pulled them—from Matthew to across the street. With the day turning into night, the dusk was deepening and growing the pool of shadow along the fabric shop's wall along a good length of the alley. As the shadows thickened and lengthened, the body of the man she had knifed to death took shape within them. She could sense his outline and knew the dead man's eyes were open and staring at her even now.

Jerking her gaze from the alley, from the vision, she faced Matthew. "Tell Mother she need not worry about me... tell Yosef too. I have asked him that in my letters, but he will believe me if it comes from you. He has enough—"

She stopped talking as the stall owner lighted the lantern above them; it had grown dark on the street too. The light above them now brightened the table and the area along the front edge of the canopy. A dim shape on the street was coming closer to them and shot a glance at the alley —as if to see if the dead man's body was still there.

"Matthew... Matthew ben Mathias?" A deep voice came from the gloom.

Miriam and Matthew both looked up at a tall man standing at the edge of the lantern's glow. Miriam knew immediately who it was, her memory casting back years—a lifetime. She froze, stunned.

"Yes," Matthew stood and took a step toward him and stopped. "Ehud?"

Ehud came farther into the light and nodded. "It's been a long time," he said.

"You moved to Alexandria... what are you doing here?" Matthew asked.

Ehud lowered his head and shifted his weight from one foot to the other as if he wanted to turn away from them. Then he spoke all in a rush: "Alexandria is not as good for Jews now. Recently there was a massacre... and now, with what is going on here, even more Roman soldiers are there, and something worse looms over us. My father worries we will be targeted. Many are jealous of his fortune, and they wish to take it from him." Ehud lifted his head, but he did not yet recognize her. "My family is in danger, and my father sent me here to begin a return to our birthplace."

"But why come here?" Matthew asked. "Soon, we'll have the might of the Roman army outside our walls. Surely your father realizes that no one in Judea—much less in Jerusalem—is safe."

"Yes, but here all—or almost all—are Jews. Father wants to bring our family home to be among more of our own faith, to return our family to its center." Ehud's eyes skittered from Matthew to Miriam for the first time, and then he recognized her. "Miriam... is that you?"

When she met Yakov and was betrothed to him, Miriam had pushed Ehud from her mind. He had never regarded her as anything but Matthew and Yosef's little sister who tagged along as they explored Jerusalem and played with wild abandon up and down its streets. But she had seen Ehud even then with the budding interest of a child entering her teens, and then through the eyes of a blossoming young woman. He had been her first love. She sat up straight and met his look. "Yes, Ehud."

"You've grown into a beautiful woman!" His tone was a confirmation rather than a surprise.

So did he see me then, too? Miriam felt the blush warm her face; few had told her that she was beautiful. Then she cooled. Zechariah had taught her to listen with more than her ears to the words people spoke. He had stressed that she must use her sight to complement her sense of hearing.

As the words left Ehud's lips, his shoulders dropped, and he swayed with weariness. He had pronounced her beautiful, yet he had no hope for what such a revelation might bring. He seemed exhausted and worn down.

His family must be in real danger, she thought.

LVI

Jerusalem

Just past dawn, the Temple attendants had already appeared in the courtyard. The square, 200 feet on a side, was as close as Israelite women could get to the Temple, and within it stood four massive lampstands almost ninety feet tall. A team of four attendants carried ladders to each and extinguished the lamps as the sun rose over the Mount of Olives.

Rebecca turned to her daughter as they witnessed the ritual. "Matthew told me last night that Ehud approached you both. What has it been... seven or eight years since he moved to Alexandria, and you saw him last?"

Miriam remained silent. Mother was working toward asking how she felt about seeing him again. More than once, she'd cried on her mother's shoulder that Ehud would never see her as she wanted to be seen. It was a weakness she did not care to remember.

"Your father and I knew his parents well," Rebecca continued, "until Meshulam was compelled to move the family to Alexandria—there his business was assured. He was very ambitious, but I know Aster, his wife, did not wish to leave." Rebecca paused as the orange-yellow ruddiness of sunrise climbed over the Mount of Olives, the moment's beauty bathing her face in the glow they witnessed, but Miriam turned from it.

"Was it that you still loved Ehud that made you hesitate with Yakov? Did he sense you and Ehud... had feelings? Yakov told us only that it must be done."

Miriam started walking, and Rebecca hurried to catch up. "Matthew also told us what you said.... about why you go to the Lower City so often. But... I think you've found someone to teach you"—she hesitated, and Miriam held her breath—"how to defend yourself."

Miriam froze but for darting a glance at her mother—*What does she know?!*

As mothers do, Rebecca continued in a rush, as if it must all come out while she had an opportunity—"I was there when it happened—the Roman attacking you in our home—where you should be safe. I understand how you must feel. Your father and I will support anything that makes you feel better.... being able to strike back. But how well do you know this man, this Hananiah... a workman? Is it safe for you to be at his shop alone?"

Oh, Mother, if only it were so slight a thing. "He's a quiet, harmless man, Mother... I don't think he would or could harm me, or anyone."

"But he makes weapons—"

"—And kitchen knives. Making weapons doesn't mean he can use them—he's just a craftsman."

They had crossed the outer court and neared the southwest corner of the Temple enclosure. Miriam was wearing the plain clothing with a simple over-robe she wore when she went into the Lower City, and both women understood she would be taking leave of her mother here.

"Mother, I can take care of myself. Don't worry."

Miriam felt her mother's eyes on her as she walked away, but Matthew was sitting with their father, and Rebecca must relieve him so he could report to the Temple. Miriam raised her hood as she stepped onto the platform and began to descend the steps.

* * *

Miriam was near Hananiah's shop when she spotted Ehud walking with a short, soft man, she recognized as Bartholomew, one of the largest property owners in Jerusalem. Her father and the Sanhedrin had dealings with him, for he owned many buildings in both the Upper and Lower City. Zechariah had mentioned to her once how the man squeezed anyone late on rent and did not hesitate to have his hired men put them on the street, keeping all their belongings to go toward payment. She was glad Elazar ben Yair had kept Zechariah's shop in his own name, so he could deal with the owner while she enjoyed the refuge for her training. No doubt the landlord treated the Sicarii leader with respect—*That is wise, to say the least*, she thought with a chuckle.

But she came to herself and looked around her quickly—she had no wish to see Ehud or be seen by him. She turned down an alley and went quite a way to reach the cross street that ran behind Hananiah's. If she continued a bit farther, she would come to the back of Zechariah's place, too—or Elazar's, as it was now.

Zechariah had taught her to keep an account of what she passed between specific points. He stressed the importance of always knowing where she was—a skill that could be developed even if one could not see. In an unfamiliar place, in the dark of a tunnel or a street at night, that sense of location relative to where she had been and where she was going was vital. There were five more storefronts or buildings before she got to Hananiah's, and she counted them once she was on the cross street. At what should be Hananiah's, wooden crates were stacked along the wall on either side of the back door. She paused to touch one with a loose top.

The scraping of the door alerted her, and she barely made it to the corner to get out of sight. She did not care to explain why she was there and not on the main street.

Carefully she leaned to peek an eye around the corner. It was Hananiah, who carried a small pry bar and opened a crate. Setting the bar on the ground, he lifted out thick, flat strips of metal. His short-sleeved tunic revealed lean arms with corded muscle as he turned to take the stack of metal inside his shop.

She gave him time to finish and decided that instead, she would go to Zechariah's first to check for any messages from Elazar. The Sicarii leader had mentioned he had targets for her coming up, and a tingle of expectation coursed through her. Romans or collaborators, it did not matter. Both remained hidden in the city, and if the Sicarii had ferreted them out, then she would strike and remove the threat to her people.

* * *

A message had been waiting for her in the hidden compartment in the floor of Zechariah's room. "I will be at HT every morning for five days after this date." She knew the location in Hezekiah's tunnel and had met there before—with Menahem ben Judah, Elazar's former superior in the Sicarii. The message had been left the evening before, but she could let it wait—she must go to Hananiah's next. Matthew might not have believed her and might check her story with Hananiah. She would speak with the craftsman as she had told Matthew she would, and she prayed that afterward if her brother checked, he would not ask how long Miriam had been coming to meet with Hananiah. The truth would ruin her story, and she could never explain it to her family.

She opened Hananiah's shop door and stepped inside. It was as dark as it had been on her last visit, and she had no desire to interrupt him as she had done then.

"Hello!" she called loudly, waited a few moments, and called again: "Hananiah... It's Miriam... if you remember me."

"I do"—the voice came out of the darkness before Hananiah did, a thin cloak now covering his work tunic—"But I was about to leave." He stepped closer to stand in the light from the still-open door. "I

wondered when you would return. Let me get your knives for you."
He turned and went to his work table and, despite the dim light,
found the one bundle among several others and returned and handed
it to her.

Miriam took a small silver coin from her purse and handed it to
him. "You didn't tell me the cost, but is this enough?"

Hananiah nodded and put it in a pouch at his waist. "I have to go
now"—he held a hand out and motioned toward the door.

Miriam did not move. "I saw how you worked with the metal," she
said, "and I know you might think me odd, but... I enjoy the feel of
metal. I like its weight, the texture, and the smoothness when it's
been worked. Someone with skill can bring out a fine edge...
transforming it. Someone I knew once told me a dull blade is as
useless as a dull person"—she cut off abruptly, realizing she was
talking too much.

Hananiah came even closer, his eyes losing their squint so that
she could see how large and clear and dark they were. He did not
blink. "Feeling that way is not strange at all." His tone—for the first
time—held some emotion. "But to hear it from a—"

"—A girl? I know,"—Miriam shook her head. She still felt the sting
of being less than whole, of being less than a man. Zechariah had
worked to purge her of that thinking, and she no longer felt that way
most of the time. Then it would creep over her, and the darkness
would return.

"I was going to say from another in general," Hananiah replied
softly, "especially a woman." He moved a lamp nearer and struck
stone and metal to spark its wick alight.

"Would you teach me more about working with metal... and how
to turn it into a knife? I can pay you."

"Yes"—Hananiah nodded slowly—"but it must be only when I
say... and only in the mornings. Later in the day and evening... I have
other things to do."

"May I come by the day after tomorrow, in the morning?"

"Yes." Some of the squint and the flatness of voice had returned.
"Your brother is an officer in the Temple Guard?"

"You heard us the other day?"

Hananiah nodded.

"He's the second in command," Miriam said, then hesitated. "If
he should come to see you... it's okay to tell him you're teaching me.
He knows."

"I don't care to talk much to people."

She hoped he would not. "I'll see you in the morning, day after
tomorrow."

He nodded again, this time a goodbye, as he leaned over the counter and with thumb and forefinger snuffed out the burning wick.

Miriam stepped out into the daylight, her eyes adjusting to the brightness. She glanced back at him in the doorway, staring at her, and it occurred to her—*He never blinks.*

LVII

"Are you well, Yohanan?" Yosef asked the priest, who had arrived just before they secured the gates for the evening. "Please, sit and rest."

"Yes, I am well, but I covered many miles in only a few days." He sank into a chair beside Yosef's work table. "I thought it best to hurry."

"How is my father?"

"I spoke to him briefly. He is still weak but wants you to find the strength to 'do what is right and not what is easy,' he said. Do that for him, and he swears he will be there when your duty is done, and you return to your home and family. Those are nearly your father's words." The priest's smile came and went quickly in his exhaustion.

Yosef felt relief course through him. "So, then, he is stronger now."

"No, Yosef. He is still weak. But I think your sister is good for him; Miriam had him sitting up for a while until he tired from talking. I saw the belief and determination in his eyes when he told me to tell you he will not die. Afterward, once your mother was no longer angry at me for agitating Mathias, she said if the stubborn streak he's had all his life holds, he'll keep his vow."

"Did you speak with Shimon ben Gamliel and find out why he demands my return?"

"I first talked to Matthew.... and he and your father thought it would do no good for me to go to ben Gamliel or the Sanhedrin. It is because of my reluctance to be part of the priests' efforts in Jerusalem—instead, I chose long ago to serve and teach in Galilee." Yohanan paused to take another ragged breath. "Mathias said he would speak with ben Gamliel when he felt better and would resolve whatever issue he has with you."

Yosef caught the change in his expression that outweighed even the old priest's fatigue. "What is it, Yohanan?"

"As I neared Yotapta, I heard about the Jerusalem envoys at my hometown—Gabara—and the Roman attack on the three towns. They say that you led 5,000 men to protect Chabolo. What happened there? Why did you tell the envoys to meet you in Chabolo when you thought the Romans would attack it?"

Yosef recognized the priest's tone: Yohanan was worried he intended to forcibly deal with the envoys as with the Romans. "The envoys wanted me to meet them—alone in Gabara—and that seemed strange... and unwise for me. I chose not to. As for the Romans, nothing happened because they were not there. As we neared the town, the Roman commander, Placidus, pulled back toward Ptolemais. I don't understand why. Reports said he had as many men as we did, and they were much better equipped."

"That seems odd," Yohanan said, "to change from raiding those other towns and burning them to ashes... to become suddenly cautious and avoid battle."

"It makes no sense to me, either. But I left 2,000 men outside the town under Levi's command, in case the Romans return. He'll patrol the area and report any other Roman activity." Yosef bent over the map spread across the table, made a note on it, and straightened. "Were you able to go to Qumran, too?"

"Yes, long enough to meet with your friend Nahum—he confirmed his man from the Essene order there—the young engineer he told you about when you last visited. The man is ready to begin surveying and documenting the location of secure sites for the Temple treasure—as soon as the command is given."

"And we cannot give that without the Sanhedrin, which means Shimon ben Gamliel must agree to it. But if he has something against me, will he allow our plan? That must come to him. Matthew would take charge of implementing the plan in Jerusalem and coordinate with Nahum and the Essenes. I would not need to be involved directly." Yosef shook his head and scratched an eyebrow. "I just don't understand it, Yohanan. Why does ben Gamliel—or anyone—in Jerusalem have a problem with me or be upset at what I'm doing?"

"The Sanhedrin will recognize there is a real risk if the treasure remains in Jerusalem. Surely, they will see the wisdom in our plan, Yosef," Yohanan replied. "So, they should be willing to have someone from the Sanhedrin work with Matthew to execute it."

"Maybe, but who? The leaders we count on all seem to make decisions based on their own interest—whatever that might be—and not our people's. Regardless of who is in charge, Yohanan, it must be done."

"Excuse me, Yosef"—Ariella entered the room—"I have a message for you from Levi."

Yosef took the scroll of parchment from her, unrolled it, and held it under the lamp on his desk. He scowled. "Is the courier still here?"

"Yes—Dalit took him to the kitchen to give him dinner."

"Please bring him here now. I must have him return tonight with my reply to Levi."

"I'll be back shortly"—she turned and left.

Yohanan ben Zaccai rose from his chair, tugged his robe straight, and leaned closer. "What is it, Yosef?"

"One of Levi's outrider patrols intercepted a rider—a Gischalan one, Levi believes—who carried a message to Yohanan of Gischala." He handed the message to the priest. "The letter acknowledged—and seemed to approve—his plans to flood Galilee with letters. He wants to tell every town and village that I intend to turn Galilee into my own puppet province under the direction of Jerusalem. Yohanan of Gischala calls me a traitor to all Galileans and wants them to abandon me and refuse my call to stand against the Romans." Yosef took the message from Yohanan ben Zaccai and rattled the sheet of parchment in his hand. "Levi thinks the courier had come from Ptolemais or near there... and—"

"Here is Galon, Yosef"—Ariella led into the room a young man still chewing on the end crust of a fresh-baked loaf of barley bread.

Yosef took a scrap of vellum from his desk and quickly wrote on it, muttering, "I need you to get a fresh horse, leave now, and get this to Levi as fast as you can."

Still chewing, the man took the message from Yosef and tucked it inside his tunic. "I will, Yosef"—and he hurried from the room.

"What do you order Levi to do?" Yohanan asked.

"I want him to block the two roads in the hills—the roads coming from Gischala—and to hold anyone who carries these letters from Yohanan of Gischala. Levi will collect all the letters and bring them and the couriers to me." Yosef turned to Ariella and said, "The envoys from Jerusalem did not come to Chabolo to meet with me. Do you know if they are still in Gabara?"

"I believe so, Yosef. I can go now, see my cousin at the inn, find out, and be back by daybreak."

"Take someone with you, Ariella—at least one guard—and be careful. Levi would not forgive me if you were hurt."

"I'll be fine, Yosef." She flashed him a quick smile over her shoulder as she left—"Do not worry."

* * *

Next morning...

"They are still there, Yosef," Ariella said, looking far too fresh to have ridden to and from Gabara between sunset and the dawn, "and

226

Yohanan of Gischala has joined them and brought 3,000 men with him."

"What next, Yosef?" Yohanan ben Zaccai asked as he stepped into the room.

"I'm not surprised the Gischalan is with them," Yosef said. The sunrise poured through the window and across Yosef's back as he began the day's work. "I will gather the letters Levi's men take from the Gishcalans as proof of how he disrupts things and prevents me from doing what Jerusalem originally sent me here to do. It jeopardizes and weakens us, and I now mean to finish what I agreed to do. I will go to Gabara with the 3,000 men I returned with from Chabolo, and I will confront Yohanan of Gischala and the envoys."

Yosef said to the priest, "Spread the word for as many Galileans who are with me to join me in Gabara in two days." Then he took a note from the table and looked at the young woman. "Ariella, bring me a rider to carry this message to Levi. I want him to be in Gabara, too. I'll need him and his men."

LVIII

LAODICEA AD MARE, SYRIA

War is pretty profitable, it seems, Sayid thought as he wrestled with the iron-tight knots of the rope while the business of the port bustled around him. His boss, Palakh—who had the concession for all vessel loading and unloading—had come off the docks himself and believed in paying top wages to hard workers. He made sure Sayid and the others earned it, but with this one additional month of labor, he could leave his mother with ample savings to help her until she returned fully to her work.

He shifted around on his knees to tug harder, got the end finally free, and unknotted the line securing the broad and heavy net. The mesh was lashed over a dozen barrels, still slick with sea spray, that had been fastened onto the deck of the ship since its cargo hold was full.

"I'm glad to get those off my deck... but gladder still we travel fully loaded these days." The ship's captain knelt beside Sayid to check the deep gouges in the deck where bronze spikes had been driven to tie down the lines securing the barrels. "Now, I'll have to see the port master about a joiner to repair these deck planks."

"What's the latest news, Captain... of the Romans and the Judean rebels?" Sayid stood and stretched.

The captain rose with him, rubbing his knees. "Three legions from Alexandria are near Gaza and will soon be encamped in southern Judea near the border with Idumea. Lord Vespasian's son, Titus, is as much a driver as his father. And this morning, as we approached our turn to enter the port, a Roman galley, traveling fast, drew alongside. Before they passed us, they slowed so we could hail each other—as we should—and I logged them. The *Aegyptus* out of Ptolemais was headed to Antioch. I could see they were loaded with legionaries escorting a general."

The shipmaster shook his head. "I saw him next to the galley's captain and think it was Lord Cestius Gallus, the former governor and commander of the 12th Legion. I've seen him many times before in Antioch when I was delivering legion supplies and equipment. He will soon be there once again, probably by daybreak or early morning tomorrow. The new governor, Gaius Licinius Mucianus, and the military commander Lord Vespasian should arrive soon, too. Then that's it for Lord Gallus—he'll go back to Rome or be ordered to"—the

228

man did not elaborate—"Vespasian and his men will move south then. Titus will move his legions up, and then this war will really start."

As the captain walked away, Sayid wiped his brow with a forearm now more muscular from daily labor than when he had arrived in Laodicea. *It is getting late,* he thought, blinking at the bright sun now angled overhead in the mid-afternoon sky. But it was not just the day getting late. It was also late—and more important—to make his decision about what he must do.

More than once, Sayid had dreamed at night or mused during the day that remaining here in Laodicea would be easy. He could work on the docks and maybe one day take over for Palakh, who had no sons or daughters—the man had taken a liking to him. *There's plenty of opportunity for me here,* Sayid thought. And he could be with his mother and aunt, the only family he had.

But what of my duty... and my friends? He had a responsibility to the legion and to those people, and that meant he must go back to what he had left behind. Sayid wondered if he should go to Antioch and see Lord Gallus first. But just as the captain had suggested, Lord Gallus now faced his fate. If he showed up to see Gallus, there was no telling what could happen. He could be held, questioned, *and who knows what else?*

His mother and aunt knew the time was coming when he must leave, and understood, but still, it would be sad for them all. Who knew when he could return once he was an auxiliary with the legion again? Sayid gauged the sun above; at the day's end, he must tell Palakh he was leaving, and that, too, dismayed him.

* * *

The house was filled with the delightful aroma of his favorite foods, but Sayid could not enjoy them because what he had to tell his family churned his stomach.

"Your mother cooked it all, Sayid," Yara said with a smile and nod at the table full of dishes and bowls.

"Yara, you talk like it's the first meal I ever prepared"—Tahir fluttered a hand at her sister.

"The first you've done in a while, Tahir... and you did not have to stop and rest at all today."

"It's delicious, mother," Sayid said with a sigh as he wiped his lips with a cloth; it was time to tell her. "I heard today the legions from Alexandria are near southern Judea and that the new governor and the new military commander Lord Vespasian arrive there soon. So, it is likely the rebels will stay more in their cities and strongholds."

"And the roads south will be safer?" Sayid's mother asked, and some of the light in her eyes dimmed, and her smile faded. "So, it is time for you to return to duty."

"Yes, it should be safer to travel. I'm sorry, Mother... Aunt Yara... I want to stay with you, but I must go."

"When will you leave?"

Sayid sighed again—he wanted so badly to stay.... to tell her he had a few more days with them before he must leave. "Tomorrow. Palakh is friends with a shipowner who returns to Ptolemais, and he sails with the morning tide."

Tahir nodded. "You have a responsibility to meet and a commitment to keep. As your father did..." She pushed the bowl away, closed her eyes, and slumped. Yara touched her sister's shoulder, and Tahir straightened and studied her son. "I did not tell you," she said, "but a year ago, I received news about your father— Marcus Sabinus. They say he is well and now a senior centurion with the 10th Legion, which was in Alexandria. If he is still with that legion, it might be one that is soon to be in southern Judea."

With that statement, a resolve settled over Sayid that calmed his stomach. Along with seeing to the safety of Lady Cleo for Lady Octavia and returning to duty with the 12th Legion, somehow, someway, with the other legions converging on Judea, the chances of meeting his father were beginning to improve.

LIX

PTOLEMAIS

Sayid left the ship as soon as it docked, noting that the port of Ptolemais was as busy as Laodicea had become. He recognized the resignation of the men lined up along the wharf—all the work ahead under a blazing sun and under the sharp eye of the wharf master. Several of the dockworkers massaged their gnarled hands as they waited to unload the ship and then load it back for its return to Antioch. Sayid rubbed his own, feeling the ridges of callus that had built up over his many weeks of hard labor, and studied the new scars his hands had acquired. He patted the only weapon he had acquired in Laodicea, though it was not intended as one. The wooden spike tapered twelve inches, from a thick round head to a flattened point. Carried in a loop at the waist by sailors and many that worked the docks and used for winding rope work and knot tying when securing lines. He'd become as accustom to having it at his belt as the short sword he had carried as a Roman auxiliary. With his hair grown longer than the usual legion cut, and in his workmen's garb, he fit in.

He knew little of Ptolemais, but he went right to the best place for information in any port—the *tabernae*. Within steps of the office were two or three of the harbor's drinking and eating spots. He checked that the documents Cestius Gallus had issued him were tucked safely inside the lined pouch at his waist, safely under his tunic. He wondered, not for the first time, whether the documents were valid since Lord Gallus had been relieved of his position. He must remain careful and not draw any attention for now, and then when he reported back to the 12th Legion, he hoped they would accept the documents and not execute him as a deserter.

* * *

It had taken longer than Sayid had hoped to find someone who could give him directions to Lady Cleo's residence. Lord Florus was less known by the locals in Ptolemais, and in his new role as an imperial tax collector, he was far less visible than when he had been the Judean Procurator in Caesarea. But a grain supplier who had delivered to his residence recalled the lovely lady and commented: "She had the major domus bring my men and me a drink... even water for my mule. That was very kind of her." The man then gave him

231

directions, noting, "It's a good distance away from town. Lord Florus wanted privacy, I've heard, and spent a lot to make the place what he wanted."

The road to it had almost no traffic, so any walker was more visible to the legionaries patrolling the area, and no doubt Lord Florus's personal detail of men. To be safe, Sayid left the road and followed the rough coastline, where wind and sea had scalloped the land, cutting into banks of earth and laying down broad swaths of fine sand, creating seemingly endless dunes. The sand was hard to walk in, and the dunes—some low, rolling, and others piled high with tufts of plants on top—often blocked his line of sight. He tried climbing one to gain height to see what was ahead, but he floundered and slid so much that in frustration, he gave up at the highest point he could find stable footing. He scanned the area. The dunes made a series of wind-sculpted terraces and hillocks of stunted trees, ascending to the level ground where Cleo's house must be.

In the distance, it seemed a lady wearing a red cloak was trailed by a boy in a gray tunic who occasionally darted in front of her. It was hard to be sure, but it could well be Lady Cleo. The path the pair followed led toward a few high dunes where it disappeared from sight.

Sayid started to cup his hands to his mouth and call to the woman, but then he saw a man crest the earthen bank where it transitioned to sand then duck down, watching the woman and boy. His stealth bothered Sayid, who stooped as well, to stay out of sight but still watch. He darted a glance toward the woman and boy, but he got only a glimpse of fine scarlet fabric in the sun, and she was gone.

The man's head popped up, and he continued following to where the woman and boy had disappeared. Sayid could not directly reach that path without being seen, so he slid down the dune and circled around to where the man had first appeared, to get behind him, hopefully unnoticed. It was a hands-and-knees crawl to remain low, and thankfully a breeze had picked up. The sigh of the wind coming from seaward carried away any sounds he was making.

Sayid reached the spot where the bank of earth gave way to sand. A gravel path led up the embankment, and Sayid thought he saw the edges of a stone walkway that ran behind a high hedge and wall. *That must be their home.* He continued to follow

It was minutes later, and if the man had not muttered a curse as he slipped from his perch, Sayid would not have seen him until it was too late to hide. The man had climbed a dune with a buried column sticking up from it and now peered at something on its other side.

Carefully Sayid crawled near—keeping his distance and praying the wind covered his movements—and lay in a patch of scrub. The man was watching an opening in a section of the wall buried in the sand. Through the opening, walking within the building, Sayid could also see the woman. The scarlet cloak billowed and swirled as she turned and paced, and the same wind sprayed the man with a dusting of sand. He softly cursed again and wiped his eyes.

A boy's high-pitched voice came through the window: "Lady, why do you keep them here and not in your room?"

"They are safer here, Elian."

Though the woman spoke Greek, Sayid recognized the tones of the Roman noblewoman. He had traveled with her—been through so much with her—how could he not know her voice?

"Is it because Lord Florus is mean to you, lady? Because he hits you?"

Anger kindled in Sayid, growing hot in his chest. The man on the sand dune ahead of him shifted, and his head came up full into the sun. *Capito!* Gessius Florus's lieutenant and loyal dog. Whatever he was doing following and spying on Lady Cleo was not good for her. *The bastard*—Sayid gritted his teeth.

Capito was slipping quietly down the dune's slope to an uneven wall. The Roman followed it, creeping to where the wall had collapsed, and the sand flattened to become a beach frothed with waves. At the corner edge of rubble, Capito pulled his pugio from his belt. The dagger's blade flashed in the sun as he disappeared.

Not caring if he was heard now, Sayid lurched up from the sand and scrambled down after him. At ground level, he staggered along the ruined stone and mudbrick wall—as Capito had—to a low drift of sand before a wide opening into the shell of a buried two-story building. Inside, the ground floor was still awash in spots and held clear tracks, Capito's deep ones that were already filling with seawater. They led to a flight of stone steps to the second level, and Sayid ran up to a landing. There, before the window through which Sayid and Capito had spied them, were Lady Cleo and the boy.

"Elian, get behind me," she pleaded.

"I'll not let him hurt you, lady." The boy held a long rod—too thin to serve as a staff or weapon—cocked and angled at the Roman before them.

"Let me have what you hold"—Capito pointed at the small olive-wood chest Cleo clasped to her chest—"and I won't kill the boy."

"I won't,"—the boy's voice quavered—"let you hurt her."

"It's your throat I'm about to slit, boy." Capito twisted the dagger and waved it at the boy and took two steps step closer. The Roman snarled at Cleo: "Give me the box."

Sayid knew from her ashen face that dear Lady Cleo had known violence and expected more. *How much passes over her face!* he thought, noting, too, that she had already reconciled to surrendering the box.

"Let the boy go," she said with a glare at Capito, "and I'll give you the letters." She glanced at the boy— "I want you to run from here... as far and fast as you can."

"No, lady," he cried, tears running down his face.

"Do as I command—he will not harm me," Cleo spat, "his master enjoys that right."

Sayid gathered himself and rushed forward, crying, "No!" He struck Capito in the back of the head with the thick-knobbed end of the dock worker's wooden spike he had pulled from his belt. He knocked the Roman forward and nearly to his knees, blood flowing through Capito's greasy dark hair.

With a swinging slash that sliced the boy's arm, making him back away, Capito turned on Sayid and charged. Sayid backed away, sliding on a thin coating of sand over the stone tile, and fell. Capito dropped his dagger and pulled the short sword that swung in its sheath at his hip. He thrust with it as he landed atop Sayid, the gladius piercing the flesh of his shoulder and its tip striking stone beneath.

Sayid screamed and twisted, trying to buck the Roman off him. Capito grunted and shoved harder, forcing Sayid several inches across the floor, the blade tearing farther through his shoulder with searing pain. Capito—on his knees and astride him now—began to withdraw the blade, no doubt intending to thrust again, likely into Sayid's heart.

But Cleo was behind the centurion and stabbed his discarded dagger into the Roman's upper back.

Capito reared, his hand releasing the sword that impaled Sayid, his hands arching behind him to claw the blade free. His mouth filled with blood, and with a gurgled curse at Cleo, he choked and pitched forward, twitching... then he stilled.

With a groan, Sayid pushed the Roman soldier's dead weight from him and rolled the body to one side.

"Sayid!" Cleo knelt and began to pull at the sword.

"No," he gasped, "it is holding back the bleeding."

The boy stared wide-eyed at Sayid, his own wound a thin red line that dripped from his forearm. Sayid caught his eye and ordered, "Gather dry wood and start a fire."

"What are you doing here?" Cleo asked. She had removed her cloak, wadded it, and lifted his head to support it. Her white hand smoothed his brow; he recalled the smooth alabaster of it, the coolness of her touch.

"I came to make sure you were safe, my lady. Lord Gallus's wife, Lady Octavia, made me promise." His eyes shifted toward the body—"But I fear I might have made things worse."

The boy appeared with an armful of branches and chunks of driftwood from the beach. He had also found dried brush and grass for tinder.

"You saved Elian's life... and likely my own, for a time," Cleo said. She reached under a nearby stone bench to bring out a small leather pouch, opening it to shake out a set of striking stones. "You want the fire for us to seal the wound, right?"

Sayid nodded. "So, you remember Nicanor wishing for a fire when we were shipwrecked?

"Yes, you and Yosef both almost bled to death." She struck the stones over the pile of tinder and wood bits. "Elian, softly breathe into it when you see the fire has caught. Blow gently..."

In a few minutes, flames licked the Roman's dagger she held over the fire, and the blade was slow to take the heat. "Hold this," she told Elian, who gripped it for her and held it steady. Cleo tore Sayid's bloody tunic to better reveal the wound, apologizing as Sayid bit his lip with pain with each tug. Cleo went to the stone bench for a goatskin and opened it, and held it for him to drink. "I'm sorry it's only water."

"It should be hot enough now"—he nodded at the boy—"Lady, you must pull the sword from me quickly and straight out." Cleo carefully grasped its hilt. "Boy—Elian—when the lady pulls it free, you must press the blade firmly to the wound, first the front and then the back. We may have to heat it again and repeat."

"What will we do... after?" Cleo asked.

Sayid looked at Capito's body. "I'm afraid the plan I had coming here must now change, my lady."

LX

Antioch, Syria

Costas watched as the two finely garbed armed escorts parted the people milling about the wharf and stepped aside, making way for the Roman nobleman. The gangplank had barely dropped to the dock before the Roman trod upon it, cloak swirling, to leave the ship. No longer merely an olive-wood trader, Costas had not been in Antioch for a month, the last time only briefly. The local Roman army chief quartermaster for the area legions had met him with a plum opportunity to transport supplies and equipment for the legions' upcoming campaign. But it meant putting to sea again quickly.

He looked up at the just-docked ship. He called to the man at the rail who was likely the captain, who watched the line-handlers and the dock-men's preparations to unload his cargo. Costas called to him, "Are you the shipmaster?" At the man's nod, he continued: "What port are you from?"

"Ptolemais... and Tyre," the captain replied.

"Carrying passengers and cargo?"

"Just those three"—the captain thrust his head to indicate the Roman and two men clearing the crowd—"and a load of cedar from Tyre." The captain paused as his line-handlers boarded, leading the workers. "We're to unload quickly and then go back to Tyre for more"—the man clapped and rubbed his hands as he turned away.

Costas's idle curiosity vanished along with his intent to next call on Lady Octavia. His last visit had been so short he could not put Lady Cleo's message personally into Lady Octavia's hands. A sullen servant at the residence agreed to deliver the message to the lady, and, in his hurry, Costas did not ask if Lady Octavia had any letters in return for Lady Cleo. Now, since his next port was Ptolemais, he had thought to check with her again. Both ladies were generous with their coin. But his priority had just changed. He'd been promised the lucrative rights to carry cedar from Tyre, from what this ship's captain had just told him, those rights had been usurped. He must find out why and get them back.

* * *

Gessius Florus detested the crowds of commoners and the smell of every port. The sweat, soiled clothes, dead fish, and the seawater-soaked flotsam that collected around the pilings of docks and beneath the piers. That swill was an offensive, brackish stench he was glad to get away from. As soon as they'd left the ship, he'd turned to one of the men Capito had hired to accompany him and ordered them to find a carriage or cart right away.

The hot early summer sun beating down on him in the open cart had not helped his mood as they wound their way up the heights of Mount Casius. "You two stay here and hold the driver," Florus snapped at his escort when they stopped at Cestius Gallus and Lady Octavia's domus.

The men, having spent that last few days at sea with his charge, knew better than to ask questions. "Yes, Lord Florus," one said.

There were no attendants at the front entrance of the governor's residence, which puzzled Florus. Even with Cestius Gallus relieved of his position and in disgrace until a formal decree came from the emperor, the man and his wife would be accorded adequate staff and servants. Florus tried the door but found it locked. A broad path of stone squares ran along the front of the residence and around the building. He followed it to a walkway with steps up to a terrace at the rear of the house. The terrace had the shape of a ship's bow that looked out upon the city below.

A portico of a dozen columns formed a broad entry framed by large wooden shutters, now retracted and folded to the sides, that opened into what appeared to be the residence's atrium. Florus crossed the terrace to enter, and his steps echoed loudly on the stone tile. Beyond a central fountain were several rooms, likely the couple's private chambers. Off to the right was a wide frescoed hallway that must lead to the dining and entertainment area, and farther on, the kitchen and servants' quarters.

"Is anyone here?" he called out. A moment later, he heard shuffling steps, and a young female servant appeared, not surprised at finding someone there uninvited.

"Yes, my lord...." the woman answered.

"I'm here to see Lady Octavia."

"The lady is not here, lord."

"I must see her today." Florus walked farther into the atrium. "When will she return?"

The woman stepped to one side but kept her eyes on him. "Never, my lord."

Florus's eyes snapped to hers. "Don't be insolent... what do you mean?" Was this some lie, given at Octavia's instruction, to avoid having to face any Romans, after the news of her husband's dishonor?

"Pardon, my lord. I mean, she has left for Rome."

That puzzled Florus, which added to his brewing ill-temper. "When did they leave?"

"They, lord?"

"The lady and Lord Gallus."

"It was just the Lady Octavia... and a man—a ship's captain she went with, I think, lord."

"When?"

"Yesterday, lord. The man called on her in the morning, and she gathered some of the other servants, both free and owned. The man said they must hurry, so she packed some of her belongings quickly, and they all left." The woman's eyes glinted, and her face tightened with a scowl. "I heard them—the servants she took with her—chattering about seeing Rome."

"Why did you not go with them?" Florus did not care but hoped she could help him. He must get some confirmation of what Octavia and Cleo corresponded about that might involve him.

"The lady... recently... came to dislike me. She told me—I think my punishment is—to remain and await her husband's return and serve him. She said that Lord Gallus would reward me for my service."

"You say she took all of her personal items?"

"I suppose those that were most important to her, lord."

"Show me to her chambers."

The serving woman momentarily studied him, calculating. He recognized that ambition. "This way, lord," she said as she led him to a room bare of personal items—furnished only with the opulence Gallus would have ordered. She watched as he hunted through Octavia's things. "My lord, what do you seek?"

Florus's anger flared. He would have to search the entire house and hope to find a secret spot where Octavia might have—in her haste—forgotten Cleo's letters and left them behind. "That's none of your concern." Florus cursed himself for not coming to Antioch sooner. "Do you recall anything special she might have carried with her?"

"Special, lord? Perhaps. A fine leather pouch I've seen with her many times when she wrote or read. It was in her arms when she left." She cocked her head to one side with a bit of a smile. "But... if there's something I know of she did not take that proves to be of value to you, will you pay me, lord? Will you take care of me, lord... if what I have is something of interest to you?"

"I give you my word."

The woman left the chamber for a few moments and then returned, handing him a piece of parchment. "This came about a month ago, maybe a few days more..."

The large letter still had a blob of red wax sealing it. Florus glanced up at the woman.

"I cannot read"—she answered his question—"and did not open it, lord."

"Good." He took the letter over to the open window and held under the sunlight streaming in. A sigil or symbol had been pressed into the wax seal—a crescent moon, bisected by an arrow. It was Cleo's pendant! He broke the seal and read:

Octavia, I hope you are well, but I know you must be full of concern for your husband. I worry, too, and fear for our future. Have you seen or heard anything of Sayid, the Syrian who brought you my letters? I have not. But he must have reached your husband in time. Has Lord Gallus mentioned anything of him? I have yet to read what Costas brought me from you this day. But if those letters do not answer what I ask in this message, please let me know as soon as you can. I fear that I have put Sayid in danger— despite his misgivings, he carried those letters to you as a favor to me. I hope you remain safe, and please take care!

He looked up from the letter to the woman nervously, shifting her weight from foot to foot. What did Cleo send to Octavia that was then carried by this Sayid—he recalled the scruffy Syrian—to Cestius Gallus?

"Lord...."

He glanced up at the woman, who had an expectant—uncertain— expression.

"Lord, you will take care of me... now?"

Gessius Florus glanced down at the letter in his hand, then back at her, and he smiled, "Yes."

LXI

ANTIOCH, SYRIA

Though it was late afternoon, Cestius Gallus felt no hurry to leave the ship, even though the past few days, he'd felt the gazes of the sailors and ship's officers, especially the captain. Since they'd left Ptolemais, he had been watched as if he were an exotic animal brought into an arena for the entertainment of the multitude. They had the same attention and gleam in their eyes—the same perverse pleasure, the anticipation, and expectation—that rippled through the crowd when the games were about to commence.

Gallus had never traveled on a ship that had covered distance so seemingly fast, and no one waited for him at the end. But what did await him was the third and final of the *Parcae,* the three Fates of all men and women. The first, Nona, had sown the thread of life for his birth; the second, Decima, the keen observer and keeper of his life's record had measured it. And soon, the third, *Morta,* would sever the thread, ending his existence—he would never see Octavia again.

He turned from the ship's rail, and those thoughts of Octavia weighed on him as they had ever since he had sent that message ahead, telling her to not wait for him. She was to go, to leave Antioch before he arrived. In that message, he'd promised he would see her in Rome—one of the few falsehoods of their decades of marriage. What hurt him most was that Octavia would realize the lie as she read his words.

Earlier, he had seen the captain hurry off the ship, darting a glance up at Gallus. Now it was his time to leave, and he looked around, expecting a centurion or at least a legionary from the galley to escort him to his home. But there were none about. He lifted his *sarcina,* the only baggage he'd brought from Ptolemais. Galerius Senna had questioned his use of the same pack used by the legion's soldiers. But Gallus had learned by serving in combat that it was best to keep things simple and light; carry only what you need and no more.

Gallus sensed *Morta's* hand near, plucking at the thread, drawing it taut... what he needed and wanted most—more time with his wife— would never be found in a pack. So his was very light.

* * *

Despite the heat that bore down even as the late afternoon grew into twilight, Gallus had decided against a cart and followed the rising street to the somewhat rougher road that climbed to what had been his home in Antioch. Now, it was just a place to wait for Lord Vespasian and Gaius Licinius Mucianus, the new governor. Then he would learn if the domus or another location would become the place of his death.

He found the front entrance secured, as he had instructed Octavia, and followed the path around to the terrace. Though he had thought Octavia would keep at least one servant there to attend him, the house was silent. Or, more likely, the one assigned to remain thought it better to leave than to serve a doomed man, and he could not fault them for that. He walked to the tip of the terrace, set his pack down, and gazed out upon the city. He and Octavia had often talked of retirement—it had seemed close, and now it would never be—while watching the sunset from this spot.

A noise echoed behind him from inside the house. Perhaps one of the servants had remained, after all. He picked up the bag, turned from the setting sun, its top arc now a dark red-orange sliver over a black strip of the distant horizon, and went inside.

There on the other side of the atrium fountain still flowing and bubbling was Gessius Florus. He tapped the hilt of an ornate dagger against the marble pedestal supporting a bronze brazier—the flickering flames relieved some dimness of the interior. The pugio's pommel of gold glinted, an inset jewel glittering.

Gallus was startled. "Lord Florus, what do you do here... in Antioch?" He stopped short of adding "in my home."

"To meet the new governor and General Vespasian... who should arrive in a day or two." The knife struck the marble harder, ringing metal on stone. "And I'd hoped to see Lady Octavia"—Florus smiled— "but I find she is gone."

"I don't understand, Gessius... why do you need to see my wife? Who let you into our home?"

"I walked in, just as you did. I don't think your wife is needed any longer, though I'm sure I can have her found in Rome." The dagger struck the marble again. "Tell me, 'Lord' Gallus... what did my wife send to Octavia that she then forwarded to you? I understand a Syrian auxiliary, one Sayid, was the courier...."

"I don't know what you're talking about. Leave now."

Gessius Florus rose from his seat, dragged the tip of the dagger up the pedestal, and across the brazier, reversing to rap the pommel hard against the bronze bowl. Stirred sparks floated into the rising plume of smoke. He walked toward Cestius Gallus and stopped in front of him. "So, you received nothing from Lady Octavia that came to her from Lady Cleo?"

"I have nothing to say to *you*, Florus."

"Interesting how you say it that way, 'Lord' Gallus." Florus motioned with his left hand—"Quintus."

A shadow appeared quickly from behind the former governor, and before Gallus could turn to see who cast it, a powerful arm yanked him back as the other arm came up with a gleaming blade that arced into his throat. The razor edge slit the soft flesh, and for a half-heartbeat, the sides held together. Then as Cestius Gallus' recognized the scarred face of the ship's captain, the flesh parted, and his life gushed out, his hands trying to stop what they could not.

"Now, you'll talk to no one." Gessius Florus glared at Cestius Gallus as he choked on blood and then was still. Florus spurned the body with a heel, then stooped and picked up the dead man's pack. "Put your blade in his hand and bring the woman out here to lie beside him."

Quintus dragged the servant's body from the shadows. The woman's throat was horribly bruised and banded with livid finger-width marks. She had died fighting for breath. Gessius Florus smoothed the sleeves of his tunic over the freshly scabbed scratches on his upper arms. "I told you I would take care of you," he muttered. "I will get the Jews' treasure, and if anyone stands in my way, I'll take my pleasure in their punishment, too. Cleo, the Syrian, and anyone else who has helped her—I'll take care of all of them."

LXII

ANTIOCH, SYRIA

Vespasian saw the rider he had sent to summon Cestius Gallus from the governor's residence, accompanied by another mounted man whose red cloak settled as they reined in and dismounted on the wharf in front of his ship.

"From here," said Vespasian to Nicanor, beside him, "I want us to conduct all meetings at the army encampment... and not among civilians. No matter what, we will show respect to Lord Gallus—"

He stopped at a stirring from Nicanor—"What's wrong?"

The centurion was staring intently at the cloaked man, now off his horse, and headed toward the dock. Nicanor's scowl was a dark cloud settling into the white seams of his old scars more. "That's not Lord Gallus, general... that's Gessius Florus."

Vespasian noted the centurion's bitter tone and observed the man approaching the ship. "The former Judean Procurator?"

"Yes, general."

"What is he doing here... and where is Lord Gallus?"

Nicanor knew no answer was expected, and he watched as Gessius Florus boarded the ship alone and crossed the deck to them.

"An honor to meet you, Lord Vespasian"—Florus's eyes flicked at Nicanor—"and I'm surprised to see you again, centurion." His attention returned to Vespasian. "Lord, I am sorry to report that Lord Gallus has taken his own life."

"What?!" Nicanor exclaimed.

Florus ignored him, still addressing Vespasian. "His body was found this morning next to a servant—a woman—he had killed. I'm sure the local authorities will report this to you soon."

"The centurion tells me you are Gessius Florus, the former Judean Procurator.... what do you do here, Lord Florus?"

"I come to greet you, Lord Vesp—"

Vespasian cut him off, "It's just general... Lord Florus, I am a soldier first, and above all other things." He noted Florus's scowl at the smile that came and went on Nicanor's face.

The scowl vanished. "I come to greet you, general—"

"—What position do you now hold, Lord Florus?" Vespasian asked, cutting him off.

Florus blinked. "I am a special imperial tax collector, lord—erm—general. I report directly to the emperor."

"And why are you here—speaking with me?"

"General, I have experience with some of what you now face—dealing with these rebels—and I feel I could be of use."

"Lord Gallus is the one I needed to speak with." Vespasian's curt tone was markedly different from Florus's smoothness. "Did your knowledge help him? But perhaps you have some insight that will be helpful."

He nodded at Nicanor—"Centurion, get the staff disembarked and to the encampment. Have Gaheris Clineas supervise my orderlies to set up a temporary command tent and quarters for me. Lord Florus, you are welcome to join us there tonight for dinner, if you wish." He turned to leave them at the ship's railing and noted that Nicanor turned with him. He felt Florus's eyes on them both.

* * *

That night...

"Lor—I mean, general—you mean you are not going to march directly on Jerusalem?!" Gessius Florus exclaimed.

Vespasian waited as the empty plates were cleared, and more wine poured. Nicanor caught his nod to the orderly to leave them, take a deep drink, and set the goblet in front of him. "It's regrettable I can't speak with Lord Gallus. The dead woman aside, I understand his choice to die by his own hand and not some executioner. But after his failure, I will not assault Jerusalem until I have destroyed most—if not all—rebel strongholds. I must kill or capture the rebellion's leaders that would otherwise stir trouble behind me once I face a siege of Jerusalem."

"But general, you have assembled an overwhelming force... they cannot stand against you."

Vespasian picked up the goblet that looked small in his great hand. "Have you fought against the rebels, Lord Florus?" The general glanced at Nicanor, who had quietly watched throughout dinner. It was just the three of them since the new governor Gaius Licinius Mucianus was dealing with the death of Cestius Gallus. "Or have you been in combat against any opponent or enemy of Rome?"

Vespasian squinted Nicanor's way, and did not see Florus's lips compress into a tight line that did not ease until he replied, "No, general, I have not."

Vespasian turned back to address Florus: "The 12th Legion's failure—and Lord Gallus's— was unexpected." Again, he turned toward Nicanor. "First-person accounts, too, tell me not to overlook or underestimate anything or anyone."

Throughout dinner, Nicanor had watched the verbal exchange between the two. It was a game he was no good at and had always chosen not to play. He agreed with Vespasian's intent and had told the general so. But he had not told him his doubts about Cestius Gallus's suicide. Lord Gallus would have requested to go to Rome to speak with Emperor Nero personally. He would not try to avoid his fate, but he would have felt it his duty to set the record straight, accounting for what had happened. The emperor should understand why he had made certain decisions.

One thing Nicanor had learned—and what made him respect the man—was that Cestius Gallus, who had been an administrator, would not die like one. He would face his fate as a soldier and fight to the last. Nicanor took no pleasure at the consternation on Gessius Florus's face as Vespasian summarized his intent for the coming campaign against the Judean rebels. He studied the man he detested—married to poor Cleo, a woman Nicanor had grown fond of, he had realized in the lonely hours of his recent duty in Rome. As he watched, Florus's expression transformed from a slight frown to sly, to open and friendly.

"General, I will help you in any way that I can"—the imperial tax collector lifted his goblet—"To your victory!" Florus smiled.

That smile worried Nicanor more than anything the man said.

LXIII

They had followed a lengthy, crooked ridgeline northwest from Yotapta. Clusters of men, in batches of a dozen or more, formed a snaking line of over 3,000, some mounted, who partway had to divert to a lower path along the base of the hills. Most walked—carrying only their personal gear, skins of water, and weapons.

They're accustomed to the terrain and moving fast, Yosef thought as he paused to drink from the goatskin of water he had slung over his shoulder.

"Dalit tells me these hills have many caves," said Ariella, stopping next to him. "Some have been used for years by bandits, but most are barely explored." She took her own swig of water and continued, "She says the entrances are usually found at the base of the hills, though some have openings higher up. Like there"—she pointed at shelves of limestone ahead, shadows beneath them of what might be either a shallow space formed by rock shearing off or a deeper recess into a much larger area within the hill—"and some of the large ones we passed closer to Yotapta."

"Levi may be upset with me for letting you come," Yosef said as he turned to face the sun low on the horizon. A thin haze of blue marked the sea—*mare nostrum*—that the Romans rightly thought as theirs. The coolness of the breeze from that direction refreshed him. Though it was only late spring, the day had brought the heat of summer. He gave a last look at the bands of pink shading to purple above the sea and then noticed Ariella studying something. Ahead of them, low in the river valley, night fires blossomed. The long trek that day from Yotapta to Gabara had wound through crests and along the sides of hills and low mountains. Beyond that valley was Gabara.

"Galon was right," Ariella commented. "Levi picked a good spot, with room behind him to maneuver his men and still be close, just outside the town." Beyond the encampment was a broader—fainter— group of lights where Gabara backed up to the darkness of the Segev forest. "He won't be upset. I'm safe enough with you and all these men, and like we've seen all day, the people of Galilee have heard your request. Many of them are coming to Gabara, too." She pointed at

246

small groups of people, the sparks of their hand torches coming alight in the twilight of the valley floor, all heading toward the town.

"You sound like a general... assessing the terrain." Yosef smiled at her and studied the encampment that was their destination by the *nahal.* "He has set camp in a bend of the river, which is good." Yosef resumed picking his way down the path. The men scouting ahead had reported they were nearing the level trail to Levi's camp and should reach it by the time full night had set in.

"My father was a soldier and is still a warrior," Ariella said with a shrug, "but he had no sons." Wiping her lips with the back of her hand, she hung the skin over her slim shoulder. "I'm the oldest, and I guess I listened and learned the most from his stories."

"Well, you're correct," Yosef said over his shoulder. "The river's likely the main water supply for Gabara, and if the Gabarans or Yohanan of Gischala's men there want to attack him, they'll have to cross to engage Levi or flank him to strike where he'll have his strongest defense set."

As the path widened, Ariella walked faster to catch up beside Yosef. "Once we've joined with Levi's men, will you attack first?"

"I don't want to fight them at all unless we have to."

"What is your plan, then?"

"I'll explain when we join Levi," he replied. Ahead the path broadened even more and flattened onto the plain. "I'm willing to try words before swords and spears—to achieve a resolution."

"Sometimes, talking doesn't work, though." Ariella shook her head. "Levi agrees with my father about that."

Next Morning...

"So, these are the men?" Yosef gestured at the line of men arrayed before him.

It had not taken long for Levi's pleasure at seeing Ariella yield to his anger at Yohanan of Gischala's continued attacks and recruitment of others. "These are the couriers we intercepted, and each carried this"—Levi handed Yosef a sheaf of parchment, each sheet of which contained the same message. "And this man we caught with a message for Yohanan of Gischala. It is from someone—unnamed and unsigned—who approved of his plan to spread these lies to the people of Galilee"—Levi shook the letters in his hand.

"Who are you?" Yosef asked as he strode to stand in front of the man. "Where did you come from, and who sent the message you carried?"

"He won't talk but has the look of a Greek to me," Levi said. He waved a hand at the others—"and these men don't know him. They say they were paid by Yohanan of Gischala personally, to go to every town and village in Galilee with these"—he rattled the parchment again—"to convince Galileans to support him and abandon you." There was more to it than that... Levi was sure the man had come from Ptolemais. "His purse was full of Roman coins."

Yosef turned toward a crowd of men he knew were not from Yotapta but who had approached the camp at first light. "Do any of you know this man, or have you seen him before?" All shook their heads. "Are any of you from Gabara?"

A stout graying man and two younger-looking men off to one side answered: "We are..."

"And do you come here, to this camp, for the same reason given me earlier by these other men?" He gestured at the larger group.

The older man nodded. "We believe you are doing what is right for Galilee... and all of Judea." He darted a baleful glance at the man found with the Roman coins. "Too many meddle in our affairs. The Romans have long stripped many of us of land that's been in our families for centuries. They want to control our farms, our crops... dictate what pittance they pay us and then place a tax on that." The man spat on the ground. "Each year under their rule, we grow poorer, and life becomes harder."

Yosef thought of Nathan and his sons, and all the other poor fishermen and farmers of Galilee. He understood the man's pain.

"And when the Roman army comes," the man continued with a glance toward the "Greek," "they're not going to care if you've been of some service to them... you'll be crushed, too." He addressed Yosef: "We are common folk, not priests, not rich. We work the land... and the sea. War will destroy what we have left. You are trying to bring us together and make even our smallest towns stronger to stand against the Romans. So most of us in Galilee support you."

Yosef saw every man nod. "In Gabara," he said, "where is the largest place for a gathering of the people?"

"The House of Yeshua," the stout man replied immediately. "It is the town's stronghold and has a large, open court right in the center of the city."

"Do you know the city leaders?" Yosef asked him.

"Yes," the man nodded.

"Take this message to them for me. Tell them—your leaders—that at the hour before sundown today, my men and I, will peacefully enter Gabara. If they will but listen to me and not believe any message that comes from Yohanan of Gischala, I will read from those letters. And then I will ask you—the people of Galilee—what you think, what you want, and who you wish to lead you."

He saw Ariella and Levi's intent focus on him, awaiting his conclusion. "Then return their answer to me, and I will know what action my men and I will take."

* * *

In Gabara, the House of Yeshua was imposing and unexpected, as was the mass of people packing the courtyard, spilling out, and filling all the streets. Groups of people filled the roofs of nearby buildings, all waiting to listen to him as he stood upon a low platform hastily constructed for his speech.

"As your leaders agreed to let me do, I have read you the letters about me that Yohanan of Gischala is spreading throughout Galilee. He claims I am a traitor... that I am a tyrant sent to represent the wishes of Jerusalem and not the interests of Galileans. He claims I'm ill-suited and unprepared to be a general, not worthy of commanding the defense of Galilee against the Romans. He accuses me of the very things he proves of himself by his actions." Yosef paused, and his eyes swept the crowd. "Those of you who have personal experience of me... or know those who have... you know that I have proved by my actions that what Yohanan of Gischala claims as truth is, in fact, lies.

"I would confront him with that accusation to his face, but when he heard that I asked to speak to you and prove to you his misdeeds, he fled with his men before I entered your town." Yosef held up the letter taken from the messenger. "This is a message approving of his efforts to undermine me and to sway all of Galilee to his side. We believe the man carrying it came from Ptolemais and works for the Romans—and that he was well paid in their coin. I believe Yohanan of Gischala was attempting to arrange a deal with the Romans to let them march through Galilee uncontested." He paused at the gasp from the crowd. "That would serve his own interests, but not yours. The only deal that would accomplish that aim is to have me removed or killed—and that has been tried."

Yosef turned to point at the envoys from Jerusalem standing behind him and shifting uncomfortably. "These men, representatives of the Sanhedrin—or at least its president—have come to Galilee to see me removed and returned to Jerusalem."

He looked down at Levi and Ariella in the front row and noted that Yohanan ben Zaccai had finally arrived and stood beside them. "Some of you know how much I miss my family in Jerusalem. The only thing stronger than a desire to return to them is my intention to do as I was originally ordered. I was ordered to command our defense in Galilee. I was ordered to do all I can to save lives by strengthening defenses and being ready for the battles to come. I will continue to follow these orders if you let me."

Yosef turned around to the envoys and beckoned, "Please step forward to hear the answer to this question I ask the people of Galilee." The men—some reluctantly—stepped forward as Yosef stepped to one side, faced the crowd, and raised his voice: "Who do you want as commander in Galilee?"

"Yosef, you are *euergeten kai sotera*—our benefactor and deliverer!" came a loud call, and thousands of voices took up the acclaim.

Yosef turned to the envoys. "Return to Jerusalem and report this to Shimon ben Gamliel and to the Sanhedrin." Then he stepped down from the platform and joined Levi, Ariella, and his old friend.

"I'm glad you were here in time to hear them," he said to Yohanan ben Zaccai, whose tired countenance broke into a smile.

"Yes, Yosef... they were loud and clear."

"Then I want you to go with the envoys. I do not trust them to do as I ask and speak the truth. Return with them to Jerusalem and report all of this to Shimon ben Gamliel."

"What if he still demands you give up command in Galilee?" ask Yohanan.

"Tell him he needs to come here and tell that to the people of Galilee. I will stay here to do the job I was sent here to do."

LXIV

JERUSALEM

The sun had cleared the eastern wall and Solomon's Porch as it climbed over the Mount of Olives, and the coolness and quiet of the shadows were replaced with warm, bright sun and the sounds of people entering and crossing the court as the day began. Miriam rose from the bench where she had spent the last hour sitting and thinking. She smoothed her robe and adjusted the clasp of her cloak. Its metal caught a sunbeam, and the dart of light from the emblem, the fingers of the *hamsa*, made her think of two things, both of which saddened her. Both concerned her brother.

Josef had found the hamsa clasp in the tunnel beneath and just outside the Temple enclosure, not too far from where she stood now. There she had been raped by the two Romans before Zechariah saved her. Yosef, later home from Rome, visited the tunnels where the siblings and their friends had played as children and had found the hamsa. He returned it to her with questions she had never answered for him. As much as she loved the clasp, it symbolized all that had been torn from her that day, and its return complicated things with the brother she had always been so close to.

Yosef's shipwreck on his way to Rome, then his experiences there, had changed him. He came home to find that she, too, had changed. He did not know that she had known things far darker and damaging than he had, but the time apart and events during it weighed heavily on them both. She could never tell him, or anyone else how hurt she still was—and how she welcomed being left alone, even as she longed for comfort. She missed Yosef and wished he had never gone to command in Galilee.

"Miriam!"

At Rachel's voice, Miriam regretted not leaving sooner, but she turned toward the sound to see Rachel's face alight with more than the morning sun and timorous Leah beside her. Leah's expression was always guarded, and her eyes mostly lowered, as if she were ashamed of something. She had a secret, too, but hers was known to just a few—Rachel, Leah's only family since their parents had died, who had told Miriam, who had mentioned it to her brother Matthew. The recent bruise on Leah's cheek had faded, but new ones around both wrists that Leah struggled to cover with her sleeves were proof Yonatan continued to abuse her.

That shared, heart-deep, never-healing wound made them sisters, even if Leah did not know it, and that truth overrode Miriam's reluctance to stop and speak with them. "Hello...." she said.

Rachel greeted her, "We were on our way to study. Will you join us?"

"I'm sorry, but I have somewhere to go right now."

"Then walk with us"—Rachel took her arm—"We saw your mother last evening, and she says your father is better. We were so glad to hear it. She said, you all hear from Yosef that he is well."

Miriam nodded, noting the difference in tone whenever Rachel mentioned Yosef. "We are all thankful Father is better, and that Yosef is doing well, too." She looked across Rachel to Leah, who had remained silent. "Leah, how are you?"

A shaky smile came and went across Leah's face. "I'm... well, Miriam."

Without thinking, Miriam pulled her arm from Rachel's and reached out to grip Leah's shoulder. "Leah, if you need someone"— she glanced at Rachel—"someone else to talk to... please let me know." *Was that too much?*

"Thank you... but I'm—"

She didn't finish, as they had reached the entrance to the House of Study.

"I'll join you inside, Leah"—Rachel paused as Leah left them—"Is Yosef in danger?"

Miriam blinked. "We are all in danger, Rachel. The Romans are coming, and they won't stop this time."

"No... I mean, I know that. But what I mean is, is he in danger from others? From our people there in Galilee? We've... Leah and I have heard rumors."

"Matthew told you?"

She looked embarrassed. "Yes, he confirmed what we'd heard. I went to ask him, and he said there were factions, our own people, working against Yosef. Is he in danger?"

"There has been trouble, but he was safe as of his last letter."

An expression of relief erased the lines that had tightened Rachel's face. "Good. I pray for Yosef's return."

Miriam had long suspected it and now must ask to be sure. Yosef must know of it, and in her next letter, she would tell him it was more than an old, childish infatuation. "Are you in love with Yosef, Rachel?"

LXV

JERUSALEM

"The iron I brought from Alexandria comes from the Roman mines in the Sinai," Hananiah remarked as he used a set of tongs to lift a glowing lump from a clay crucible he had pulled from the furnace. The heat in the room was fierce.

Miriam felt the fierce temperature even from several steps away. The sweat-shined muscles in his forearms ripples as he handled the metal, and she wondered how the heat could seem like nothing to him.

"I'll re-work the sponge metal and re-forge this to get rid of its impurities," he explained as he set the lump beside several others on a rack of rough iron bars. "Then I'll fold the metals as I re-forge them in alternating layers of steel. Then I'll form them into rods I'll twist together, heat and beat to flatten them, then forge again to shape it all into a blade." Hananiah stepped away from the rack, picked up the hand bellows, and tucked it away, then removed what he had called *caestus*. He had altered the thick leather gloves worn in the arena by Roman, thickening the pad of leather at the palm and extending the fingers for better coverage. "Do you want to see one that's finished?"

"Please." Miriam had followed with fascination each step he had shown her and was excited to see the result.

From another rack, he lifted a sword, its pattern of swirls and whorls revealed in the firelight and lamplight. Arcs, spirals, and wavy, shaded lines—the design seemed organic, unplanned... and it was beautiful.

"This is my version of a Roman *spatha*, their long sword." The straight blade, longer than his arm, had what looked like a bleached-white bone for a hilt, the grip wrapped in black leather straps. "Stay clear," he warned and moved into an open area of his workroom with the sword at his side, point down along his leg. He picked up a square of what looked like silk and tossed it into the air. Effortlessly, he spun on a heel, the blade flashed like an adder strike of lightning across a midnight sky, and it sliced the fabric in half before it could fall to the floor. He stooped and picked up the pieces and brought them to her. "Look...."

The two rectangles were so cleanly cut the edges of cloth were not frayed, showing not even a loosening of thread until she handled each half. She touched the blade still in his hand. "Beautiful."

"Yes," Hananiah agreed, "something so splendid and deadly created from such a brutal process. The addition of some charcoal, and heat and pressure. The pounding metal-on-metal of repeated blows.... an interesting means of creation, is it not? I was taught this method in Alexandria; it's not well-known yet across the Roman empire. The Greeks call the resulting metal *chalbys*."

When Hananiah handled blades was the only time Miriam had seen any expression in his eyes—and this was joy. She did not reply because she had thought of the analogy before Hananiah spoke of it. The harsh progression of creating such a weapon had resonated with her. "May I?"—she held out her hand.

Hananiah passed her the hilt. She felt its balance, turned, and rotated it to let the pattern within the metal catch the light and form a flicker of iridescence that ran the length of the blade from her hand to the tip. *Beautiful*, she thought again and looked up at him.

His unblinking eyes were not on the sword—they were on her. His look sent a shiver through her.

* * *

It was late when she finished her letter to Yosef. She did not know whether Yohanan ben Zaccai would return to Jerusalem soon, to be able to take it to Yosef for her, but she knew it had to be written and ready. She had hinted to Yosef about Rachel's confession of love. There was nothing Yosef could or even should do while he was in Galilee, but if the rumors proved accurate, and Yosef was ordered back to Jerusalem, he must know so he could decide what to do about it. She sealed the letter and set it aside to pick up a scrap of parchment.

After her time at Hananiah's shop, she had stopped at Zechariah's to find that Elazar had left her a message: "Meet me tomorrow after sunrise, where you met Menahem ben Judah in Hezekiah's tunnel." *Good*, she thought, clenching and releasing her fist. *I hope he has work for me—and I want to ask about punishing the Jews who are as bad as the Romans.*

The lamp Zechariah had made for her sputtered, and she quenched the wick. Opening her shutters to let in the night wind, she stretched out on her bed and fell asleep dreaming of the gleaming, dancing metal.

LXVI

PTOLEMAIS

Hidden from the house by the dunes, Cleo set down her bow and a quiver full of green- and blue-feather-fletched arrows. She could not be too often out of Glaucio's sight, so she had let the major domus know she would be practicing. Cleo hung the bow over her right forearm and slipped on her new leather arm guard and the thumb ring from the quiver. She stepped to her firing point ten steps farther than the spot she had fired from before.

This arrangement for her archery practice, a broad level area between the rolling dunes, was not as good as what she had set up in Caesarea. And that was a poor version of where she had learned archery at her father's home in Rome. Though she had thought much differently at the time, her life then was so much better than now. Everything in her world had changed when her father arranged her marriage to Gessius Florus. When he told her, Cleo had resigned herself to the inevitable loss of freedom her now-dead best friend had explained to her. Poppaea had become Emperor Nero's wife, and she had a distinctly pessimistic viewpoint about husbands. Cleo had adjusted to married life, but once they were in Judea, Gessius Florus had shown his true nature, and her life had worsened from that point on. Now she feared for her very life and felt threatened by the man she had married.

She took the bow in her hands and entered the familiar act of concentration to aim, breathe and hold it, then smoothly draw and release. But the routine did not calm her as it always had before. Beyond her usual worries, she now had Sayid to care for until he healed. She hated to leave him alone in the dune-buried building, but there was no other place to hide him. He must remain there until he was healthy enough to... well, she was not sure what his plans were. But the longer he stayed, the more likely he would be discovered, and that possibility frightened her. Sayid would be killed, and... she did not know what would happen to her.

She nocked an arrow, took a deep breath, held it, and focused on the driftwood target, pausing for the wind to lessen. It was a blustery day with a darkening canopy that was drawing closer to the land. She released her breath and the string, and the arrow streaked true, striking dead center with a satisfying *thunk*. She went to the target and, with a firm tug, pulled the arrow free and checked its point and the fletching of green. All were solid—*Good*, she thought with a smile, pleased at her improving skill assembling her own arrows.

Walking back to the firing point, she set the bow down against the pedestal holding Cicero's cage. The shifting winds had ruffled his feathers and made him cross, he shuffled back and forth on his perch. Once they were inside the house, she would ease him with his favorite treat, the hard nuts he enjoyed cracking.

She reached inside the cage and smoothed his head and neck feathers. As she started to withdraw her hand, Cicero stepped from the rod to the lip of the cage door, raised a claw to touch her arm first, then stepped up and onto her forearm. He dug in, and she gritted her teeth, glad she still wore the leather bracer for a bit of protection. She smiled as the bird spread his wings and preened.

Suddenly he stiffened, his head pivoting and searching; the parrot's stare locked on something behind her, and a second later, he squawked and clicked his tongue loudly. And then she heard Glaucio's call as he came closer.

"Lady Cleo...." He always ran the two words together as 'ladycleo,' and it sounded a jeer from his lips. She did not answer, but in a few more seconds, he appeared around the bend in the path.

"A message has arrived from Lord Florus," Glaucio announced.

"For me?" Cleo replied.

Glaucio's smirk was as derisive as his tone. "No, it is for the centurion... but I cannot find him."

"He must be in Ptolemais." Cleo had known it would not take long for Capito to be missed—his dead body remained with Sayid in hiding—but she had hoped that with Florus still gone, there would be more time before his absence became an issue.

"I've checked, and he is not in Ptolemais."

"I've not seen him," she said dismissively, then saw Glaucio's eyes on Cicero, who stared at the man like he was an unusually large nut to crack. His head cocked to one side, the bird's clicks and squawks were as sharp as his fixed look at the major domus—he did not like the man. She moved toward Glaucio, who took a step back, his eyes still on the parrot on her forearm.

"If you see him, please tell him to see me"—he turned from her without courtesy, his usual way unless Gessius Florus was present—and hurried away.

* * *

The sunset had been washed away by the sheets of rain that swept in from the sea. The wind had strengthened, gathered the rain, and driven it down, angling in and pounding from a sky covered entirely with low clouds that disappeared into the darkness as she watched the night fall. She pondered Florus's message to Capito. *What could it be about?* Likely something to do with his business in Antioch. She worried for Octavia and prayed to the gods she was safe. Sadly, Lord Gallus would soon face the new governor and military commander. She knew what would happen to him resulting from that meeting, but what of Octavia?

After dinner, she had heard Glaucio go to his quarters—or to the bed of one of the female servants—and wondered if he had left the message for Capito in her husband's office. Glaucio thought little of her, a mere woman, and might have left it there without worry. It was late, so he probably would not be skulking about. *I must see if I can.* But Glaucio could have instructions to take extreme measures with her if he caught her spying. Cicero clucked and bobbed his head as he watched her.

"You will be my alarm, my friend," she told him. She tucked several treats into a fold of her robe and slid the leather bracer over her arm, turning it, so the laces were underneath. Extending her arm, she invited Cicero to climb on and set his grip. Her sentry was ready.

* * *

Nothing, Cleo thought and checked again to be sure Cicero had not left droppings on her husband's desk, as much as the thought amused her. There was nothing of import here—the scrolls and sheets were only inconsequential records and mundane reports. Glaucio must have kept with him the message for Capito. She glanced at Cicero, who was content with working on the delicacy she had given him. She held her arm out, and as he stepped up on the armguard, he dropped his nut and let out an irritated squawk.

"Shhhh... Cicero"—Cleo quieted him and knelt to find the nut and shell fragments. The bird swayed on her forearm and stretched his neck to aid in the search.

"There..." It had bounced and landed beside a woven reed basket. She picked up the nut and saw a scrap of parchment beneath the basket, a corner protruding that almost matched the color of the stone it sat upon. She slid it out and rose. The writing was her husband's, but she saw names that seemed Jewish or Judean.

Cicero cocked his head over his shoulder and squawked, alarmed enough to clench her arm painfully even through the leather armguard. She hurried to the doorway and out into the atrium.

"Lady Cleo!"—the loud whisper echoed through the silent house now that the wind had abated. As she rounded a corner toward her sleeping chamber, there was Elian in a pool of light from an oil-lamp sconce on the wall. He was soaking wet. "What's wrong, Elian?"

"It's Sayid! Come quickly!"

LXVII

PTOLEMAIS

Cleo's cloak had done little to keep out the rain. She was drenched, and the night's coolness prickled the skin of her arms and legs. Too focused on shielding the small lamp she carried to tug the robe free, the heavy fabric clung to her legs as she stumbled through the dark. The ruin's outline was faint against the deeper shadows as she entered the ground level and heard the wind moan through the cracks and fissures in the crumbled walls and collapsed or sand-buried window openings.

She wished the sounds came from her friend above, but Elian's panic pulled from him the fear he confessed—that Sayid might be dead. The boy—as foolish as it was—had done what she should have but had not. Not asking her permission, which she would have denied, Elian had checked on Sayid when the storm's ferocity peaked. With Glaucio's eyes upon her, she had thought it too risky and unnecessary. When she had left Sayid the evening before, he had been resting comfortably—at least as possible with such a wound— and had food and water within reach for a day or more. But with the storm, Elian had been right to worry and to check on Sayid. She hoped the boy remained silent in her room with Cicero until she returned.

The second-floor room was still lighted by the lantern Elian had left behind. In its flickering flame, she saw Sayid sitting near the lamp, leaning against a bench, eyes closed. The front of his tunic was soaked in blood that had run down his side and pooled into a darker red, congealed puddle that reached the base of the lantern. Even squatting next to him, she could not detect any breathing; Sayid was still. *Elian was right—what have I done?*

The tears came and filled her eyes; every friend she cared about was dead or lost to her. With a wipe of a wet sleeve, she shifted from back on her heels to kneel beside him. "Sayid"—she touched his shoulder but received no response, not a movement. Pulling away the tunic from his chest, the dried and damp blood still sticky, she saw the bandage had slipped, and the wound gaped open again.

Sayid's face was clammy and cold to her touch. "Sayid"—she leaned closer. Was there the barest flutter of breath? With the flat of her hand on his chest, she sensed a faint heartbeat, and with the other hand, she smoothed the long, tangled curls from his face. "Sayid..."

Dark, long-lashed eyes flickered open, closed, and opened again but were unfocused. "La... Lady Cleo?"

* * *

The small fire had driven away the night's chill after the storm, and the water she had heated and had him drink seemed to have warmed her friend. Sayid was weak and pale, but his eyes had lost their dazed appearance as he ate some dried fruit.

Cleo got him back onto the long bench and re-bandaged his wounds before she noticed what was missing. "Where is Capito's body?"

"I thought it best to get him—it—away from here. I dragged it to one of the dunes down the beachfront, dug into it, and shoved his body in. Then I scraped more sand down to cover him."

"You should have waited for me to help."

"My lady, I couldn't let you... you must not do something like that." Sayid shook his head, then stopped and pressed a hand to his brow. "It was for me to do."

"And the result is you tore your wound open and nearly bled to death."

"I should have come here sooner..." Sayid tried to sit up, but he winced and halted the effort. "I'm sorry, my lady."

"About what?"

"Lady Octavia was worried about you and asked me to check on you. But I took too long... I didn't know Gessius Florus was mistreating you this badly."

"Sayid, I also said you did what you must—you took care of your mother. And you arrived here in time to save me. If Capito had taken those letters to my husband, Florus would have done more than strike me. I would likely be dead and Capito alive."

"What will we do now?" Sayid closed his eyes.

Cleo wrapped a blanket around him. "Rest now. It's near dawn, and I have to be back before someone discovers I'm gone."

His eyes opened, "No, lady. I mean, how do we get you away from Gessius Florus and to someplace where you can live safely?"

"I don't know, Sayid, and trying to figure that out has consumed me."

"I wish Nicanor was here—he would know what to do. But I'm glad he is in Rome and no longer has to fight. He is a good man, and I miss him."

"I am glad, too. He deserves to rest, to be at peace." She rose from the bench. The storm had long since passed, and gray light came through the part of the window not obscured by the dune. "I must go... but I will come back later with food and medicine. We must get you better first, and then we'll figure out what to do."

* * *

Cleo thought as she climbed the path and passed through the dunes. At her crude archery range, she paused and decided, *I am done with feeling helpless... and with others—even a friend— thinking I am.* Where the rough dirt and sand path turned into gravel, she stopped and scanned the back expanse of her house. All seemed quiet as she hurried to the portico's entrance into the house, slipped her sandals off, and walked inside, trying to be quiet. In her haste to grab her cloak, settle Cicero in his cage and instruct Elian to remain with him while she rushed to check on Sayid, she had left in her room the scrap of the letter she had found in Florus's office.

"You're up early, Lady Cleo," Glaucio greeted her, stepping from the shadows of the atrium.

LXVIII

JERUSALEM

Even in the dim gray light that heralded the dawn, Miriam was sure-footed on the path that descending into the Tyropoeon Valley from the Lower City. She had crossed from the Upper City to take that roadway, which was far more frequented and more accessible than the steeper descent direct from the Upper City. It was still night-black at the base of the old west wall of the City of David, where she entered the tunnel that ran parallel to Hezekiah's. The same workers had dug both to bring water into the city from Gihon Spring. Zechariah had drilled into her how to count her stride and measure distance in the darkness, and she had made this same traverse before. She knew how far the markers for that entrance were from where she stepped onto the valley floor, and she found the small opening and entered.

Once inside the main water tunnel, she lit her lamp. Though she was not an overly tall woman, Miriam kept her head angled down to avoid catching her hood or striking her head on any of the sharp rocks projecting from the rough ceiling above her. Many minutes later, she entered the natural cavity the miners had enlarged to create an area where they could rest, stretch, eat, and drink, yet remain close to their critical project. Some 700 years ago, they had completed the project—redirecting of a seemingly endless supply of water to within the southeastern wall of Jerusalem. She had been to where the spring itself came to the surface just outside the walls, on the steep slopes that overlooked Kidron Valley. It had been covered with large stones and, more recently, masonry. It was sealed to protect the supply if an enemy laid siege to Jerusalem.

Just as she remembered from her last meeting in that chamber, the round stone cistern in the corner remained dry. And the benches and shelves carved from stone were long and wide enough to lie upon. She moved to one of them and sat. After several minutes in the dimness, she oriented to the southeastern entrance to the tunnel from outside the city walls. She heard the sizzle and pop and then smelled a burning torch's pitch-soaked head before she saw its glow grow as it came around a bend in the tunnel. A cowled and cloaked figure—much like her—entered the chamber with the torch held at arm's length but low and to one side, the light not reaching the face. Miriam slid both blades from her forearm sheaths, and the hiss was loud in the eerie silence one finds only when surrounded by rock buried deep underground.

The figure, a man by its bulk—hearing the sound—dropped the torch which rolled to the side and under one of the shelf-like benches, its illumination now confined to a small space around it on the floor. The man breathed heavily but did not move for a handful of breaths and then stooped and picked up the torch. In its light, she saw the sheen and glint from a curved dagger like hers in the man's left hand.

He walked toward her, and, in the torch's ruddiness, Elazar ben Yair's eyes met hers. "You waited in the darkness?" he asked, his tone showing he recognized her.

"It doesn't bother me," Miriam lied. For her, darkness would always be filled with fear and pain, but that was what fed her hatred of Romans and those who helped them—and in turn, gave her strength and courage to do what she must. Zechariah had told her that was what bravery really meant: doing what you had to even when frightened. She would never regain what she had lost, but she would never again be a weeping and helpless victim.

Elazar nodded once at her blades as she slid them back into their sheaths within the sleeves of the robe. She was glad to show him her readiness, and she had noted herself the ring of authority in her own voice. She left unsaid what would have happened if he had been a stranger.

"I have little time," she told him. "My family, though they disapprove, know I go for walks at dawn. They will only challenge me about it if I am not home soon after they arise. Zechariah's shop is closer—why do we meet here?"

Elazar remained standing, studying her in the flickering glow. "I am worried that Roman spies or those who would seek a means to gain Roman favors—should they be victorious—are among the workers in the Lower City. Kefa, the leatherworker who watches Zechariah's old shop for me, has seen a man skulking about. He seems to be waiting for someone to appear there. I think he knows it is a Sicarii meeting place. We will not meet there again."

"What use could the Romans have for a spy in the Lower City?" Miriam asked. "Any spies would want to be where they could see or hear things of importance to Romans—that would be among the people of the Upper City."

"—Or within the Sanhedrin, as you discovered with Yehudah ish Krioth. That is the reason for this meeting."

Miriam's eyes flashed in the torchlight. "Is there another spy in the Sanhedrin?"

"I have had a report that Esau ben Beor—Sanhedrin friends with Shimon ben Gamliel—was seen meeting in Azzah with a man believed to be a Roman. That man has been seen in Caesarea and now in Ptolemais, in the company of Gessius Florus, the former Procurator. I want you—as The Hand, or as the daughter of someone who has influence with the new government and the city leaders—to watch him as best you can."

Miriam stood, adjusting her cloak and securing the hamsa pin. "And what if I should see that he is a spy? Should I report to you before I—"

"—Kill him, Miriam. If you have no doubt that he is what I suspect, you—as The Hand—are a Sicarii, and you become his judge and executioner. If he is a spy or a Roman collaborator, kill him. There are others we are watching in Jerusalem as well, and they may become your targets, too."

LXIX

JERUSALEM

Though she did not have time for it, Miriam paused on the viaduct that spanned the Tyropoeon Valley to watch the dawn. Shafts of sunlight pierced a scattering of low clouds and began to reveal the valley floor far below the Lower City, and the steps up to the Temple enclosure and across the viaduct to the terrace of the Xystus.

The Xystus anchored the agora and marketplace for the Upper City. It was there, on its tiered terrace, that a little over a year ago, over a thousand citizens—mostly Upper City residents—had gathered to hear King Agrippa speak from the platform below the western wall. The leaders of Jerusalem had not heeded Agrippa's request for peaceful resolution with the Romans, and his words decrying their revolt against the empire agreed with Yosef's own judgment. And now Yosef was in Galilee doing his duty to support their mistake, their rebellion forcing Rome against them. Both the Galileans and the Judeans would ultimately lose; no people could long stand against Rome's military might—let alone a people with a thrown-together rebel army.

Even over the men loudly chattering outside the shops along the Xystus and the western cloister of the Temple, she could not help but still hear Agrippa's voice from that day, as if it were still echoing off the buildings. Had the leaders listened to Agrippa, Yosef could have prevented what had happened and what was to come. She would always remember the Roman attack after Passover—the new tyrannical Procurator, Gessius Florus, had set loose the troops, and these familiar streets had been covered in bodies and blood.

And within the supposed safety of her home, that Roman soldier had attacked her. She shuddered to remember being forced to kill a man for the first time as her mother and Rachel had hidden. She pushed that awful memory back down into its dark recess with the others and hurried through the agora to where the street led from shops to homes.

"You are out and about early, Miriam."

The voice behind her was familiar, but she had not heard it lately, Miriam turned around to see Yohanan ben Zaccai walking fast to catch up with her.

"I did not know you were back," she said in greeting. "I mean, it's good to see you... and how is my brother?"

"I arrived late last night... and Yosef is well," the old priest replied with a smile. The morning sun emphasized the deep-scored lines of age and set his white hair glowing.

With a start, Miriam realized that though the two men were about the same age, illness had added another ten years to her father's appearance.

"I am coming to see your father—may I walk with you?" He stopped beside her to ask the next question: "How is Mathias?"

"He's better—still weak, but able to be up for short periods." Miriam began hurrying again, hoping he would match her pace.

With a sigh, he moved into step with her. "Good. I'll try not to tire him too much."

"I have a letter for Yosef if you are returning to Yotapta... " Miriam saw how weary the priest seemed and slowed her pace, and all would be well since she could use Yohanan ben Zaccai's arrival as an excuse for any delay her mother might fret over.

"I will return, but I'm not sure when. I have to talk to some people here on Yosef's behalf, and it might take a few days. I'll be sure to get it from you before I leave"—he glanced sideways at Miriam and hesitated before his next words—"Yosef worries about you."

Miriam was aware all of her family were concerned, but Yosef's qualms indeed had the most impact on her, as the old priest no doubt knew.

"Me?" She squinted to see if she could read his attitude. "There's nothing to worry about. There are many more reasons for all of us— our whole family—to worry about him." Miriam steered the topic away from her concerns: "Is Galilee still conspiring against him?"

Yohanan ben Zaccai shook his head, accepting her deflection. "What you have likely heard is not true—Galilee is mostly with Yosef. A very few towns fail to support him, and only one leader continues to stir trouble—Yohanan of Gischala remains a prickly thorn."

His silence at that point hinted at what Miriam suspected—that prickly thorn was especially dangerous, perhaps poisonous and even worse than it appeared.

"And then there is Shimon ben Gamliel here"—Miriam waved a hand toward the Temple enclosure—"who does not believe in Yosef and wants him removed from command." She caught the priest's surprised look. "I overhear my father, mother, and Matthew discuss what's happening," she explained. "And there's talk among the people—those who listen to Gamliel's rant without waiting for the truth—that Yosef should not command in Galilee. I cannot miss hearing these opinions. But the people do not say such things to our faces. They can believe what they want. If it brings Yosef home, I am for it, no matter the reason or the person who calls for it. Yosef can fight the Romans with us from here, in Jerusalem—where he should be."

They walked for several minutes in silence, and as they reached her house, she gripped the old priest's arm before entering. "Men like Yohanan of Gischala and those who would weaken us by spreading dissension—or those here who collaborate with Romans—they are all just as much our enemy as are the Romans."

Yohanan ben Zaccai paused outside as Miriam stepped into the house, and as she looked back, she saw he shook his head sadly in the aftermath of her bitter words. She herself remembered the hatred in her own voice. He must wonder, "Where has the little girl gone who laughed as I bounced her on my knee? What has happened to her?"

* * *

That evening...

"Rebecca, it's decided"—Mathias leaned toward his wife at the opposite end of the table—"You heard me tell Yohanan this morning that I will go with him tomorrow morning to meet with Shimon ben Gamliel. If the Sanhedrin president doesn't listen to him, I will make him listen to me."

"Then, Matthew will go with you." Rebecca looked at their son and lowered her voice to a command: "You must stay by his side."

"Of course, Mother," Matthew said and turned to his father. "Father, you'll be hard-pressed to get Shimon Gamliel alone... to talk in private." *Much has changed since he was last at the Temple,* Matthew thought. The tensions between the factions had risen even higher, and many who should lead for the good of all, instead sought whichever side benefited them most.

Mathias straightened. "What do you mean?"

"I've talked about Esau ben Beor," Matthew replied, "how he makes me uncomfortable insisting on being involved in things better kept to just a few people. Now he spends a lot of time with Shimon ben Gamliel... he is always with him. It has come to the point that I wonder who is really the president of the Sanhedrin. Even Eleasar ben Ananias has complained to me about ben Beor sitting in on all meetings, even those that do not deal specifically with Jerusalem's defense. He is supervising all the production and delivery of material for the new fortifications."

"Eleasar is not the most diplomatic guard captain—he's not used to dealing with people," Mathias said, "I can sway Shimon—he will listen to me."

Matthew did not refute his father's claim, but he was not so sure. He had learned to his dismay that most people are influenced only by what benefits them. What could Mathias offer Shimon ben Gamliel? A return to rationality? A chance to do what was right for Galilee? Of course, that would extend to being the right thing to aid Jerusalem's defense, as well. He doubted those considerations would serve as an enticement. Even as he questioned his father's belief, he wondered what Esau ben Beor was up to that Gamliel had chosen to so align himself with the man.

Miriam had silently sat across from Matthew through dinner and the conversations afterward. As he had talked, he had looked toward her a few times—to invite her comments. But she had seemed very far away, even as she sparked keen interest at every mention of Esau ben Beor. *Why is that?* Matthew wondered. What did she know and how... and why?

"Mother, I'll go with Father and Matthew, too," Miriam announced, and Mathias started to object, but she continued quickly—"I mean, while they are in their meeting I'll await them in the Court of Women, and after it is over, I will help father so Matthew can attend to his duties."

Somehow, Mathew thought, I expect she has something else in mind, more than just caring for Father.

LXX

JERUSALEM

"It's a beautiful morning."

Miriam looked up as her father slowed and tilted his face toward the sky on his first day outside their home in weeks. His stride was steady, though Matthew had a firm hold of his elbow. Beneath the cloudless blue sky above streets still mostly shrouded in early morning shadows, the shopkeepers were just unfurling their awnings.

It had been a long time since she had considered her surroundings beautiful. For her, the cycle of dawn and day became twilight and night, the warmth fading to the coolness of night. But illness at her father's age must surely bring thoughts of mortality. Now that he had some of his strength back and a purpose for the day, and he could witness and appreciate what she could not.

Except for rare moments, she no longer felt alive, but even with her dead heart, she, too, was filled with a purpose—a grim one. *Will my life always be like this?*

"There's Ehud"—Matthew pointed ahead to where their friend was speaking with a shopkeeper setting up street-side tables with glassware. Miriam dropped back as they neared Ehud, trailing her father, hoping Matthew would keep walking.

"Good morning!" Matthew called out cheerfully, then stopped, which meant she and her father must stop, too.

Ehud turned toward them, and to her discomfort, she noted his eyes went first to her and then to Matthew and Mathias. "Good morning—it's good to see you, sir, and that you're better." He turned from Mathias to grin at Matthew. "Hello, my friend.... and"—his eyes went again to her—"Miriam, how are you?"

In the silence, Mathias glanced at her and then nudged her with an elbow, raising an eyebrow as he often had when she was a child. She smiled for him, and reluctantly greeted Ehud. "I'm well, Ehud." She felt her father's elbow move lightly and added, "How are you?"

Ehud's grin became a softer smile. "I'm good, as you can see"—he half-turned back toward the shop's tables—"These are the first results from the small glassworks I've set up."

"So, will your father bring his business and all your family back to Jerusalem?" Mathias asked bluntly.

The smile dimmed as Ehud blinked and seemed uncomfortable. "We hope so, but so much is unsure and unknown... you know... about what's to come." He paused and met Mathias's look. "Is there any hope for peace with the Romans?"

Miriam stiffened as Matthew shot her a quick look then squinted back at Ehud. "Present circumstances and attitudes make that seem unlikely, but we can hope."

Mathias shook his head as if casting a wager against that possibility. "We must go, Matthew. Ehud, perhaps you will come to see us. I'd like to hear more of your father... he was a friend." The last carried regret for something gone but also hope it might return.

"I'd like that." Ehud then spoke to Matthew: "Let's get together soon and catch up." He avoided looking at Miriam and nodded to Mathias. "Thank you, sir... I'd like our families to be friends again."

They walked in silence for many minutes through the marketplace, climbed the stairs, and crossed the bridge, then entered the Temple enclosure at the Kipunos gate. "I see someone has finally done it"—Mathias pointed at the damaged golden eagle, the sign over the entrance stating that the Temple was under the protection of Rome.

"Its message no longer holds true, Father," Matthew said as they climbed the stone stairway. "We must protect the Temple and its treasure from those the eagle stands for. There is no one else to count on for help."

At the top, they followed the portico eastward along the northern wall, passing column after column carved from single massive blocks of white marble, the shading ceiling above them also serving as the walkway above—thick cedar tightly joined in a seeming continuous sheet of polished, curiously graven wood. The markings were too high for most people to discern their meaning or appreciate the craftsmanship, but its richness added to the atmosphere of power and elegance—the mysteries—the Jews so revered in their Temple.

Each one lost in his or her individual thoughts, the family, had reached the spot near the steps to the Lower City, where Miriam had killed the traitor Yehudah ish Krioth. Then Zechariah had died saving her from the Roman mercenary intent on killing her in revenge. And she had brought it full circle by taking that life, too, with her own hands. She had not been in this spot since that day.

"Miriam?" Matthew called.

Shaking off the memory, she looked up and saw that Mathias and Matthew were now over at the foot of the Mishnah, also called the *chel*, a terrace that ran along the outside of the wall of the inner Temple complex. Yohanan ben Zaccai had joined them there.

Matthew beckoned to her, and she followed as they ascended the terraced steps to enter the inner courts.

As they crossed the Court of Women and approached the gate of Nicanor, Mathias and Yohanan were slightly ahead of Miriam, who walked beside Matthew. For Miriam, the gate's name recalled the brawny centurion Yosef had introduced to his family at Passover over a year ago. The two men might be fast friends after surviving a shipwreck together, but being so close to a Roman soldier again had made her skin crawl. And the Roman lady, the soldier accompanied—also a survivor of the shipwreck—Yosef seemed fond of her. *Doesn't he understand they are our enemies?*

"What is it?" Miriam looked at Matthew, reflexively answering the question he had whispered and to which she had not paid attention.

"That's Esau ben Beor standing with Shimon ben Gamliel," he pointed to where the Sanhedrin president was talking with a burly thick-shouldered man. They were close enough now to hear Esau say to Gamliel, "You are of the line of King David, are you not? Then act as strong as he was, become as strong"—he cut off his admonition when he saw Mathias and Yohanan.

"Shimon, we must speak with you," Yohanan said as they went up to the two men.

"What about?" Shimon ben Gamliel replied curtly. Esau ben Beor remained beside the Sanhedrin president and stared coolly at Mathias.

"—A matter that concerns only you, Shimon." Mathias shrugged off Matthew's hand and stepped closer and locked eyes with ben Gamliel.

The Sanhedrin president's eyes slid sideways toward Esau ben Beor, then back to Mathias and Yohanan. "Mathias, there are no private matters to discuss. Now we must go to our council meeting to review progress on Jerusalem's defense." Shimon ben Gamliel and ben Beor turned from them and walked through the gate, then continued into the narrow hall filled with the elegant columns bordering the Court of the Israelites. Within that court was the Court of the Priests, and there was located the altar of sacrifice. Beyond the altar, toward the western wall of the Temple enclosure, was the Hall of Hewn Stone and the meeting place for the Sanhedrin. Miriam could never enter these places, and only the priests could venture farther than most men of Israel.

"I told you, Father," Matthew said. "ben Gamliel won't meet alone with anyone, and Eleasar ben Ananias told me that Esau ben Beor has usurped this morning's briefing. It was supposed to be about local defenses."

Mathias nodded and looked at ben Zaccai. "Yohanan, did you ask them to come, as I wanted?" He took his friend's arm to steady himself as they entered the gate.

"Yes, Mathias. I brought the envoys here before meeting you, and they await your call for them in the Chamber of Broken Knives."

"Who is the 'them' you ask about, Father?" Matthew asked.

"That chamber seems appropriate, considering"—Mathias nodded at Yohanan and glanced at Matthew—"How appropriate it is for Shimon ben Gamliel's envoys to wait there. They failed, too, to remove Yosef, and it is right that they should wait for me where the dull knives are stored until they can be made useful for Temple service. "Do you think they will speak out, Yohanan?"

"As we traveled from Gabara, I discussed with all of them what had happened. I believe those who have shown up here will report the truth of what they've seen and heard in Galilee."

Mathias nodded again. "Good." He looked to Matthew—"You'll hear from 'they' and 'them' shortly, son."

"Father?"

They all turned toward Miriam.

"I'll be here"—she waved a hand toward the central area of the Court of Women—"or atop Solomon's Porch."

"We'll come to find you when we are done," Matthew said over his shoulder as they passed through the gate of Nicanor.

LXXI

JERUSALEM

The meeting hall and chambers for the Sanhedrin had been built into a wall of the Temple—half-inside and half-outside the space designated as the sanctuary. The sanctuary itself had been constructed according to the law from uncut stones untouched by iron, and the Hall of Hewn Stone functioned as a sovereign court and the center of political and religious leadership in Judea. With the coming of the rebellion, it was also the principal center where factions vied for power—whether out of a belief they best represented the will of the people or deluded because their control served their own interests. The coming of the Romans had done little to reduce internal maneuvering and manipulation.

"I must speak"—Mathias interrupted the senior members of the Sanhedrin, who turned as he entered the hall with Yohanan ben Zaccai and Matthew on either side—"on a matter of public import."

"This council session is for the discussion of work being done for Jerusalem's defenses, Mathias," Shimon ben Gamliel announced. "You can speak another time." He turned to resume from the point at which he had been interrupted.

Matthew could not stop his glare at Shimon and Esau ben Beor, who sat side by side at the head of the chamber. But Mathias spoke before Matthew had the opportunity to say something he should not.

"I will speak now," said Mathias, undeterred, "and then you can continue your meeting."

Eleasar ben Ananias scowled at the Sanhedrin president. "I welcome hearing Mathias... let him speak."

A flush of anger bloomed on ben Beor's face.

"Some"—Mathias pointed solely at ben Gamliel—"have heard Yohanan ben Zaccai report of what happened recently at Gabara. But not all of you have... and you should since all of Galilee is important to Jerusalem's defense. Yohanan, please come forward and give your report to these men of the Sanhedrin."

After taking the floor and speaking several minutes, ben Zaccai concluded with a description of the thousands of Galileans who had cheered Yosef. "So, those who have seen it in person believe Yosef can lead Galilee. He has gained their trust."

"And he should have yours," Mathias's voice echoed in the chamber.

"Do you have proof of this letter that casts suspicion on Yohanan of Gischala?" Shimon ben Gamliel asked.

"As I told you before, Yosef has that letter, Shimon," ben Zaccai replied.

"So, you make claims without proof."

"Yosef wanted to keep it safe, and my good word is my proof."

"Safe from who, Yohanan?" ben Gamliel turned from the old priest to Yosef's father. "Mathias, we are all on the same side. We all face the same threat. Do we not?"

"That letter alone proves that some are not on 'our' side, Shimon," Mathias replied. "Some play their own game. That letter is addressed to Yohanan of Gischala and confirms his plan to continue to spread dissension among Galileans, to increase their distrust of my son, and to convince them to follow someone who it now seems could be favored by the Romans."

"Yet, we cannot see that letter with our own eyes." Shimon shook his head and held out his hands, palm up.

"Your envoys—those you, Shimon, sent to remove Yosef—have seen the letter. They will attest to its contents."

"But they are not here to speak."

"Some of them are"—Mathias turned to ben Zaccai—"Please bring them." Then he swung back to the Sanhedrin president. "Some have disregarded the instructions given them when they returned... instructions to leave Jerusalem." Mathias studied ben Gamliel for a moment. "They are willing to speak before you. They did not flee as Yohanan of Gischala did when my son tried to confront him with his treason. Your envoys heard the people of Galilee, and each of them saw and read the letter. They met the man who carried it—a man coming from Roman territory, who had been paid in Roman coin."

The sound of two dozen men entering the hall made all turn to face them. "Each of you," instructed Mathias, "please tell all here what you witnessed."

* * *

Though Mathias now sat as each man stood before them and confirmed all that ben Zaccai had reported, Matthew noticed how his father seemed to weaken. When the last man finished, Mathias struggled to stand, Matthew, helping. "What do you say now, Shimon?" Mathias's voice shook.

Esau ben Beor, who had not spoken, leaned toward the Sanhedrin president and whispered in his ear.

Shimon ben Gamliel straightened in his seat. "Yosef ben Mathias shall remain in command in Galilee. But this letter you and the envoys speak of, the letter you believe came from the Romans—we believe it to be a ruse, a ploy to sow discord and suspicion among us." He stood and dismissed the Sanhedrin—"We will break for now and reconvene this afternoon to discuss the matters we had planned for this morning."

He remained standing and watched as the hall emptied, and Matthew and ben Zaccai waited for the crowd to clear, then rose from their bench to leave.

"Mathias"—Shimon ben Gamliel called to them. Behind him, Esau ben Beor retreated into the small alcove off the main chamber. "You have what you wanted"—he turned to frown at Matthew—"and I look forward to reports of your progress—with Esau—with the plans to protect the Temple treasure."

* * *

From Solomon's Porch, Miriam could see Jerusalem's sprawl to the south. The double-high, double-wide colonnade lined the sanctuary's entire southern wall, with a walking lookout platform on the roof. Beyond her line of sight, she could envision the uppermost part of the terraced western ridge of the Tyropoeon Valley that ran through the center of the city and climbed to the Upper City of the affluent citizens of Jerusalem—there white marble villas and palaces stood out like patches of snow—and two large arched passageways spanned the valley, crossing from the Upper City to the Temple. The Lower City, south of the Temple, was filled with limestone houses, yellow-brown from years of sun and wind. Narrow, unpaved streets and houses sloped downward as if sliding into the Tyropoeon Valley.

The two cities were like two sides of the same coin. Off to the east was the garden at the foot of the Mount of Olives, just beyond the Kidron Valley—*Gat Shmanim*, or Gethsemane as the Romans called it. Mathias had told her the story of the rabbi Yeshua ish Nazrat—whose followers still believed him to be the messiah. He had been arrested there over three decades before. The Romans had horrifically executed him by crucifixion, as they had so many other Jewish patriots and bandits over the years. It was a brutal way—one of many they used—to intimidate by fear those needing to be controlled.

Miriam wondered at the concept of a new life held by those followers of Yeshua ish Nazrat... to rise from the darkness into the light. She turned from the view and scanned the Court of Women.

The three men she awaited were strolling toward the steps up to Solomon's Porch. A minute later, Matthew came onto the landing of the porch and waved to her. She went to join him and had a fleeting thought of Ehud.

LXXII

At first, Nicanor had been surprised to find the horse trader that had sold him Abigieus still near Antioch. But then, seeing the man's robe of excellent quality and good mood, he realized this war—not yet fully unleashed—brought him wealth supplying mounts and pack animals for the Romans and allied forces. The trader now held the largest auctions in Antioch and made direct sales to the Roman army. And he remembered Nicanor and Abigieus: "The finest horse I ever sold, centurion... you have to attest what a fine animal you bought from me." The man's glee had slipped at learning of Abigieus's death but then returned when he realized Nicanor needed another horse.

The animal presented to Nicanor was as large as Abigieus, and though a mare, even thicker in the chest. Dark-eyed with an ebon-coat from nose to tail, the silky mane slid through Nicanor's fingers and draped like nightfall along the horse's muscular neck.

Nicanor had paid more than he wished for the horse. The trader—flush with prosperity and no longer in a financial bind—saw little need to haggle. But Nicanor had earned more and saved much during his time in the Praetorian Guards. And he liked the glint in the animal's eye and its quick, testing snap at him as he checked the soundness of legs, hooves, and those teeth. The big black mare was young, just reaching mature size. The creature snorted and watched, head turned, and unblinking orbs fixed on Nicanor as he transferred bridle and saddle from the camp stock mount he had ridden to the stables. The camp horse was older, smaller, stolid, and utterly apathetic about Nicanor. This big black studied his every move intently as the man adjusted the bridle and saddle, but let him finish without shifting or blowing restlessly.

Nicanor secured the halter and lead rope to the camp horse, holding the line in one hand as he stepped up and onto the mare. The young horse then proved she was patient... and had been waiting. Nicanor had half-turned in the saddle to wave goodbye to the trader when the black took off like a bolt fired from a crossbow. The sudden surge and slow response from the camp horse yanked Nicanor backward and almost unseated him. He centered and clamped down with his thighs and knees, then eased back with a light pull on the reins. The mare—having tested the man again—responded and slowed to a canter.

277

Nicanor beamed, the seamed scar across his brow pulling down into a chevron. He leaned forward and patted the horse's thick neck as it moved in perfect tempo with the thud of hooves on the hard-packed road. "Give me a day or two, and I'll come up with a name for you, girl...."

* * *

Nicanor's tent was on the east perimeter of the camp, and he was glad Vespasian had let him set up there instead of with the other staff around the central command tent. He could thus avoid the gossip and other chatter of staff officers. But the main reason for his choice was keeping his new mount near him. He wanted to form a bond by tending to the horse himself. After returning the camp mount to the stock pen, he dismounted and began to remove the saddle and blanket to groom his new horse.

"That's a big, dark one...."—a familiar voice sounded behind him.

"Aulus, what do you here?" Nicanor turned to the friend he had known since his early days in the 12th Legion.

"I heard you were on General Vespasian's staff and thought I'd come to see if you had picked up any new scars in Rome. I've heard many men say the wenching and drinking is a dangerous duty there."

"No"—Nicanor rubbed the long scar on his face—"I allow new wounds only when you're around to sew me up. I trust no one else." He grasped his friend's hand. "How is the 12th, and why aren't you with the legion in Ptolemais?"

"The men are still bitter about Beth Horon. Their physical injuries are healed, but they remain heartsick. All are glad Cestius Gallus is gone, but many of us feel that Galerius Senna is little better as a military commander... and he is a far worse man. He focuses more on polishing his armor—or having that done for him, I should say—than on working with the men. Lord Gallus at least would walk among us, ask questions, and just talk. Senna has no interest in that—he is above us, plain soldiers. He prefers to stay in his tent either alone or in discussion with Tyrannius Priseus—who is still the Camp-Prefect.

"Or Senna spends time in town with officials and other wealthy Romans—there and along the coast to Caesarea." Aulus gave Nicanor a half-grin. "Lord Titus stopped on his way to Antioch for provisions—you know he's commanding three legions for the Judea campaign, right? Lord Senna all but demanded he accompany him to meet with General Vespasian. Lord Titus gave him an hour to be ready or be left behind. My *contubernia* was near where they met, and Galerius Senna ordered the eight of us to serve as his escort. So, here I am."

"What's your impression of Lord Titus?" Nicanor asked.

"He is nothing like Galerius Senna. While we were at sea, he ate with his men. When we boarded, he made a point of including us. He met separately with each of us from the 12th and asked about what happened in Jerusalem and at Beth Horon. He made sure not to cast blame nor dishonor upon us. His questions were not idle—he was considering the tactics of the rebels and the outcome. He understood what we told him. He has sharp eyes—and comments."

"Interesting—he sounds much like his father, then." Nicanor stripped the bridle from the horse and slipped a halter on to replace it. "And how is Sayid—remember the young auxiliary you patched up along with Abigieus?" He patted the horse, "What would you call this one?"

"Too bad about Abigieus," Aulus said, then gestured at the black horse—"So, you chose a mare... this one's big and dark." Aulus stepped closer, and the horse's eyes locked on him, wary but unafraid. "She has an ominous look, too... like when the air changes to foretell the coming of a storm, *magnus tenebris*... like a thundercloud looming in the sky."

Nicanor laughed. "My friend, I think you have given her a name—*Tempestas*... the goddess of storms she shall be."

Aulus held the horse's head by the halter as Nicanor rubbed her down with the blanket. "You asked about that Syrian auxiliary...."

"Yes, how is he? I look forward to seeing him in Ptolemais." Nicanor glanced at his friend as he moved around the horse.

"He has not been caught yet, and it is best he is not. Lord Senna would have him executed. Your friend should not return if he wants to live."

Nicanor turned from the horse with a puzzled expression. "Caught... executed... what do you mean?"

"I thought you knew—that you assumed he had been captured and held for punishment. Shortly after you left for Rome, he disappeared and has not been seen since. Once Cestius Gallus left for Antioch, formally turning over command of the legion, Galerius Senna announced and sent dispatches to all units that Sayid is a deserter and can be killed on sight."

A camp runner came to a stop in a swirl of dust. "Centurion... " he said, looking at Nicanor.

"Yes, what is it?" Nicanor blinked, his thoughts still on what Aulus had just told him.

"General Vespasian calls for you to attend a meeting at the command tent."

Nicanor surveyed his worn field tunic and breeches. "When does the general require me?"

"Right now, centurion. I will tell him you are on your way." The runner turned and trotted back into camp.

Nicanor wiped his brow with a sleeve. "Aulus, can you take care of Tempestas?" He gestured at the animal's provisions he had prepared earlier and stowed beside his tent.

Aulus nodded. "Surely, and I will wait a while to see if you get back in time to talk more... I want to hear about Rome."

* * *

The sun had long set, and the dark night had fallen before Nicanor returned. The meeting had lasted longer than would be expected just for Vespasian to introduce his son. Titus struck Nicanor as a younger and leaner version of his father, and he clearly did not mind the centurion's appearance. He had greeted Nicanor: "I have heard good things about you."

Nicanor had left the meeting agreeing with Aulus—Titus asked the questions a soldier and a good battlefield leader would ask. He felt much better about being assigned to serve under Titus but still reserved his opinion until he was able to see more of the man.

Back at his tent, he found Aulus had erected a canopy and lean-to secured to the four tall posts sunk next to his tent. Underneath, Tempestas chewed mouthfuls of fodder next to a large, now-empty goat-hide bucket of water. The horse's dark eyes reflected the flickering light from a large lantern Aulus had secured to the outermost post. Nicanor stroked the horse's neck and felt the animal relax, its breathing settling into a deep rhythm.

General Vespasian had insisted Nicanor join him and his son for dinner, and Nicanor wished that meal could have settled with his thoughts so he could sleep. He had an early staff meeting for planning the route to Ptolemais and to set the order of battle of the allied forces marching with them into Galilee. But since Aulus had mentioned it, he could not stop wondering what had happened to Sayid. His mother was in Laodicea—should he search for him there to warn him before they marched to Ptolemais? No. If Sayid was there... better to let him remain. Nicanor prayed Sayid was alive, and that he would not try to rejoin the legion.

LXXIII

"Lord Florus, I have a staff meeting shortly with my commanders." Vespasian did not ask what Gessius Florus wanted, knowing the man would immediately bring it up. He nodded to his aide Gaheris Clineas to let Florus into the section of his command tent partitioned for his office and sleeping quarters.

"I understand, general. This will take only a moment,"—Florus glanced aside at the aide—"if we could talk privately."

"Gaheris, let me know when all the staff is here for the briefing," Vespasian said, then sat behind his campaign desk and studied Gessius Florus. He was still unsure what to make of this man who Emperor Nero apparently favored for some reason. "Well?"

Florus stepped closer toward the desk. "What if I told you it was possible to have Galilee surrender?"

Vespasian shook his head. "You have declared that before, but my plan remains unchanged."

"I don't think we have discussed any of the details of what I stated, general"—Florus pulled a chair out and sat in it, not waiting to be invited.

A vexed expression formed on Vespasian's face. "What do you mean?"

"There is a strong possibility we can arrange the surrender of Galilee before any conflict arises with the Galileans."

"How could that happen, Lord Florus?" Vespasian picked up the nicked and scarred wooden cudgel from his desk. Leaning back, he tapped its tapered, bronze-tipped and ferruled end into the palm of his right hand. "And you refer to the Galileans as if they are separate from the rebels we face. Are they not joined as one... all Jews—Judeans—who revolt against Rome?"

"The Galileans are mostly Jews, general... but not necessarily aligned with the rebels in Jerusalem. Galilee and Jerusalem are distinctly different regions and people. Many Galileans share a great loathing of Jerusalem—they see Jerusalem wishing to rule over them."

"How can you assure a surrender, solely by the Galileans, that is honest and not a ploy, a decoy to make us vulnerable to attack?" For a moment, Vespasian considered whether such a thing had happened with Cestius Gallus, if he'd been lulled into a belief a peaceful resolution was possible, to the point that he let his guard down. He must speak more with Nicanor—see what he knew about the strength of the factions among the rebels.

"When dealing with these people, nothing is sure or certain, general. But I know that dissension exists. It is not just in Galilee, but within Jerusalem as well. I believe many of the people can be won over to break from Jerusalem. One way to do that is to capture or kill the current military commander in Galilee, someone who was put in place by Jerusalem. A strike against the military commander in Galilee could remove the tie of the Galileans with Jerusalem against Rome. If you cut off the head, the body dies, general.

"There are ways we could then convince the Galileans that their commander was a traitor all along. That, sir, will drive a wedge between Galilee and Jerusalem that cannot be dislodged."

"General, the staff is ready," Clineas called from the entrance.

Vespasian was glad for a means to break off the conversation. Duplicity was one thing he detested in Rome's leaders. "Lord Florus, my plan remains the same"—Vespasian rose and lifted his loculus from the table behind him. Tucking the satchel under one arm, he walked into the larger meeting area, to a sizable map-covered table where Titus and Nicanor and the rest of the staff awaited him. As they entered, Vespasian saw Nicanor's eyes narrow when he saw Gessius Florus.

"General"—Florus stopped beside Vespasian—"may I travel with you to Ptolemais?"

Vespasian nodded and noticed Florus exchanging a look with Galerius Senna. "Gaheris," the general said, "arrange a horse and orderly for Lord Florus, and any equipment he might require, so he can join us." He turned to Florus—"We march tomorrow."

* * *

The briefing had concluded, and only three men remained around the table. The legion and unit markers Vespasian had used in Rome stood at various positions on the map, and trailing behind them were smaller indicators of the march route. Flags marked points where the forces would camp overnight.

"So, with Agrippa's troops and allies, we will have a force of 60,000 men"—Vespasian glanced at his son—"You will sail today for Azzah and take your legions north. The 15th Apollinaris will join with the 12th Fulminata in Ptolemais, forming our main center of operations until we secure Galilee. The 10th Fretensis and 5th Macedonica will move to Legio—occupying the Roman camp Cestius

Gallus vacated—and pull legionaries into Ptolemais. This secures our southern exposure until we wheel toward Jerusalem."

Vespasian pondered again what the former commander of the 12th Legion might have told him about his retreat from Jerusalem, information that was not in the reports he had received. Something— he was certain—something had driven Cestius Gallus's odd command decisions.

"Titus, it's a six-day ship transit for you from here to Azzaah and your legions nearby, and then four days to fast march the 15th to Ptolemais. A day less to Legio for the 5th Legion." Vespasian turned to Nicanor—"You have force-marched before with allied units— Agrippa's especially. What can we count on as their best pace? Roman legionaries can cover the distance from Antioch to Ptolemais in seven or eight days at the most."

"They're not legionaries, general... you should add at least a couple of days for them."

"So"—he looked from Nicanor back to Titus—"in ten days all legions, auxiliaries, and our allied forces should be positioned where I want them."

"Yes, general," Titus nodded.

"Nicanor, do you agree it is better to work our way through Galilee first? And that we should not bypass Galilee to drive directly to Jerusalem?"

"Yes, general. The rebels have a few competent combat commanders that will take every advantage. They are familiar with the terrain, and they are able as small units to strike quickly and minimize their losses by spreading out into the countryside to reform, then attack any weaknesses in our formations. So you must make them flock to their strongholds—fixed points they must defend—and there we can bring their walls down upon them and take out the leaders."

"If their leaders are eliminated, will their people surrender?"

"I don't know, general. The Judeans are difficult people to assess. Some are very strong-willed and will not give up. Others are weak and driven by personal needs or gain. The latter will go whichever way the winds blow them—any way that serves their interest in profit or survival. The Judeans can be complex and confusing, as my friend Yosef used to tell me."

"Yosef is the Jew from the shipwreck? The one you parlayed with in Jerusalem—at the order of Cestius Gallus?"

"Yes, general. Yosef's family are priests and civic leaders in Jerusalem, and he told me Jerusalem's internal politics often interfere with rational decisions. That has led them to mistakes and misjudgment. Back to your question... if you remove their competent leaders, all the rebels will be far less effective in combat. While they may not surrender, they will die more quickly and kill fewer of our men."

Not that different from what Gessius Florus just told me, Vespasian thought. *I will speak again with this man on the march to Ptolemais.* "Then, we are set," Vespasian announced, turning to Titus. "I'll see you in Ptolemais,"—he gripped his son's shoulder.

"Yes, general." Titus bowed his head as Vespasian turned and entered his private quarters.

* * *

Nicanor was curious why Titus never referred to Vespasian as "Father." His address was always formal—as a junior to a senior officer.

"You did a fine job with the plan," Titus said, gesturing at the map.

"It helps to have traveled much of it before," Nicanor said. *What happened in Florus's meeting with Vespasian?* He had watched Florus's eyes go directly to Galerius Senna when Florus and Vespasian entered the staff meeting. He trusted neither Florus nor Senna.

"You dislike staff meetings, don't you?" Titus asked.

"They're necessary, Lord Titus."

"Please... unless we are at some function or in the field—in private, just call me Titus." He studied the brawny centurion—"You are more comfortable in the field, right?"

"Yes. I'm not much for talk, and I'm more used to getting things done with this"—Nicanor patted his gladius. He was one of the few who wore his at all times, even while in camp. He held a finger to his temple—"And with this." He then slowly brought his hand to his heart. "But most of all... with this. The gladius, the mind, the heart—they're all I have that I value... in myself and in others."

Titus nodded and held his hand out—"Nicanor, those are the things I value, too. I look forward to seeing you in Ptolemais."

Nicanor watched the young man leave and realized what he liked about him, and why he—in public, or privately with others present—did not speak familiarly with his father: Titus was not a general's son—he was a soldier.

LXXIV

Maybe it's my age, Vespasian thought, as the growing shadows of twilight encouraged the lighting of lanterns. Or perhaps it was the time since his last military campaign or the break from Rome's intrigues while in retirement that had heightened his perception. But something about this campaign suggested some hand tugging strings behind a curtain. Either someone was controlling Gessius Florus to influence Vespasian's decisions for the coming combat against the rebels... or Florus was seeking his own purposes. Had Cestius Gallus been entangled in those strings? Was that what had tripped him up and led to his downfall. *And what of his death?* Vespasian almost whispered aloud. The darkness gathered as he sat thinking about that, then he called for his aide: "Gaheris...."

The man appeared almost instantly. "Yes, general?"

"Send a runner to Governor Mucianus and tell him I will dine with him this evening."

* * *

"So, you chose not to move into the governor's domus?" Vespasian eyes swept the dining area and lingered on the broad open terrace that overlooked the city. This residence sat upon the same ridge as did the official governor's domicile of Cestius Gallus, but this was smaller and more easterly, built on a lower shelf carved from the mountainside.

"Too much of the man and his Lady Octavia remains within it—it is as if she left quickly. Perhaps when she settles in Rome, she will send for their personal possessions"—Gaius Mucianus handed another goblet of wine to Vespasian over plates now emptied of food.

"Did you find out anything about Gallus's death?"

"You mean anything inexplicable... no. I had men speak with the servants who had remained here with family, choosing not to go with Lady Octavia. They said the dead woman found beside Lord Gallus's body was a servant who had recently fallen out of grace with Lady Octavia and was—as they put it—an unpleasant person to begin with. She had not been selected to go to Rome with the lady. Perhaps Cestius Gallus found her stealing once Octavia left. Perhaps he

285

punished her in anger and then committed suicide rather than face the emperor's judgment."

"But why strangle the girl with his own hands?"

Mucianus shrugged. "I don't know, general. Did these questions prompt you to accept my open dinner invitation?"

"Partly," answered Vespasian. "Though we both know of many who've run afoul of emperors, many who have chosen suicide as their atonement, or as a means of escape from a more painful death. But it strikes me that Lord Gallus had more to say before he would have faced his punishment at the command of Emperor Nero. By all accounts, he and Lady Octavia were happy and still loved each other." He paused to let that thought take its space in the room.

"Did he know she had already left Antioch?" he continued. "If so, there was no need for him to come here... why not kill himself in Ptolemais, if that was his intent? Or if he did not know she was gone, why kill himself without finding out what happened to her? If she left him a note explaining her departure, where's the note?" Vespasian emptied the goblet and set it on the table. "But perhaps the answers to my questions are unimportant at this point. Have you any news from Rome?"

"Only that many are displeased with Nero... especially at his decision to visit Greece. It is unseemly to be feted there, while his people protest—when there is so much that requires attention in Rome and within the empire. The Arval Brethren report the growing unrest and are increasingly concerned that the old ways that made Rome strong are now at great risk of being lost or destroyed. The emperor does not seem to value the sanctity of oaths and rituals, the *pignora imperii*, nor the sacred objects. The *fratres arvales* also tell me that much of the enmity among the people is sown by the resurgence of Gaius Piso's supporters—their failed conspiracy never met punishment by Nero."

"Is it known who they are?" Vespasian picked up the empty goblet and rotated it back and forth in his hands, shaking his head to decline the offer to refill it.

"I have suspicions"—Gaius smiled at the general's quizzical expression—"suspicions that are best kept until I know more about the political situation. I know you have little interest in that."

"—Only if it should affect my family or military decisions." Vespasian rose from the table and walked out onto the terrace to stand at the balustrade. The lights of nighttime Antioch spread before him. Just beyond the city, the glow of the encampment's cook fires was beginning to transform into reddish embers. He recalled his last meeting with Emperor Nero.

The emperor had told him that removing Cestius Gallus from command was the right decision, and then he had asked Nero why Florus had not been recalled to Rome for his part in fueling the fire of open rebellion. Nero had replied: "Lord Florus is to collect what is owed to the empire. Your job is to subdue the rebels and defeat the rebellion. Ensure Lord Florus has your support to do his job. Can you do that, General Vespasian? This job the empire requires of you?"

Those were not a questioning of his expected duty but clear directions from the emperor and a veiled threat if he proved inadequate for the task. Recalling that last meeting with Nero, Vespasian gripped the stone handrail with both hands. He had always done what the empire asked of him, and he would do his duty. He had no doubts he would crush and punish the rebels. They must show other provinces the futility of revolt against Rome. But what if what was asked of him was not just for the good of the empire—was more for the benefit of a select few?

He noticed off to one side of the terrace, between two couches, a gameboard. He walked over to examine it. Made of flat stone mounted on a low pedestal, its counters were one set of black stones and the other white, like his own set back home in Falacrine. He looked down at the *latrunculi* board and thought of Antonia. That last night he was home, she had said, "You play this game well, and just as on the field of war... you win much more than you lose. Before you leave for Rome, I want you to remember something and always keep it in mind. Focus on who you are and put this in perspective, even if any coming battles are not to be fought on fields of dirt, grass, and stone." Her last word—as she paused to study him for a moment, a smile on her lips—still lingered: "Do not become drawn into the disorder. Do your duty. Win the battles before you... and should a storm sweep through Rome... let it all pass you by. Then return here to your family and fortune... and to me." She had finished and hugged him tightly.

Vespasian's reverie faded with the feeling of Antonia's arms around him, and he turned to the governor who had followed him onto the terrace, speaking words he had not caught. "What did you say, Gaius?"

"I was just saying that I wondered if the hastae martiae in the Shrine of Mars in Rome are shaking yet. It seems they might yet tremble."

Vespasian nodded, feeling that likely too, but he would leave the political rumblings in Rome to the politicians. As Antonia had advised, he would not become drawn into the disorder. All he cared about was letting it—whatever it might be—all come to pass. As long as he could focus on the battles to come, to defeat the rebels, and then return to his home and Antonia, he would be satisfied. But was he one of the counters—a piece in the game—or was he someone who had control over moving the pieces? That question troubled him.

LXXV

PTOLEMAIS

"How is Lady Cleo?" Sayid asked Elian as the boy entered the second level room carrying an armload of driftwood. It had been days since Sayid had seen her—not since the morning after the storm.

"This is drier and won't make as much smoke," said Elian as he set the wood in the corner across from the remnants of a small fire Sayid had let go out before dawn. "Lady Cleo told me to tell you all is well, and that Lord Florus is still away, which is good. But since the night of the storm, Glaucio is watching her—he walks through the house at night. So she goes out only to shoot or to walk on the beach. She doesn't want to come here. Glaucio follows her, or Eris from the kitchen. She says maybe they will get tired of watching her."

Elian came over to Sayid and squatted on his heels to check the bandage. He carefully loosened it and looked at the wound. "Lady Cleo worries the wound will sicken, but she says if there is no redness, that means the medicine salve she had me buy in Ptolemais is working. When I come back tonight with your food, I'll bring more—and fresh bandages."

"Have you heard anything of the Romans or the 12th Legion's movements?" Sayid asked. "Any news at all?"

"No"—the boy shook his head—"Since Lord Florus has been gone, no one has called, and Glaucio now sends a cart to town for supplies... so, Lady Cleo has no one she can talk to."

With nothing else to do, Sayid had spent the days in thought about what could be done to get Lady Cleo away from her husband—and away to safety. There was only one way—he must return to the legion. In Laodicea, he had heard the talk about General Vespasian, and much of it had been about the man's honesty and fairness, especially when dealing with the men serving under his command. The men who shared the stories, and a few who claimed to have served under him, also talked of his regard for facts and not gossip or opinion.

If Vespasian was the man they described—someone who could see into the truth of things before committing an act or making a decision—then he was the one Lady Cleo should tell her story to... and share her letters and information about Gessius Florus. Sayid could tell General Vespasian about how Lady Octavia had also stressed the need for Sayid to get the messages to her husband before he attacked

289

Jerusalem. He would explain how he had delivered them to Cestius Gallus after the attack had started and how the letters seemed to have an impact on him. He stopped the attack and attempted to talk to the rebels and secure a peaceful resolution.

He could also tell Vespasian about his special mission from Cestius Gallus—to take his notes and a copy of his complete report for the emperor to Lady Octavia, for safekeeping. Lord Gallus had not told him why, and he would never reveal such to a mere auxiliary, but Sayid had seen the worry in his eye that showed the importance of his task. Sayid could provide General Vespasian an idea of the contents, and then the general could discuss it with Lord Gallus or even Lady Octavia.

If the general was the man he had heard about, Vespasian could protect Lady Cleo from Gessius Florus until her long-term safety was worked out. But Sayid needed to know when Vespasian would arrive Ptolemais. And to do that, he must get to the port—the center of all incoming and outgoing gossip and news of the empire. Surely some captain or sailors had heard where General Vespasian was right now and when he was expected to arrive.

"Elian, tonight you must bring me some clothes," Sayid said, checking his filthy but serviceable breeches. "At least find me a clean tunic and a cloak with a cowl."

The boy was puzzled. "Days ago, I brought two more blankets for you. I know they are from the donkeys in the stable, but they're clean and will keep you warm at night."

"No, Elian. I need clothes because I must go into town and learn what I can of General Vespasian and the legion's status. I can't go looking like this."

"You're still hurt, Sayid—you can't do that!" Elian protested, shaking his head. "You must stay here as Lady Cleo told you."

"It's the only way, Elian. I have to get Lady Cleo to someone who can protect her... and the only one with that kind of authority is General Vespasian." —*If I don't get locked up or worse before I can see him—and if he will listen to me*, Sayid thought.

"No, Sayid... I can't"—the boy had not stopped shaking his head—"Lady Cleo will not like this."

"Elian, do you care for Lady Cleo? Do you not want her to be safe from harm?"

"Yes. She is nice to me... the only one who is... other than you." The boy was white-faced as he met Sayid's gaze.

"Then help me help her.... you must, Elian. It's the only way." Sayid tried to ignore the terrifying thought of what would happen to him after he took Lady Cleo to Vespasian.

* * *

That evening, in the wind's lull, his hearing heightened, Sayid heard below him the shuffling steps of someone larger than Elian cross the ground floor and begin climbing the steps from the first level. With a groan, levering himself erect with his good shoulder, he stood clasping his right arm to his chest and, and with his left hand, picked up a forearm's length of driftwood from the pile and faced the entrance to the room.

"What are you doing on your feet and holding that piece of wood?"

"Lady Cleo! I was expecting Elian, but it did not sound like him"—Sayid lowered the chunk of driftwood and dropped it back on the pile.

"You must lie down, Sayid... or at least sit and be still so I can check your wound." Cleo carried a basket with fruit, salve, and several folded squares of cloth, and over her shoulder, she had slung a goatskin bladder of fresh water.

"But what of Glaucio?"

"A messenger arrived... calling him away to some errand at the port, from what I overheard."

"Then is Eris, the kitchen woman, watching you?"

"I've learned she drinks heavily every moment she can when there's wine at hand, and after Glaucio left, she began exploring a cask of wine she believes won't be missed." Cleo smiled. "Elian watches my watchers and reports on them, but I must be quick." She helped Sayid lower himself to recline against the stone bench beside the ashes of the small fire. "So I came to tend to you and ask you not to do what you told him you must do."

Sayid leaned back and closed his eyes, "Elian told me he would not tell you."

"And he did not. But when I saw him with a bundle of clothing, he couldn't lie to me." She knelt and lifted pieces of the tattered tunic covering the bandage. "You're wound is healing well now, but it will easily tear open—again—if you strain yourself."

"I can walk to the port without doing that,"—he winced as she carefully removed the bandage, parts of it sticking to flesh that tugged at the wound.

"You know it's not a short walk nor an easy one, especially since you need to stay off the road. Florus's men stop and question everyone. Our suppliers were glad to no longer have to come out here and deal with that. And what if you have to run... or defend yourself?"

"I won't have to do either, Lady Cleo. I'll be careful."

"You can't know that—and for you to even consider doing something like this—while planning to not tell me—shows you are not taking care. You're not thinking of the consequences."

"But I am my lady. It's the only way to protect you." He opened his eyes to catch her gaze. "Please let me do this for you."

"Sayid, you need more time to heal, and I need to see if there's more information I can find that is timelier and of value. This General Vespasian may not care what has gone before or care anything about Cestius Gallus's concerns or my own suspicions about my husband's activities since coming to Judea." Cleo dipped a square of clean cloth into a bowl she had filled from the water skin and washed the wound, reapplied a coating of the salve she had brought, and re-bandaged. "There..." She sat back. "I must go soon, but I want you to wait and heal more before trying to go anywhere or do anything. Will you promise me—on your honor—you will stay until we talk about it, agree, and decide together?"

"Yes, my lady...." Sayid was silent for a moment. "Lady Cleo, do you ever dream of what life was like before the shipwreck of the *Salacia*?"

Cleo sighed, "Yes, but if that had not happened, then there are some good things that would never have happened to me."

"Like what?" Sayid closed his eyes again.

"Well, meeting you, and Nicanor... and Yosef. I have not had many friends. Really, I had only one before all of you. You told me Nicanor is in Rome, and I am thankful for that. But I sometimes wonder about Yosef in Jerusalem. I'm glad he is relatively safe there... for now. I pray something can be done before this war reaches him."

Sayid blinked. "Yosef's not in Jerusalem, my lady. I thought I told you—but I must not have—he is the rebel military commander for Galilee. He is in Yotapta... not that far from Ptolemais. That is why I think Vespasian will come here and make Ptolemais his headquarters. He will bring the legions to bear on the rebels in Galilee before attacking Jerusalem. There's nothing I can do to help Yosef. The Fates—and all that has happened since we got to Judea—seem to have fixed that, and nothing will change it. But I can help you even if that means getting you to the man who delivers what the Fates demand. Even if that falls upon our friend Yosef and his people."

LXXVI

SOUTH OF ANTIOCH, THE COASTAL ROAD

When the rider had fallen back to give Nicanor the general's request to join him, the centurion had been thinking about Sayid. As they had passed near Laodicea ad Mare after leaving Antioch two days earlier, Nicanor had wanted to make a brief side trek to see if Sayid was still with his mother, and then catch up with the formation later. But that would have required an explanation he was not ready to give. Now Laodicea was nearly two days behind them—*And that's probably best*, he thought as he reined in Tempestas to match the pace of Vespasian's magnificent white mount at the vanguard. Riding next to the general were Gaheris Clineas and the standard-bearer.

"You called for me, general?"

"Yes, Nicanor"—Vespasian turned to the aide—"Gaheris, you two go ahead of us."

"Yes, general"—the aide caught the bearer's attention, motioned ahead, and nudged his horse into a trot, with the standard-bearer following.

Vespasian slowed his horse to create distance also between them and the main body of the formation so they could speak privately. He glanced over at Nicanor as he flicked a horse-hair whisk against the black flies landing on his perspiring face. "Lord Florus is a man of many questions... and suggestions. This morning he asked why we do not take the road to Damascus, which is better maintained and a somewhat easier ride. I told him your route to Ptolemais was also intended for conditioning our allies—an excellent idea of yours—so necessary. Though it's only our third day, he seemed already saddle-weary and not at all appreciative of his privilege riding—not marching like most of the men." Vespasian's lips curled into the slimmest suggestion of a grin revealed by his helmet's cheek guards being hinged up to let air better circulate.

"He asked if I thought you a good advisor.... and it struck me there was an undercurrent—a tone to his question." Vespasian looked inquisitively at the centurion.

"I don't think Lord Florus likes me," Nicanor said in response to the real question, " and that matters little to me... but I hope that does not cause a problem for you, sir."

"He has been appointed directly by Emperor Nero... in a role with some authority, so I have to listen to the man... consider what he says... to a degree. But why does he seem to dislike you?"

Nicanor replied with most of the truth: "He senses that I do not respect him... something I should have done more to hide, general. It's difficult for me."

"And why do you not respect him?"

"Lord Florus has not earned my respect, general. I think he made some very poor decisions as Procurator in his dealings with the Judeans. He forced a reaction from them that has led to where we are now. I could not prevent my opinion from affecting how I behaved toward him in the past, though I never thought I would have further dealings with him." Nicanor left unsaid that Florus was unworthy of Lady Cleo and—more important to Vespasian—that he had likely undermined Cestius Gallus. Thousands of Roman soldiers had died, hundreds of them under his personal command. *Not to mention Cestius Gallus would not have killed himself—odd that Gessius Florus would show up in Antioch to report the death to the general...*

"You don't have to be involved with him directly, Nicanor... but I do. And indirectly, your opinions, which matter to me, have an impact." They rode in silence for a while. "Setting aside his insistence on marching straight to a siege of Jerusalem... what do you think of Lord Florus's suggestion? I mentioned it to you the morning we left Antioch—he suggests that he could destabilize Galilee, bring it to heel, by striking specifically at rebel leaders?"

"General, there are things I doubt about Lord Florus—mostly his intent—based on some of what he's done in the past. But as I told you after the briefing in Antioch, killing the rebel combat commanders is a sound strategy. If we can find and isolate them, they should become our targets."

"Galerius Senna was with Lord Florus this morning and told me he has confirmed that the headquarters of the military command for Galilee is in a fortified town—Yotapta—and that he had identified the rebel commander for the region."

"That's not far from Ptolemais," said Nicanor, "and if it's true, that rebel leader would be an excellent target for the legions. That should be one of the first objectives."

"When we arrive in Ptolemais before I detach you to serve under my son, we will plan our assault on Yotapta to capture or kill this rebel commander." Vespasian lifted the whisk again to flick at flies. "In Rome, you told me Tigellinus wanted you to send him secretly your private reports of what I am doing. How does that work?"

"Lord Tigellinus told me a man will contact me once you've set up your base camp headquarters. So, I assume that will happen when we reach Ptolemais. That man will give me instructions on the process and take my first report."

"Have you written one yet?"

"No, general. I have not and will not until I discuss it with you."

"Go ahead and write a report about our plan for the Galilee stage of the campaign. Say that our first aim is to attack a rebel stronghold in Yotapta, said to be the headquarters of the region's military commander. That will match what I put in my official report to the emperor, which will also pass through Lord Tigellinus. As the Praetorian Prefect, he will no doubt read it before the emperor does. But in your report to Tigellinus alone, add that Gessius Florus has been meeting privately with me to offer advice about dealing with the Judeans. I want you to always include something that I do not have in my official reports. You and I, and eventually Titus, will coordinate what that is. That should make Tigellinus feel he is getting good service from you, and that opinion may be of help to us at some point."

Nicanor was relieved he had not been asked to do more than tell the truth. "Yes, general.... did Lord Senna say if he knew who the rebel commander was in Yotapta? It's likely Yohanan of Gischala. When I was here before, he had been reported as wielding a lot of influence in Galilee—choosing his home town of Gischala for his headquarters. Or it might be Simon bar Giora, the rebel commander who harried the 12th Legion to and from Jerusalem." Nicanor paused, "It was he who commanded the rebels at Beth Horon and took our aquila. I hope it is him.... nothing would be sweeter than killing him and taking our legion standard from his own dead hands or those of some other rebel."

Vespasian was so silent that Nicanor shifted in his saddle to face him. "General, did Lord Senna know the name of the rebel commander?"

"Yes, centurion"—the general reined in and came to a stop. Nicanor stopped with him, wondering at the expression on Vespasian's face. "The rebel military commander for Galilee we must kill is Yosef ben Mathias... your friend from Jerusalem."

LXXVII

Matthew had almost asked to meet Ehud in the Upper City, but he was glad he had agreed with what Ehud suggested. It was so easy to fall into a routine of the same places and the same faces. The contrast as he had watched the busy people of the Lower City throughout the afternoon had given him a new perspective.

Where he lived, the always-swept-clean streets of the Upper City were long, broad, and lined with the prominent homes of the wealthiest in Jerusalem. The people there were worried about the Romans. But once he descended past the gates from the Upper City, up and down the hills of the Lower City, he was in a warren of sand-strewn streets and alleys. Closest to the Temple, all along the central road, the craftsmen worked, some in open-air shops. Then he came to a colorful bazaar where merchants sold fruits and vegetables, dried fish, and the sacrificial animals raised locally. Other tradesmen offered clothes, perfumes, and jewelry. Off the main street were the manufactories and homes of those workers and their families. The Lower City was full of sensations: the clatter of donkey carts, the enticing smells of cooking food and the sounds of voices of the people enjoying it, the blur of shop owners displaying their wares, the sights and sounds of tradesmen and customers haggling, and the call of women after their quick children. Only on Shabbat were these streets empty and quiet.

Maybe it was because of the influx of people into the Lower City seeking the safety of the city's walls or the plenitude of work and trade opportunities. But those in the Lower City did not talk and debate as many in the Upper City did—as the Sanhedrin did. These were too busy with the making and selling of things... with living. They did not endlessly contemplate the material things they stood to lose when the Romans arrived. They might have fled within these sheltering walls, but they just wished to live.

The Lower City had many taverns that offered fresh or salted fish, fried locusts, vegetables, soup, pastry, and fruit that could be washed down with water, wine, or beer. Matthew and Ehud had gone to one of these taverns after visiting Ehud's glassworks.

"That was interesting, Ehud"—Matthew took the cup of *chamar medinah*, the diluted wine they had ordered, and drank. The first sip was enough for him to decide he did not care for the thin wine. He

296

knew little about glassmaking, but in the shop, Ehud had explained what his workers were doing, and that proved fascinating. "This is an old way of forming vessels"—Ehud had pointed at one worker winding a rope of glass around a shaped core of sand and clay over a metal rod. "Next, he'll add to it—with thin rods of colored glass—and fuse it, creating a solid piece by reheating it several times."

As Matthew had watched, by varying the windings, the worker created patterns that he pulled into place. The container was then rolled on a polished stone slab to press and smooth the decorative threads into the body of the vessel. The worker attached pre-formed handles and shaped the base so it would stand upright once cooled. "When he is done," Ehud had told him, "he'll pull the rod out as the glass slowly anneals and then scrape out the core material." He walked over to another table and worker. "This man is creating molds—we have dozens in Alexandria I could not bring with me—for some of our glass products. Until they are done and suitable for use, once the completed pieces are cooled and set, we'll rely on techniques borrowed from stone working, grinding and carving the glass to get the final shape we want. As soon as possible, I want to bring a glassblower from Alexandria." Ehud had gone to a table against the wall and lifted a long tube to show him. "He will be able to teach others so we can improve production and quality to match what we have in Alexandria."

Matthew almost regretted that he'd spent the middle part of his day on such diversions, but the break was worth it. He studied his friend across the tavern table. "Why did your father move your family to Alexandria?"

"My family originally came from Megiddo, and my father's father moved to Jerusalem," Ehud answered with a sad cast to his face. "I did not want to go to Alexandria, but I understand why my father wanted to go there—where he could learn more about our family's craft."

Matthew had to state it: "Many believe you've gone over to the Romans because of the money."

Ehud sighed. "When people don't know the truth... they imagine or concoct things to explain what they don't know. My father did not ally with the Romans, and neither do I. But once everything important to us relied on them"—he counted off on his fingers—"the market the empire represents, and other things we could not risk losing"—Ehud looked down at his hands and did not finish. "I'm here trying to save what I can."

Matthew did not press his friend. It had taken the experiences of the last few years for him to understand how outside parties and interests wielded influence and control. He got up. "I want real wine," he said. He took his goblet and started to reach for Ehud's—"How about you?" At Ehud's nod, he took both cups to the bar and returned with two new goblets and a fired-clay pitcher of wine. He filled both cups, slid one to Ehud, then sat and drank from his. "Better... much better," he smacked his lips.

"I heard your father got the Sanhedrin president to relent," Ehud said, "and not push to have Yosef removed from command in Galilee."

"Yes"—Matthew paused, hesitant to comment, but the words were too sour to hold—"for a price." As soon as he said it, Matthew recognized in his own voice the bitterness he'd heard in Ehud's tone just moments before—compliance comes with a cost.

"What do you mean? What price?" Ehud straightened in his chair.

Matthew dipped a finger in his wine and drew circles on the wooden tabletop. "I now must work with Esau ben Beor... a man I do not care to work with."

"I don't know the name or man... is he in the Sanhedrin? Why do you dislike him?"

"There are reasons... but let's not talk of him or them." Matthew raised his goblet. "I'm glad you've come back to Jerusalem and hope you stay. Let's talk of happier days."

* * *

They talked until late afternoon faded to twilight, and the lighting of the night lanterns made Matthew realize how late it was getting. He got up from the table, took their cloaks from a peg by the door, and handed Ehud his. "It's time we go home." He shook his dizzy head, regretting all that wine, as they stepped out into the street. "We had such fun as children"—he hesitated then went ahead, emboldened by the wine—"I think my sister is still fond of you."

Ehud cast him a quick glance. "Miriam's grown into a beautiful woman... I remember how she used to hide her scraped knees—she loved following us into some of the old tunnels. Your mother disapproved of her chasing after us."

Matthew laughed. "Miriam is still headstrong." Then he said what he hoped would help: "You should call on her sometime."

"Would she like that?"

"I think so, but that's for you to find out." The evening shadows on the street were too dark for Matthew to clearly see Ehud's face, but it seemed twisted in conflict. Coming back to Jerusalem, leaving his family in growing danger must be hard on Ehud. Matthew hoped they were able to soon move to Jerusalem. That's truly where they wished to be since they had sent Ehud ahead of them.

* * *

Behind them, unnoticed, Miriam had just left Hananiah's shop and stopped near the door of the tavern, her night-sensitive eyes recognizing them as they came out. Too far away to hear what Matthew said, she saw them pass under a large street lantern near the gate to ascend to the Upper City. Ehud turned his head, and in his profile, she saw a man in pain.

LXXVIII

Since the Sicarii leader had told her someone had been watching Zechariah's shop, Miriam had been very careful entering and leaving. She scouted the area as she approached, studying everyone on the streets, and had yet to see anyone suspicious. She had avoided Ehud's glassworks nearby and kept out of sight while noticing Ehud appeared to be in the Lower City two or three times throughout the course of a day.

Each day brought more rumors of the Romans—where they were, and how fast they were closing in on Jerusalem. Miriam's family was alone in worrying about the people of Galilee, it seemed. But then most who had family in Galilee had already brought them to Jerusalem for protection. Soon the real war would be upon them, and that tension was in the air and on people's faces. She worried about Yosef but felt ready for what was coming. She had maintained her practice of Zechariah's training, and the moves had become second nature, a reflex requiring little thought.

Months before, Miriam had watched as Matthew and Eleasar ben Ananias, the Temple Guard captain, implemented daily training to strengthen the city's militia. She had followed a similar regimen in Zechariah's shop.

She could not run in the confines of the shop, but there were other ways to improve her wind; she whirled and danced within Zechariah's old workroom until she had to stop for breath. And now she could last for a long time before having to slow or stop. To strengthen herself, Miriam did lunges and strikes with Zechariah's staff—just as he had taught her—until her thighs and arms burned. Lifting baskets of Zechariah's special clay built up what he had said was the foundation of a warrior's power in combat. Taking the laden baskets, she crouched, then lifted them onto the table, paused, then raised again to squat and lower them to the floor. As she got stronger, she added a twisting motion, holding the baskets longer and rotating her upper body before setting them down.

The minutes that grew to hours of exercise over the days, weeks, and months had changed her in ways that she hid by continuing to wear clothing now too large for her. The one thing revealed to all was her face. It had lost all of its fullness and now showed a sharp jawline above a taut neck connecting to shoulders less rounded but broader.

She marveled at these muscles when she bathed. So too were her arms more defined: upper arms and forearms leaner with the play of muscle noticeable underneath her pale skin covered by long-sleeved robes.

Miriam stood in front of Zechariah's mirror—the one Elazar said he had made for his wife—and used a wet cloth to wipe the sweat from her naked body. Her breasts were firmer, sitting higher on her frame, and she ran a hand across the flat of her stomach, feeling the band of muscles there, too. Her stomach had less of a curve, and she would have to add more padding to it for her disguise. And that would be soon.

She dressed and gathered her things. Removing a man's clothing, the padded girdle, and the false beard from their spot in the hidden compartment in the floor, she rolled them tightly together and tucked the roll into a bag. Smoothing her hair and settling her head covering, she slung the bag over her shoulder to carry it as women did. With her mother, father, and Matthew so preoccupied, she wanted the disguise with her at home. She wanted to be able to change into it when an opportunity presented itself—without having to come to Zechariah's. With the bag over her shoulder, mostly hidden by the folds of a now-too-large robe, Miriam opened the back door to the alley that led to the street, checked it up and down, and then stepped outside.

Moments later, she was on the street lined with craftsmen closing their shops as the setting sun cast its long shadows. She had just glanced at Hananiah's darkened shop as she passed it and wondered if he was inside when a voice called her, and she turned.

"Miriam"—Ehud hurried toward her—"may I walk with you?"

In the past, before the frightening constant reminder of their mortality now subject to Rome's power marching toward them, if observers knew a young woman and a young man to be unmarried, it would have been frowned upon by many for the two to walk together. Now, most people on the streets no longer noticed such things.

"Yes,"—she nodded at Ehud, who now was beside her. As they walked, she noted his sideways glances at her. They approached the lanterned gate to the Upper City, and in its light, she saw on his face a pained expression, quickly replaced by a smile.

"Matthew asked me to join your family for dinner this evening," he said, "and I'm headed there now. I hope you don't mind."

"Why would I mind? You are his old friend—and welcome." Miriam shrugged, and the bag's strap slipped along her shoulder. She shifted it back to ride higher and gave him a sharp glance that caught the flicker of discomfort on his face again.

"Am I not *your* friend, too?"

Ehud's plaintive tone slowed her, and she half-turned back toward him. At the base of the steps, the gate lantern's glow caught the blink of his eyes. They glistened but held steady on hers.

The breath she held first fluttered, then escaped with a sigh. Suddenly she was that young girl—still whole—who had secretly fallen in love with him.

"Of course," she said, mounting the first of the steps, and at first, he followed behind her, then he drew next to her as they walked onto the terrace of the agora.

* * *

The dinner conversation had been mostly about the latest news of Vespasian's and Agrippa's men approaching Galilee from the north, and the stirring of the Roman legions camped around Azzah southwest of Jerusalem.

"I'm glad Eleasar insisted on using our men as couriers between Yosef's headquarters to our southern outpost near Azzah," said Matthew. "It upset Esau ben Beor, who wanted to use his Idumeans." He had arrived for dinner angry and had remained so. "It was good to see him denied... the man knows too much and seeks to learn more about—"

Mathias had reached over the table and tapped his son's hand, catching his eye and then Ehud's. "Let's continue our talk in the courtyard so the ladies may clean up."

* * *

Miriam fumed at having to clear the table and wash the dishes, but there was no arguing with her parents. She finished as quickly as she could and went upstairs, knowing she was not invited to the courtyard. She carefully cracked open one-half of the window's shutters and pulled her chair closer. The night was still, with just a hint of a breeze, and she heard her father below.

"You may call on us, and we welcome you visiting more often... but what are you seeking, Ehud? Miriam has changed in the last three years, even more since you last saw her many years ago."

"Thank you, Mathias," Ehud said. "I know she's become a woman... and I must—"

Her father started to reply, cutting Ehud off, but Matthew interrupted first: "Father, I think it would be good for her... she needs someone—other than family—who cares about her." Matthew moved, and Miriam saw his face come into the lamp's light. "Ehud says he believes that eventually, his father will bring all of his family back to Jerusalem."

Ehud shifted in his seat, leaned away, and looked off into the darkness beyond the pool of light at the table, then moved his chair forward again. "Matthew, I've heard you talk about this Esau ben Beor—with some anger or frustration—and you mentioned he was Idumean. My father knows many Idumeans who trade heavily with the Romans in Alexandria. Is that what you've learned about him— his people—that has made you so angry? Or does ben Beor know something you feel he shouldn't?"

Miriam had become agitated at hearing them speak of her, and Matthew was out of line to encourage Ehud to rekindle some flame long extinguished—*I will resist that manipulation,* she almost said aloud. But that personal anger passed at hearing Esau ben Beor was an Idumean, and there was a connection between Idumeans and Alexandrian Romans. Elazar believed that, too, and he'd told her to watch Esau and his people south of Jerusalem. Idumea was a region of mixed races and creeds, and few were loyal Jews.

The next day she would get a message to Elazar about what Ehud had said... and she would begin following Esau to get proof.

LXXIX

NEAR PTOLEMAIS

The setting sun made a darkening orange that tinted red along the horizon behind Nicanor as he entered General Vespasian's field tent. This space was half again as ample as the tent he had just set up for himself. That morning they had bypassed ancient Tyre, that city having been allowed to keep much of its independence as a *civitas foederati,* an ally of Rome that also served as the closest seaport to Damascus. By sundown the next day, they would be in Ptolemais.

Within the tent, General Vespasian sat studying a map held down on the sides by the wooden cudgel he always kept near, and Nicanor stood quietly, waiting for the general to recognize him. At the center peak of the tent hung a lantern that cast a glow that faded into shadows climbing the walls. A simple cot at one side left just enough room in the center for the foldable table and two camp stools. Vespasian then looked up at Nicanor and then down again as he sifted through the sheets of parchment for a particular one.

"Centurion, as we set up camp this evening, Galerius Senna brought a representative from Sepphoris who carried this message from that city's leaders—they declare that they do not stand with the Judean rebels against Rome. They claim to be an independent city-state." He set the note down, glanced up, and pointed Nicanor toward the second chair. "They wish to be left out of any conflict."

Nicanor nodded as he swept his cloak aside and sat. "That's also what I had heard of them, general, when I served here before. And no word came—I know—that Sepphoris was involved in any of the attacks on the 12th Legion or sent men to support the rebels. I believe Lord Gallus did not consider them part of the rebellion."

"Then we'll leave them alone for now, unless we discover otherwise." Vespasian picked out another sheet—"But our scouts and patrols inland and farther southeast—checking that our route ahead is clear to Ptolemais—report skirmishes with the rebels, who strike fast and disappear." He pointed out two locations on the map. "I asked the Sepphoran about any news he had of rebel activity, and he mentioned these two towns—Tiberias and Tarichaea. He says they are well-fortified and likely where the rebels originated. These men are led, they believe, by a rebel commander named Yeshua ben Shapat. We arrive in Ptolemais tomorrow, and the next day I will have Titus lead a force to hunt down the rebels hounding us from those towns and put a stop to them. They are like dogs snapping at our heels."

"More deadly than dogs, general. They did the same thing to the 12th Legion under Cestius Gallus. With great impact. They killed many men and gave me this," Nicanor rubbed the long scar still prominent against his sun-browned cheek and neck. "If we don't deal with them, they'll tear at us all the way to Jerusalem."

"I've said as much again to Gessius Florus, who now seems particularly focused on your friend Yosef in Yotapta." Vespasian studied the centurion for a moment. "You've not said anything since learning he is in command of the rebels in Galilee."

"I have nothing to say about it, general," Nicanor replied, not mentioning his lingering private thoughts since he had heard about Yosef. "I follow orders to defend Rome against all enemies. I regret that it is my friend, but that won't stay my hand nor affect my duty to you and to Rome."

Vespasian nodded. "Very well. Have you prepared the report for Lord Tigellinus, so it is ready if someone approaches you for it when we arrive in Ptolemais—as you expect will happen?"

"Yes, and it contains the points you intend for the Praetorian Prefect." Nicanor hesitated—"What are your plans for Yotapta?"

Vespasian rolled the cudgel on the table under the palm of his right hand. "Tell me what forces you recommend we wield from Ptolemais to destroy the rebel leadership in Galilee."

"Without committing the entire legions, general, I would say eighteen cohorts of light and heavy infantry and the squadron of cavalry from Caesarea, along with the five squadrons we brought from Syria. Agrippa has also provided 2,000 bowmen and 1,000 cavalrymen. Another local ally king—Malachus—according to his report to you, has sent 1,000 cavalrymen and 5,000 infantrymen to join us in Ptolemais. We won't know if those are light or heavy infantry until we see them."

"That is more than enough. Titus can use the bulk of them to go after the rebels in Tiberias and Tarichaea. I doubt they can field a force large enough to stand against him. We will go to Yotapta with the rest of the men and siege equipment and prepare for that battle. Titus will join us there, bringing his force for the assault." Vespasian flattened the map again and studied it, then picked up another page of notes. "You have said the terrain inland from Ptolemais gets hillier, with many steep grades closer to Yotapta... that will make our movement difficult."

"Yes, general. It will be hard. I've seen some of the land surrounding Yotapta, which sits atop its own hill, surrounded on three sides by deep ravines. I was told that walled city is built on levels ranging from 150 to 300 feet above those ravines. The only easily accessed route is through a saddle between the city and the larger hill to the north—and that area has the only road that connects to the city."

"So, we must first plan how to take the city without having to claw up steep slopes from the ravines." Vespasian stood, lifting the cudgel to tap it on the map, "Find the commander of the engineers we brought from Antioch and return with him. We'll then locate where to place our *castra*, settling and fortifying that base for our attack on Yotapta. It seems we'll have plenty of raw materials for it—earth, turf, and timber—and we have a cohort of auxiliary *immunes* not assigned other duties—they can focus on camp construction. Once that is done, the engineers can prepare the road for the siege equipment and move men into place to break through Yotapta's ramparts and any barriers the rebels have erected."

"Even once we're through the walls, general, we'll be fighting the rebels all around the sides of the hill. It will not be easy." Nicanor shook his head and hoped that when they got there, he would find that Yosef was not in Yotapta and would not be caught in its inevitable destruction.

LXXX

NORTHEAST OF PTOLEMAIS

What General Vespasian had ordered the next morning, after sleeping on their previous evening's discussion, made sense to Nicanor. Nothing in battle could become more of an equalizer—or advantage—as choosing where the battle was fought and using the land best. Any seasoned field commander would want to see the terrain or its like so that his observations factored into future decisions. Vespasian's determination to march inland some distance to at least glimpse a portion of what northern Galilee presented them made confronting the rebels even more difficult, but it was what any experienced combat commander would deem worthwhile.

Nicanor wished Vespasian had let him go with the forward cavalry elements that had screened ahead of them and on their flanks throughout the day. But then he might have missed Placidus—leading his patrol squadron of cavalry and infantrymen from Ptolemais—who had joined them just before sunset. The officer had reported first to Galerius Senna, and he had, in turn, requested that Placidus brief General Vespasian and his staff after the evening meal.

Once dinner was over, the sides of Vespasian's field tent had been rolled up to accommodate the large group of men and to let the evening sea breeze cool those standing inside. Nicanor looked at the cavalry officer in front of them and recalled the man from when he had served in the 12th under Cestius Gallus. Placidus never looked comfortable unless he was on horseback.

The man was uncomfortable now and shifted from foot to foot as he spoke. "General, since arriving in Ptolemais, the units I command have encountered the rebels several times. It is vital for you to know what I've learned in the field from a man—a Sadducee from Gischala—who told me what he knows of the rebels' plans. The rebel leadership is determined never to face our combined legions in the field, and their activities in Galilee will be defensive. They know they cannot push us out of their country but hope to wear us down until—they hope—we leave.

"Many of the towns have been fortified, as ordered by the rebel military commander in Yotapta. His orders are to wait for the Roman army to come to them. We have attacked and destroyed several of the smaller towns and villages and must admit they put up a formidable resistance that has infuriated my men. Apparently, according to this

Sadducee, Galileans are fiercely independent, and that independence has increased over recent years as they have seen their territory and wealth shrink. That has been a result of rising hostilities with non-Jews and those who have aligned with Rome, as well as with Roman taxes and levies. When Lord Gallus brought the 12th through Galilee, the farther south we moved, the more contact we had with rebels following behind us, waiting to strike." Placidus nodded at Nicanor—"The centurion knows what I speak of. Once we entered Galilee and Judea under Cestius Gallus, as we neared Jerusalem, the rebels we had seemingly bypassed or overlooked became bolder and their attacks more effective."

"We already see that again, Placidus," Nicanor replied. "We've had to strengthen the rear and sides of our formation. The rebels seem even more persistent than on our march to Jerusalem."

"What—who—are these Sadducees you mention?" Vespasian asked Placidus, his glance also going to Nicanor. "And can you bring this man to me?"

"I'm sorry, general"—Placidus paused, his eyes flickering toward his commanding officer—"The man was captured by the rebels and has not been seen since. The Saddu—"

"As I understand it, general," Gessius Florus interrupted, "the Sadducees are a sect made up of mostly affluent Jews—the high priests and leaders of Judean society. They make up the nation's internal administration, so their role goes beyond religious responsibilities—it is also political. Many have proven to be loyal to Rome, but as I discovered when I was the Judean Procurator, other factions, like the Zealots and the Sicarii, have fought against their wishes and created the schism that has led to this rebellion."

"Thank you, Lord Florus"—Vespasian nodded and turned to Nicanor, who struggled not to say something. "Centurion, when I decided to swing inland to view some of the area of Galilean hills and mountains you spoke of, you said we were headed toward one of the larger towns—is that the Gischala that Placidus mentions?"

"Yes, general, it is in that direction, but many miles to the east and deep into the mountains. There are steep foothills surrounding and leading to that city."

"If the Sadducees are in power there, would they be on our side? Or would they be like those in Sepphoris and declare they are not part of the rebellion but neutral? Perhaps we should make Gischala one of our objectives."

Galerius Senna spoke up: "Gischala could become an ally, general. They could help us in Galilee."

Nicanor had seen the sideways glances Galerius Senna, and Gessius Florus had exchanged and knew he must speak up. "But, Lord Senna, as I remember from before I left Ptolemais for Rome, the Gischalans, with a force of several thousand men, had aligned with Jerusalem. The leader of Gischala presumed he would be the commander of all of Galilee. We now know that he did not become the military leader for the region, but we should still assume he is with the rebels."

"I agree with Nicanor, General Vespasian," said Placidus. "No town in this country should be relied on—where their allegiance rests depend on where their interests lie, and those may not always be with Rome. Gischala should be one of the cities you break or bring under control, but do not trust them."

He paused as if scaling back his vehemence. "That decision is above me, of course. I know only what I have learned from fighting the rebels. We must deal with them in Galilee, and though most of the main roads are Roman, the paths and cross-country roads follow the dry season rills that run in the valleys. The heights above those paths are thick with rebels. Any slow-moving formation is at risk of losing many men unless you sweep the rebels from the slopes and flush them out of caves and off their ledges."

He addressed his old comrade: "And one thing is different from before, Nicanor. The rebels now move, attack, fire, and withdraw more as disciplined units than before. They bring attacks to bear from all directions, wherever they can do the most damage while taking the fewest losses. So, I think we should not chase them into their hills... We should kill them where we can pin them down, then go to their strongholds and bring down their walls upon them."

Vespasian walked to his desk to look down at the map. He turned to face the assembled officers and said, "Then let us not get too far ahead of our original battle plan. In the morning, we'll turn back toward Ptolemais and join with Titus before pushing into Galilee and crushing the rebel-held towns. We'll not repeat past mistakes—we'll listen to what's been learned. Lord Senna, send a rider to Ptolemais with advance notice that we are a day or two away."

"General"—Placidus stepped forward to point at the map—"from where we are now, we should travel due west and avoid Meroth to the south. It has been fortified by the Jewish commander in Galilee and sits upon the slopes of the highest mountain in the region. The rebels there sweep down quickly to strike when we come near and then retreat and regroup. They know the mountain and move faster so that we've been unable to catch them."

With a nod, Vespasian ended the briefing with orders to Placidus to split his men into three elements to further protect the main body of men, animals, and equipment on the march to Ptolemais.

As Nicanor left for his tent, he wondered if the time he had spent with Yosef in Rome—so much of it on the training fields—had led to Yosef becoming a competent military planner. He was naturally a leader and likely had instilled some fighting discipline in his men. The centurion struggled with the thought that the days and weeks to come would be very hard for both of them.

LXXXI

As they approached Yotapta's gate on their return from Gabara, Yosef had noticed Dalit herding her goats in one of the stone-pocked scrub fields of already browning grass, bringing them before sundown to the new pen constructed within the town's walls. Ariella had told him about Dalit's knowledge of the caves that riddled the hills in and around Yotapta, and he sent for the girl that evening and gave her a mission: find a suitable cavern underneath the town to serve as a refuge—the last redoubt for the defenders of Yotapta—should the Roman attack overwhelm the walls.

He knew they would eventually need it.

Two days later, Dalit went to him, abstractedly turning a goatherd's rod as she spoke: "One of my young goats fell into a shallow gully along the edge of a rocky outcrop on the western slope. I found a long, low arch of stone capped by turf. It has an opening just under the ridge you can see only from within the gully. Grass grows thick in front of it, and the greedy little goat had already eaten enough to reveal part of the entrance. I went back this morning and climbed down into it. It's big, but I need help to see how deep and far it goes."

Now, a month later, Levi's workers had cleared the entrance and followed the cave as it descended and came out below the western wall of Yotapta on a narrow-ledged path above the deep ravines.

The work had progressed to where Yosef could inspect it. He passed the series of stone cisterns that had been placed in dugouts in the eastern slope to catch the rainwater runoff—throughout winter and spring—fed through runnels of stone. An army of water bucket carriers had emptied their contents to fill the cisterns within the town walls where there was little runoff. There would be little rainfall during summer, and he and Levi had already discussed rationing plans.

As Yosef stepped onto the level ledge and came upon the entrance to the cave, he saw the opening was filled with the largest man he had ever seen. The giant nodded, came fully out, stepped to the side, and immediately cast a shadow over Yosef as Levi came out from the cave.

"Yosef, we've finished clearing both the upper and lower openings to more easily enter the cave. A fall of rocks and dirt is now set... and with the tug of a rope secured just inside... we can bring down enough to seal both entrances."

Levi reached up and clapped the giant on one massive shoulder— "Dov moved the heaviest pieces into place. He has worked in the stone quarries of Cana and knows about planning and setting framing timbers to line shafts and shore up tunnels."

"I'll go to the peak now and see to the digging of the other airshafts," said Dov. "Then, I will show their location to you so they can be hidden." He nodded again at Yosef and left them.

"Come inside, Yosef, and let me show you what Dalit found." Levi turned back into the entrance and stepped inside and down, and Yosef followed into the darkness. A minute later, illuminating the way with a large lantern, Levi took him into a level area that could easily hold nearly a hundred people. "It's big but not large enough," he commented.

Yosef walked to the far wall—leaving the arc of light—and ran his hand along the wall of rough stone. "Hundreds come to Yotapta for safety each day. There's no place immense enough to protect them all. But this could save a few. We must also tell everyone that if the Romans breach the walls, they must flee. The Romans will come from the north, so they must make their way downhill and then south toward the next closest hill or fortified town where they can turn and fight. If the Romans had only given us enough time, we could erect fortifications there."

"Yosef, don't we have enough time?"

"No"—Yosef shook his head—"Yohanan ben Zaccai has returned, and there is confirmed word that a Roman general, Vespasian, has arrived in Ptolemais from Antioch with an allied force and enough men and equipment to reform the 12th Legion. Another general has brought three legions from Alexandria through southern Judea into Galilee. It will not be long before they come against us."

"We'll keep preparing, then, but we have done most of what we can," Levi said. He pointed up at the ceiling, and Yosef saw the rough circle of gray above them. "Like Dov said, we'll dig more airshafts. He also found what seems to be a vertical fissure—it forms a natural tunnel that climbs higher, then goes under the walls, and ends inside the town. Dov has a crew of men working to secure and extend that tunnel into the cavern. As with the entrances, he'll rig it so we can collapse the opening if we must to keep the Romans out. Jerusalem faced one legion. We will see more."

"So, we might have to bury ourselves to stay alive." Yosef stepped beneath the airshaft, looked up, and whispered, "But for how long?" A wave of vertigo passed over him, and he faltered.

"Yosef"—Levi came to his side to steady him—"are you sick?"

"I'm fine..." Yosef tried to shake off the feeling he had been there before—in this very spot looking up at the airshaft. He knew its smell of damp earth... the sound of his sandals scraping on the grit over stone as he shifted his feet. Through the shaft, he sensed the faint echo of screams... and a stronger smell of blood. Down the shaft came the memory of a voice he knew that pleaded with him. It had been some time since he had dreamed that.

He wiped his face with the palms of his hands and rubbed his eyes. "It's nothing, Levi, and it has passed. Let's return to daylight... I must speak again with Yohannan ben Zaccai, and he has brought letters for me from my family... I could use that comfort right now."

* * *

That night...

The resonant voice from the shrouded figure had faded, but Yosef recognized it as one he had not heard in nearly ten years—Bannus, the Essene he had studied and lived with for three years before he was twenty. Bannus had explained all the messianic beliefs of the Essenes as he studied their scrolls. As his long-ago mentor disappeared, the shadow of another man replaced him. This one he knew was prophesied to come out of Judea to rule not just that land but the world. As he came near, Yosef's foreboding grew that this man would cause Yotapta to suffer through a bloody siege of several weeks, ending in its fall. His friends and the defenders of Yotapta would not survive, but it seemed that somehow Yosef would.

He shuddered awake, his outthrust arm knocking his unlighted clay lamp to the floor. The lamp's seal must have broken, for he smelled then touched the oil spreading over the woven goat-hair mat beside his bed. The odor wiped away by the memory of his dream, of the screams heard in darkness and the reek of blood. His senses cleared as he came awake, and all faded, but the ghost of a voice Yosef still heard calling to him: "Yosef... are you there?"

LXXXII

Yosef, still shaking off the dream, walked to the window. It was gray dawn, and a blanket of mist hung low to the ground with streaks of paler light revealing work crews already forming in the square. The men waited in the knee-deep fog to better prepare Yotapta's defense. In Yosef's mind—in the dream—it had been a drapery of smoke. Down in the square, Dov was easy to identify by his size, and he shouldered a thick bundle of what seemed to be long iron rods. In one hand, he held a massive hammer, its head as large as his fist and its handle as long as his thick-muscled forearm.

As Yosef looked down on the men, the voice returned. No, it was not inside his head, but was Levi's calling him. Yosef turned from the window as his lieutenant came through the open doorway without hesitating, the out-of-breath captain of the scouts with him.

"Yosef, the Romans come"—Levi's expression was strained, but his voice calm.

A pain churned Yosef's stomach. "How many and how far away?"

Levi glanced at the man with him. "The patrol counted 1,000 cavalrymen supported by a cohort of what looks like light-infantry..."

"Fifteen-hundred men is not enough"—Yosef shook his head—"Are you sure?"

"It sure looked—like a lot of Romans—to me," said Galon between gasps. "They filled the path—between the hills to the north. Ahead of the cavalry, the infantry—the infantry climbed each slope and cleared them. I had our men fall back as they advanced—and now the Romans have stopped at a hill a few miles north of us."

"A second patrol reported a cohort of what looks like auxiliaries following them with carts," Levi said, "most carrying shovels and armed only with short swords and spears. Our men had scattered by then, and we did not have enough there to stop them, anyway. They're now atop that hill, with the infantry and the horsemen encircling it."

"That's not enough men to press an attack against us," Yosef explained. "This is just the beginning. The auxiliaries will construct the Roman base camp close enough so the commanders of the larger force can see the battleground and study us. Galon, stop all patrols and send runners to watch for any still out and order them to return. Pull all our men back, and get everyone inside the walls. They must be back in by sunrise tomorrow. Many, many more Romans will come along that same route."

Galon took a deep breath and left, and Yosef glanced at the window. "Levi, I just saw Dov with his workmen..."

"They're working within the walls today to dig the last of the airshafts."

"What of the crews gathering building materials?" They would be needed for repairs and to shore up weak or damaged parts of the wall during an attack.

"Dov's men have stockpiled enough stone and timber to erect a new wall inside the old. And he's had men collecting smaller stones to hurl at the Romans should they come near enough to our walls."

"You can count on that," Yosef said. "Once the Romans' fortified camp is in place, the soldiers—likely the cavalry—will move to seal off Yotapta and test our defenses." He turned to his desk and picked up a sheet with a list of items. "What of our supply of oil and arrows?"

"Ariella and the women have been making arrows for weeks now. We have thousands."

"Get them distributed to the towers and ramparts of the walls. We'll need every one of them... and the oil?"

"Every olive press in Yotapta has been in use since we returned from Gabara. Near the walls, we have set up iron cauldrons as you showed me—affixed on small beams, so two men can handle them. They can be filled as they sit over the fire pits. We have enough cut wood to heat all we have. Once it's all ready, the rigging is in place to lift each to the ramparts to dump hot oil onto the Romans."

"Good"—Yosef nodded—"Everyone is to keep working... making more arrows... digging up more stone, but only from the fields within the walls or what can be quarried and brought up from the cave beneath us.

"This Roman General Vespasian will not be far behind these men, and he will bring at least an entire legion with him."

* * *

"Old friend, I have one last task to ask of you... to take these letters to my family." Yosef handed Yohanan ben Zaccai a packet of parchment—three folded squares sealed individually and wrapped together with a leather cord. The letters to his father and mother and to Matthew had been easy to write. He had written that he loved them and hoped they would one day be together again. In Matthew's, he added that he should trust his instincts to not have faith in Esau ben Beor and that he should deal directly, quietly, with the Essenes. There had been too many examples of men within the Sanhedrin working to serve their own purposes and not that of their faith. They would not do what was needed to protect the Temple treasure.

Despite all that surrounded him, Miriam was on his mind more than anyone. In her last letter, she had told him of Rachel's professed affection for him and of Leah's dire predicament with her abusive husband. In his reply to Miriam, he had not acknowledged that news—he felt terrible for them but had no way to help. This was no time to think about what could be done in Jerusalem when the Romans were at Yotapta. All he had to help Miriam were his words... that he loved her and wanted her to find a way to be happy. He prayed she would and had asked Matthew to encourage Ehud's interest in their sister.

"Gladly, Yosef"—the old priest started to go—"I'll leave now and return as quickly as I can."

"No, Yohanan. You've heard that the first elements of the Roman army are here. I can even now step upon our battlements and see the campfires on the northern hill where they build their encampment. You must wait until the deep of night in case they have patrols out. And when you are gone... do not return. Stay in Jerusalem with my family or go where you feel you will be safe."

Yosef handed him another letter, this one sealed in wax. "You can show this to my father, but it is for Shimon ben Gamliel and the Sanhedrin. In it, I ask them to send more men to withstand the Romans. Or to change what is bound to happen to more cities than Yotapta—by letting me attempt to talk to the Romans. I have hope to negotiate peace if that is still possible. Otherwise, the Romans will force us behind the walls, and then they will eventually destroy and bury us beneath them."

Yosef sat down and looked up at his friend. "At midnight, Levi will come for you and take you into the tunnels under the southern wall and then down into the valley outside the city."

* * *

Yosef was up before dawn and writing in his journal. It was one he had created himself, the vellum pages bound between two pieces of wood with a cord. He would soon need to release the cord to add more sheets. He had just filled a page with his notes about the recent dream and the news of the Roman army's arrival.

The room had brightened as he wrote, so he blew out the lamp. He sighed. Yohanan ben Zaccai should be well on his way to Jerusalem by now.

"Yosef...."

"Yes, Levi?" The man looked as if he had not slept, which was probably so.

"Our last scout has come in... and has news that the Romans have attacked Tiberias and Gabara. They have killed all the males—even the young—and burned the towns."

"Are there any survivors?"

"Yes, but the scout reports that the Romans shackled them, and he heard the soldiers boast they will sell them into slavery."

Yosef closed his eyes, and the vestiges of his dream taunted him.

ACT III

LXXXIII

The hills, more like young mountains around him, made Nicanor uncomfortable. He trusted they had been cleared of rebels, as Placidus, the *praefectus alae* leading the forward element of the 12th Legion, had just reported. —But he still did not like being among those hills. His concern increased when their already frustrating crawl came to a halt.

Vespasian noted Nicanor's unease. "I don't like holding here either, centurion"—he leaned forward in his saddle toward Placidus, who had ridden out to meet them—"So the camp is ready, and you have sealed the city?"

"Yes, general, and we've scouted Yotapta's defenses. The engineers will have the report ready when you arrive. My decurion Aebutius has encircled the town with a rank of the *cohortes equitate*, backed by the cohort of light-infantry. They're spread thin, but no one can escape the town without alerting them, and they have riders to report in throughout the day and night."

"We'll reinforce that line with a regiment of *sagittarii* and more infantry"—He glanced at Nicanor, who nodded his understanding— "The mounted archers will deploy before we begin assault preparations, then the infantry will move up." Vespasian shifted to study the declining sun over his shoulder. "How much longer to get the replacement mounts up from the rear?"

"General, a dozen men are exchanging the horses that have gone lame from trodding on these cursed rocks," Nicanor said with a scowl at the steep slopes climbing from their narrow path. "This is barely a goat track. The men can manage, but it's taking a toll on the horses' hooves." He clamped his knees against Tempestas's sides and raised up to look back at the men and horses moving behind them. "It should not be much longer."

"Good. I'll be glad to get to the camp if only to silence the men's cursing... and I do not blame them. Placidus, ride ahead to the camp and return to your men. At our pace, it will be nightfall before the first units reach you. Titus is coming from Legio—with units from the 5th—and should pass west of Cana through the Plain of Asochis

319

tomorrow. He will join us within two days to take a position at the southern end of Yotapta."

* * *

Nicanor was thankful for the cloudless night. The moon cast enough light for him to follow the rough path, but the treacherous footing forced them all to walk now. "We should be there soon, girl," Nicanor told Tempestas and cupped a handful of barley from his pouch to the horse's mouth. Neither Abigieus nor Tempestas had needed the harsh iron-bit most Roman soldiers used to control their mounts— Nicanor had gentler methods to cultivate immediate acceptance from his animals. Abigieus had responded even when terribly injured—the horse had served him well, saving him by not falling at Beth Horon. Then he had saved Sayid's life when the pair had remained to command the decoy unit so the legion could escape—Abigieus had carried the auxiliary from that valley of death despite having suffered fatal wounds.

Nicanor hoped he would never have to ask that of Tempestas.

Behind them came the snorts and snaps of the less fortunate horses and the mutters of men who were footsore, hungry, and tired, too.

A pale gleam shone fully on Vespasian's helmet when the general turned to glance at Nicanor as they walked side by side. Their mounts, flanking them at the borders of the path, served as shields against any threat that might lurk in the darkness to either side. "Tomorrow, early, we will prepare for a siege of the city," said Vespasian. "We take this Yotapta, and no other Galilean stronghold can consider itself impregnable, nor its defenders think themselves safe."

When the path narrowed, Nicanor would, by instinct, move ahead through puddles and curtains of shadows, unable to see more than ten feet ahead on the trail and no distance at all up the dark heights around them. In those moments, he wished Vespasian had allowed them to carry torches. But then the hills looming above might not be as devoid of rebels as they had seemed in the daylight, and the Romans' own lights could target them.

"The message from Placidus says the walls and defenses are impressive for a city hidden among mountains. The town sits atop a hill like a bowl turned upside down. The farther you travel from the center, the steeper the sides get. Your friend"—Vespasian glanced at Nicanor—"has apparently done well at fortifying it... and some of the other towns in Galilee."

"Yosef is a brilliant young man, general. We must not underestimate him."

"I won't. When we capture or kill him, that will send a message to Galilee and all the rebels in Judea. This time we will secure Galilee first, then we will secure the rest of Judea before taking Jerusalem. But I believe most of the Judean rebels will flee to Jerusalem after Galilee and its stoutest stronghold have fallen."

"The walls of Jerusalem are not like those of any town in Galilee, general. I have seen them and know how hard they are to breach. The Jews have now had far more time to prepare than when the 12th Legion attacked before. The city's defenses will be even more formidable."

"You sound reluctant, centurion."

"It's more of regret than reluctance, general. It's necessary—we do what we must do—but I do not look forward to that challenge."

"And what of Yotapta?"

"I do not look forward to this, either... but I will do my duty, general."

As they entered an open area between the arc of hills surrounding them, a glow was visible atop a shadowed plateau, the familiar shape of a Roman encampment's night fires. The frame of bonfires was repeated around the base of the hill and showed many men had secured it.

"There's the camp, general," Nicanor said.

By morning the level area between the mountains would be full of the soldiers, horses, and equipment now trailing behind them far into the darkness.

* * *

Next morning...

Awake before the call to duty, Nicanor had inspected the perimeter, and the stiffness of the long ride and short sleep had faded. He walked more easily now, but his ongoing slight limp remained as he joined Vespasian and Placidus at the edge of camp on the rim of an overlook. The sunrise tinted the sides of their sun-darkened faces an orangish-red. Vespasian's face—lighter than the others—had a band of paler skin just above his brow protected by his helmet now tucked under one arm. They looked down at the thousands of Roman soldiers and dozens of carts full of weapons, arrows, and lead pellets for slingers, provisions, and siege equipment.

"I hope this sight the rebels awake to fills them with terror," Vespasian said, holding up a hand to still Placidus's pointing. "I see it." They watched as the sun slowly revealed the town, and Vespasian compared it to the sheet of vellum in his hand. Placidus had given him the engineer's sketch and notes of the town's situation upon the terrain and its defenses.

Nicanor studied Yotapta in the growing light. The city covered the top of a nearly isolated rounded hill with bare limestone visible in places around its edges. Steeply flanked gorges guarded the town; he could see its western side for himself, and he had been told of the southern and eastern sides much the same.

Vespasian handed the notes to Nicanor. "So, it's protected on three sides by ravines, and we'd be foolish to scale them into the teeth of its defenders. The lower part of the city sprawls southward, downslope, to a ridge defended by a wall over the southern drop. That means the town can be attacked only from the north." He paused and rapped his cudgel against his right thigh—"It will require some work to get our siege engines in place—the road to the northern gate will need to be improved."

"Yes, general," Placidus said and gestured at the notes in Nicanor's hand. "The northern approach is protected by a casemate wall—scouts have reported bowmen lined up on top and within. Where it becomes a single solid wall, it's reinforced with parapets and a few towers. The wall closely follows the contour of the hillside and, in some places, has been built into or through some of the buildings, which have themselves been fortified. The rebels have a solid defensive position that will prove a challenge for us. But the city has a weakness." He paused to be sure he had Vespasian's attention. "After we had the camp erected, I sent *venators* out with an escort patrol—they found game nearby to add to our provisions, but not any springs. There is no source of water close to the town."

"Could there be one within the walls?" Nicanor asked, remembering Jerusalem's Gihon Spring.

"The hunters did not think so," Placidus replied. "They are experienced in finding signs of water, and of course, hilltops like this do not have springs; Yotapta is likely dry and dependent on spring rainfall to fill their cisterns. The only other water source we've found is at some distance. We have secured it and found a heavily-traveled trail to Yotapta. We should strengthen that position and patrol that trail. They may have a few wells, but as at my home in Italia, they may dry up during the summer."

"Nicanor will assign you more men to guard the spring"—
Vespasian turned from Yotapta to face the two men—"Have
Aebutius's men reported anything?"

"They checked in before dawn. All quiet, general. Some
movement was seen on the ramparts but nothing outside the walls."

"Very well. Nicanor, send out the regiment of sagittarii to
reinforce Aebutius. Placidus, muster your immunes—I want the road
from here to Yotapta improved and a foundation set for the
construction of a siege ramp. If the workmen need more, we have a
supply of material for *opus caementicium* to construct its retaining
wall."

"Yes, general... we'll need more rough material for fill, and we've
found a nearby gully that seems has been used for years as a dump
for broken pottery. That will serve well in the ramp's base. We've also
spotted a site to quarry stone for the *ballista*."

"Then prepare the men and await the *bucinator's* signal."
Vespasian dismissed the officer. "Nicanor, after you deploy the
sagittarii, I want you to join the architecti and *armicustos*, who
should already be at work below. See to our siege engines—assemble
whatever was disassembled for travel. Move up the smaller ones and
position them with support auxiliaries behind Aebutius's line. Have
the larger engines readied to move into position as soon the ramp is
ready."

* * *

YOTAPTA

"Have you ever seen so many Roman soldiers?" Levi asked.

Yosef shook his head. "Not since the training fields outside of
Rome. They had nearly a full legion at Jerusalem last year. There is a
full legion here—and many auxiliaries—and I fear another legion is
on the way." He scanned the Romans forming in ranks down the hill,
outside the range of the archers and slingers of the north wall, where
he and Levi stood. The Romans' small fires were being extinguished
as the men mounted horses or relieved those who had watched
through the night.

He looked up toward the Roman camp, visible nearly a mile away.
As they watched, he had heard the buccinator's first sharp trumpet
call that carried and echoed in the morning stillness. Levi twitched,
and Yosef almost grinned. "The Roman army does nothing without a
signal—that's how they coordinate the movement of such large
numbers of men across broad fields. And the units with orders are all

323

trained to immediately respond. Seeing that, I've wondered... is the reaction so deeply embedded in them that even their dead would answer? The first trumpet means they are preparing to move out of their camp."

It did not take long for the trumpet to sound again, and Yosef explained: "That orders them to get ready to march." Soon came the third signal—"Now they will move out." From the not-too-distant hilltop and its base camp below came a thousand cries far louder than the sound of the trumpet that had sent a chill through him. Yosef knew the soldiers would have their right arms raised, fists clenched and held high as they shouted, "We are ready."

Yosef sensed Levi's nervous flinch again, though the Romans were nearly a mile away. All in Yotapta had done what they could with what they had. He and Levi turned to view the town behind the wall, the clusters of men at their stations. Dov was at a line of carts, lifting stones that no other man alone could raise and stacking them near the hoists at the foot of the wall. Close to him, Dalit and Ariella stood with a group of women, and Ariella smiled and waved up at Levi, who returned both her smile and wave.

Levi had told him they wished to be wed as soon as possible. He understood the urgency of such a love... but he also knew that Levi and Ariella's marriage would last only as long as Yotapta could stand against the Roman army.

LXXXIV

Nicanor walked Tempestas down the steep grade. Unlike the other officers—even General Vespasian—he had not left his horse to be corralled with the other animals of the legion in the field camp at the base of the hill. Tempestas had proved good company, and he preferred to keep the horse with him. With no social expectation of conversation with Tempestas, Nicanor was content in the silence—he had much to think about.

"How many are ready, Nicanor?" Vespasian had asked him earlier, without preamble.

"Most of the 160 we brought, general. All the smaller siege engine pieces we can move—with donkeys and men—over the road as it is now, and they are ready to go. The heavy machines—the *ballistae* and the largest *catapultae*—will be ready in another day. I ordered the *scorpios* with a stockpile of heavy-bolt arrows and the small catapultae to move into place. The armorer is preparing the firebrands—he has oil and cloth ready for them, and the quartermaster's work crew is bringing wood for the flammable bundles. They will also bring the cartloads of stone to a point behind Aebutius's line, facing the north wall. Loaders there will chisel the rough rocks to round them off as much as possible."

"Good." Vespasian had nodded at the report and half-turned so as not to squint into the sun. "The missile stock for all siege artillery is to be continually replenished. Make sure the quartermaster knows this and keeps making more. I want to rain rocks down on the walls of the rebels but reserve the heavy bolts and firebrands for their towers and parapets. Direct the men on that and to not waste their shots on other things. We'll drive the defenders from their posts and test what seems the weakest section of their wall—or at least the one with the easiest foreslope to climb."

"When do you want to be ready for that attack, general?"

"Today... as soon as the scorpio and ballistae are in place and begin firing. I want you to be in command of that effort."

"Yes, general."

"And Nicanor, I want you to command the cohort of heavy infantry to protect the siege engines." Vespasian studied Nicanor's face for a moment, then glanced at the centurion's bad leg, "You can serve in the field for me, can't you, Nicanor? It's important not to let the rebels have any more time. I don't expect them to try anything, and I believe they will remain behind their walls."

"All I have ever been and ever will be, general... is a soldier. I can fight."

Vespasian nodded and walked away, and Nicanor turned to Tempestas and went down to the field camp to carry out his orders. Nicanor meant what he had said—he would always be a soldier—but he got a sense that Vespasian was testing his willingness to fight against Yosef. It was true that a recurring qualm had run in the back of his mind since learning Yosef was the rebel commander in Galilee. Even though Nicanor's duty was defensive and he would not be leading the attack, he breathed a constant prayer that he would not have to face his friend with weapons in hand.

Nicanor shifted one section of his *lorica segmentata*—it chafed him despite the padded undertunic. He had not worn combat armor and battle gear since Beth Horon, and it was far different from what he had donned as a Praetorian Guard in Rome—that had been lighter and more ceremonial than functional. He dropped Tempestas's reins to adjust the scale armor to sit more comfortably. The horse cocked her head toward him and stretched her neck to be scratched under her chin.

"Don't worry, girl. I can still fight if I must," Nicanor muttered as he reached the base of the hill at a broad, stone-strewn path and mounted the horse. They soon reached the staging area for the siege engines.

Dozens of men maneuvered the small cart-mounted catapults that could quickly fire armor-piercing bolts or stone balls at a very high velocity, propelled by the torsion release of multiple strings of twisted catgut. Passing him to join others off-center of the line was a scorpionarius who trundled along beside the mule-drawn cart upon which was mounted the giant crossbow that was his charge. The man was personally responsible for positioning, aiming, firing, and maintaining the weapon in the field. On the other side of the cart was his loader, an auxiliary. Each man had a short sword at his hip and held an infantry *scutum*, the large Roman shield curved to fit the body. Before leaving Antioch, he had recommended to Vespasian that all men have and carry one, even before combat, to ensure the men got used to its weight and handling. They had emptied the armory of the shields, but he felt better seeing them on the arm of every man who could wield one. At Beth Horon, too many had lost their shields or had never had them, especially auxiliaries like Sayid, and they had been raked by arrows and javelins. That valley floor had been littered with the dead and dying. His sleep was still broken with nightmares of that time and place.

Nudging Tempestas, he cantered the line to make sure all was ready for the attack signal. He leaned forward to pat the horse's neck—"We'll be all right, girl."

* * *

"How is your arm, centurion?" General Vespasian asked from behind his field desk as Nicanor entered the command tent.

"It hurts, but it's healing, general." Nicanor rested his heavily wrapped right arm on his lap—spots of blood had seeped to stain the bandage. Five days before, during that first attack to test the rebels, the Jews had sortied through their gate—to Vespasian's surprise and his own. Supported by a shower of arrows from archers, piercing javelins, and a hail of lead pellets from the slingers on the walls, the rebels had stopped the Roman attack. Under the cover of that fusillade, the Jews had attempted to take the siege engines closest to them.

Not waiting for support, Nicanor had surged forward with his men. In the fighting, a rebel had taken up one of the many javelins littering the ground like kindling and charged at Nicanor. The centurion had tried to yank Tempestas around to free his sword arm, but the horse had stumbled in a wheel rut and nearly gone to his knees. Nicanor had been vaulted from the saddle, and the rebel's thrust had caught his forearm cuff and skittered along his arm, tearing a deep furrow up to the elbow. He spun, deflecting another jab of the javelin, and skewered the rebel with his short sword. Then he cut down another rebel while trying to avoid Tempestas's flailing hooves. It was man-to-man and hot work for a time before the rebels retreated.

Afterward, Nicanor had found his medicus friend, Aulus, who had shaken his head at this new bit of work and told him, "One day, my friend, you'll suffer a wound I can't stitch up or heal... and that—the gods help me—will be a sad day."

Nicanor used the wounded arm to reach for the cup of wine the general offered him.

Vespasian leaned back. "These Jews are braver and bolder than I thought, and now I better understand what Lord Gallus—and you— faced before. Each day they have come from behind their walls, come out against us, and failed. We've killed or wounded hundreds."

"General, there are believed to be several thousand within the walls. Placidus reported that all the fighters in this area came here once we left Ptolemais and were headed toward Yotapta. We need the ballistae and largest catapultae to batter their walls. We must hurl barrels of rocks to scatter the defenders from the ramparts and firebrands to burn that cursed platform they built. It gives them a perfect angle to fire down on our engineers and sappers working on the siege ramp."

"They've completed almost enough of it to get our larger siege engines close," replied Vespasian. "We've cut down a lot of trees on and around every nearby hill, and the stream of carts loaded with stones, dirt, and pottery shards has not stopped. Tomorrow morning, the engineers will pour more concrete for the thicker revetment needed to raise the ramp even higher. We'll have them work under a *testudo* formation—shields above and at the sides—in a stout framework of wood and hide—that should protect the legionaries well enough to let them finish it."

Nicanor carefully tugged at the bandage and tucked a loose end under. "I hope so, general. The rebels seem to have an endless supply of arrows, javelins, and rocks." Feeling Vespasian's eyes on him, he flexed his arm without outwardly wincing.

"Centurion, once the ramp is high enough to allow us to clear and scour their walls, we'll bring a ram to their gates. Then we'll end this for them."

* * *

Yosef was moving, but his legs were numb with fatigue. Despite the Galileans' attempts to reach the siege engines, the Romans had fired on them nonstop for days. The Jews had killed many Romans, but the city was filled with the cries of the hundreds of their own wounded they had pulled back within the walls. For the last five days, he had slept little and did not know when he would be able to. Besides himself, Levi, and Dov—the big man seemed unstoppable—there was no leader willing to leave the safety of the walls and risk death to seize or destroy the Roman siege engines.

Though the pace lessened at night, the Romans still fired on them by torchlight. The sound of rocks and heavy bolts striking the walls and parapets—most did not cross over the wall—had become as steady as the moans coming from the suffering who filled several buildings around the town square. He had just visited a dozen of them. Leaving the square, he had come upon Dalit and Ariella, exhausted and bloodstained from helping tend to the wounded and working with the hides of freshly slain oxen. The still-bloody, uncured hides were wrapped, stretched, and sewn onto frames to form a relatively flame-resistant barrier. They used these to shield the wooden platform atop the walls from the incessant firebrands that flew from the Romans' small catapults.

Once the Roman ramp was done, larger stones and firebrands would fall, and they had no way to stop them other than to attack the machines again with a hope and prayer to destroy them.

Yosef stopped to greet the two women. "Ariella, you must prepare... it is soon." They had found an old priest named Shaul for her and Levi, and the time for their wedding had come. But in the circumstances, happiness was difficult, and Ariella had grown increasingly silent. Yosef understood her glance at Dalit's blood-streaked form and then down at her own stained robes and the smears of blood covering her arms from hands to shoulder.

She shook her head without replying, and he regretted there was no water to spare for them to bathe as they should.

"I'm sorry"—he had shaken his head—"I will see you later."

Once night had deepened, he would join Levi and Dov... And Shaul would perform the ceremony and document Levi's marriage to Ariella. Yosef hoped the Romans would do nothing to disrupt the rite and that Levi and Ariella would have at least this one night. No one knew what tomorrow would bring—other than more blood and tears.

LXXXV

"While we do nothing, the Romans make more progress on their ramp," Levi grumbled, lying flat on his stomach next to Yosef in the space within the top of the casemate wall. He jutted his chin toward the small opening through which they peered down at the Romans at work. The Roman engineers had set a new layer of the concrete retaining wall and begun filling it to raise the ramp level. Each day it grew incrementally higher as other workers packed and smoothed the fill and leveled the material already in place. As it rose, the framed shelter erected to protect the workers grew higher.

Yosef shook his head. "No, it's good. Let them make progress—as the ramp gets higher, they must lessen their firing or even stop the siege engines altogether, lest they risk striking their own men. Until they move the weapons onto the ramp to fire over them, we are safe. I want them to think we do not have the will to come from behind our walls again—perhaps they will let down their guard."

The two men belly-crawled backward until they could slip onto a ladder and climb down. They reached the ground, and Yosef turned to Levi. "Dov thinks it's better to destroy it once they are closer to finishing. The rubble and wreckage will slow them down when they try to rebuild. They will want to keep the ramp at our weakest point, but they must first clear the debris or work around it. With thirty men, including several of his best stoneworkers, Dov says he can do enough damage to set them back considerably, or maybe make them switch to a spot we can better defend."

"When will we attack?"

"Tonight. The Romans keep their turtle formation in place under the *vinca*, what they call that fireproof wooden shelter over the workers. That legionary unit guards them, but they must periodically rotate to rest the men. I've watched and know the Romans—true to form—change the guard at the turn of a standard Roman watch. Tonight, we'll attack at the end of their second watch... just before midnight."

"I'll be ready then." Levi's expression tightened, then eased as he took a deep breath and let it out. "I need to find Ariella and let her know."

"No." Yosef put a hand on his friend's shoulder. "I'll command the men tonight, and you will remain here."

"I will not Yosef. We cannot afford to lose you, and I should lead the men tonight."

"This is my order, Levi. You remain here." Yosef looked Levi in the eyes—"I would not have Ariella become a widow." He did not say the words that almost slipped out: *Tragedy might come soon, and though I have no wife to make a widow...* his family would have lost a son and brother. For a fleeting second, Leah, Cleo... and even Rachel flashed in his mind. They might also mourn him... but he knew he would never be more than a memory to them. Here—in Yotapta—was his reality and fate.

* * *

OUTSIDE YOTAPTA

Nicanor had not lost the habits of commanding men in the field, and though it meant getting less sleep, he had made a point of speaking with each squad at the turn of the night watch before they relieved the men at the siege ramp. He was with them at this change of the guard when firelight suddenly bloomed in the distance, and then he heard indistinct shouts and the sound of a man running from the blackness in that direction. The cries grew louder as the runner entered the nearby shadows and then stumbled and halted before the campfire.

"The rebels are attacking, and they have a giant!" Behind him, the light of fire spread, and now were added different shouts and the screams of men... and the sudden faint clang of metal striking metal, and the bashing of metal on stone.

Ignoring the frantic man, Nicanor turned to the men. "Shields and swords ready—follow me...." He ran toward the fight, and they followed.

Minutes later, breathing heavily and thankful Aebutius's line had moved closer to tighten the encirclement of the town, Nicanor stopped at the edge of the light cast by the fire. The shelter of wooden framing blazed, and the hides strapped to it were smoking. A vast stack of wood the Romans had gathered to be used for shoring up the ramp was also ablaze.

Taking a moment to study the situation before rushing in, as had been drilled into him, Nicanor scanned the area. Two dozen or more rebels were locked in combat with the legionaries guarding the ramp work. Men from both sides fell to the ground in just the moment his eyes swept the scene. His gladius already out, he stooped to take up a shield from a dead legionary's hand. He strode into the flickering and shifting light, and his shock at what he saw—*It IS a giant!*—almost caused his death.

The stroke of a *spatha* arced from his right, and for a split second, Nicanor wondered where the rebel had gotten a Roman long sword, then it cleaved the crest of horse-hair from his helmet. His gaze at the giant had blinded him to the more immediate foe. So powerful a blow skewed the helmet around on his head and half-blocked his sight. He had to drop his shield to straighten it, then frantically blocked the next strike with his gladius, the force of the Jew's blow nearly knocking the short sword from his hand. The rebel was as big as he and even more stoutly built, muscled like a stoneworker or quarryman. But he had no skill, and that was the rebel's downfall.

Nicanor spun as the man brought the long sword around again— too wide—and let the man's momentum from the overstrike carry him off balance on the uneven ground. That exposed his neck, and Nicanor thrust into it, his sword grating on neck bone as it went through the other side. Pulling his weapon free, Nicanor sidestepped the rush of another rebel and slashed low to hamstring him. As the rebel's legs buckled, Nicanor's pugio tore into his throat, ripping it open with a spurt of blood.

Nicanor straightened, and there before him was a giant swinging a massive sledgehammer, his enormous figure silhouetted by flames. This Jewish Hercules had bashed the concrete foundation of the ramp into a web of cracks, and then it crumbled. Large chunks fell away, and the bulk of the ramp spilled out of its framework to spread across the ground. The giant turned toward Nicanor with a grim smile of satisfaction. The enormous rough-shaped iron head of his hammer and its thick wooden handle were slick with a red sheen. The rebel colossus walked toward him with lumbering steps, the sledgehammer held at his side.

"Futuo!" Nicanor cursed and backed away, trying to find better footing. He had only a short sword and a dagger... *Gods know I need a crossbow*—with plenty of heavy bolts and enough time to sink five or six shafts into this bear of a Jew. From the corner of his eye, he saw a Roman soldier and Jew exchanging sword strokes by firelight. A second, then a third legionary joined the fray, driving the rebel toward him. *The Jew will be cut down soon, and then they can help me against this giant.*

"Dov!" the Jewish rebel shouted as he came fully into the light. "Help me...."

The giant turned from Nicanor and moved with a roar to the other rebel, who twisted to the ground under the raised swords of the three Romans. The cry turned them and shook Nicanor, as the Jewish giant's mighty chest expanded and released another. In two strides, the behemoth had reached them, and his hammer struck a helmeted head in a burst of bone, brains, and blood. The huge Jew twirled the long-handled hammer, reversing it, and jabbed the handle end into the cursing mouth of the second Roman soldier, who fell choking on splintered teeth and blood as Nicanor ran forward to stab at the Jew's enormous back.

Pulling the hammer free, the giant spun it again, and with a short-gripped punch of its iron head struck the third legionary in the chest. The scale armor gave a metallic crushing sound that ended with a gasping rattle from the dying Roman soldier. The giant reached down and with one large hand gripped and lifted the other Jew and draped him over his broad shoulder. Blood flowed from a deep wound in the man's scalp, but he was conscious. His face came into the light, and his eyes opened upon Nicanor. Their stares locked as they recognized each other.

Stunned, Nicanor had but a millisecond's warning from the wind-swish sound of the hammer shrieking toward him and grabbed the shield at his feet, swinging it in one move tight against his body as he twisted to ride with the hammer's glancing strike. He was still knocked off his feet, and his shoulder and arm numbed with the blow. It took a second to stagger up, and he tried to raise the shield again and face the giant.

But the colossal rebel had turned from him and quickly—for such an immense man—headed toward the wall. A dozen rebels came from the shadows and surrounded the pair as they disappeared through the narrow gate.

Arrows and javelins had begun showering down from the rebel defenders on the wall, and Nicanor staggered away from the light of still-burning fires and kept to the shadows as he searched for any of his men still alive. He could not help but wonder if Yosef was badly wounded.

LXXXVI

"We don't have a line of sight, general," reported Galerius Senna, "but it seems the change in the ballistae's mission is having an impact."

The 12th Legion commander had arrived the day before with a thousand heavy infantry escorting a long pack train of mule-carts loaded with more equipment, arrows, and lead pellets from the latest Roman shipments into Ptolemais. They would need all they carried. Vespasian had ordered 500 archers and 500 slingers from the auxiliary forces to join them in Yotapta, and they should arrive soon. Unsurprising to Nicanor, Senna had immediately placed himself between Vespasian and the centurion.

"That was Nicanor's idea," said Vespasian with a nod to him. Nicanor had agreed with the general's order to pull back to regroup the engineers and construct new protection and siege towers for renewing the work on the siege ramp. But he had not believed that stopping the bombardment and merely blockading Yotapta was a good idea. His soldier's intuition told him they should press the attack despite the rebels' success in severely damaging the siege ramp. But Vespasian had decided to starve the rebels into submission. Perhaps that was best, though.

Nicanor had not reported to the general his brief sighting of Yosef nor that the rebel commander of Yotapta appeared to be wounded. He was conflicted about the attack's inevitable end, which would also likely mean the death of his friend. And as more time passed, it became too late to report because Vespasian would then ask why he had not told him sooner.

Accepting the order to pull back and cease firing on the rebel walls, Nicanor had recommended the small ballistae, which could be maneuvered and more easily protected, fire in a higher arc, and carry the projectiles over the walls instead of battering them. Their smaller stone loads had not proven effective against Yotapta's thick walls, anyway. Instead, they should target inside the town to strike the tightly packed rebels and especially with a hope to damage their cisterns: "The rebels likely have plenty of food stored, general, but not enough water," he had told Vespasian. "If we must cordon off the town... we should focus on that. Damage what they have for water

334

storage and make it risky out in the open within the city walls. We should also let the rebels think we have become lax in guarding that spring Placidus's hunters found. If the rebels become desperate—and I think they must—they may try to reach it. We can let them... then trail their men back to find how they sneak from the town. They surely have some secret way in and out, and we must discover it."

Vespasian had agreed. Nicanor had heard the talk in the camp that morning, and what Galerius Senna reported now had proved him right and confirmed the worth of his suggestion.

"A dozen rebels crept down to the spring in the middle of the *quarta vigilia noctis*, before dawn. The few men posted there had, as ordered, gathered away from the spring near a cluster of rock and scrub trees." Senna darted a glance at Nicanor, yet spoke as if it had been his idea. "They built a small fire and pretended to be absorbed in their game of dice. The rebels reached the water through a narrow, irregular gulch that arcs around the hill and climbs the slope up to the town. Its outer border—the one away from the mountain—is lined with scrub grass and brush that hide it until you are right upon the gully's edge.

"Our men hidden around the spring spotted the rebels," he continued, "who wore sheepskin cloaks and caps... each carrying two large water-skins. They left the gulch and crawled to the spring. Our men did not attack"—again, Senna's eyes shifted to Nicanor—"since we wanted to track the rebels back to the town. They filled their skins and crawled back into the gully. Our men followed them to a flat sheet of sheer rock with handholds carved for climbing. One rebel spotted a legionary who'd gotten too close and shouted an alarm. Our legionaries killed the rebels and scrambled up the rock face themselves. They discovered a small entrance in the wall—you'd have to crawl into it—but arrows flew at them from there, and as they drew back, the rebels filled the hole from the other side, sealing it with rocks."

"That way into the city is lost to us then," said Vespasian, "but not of great use anyway. We could never get many men through it, not enough to be worthwhile. But the rebels cannot use it now, either. Keep men posted there to guard it, commander." Vespasian dismissed Galerius Senna, who seemed reluctant to leave as the general turned to Nicanor. "Centurion, bring the architecti and quartermaster. I want them to prepare for when we have the additional archers and slingers here. They'll be able to keep the rebel defenders at bay when we rebuild the siege ramp and position the ram."

* * *

INSIDE YOTAPTA

"We are cut off then." Yosef shook his head wearily.

"We had no choice, Yosef." Levi read from a sheet of parchment in his hands: "four broken cisterns, choked with stone... others damaged, losing the water they held. Thirty-two men and a dozen women have died trying to salvage what we could from them."

Neither man looked up or flinched at the crash of Roman projectiles. They heard the stones land on buildings and on the street outside, and then the familiar cries of people struck directly or by fragments of rock. The din had no rhythm, and there were moments of relative quiet when nothing fell, but those were few, and then the bombardment continued.

"I should surrender myself to them... it's me the Romans want."

"No, Yosef... You've offered the people Yotapta that option—and received their answer."

"Then, I should go and raise an army to return and save Yotapta... it's the only way, Levi."

"Jerusalem never replied, did they?"

Yosef knew Levi meant it as a statement and not a question; no answer needed but shook his head. *No, Jerusalem will not send us an army.*

Levi continued: "And Tiberias and Gabara are destroyed... those towns' men are all killed or enslaved. Yohanan of Gischala—with all of his bold talk of being the man to lead Galilee—hides in his town with his men. Sepphoris will never fight against Rome. Among all the other villages of Galilee... there is no army to be raised to save us. This"—Levi waved his hand around them—"is all we have, and we need you to lead us."

"—To death from thirst." Yosef turned to the window as more screams came from near the wall. "The Romans will continue to break us down... bit by bit... until we are weak and can no longer fight. Many will not last long enough to even try... "

Levi set the parchment down on Yosef's table. "I pray we do not die that way."

"Then, we have no options. We must make them attack us now," Yosef said, the matter decided.

* * *

336

OUTSIDE YOTAPTA

Nicanor watched the engineers finish assembling the ram. Its shaft—a baulk as large as the mast of a ship—hung by heavy lines from scaffolding and a heavy-beamed frame. At its tip, the impact point was fitted with a massive piece of iron in the shape of a ram's head. The whole thing was mounted on four large wheels broad enough to traverse dirt or semi-packed sand with enough men or animals to pull it. Intended for Jerusalem, the ram was the largest Nicanor had ever seen; its parts had come on one of the supply ships with Galerius Senna.

Vespasian would join him shortly to witness firsthand the surprise sunrise had revealed. At the north wall and its buttressed gate, hanging from the parapets were dozens of blankets and assorted pieces of clothing—all soaking wet and dripping.

"What madness is this?" Vespasian asked as he reined in beside him and pointed at the rebel walls with the tip of his cudgel. "They certainly must have a well."

* * *

Whether the display was an insult or statement of resistance, Vespasian had not wasted time in canceling his plan to starve out the rebels and bring full strength to bear on them. All ballistae, with the additional 500 archers and 500 slingers, began firing. The team of men pulled the ram under its protection of uncured hides, thick timber, and wicker hurdles. This shed was far more substantial than the one used for the siege ramp work, and surrounding the team pulling the ram was an expanded testudo formed of two ranks of heavy infantry armed with swords and spears, and carrying their shields above them or at their sides. Foot by foot, the turtle formation moved between two newly constructed siege towers 50 feet high and iron-plated to protect them from fire until the ram was in a position to reach the wall.

Nicanor watched at the ram was secured beneath its cover. Two men released the blocks and wedges, and it swayed slightly before the men chocked the wheels to secure the ram firmly against the coming recoil. A team of eight men, muscles straining and feet digging in, pulled back on the tethers affixed to the massive ram and released. The ram's huge iron head struck, and the whole wall shook. From within the walls, an awful shriek and wail of women came as the first toll of the destruction to come.

LXXXVII

Julius 67 CE

Galilee

Inside Yotapta

Throughout the late afternoon, Yosef watched Dov's immense shoulders heave as he lowered huge bags, one after another, filled with dirt and chaff to provide a buffer between the wall and the striking of the Roman battering ram. Men not as strong as he had tired and been relieved and gone below or had been wounded and fell aside or from the parapet and then were carried away. Dov remained at his task. The cobbled-together protection he wore—Roman scale armor crudely reworked to fit his large frame, with leather forearm guards and a too-small helmet, had been struck by countless arrows, javelins and slingers' lead so often those near him claimed it sounded like an unending hail storm. One massive arm swung the line to keep the bumper high enough and in front of the ram as his other hand wiped away the blood that streamed from a deep gash in his brow.

Yosef felt Levi lean closer to speak over the cacophony of the Roman assault and the shouts and screams of men and women within the wall: "The Romans are using hooks on long poles to yank the bags of chaff aside," he said, "though sometimes they still shield the wall. But that's not stopping the steady hammering."

Yosef nodded without reply and looked away to inside the wall where Dalit climbed a ladder. There was no room for her on the parapet next to Dov, so she reached a sweat- and blood-streaked arm up to tug at the big man's leg. He scowled down at her—fiercely enough to make Yosef blink a dozen feet away and want to step farther from him—then changed to a smile. Quickly wrapping the rope, he held around the end of a post to secure it, he knelt and lifted her to dangle above the ladder. She touched his face, and Yosef wondered how he had not noticed their affection for each other before. The big man kissed her hand and said something, his whisper brushing her ear. Dalit's other arm came up around his thick neck, and Dov drew her close. Then slowly—regretfully—he lowered her to the rungs of the ladder until her feet found them. Then he waved her down.

Dov straightened and half-turned toward Yosef with a sudden shout: "The wall cannot hold!" The Romans manning the ram must have heard, as its next blow was even more powerful, and the cries of the legionaries grew louder.

The wall shook, and Yosef could see the old sections and quickly-built new ones around the gate crumble from the relentless pounding. The platform of the parapet shook, making Yosef grip a corner of the watchtower to steady himself. "Levi, have the men bring up more stone and timber to reinforce the walls."

Minutes later, his lieutenant returned with a dozen men pulling hand carts loaded with rocks and wood. They started unloading, the two largest men struggling to lift the biggest stones to set near a stout net used to raise materials and weapons to the ramparts.

"Levi!" Yosef called down to him. "Is there enough bitumen and brimstone to mix with the oil to use on their siege towers and the ram?"

"Not to set fire to both the towers and the ram, Yosef."

"Get what we have prepared and split it among three strike teams, then have them muster at the sally ports. When they're ready, let me know and watch for my signal to attack."

Dov crouched as low as he could to come to Yosef. "What's the plan? The gate wall will not take much more."

"Levi will lead an attack to destroy the two siege towers and the ram. There's not much pitch left to set them all afire"—Yosef shook his head—"but we must try."

The wall shuddered again, and Dov glanced over his shoulder at where he had tied off the bags of chaff. "Have them focus on the siege towers, Yosef. But they are iron-clad... so Levi's men must get inside that cladding to the wooden frame, douse it and set alight."

"What about the ram?"

"I will take care of it."

"How?"

"I'll do what I can... or at least do enough damage to it and the men handling it, and then others can reach it and do more. When Levi and his men are ready, signal me, and then let me do what I will do. I will tell you when to have Levi and his men attack."

As Dov walked away, he shouted down at the men handling the stone below: "Get all of the largest, as many as you can—ready to haul up to me. Set them on the net's platform and when I tell you... pull to raise and when I have it... lower and load again. Keep doing that until I tell you to stop... or until your arms fall off." He returned to his spot at the wall over the ram and leaned down toward the men. "And I will not tell you to stop!" thundered the bear of a man.

Levi approached Yosef with three groups of men, all carrying torches and bulging goatskin bags he knew were full of what

339

remained of the viscous, sticky flammable pitch. Levi directed two of the teams to fortified portals in the walls within his line of sight as he positioned his own in front of the sally port closest to the gate. He looked up at Yosef and raised his right arm.

Yosef nodded and called to Dov, "Levi is ready!"

Dov leaned down to the men at the base of the inner wall—"Pull!"

The stoneworkers already had the first boulder positioned and began hauling on the line. As it reached the level of the rampart where Dov knelt, the giant got his arms around the stone, lifted it, and stood with the rock chest-high. Bunched and bulging muscles strained the cords tying his leather forearm guards in place. One, then two of the armor plates protecting his shoulders sprang loose. As Dov rotated and turned to face out from the wall... more scale plates came free, rippling loose from his upper chest. He looked like a massive bird presenting ruffled feathers in anger. Dov raised the stone over his head, moved forward until his chest was pressed against the outer bulwark of the parapet, and threw it down on the fortified shed protecting the Romans and the ram. The weight of the stone, more than the shed's covering could withstand, broke through the timbers, and Yosef heard cries from below.

Dov kept moving and had barely thrown the first when he stooped to grip and lift the second. He cast it, and more of his armor loosened and fell from him. He reached for a third stone as Yosef moved toward him and stretched flat at the parapet's peephole to peer down at the Romans. The testudo was shattered, and several Romans within the formation were injured—one not moving and the rest in disarray, trying to reform. The third boulder landed to crush a legionary at the ram's head. Dov was going to bury the ram in rocks.

Yosef heard Dalit's scream and almost turned toward her voice but stopped. Dov had the fourth rock over his head when the javelin pierced him. Rocked back on his heels, he steadied and planted his feet and threw the stone. Yosef quickly put his eye to the hole and saw it strike the ram's metal head and heard the loud cracking of its shaft. His eyes went to Dov just as a second javelin struck the giant. Dov stood still, arms at his side, then brought a hand up to tug at one, then the other spear. The first had gone through his thick shoulder and came free in a shower of blood. The second—penetrated deep into his thick chest—must have caught on bone, and Dov's blood-slick hands could not pull it out. He snapped its shaft, so only a foot protruded, stooped and raised the fifth stone.

"Now, Yosef..." he said as blood gushed from his mouth.

Yosef barely heard him but saw it in the enormous man's wide eyes. Yosef slid to the inner edge of the rampart and shouted to Levi:

340

"Go!" He looked back at Dov as the man threw the most massive rock yet. Yosef quickly put his eye to the peephole as the stone landed squarely on the ram's head, breaking it off. Dov's roar brought his head up. Another shaft now protruded from Dov's chest. Below, one of the stoneworkers held a scratching, screaming Dalit, who was trying to reach the ladder to climb to Dov. Ariella ran toward them. A roar choked with blood made Yosef's eyes return to Dov, who shot Yosef a final look and nod, then he jumped from the wall.

LXXXVIII

JULIUS 67 CE

GALILEE

OUTSIDE YOTAPTA

Even though others had seen the giant rebel, too, and reported it to General Vespasian, Nicanor thought the general had disbelieved his report of the night battle at the walls when he mentioned to him: "Centurion, I've known men to see—or believe they've seen things in battle that just were not so. In the light of day, they saw differently, or things were proven otherwise afterward."

The comment had chafed Nicanor like the poorly fitted forearm cuff the armorer had made that reached his elbow to protect the fresh injury. He would fix that cuff if he had to do it himself. That night encounter with the giant rebel had torn open the wound, and Vespasian had ordered him to turn over to another centurion his command of the units defending the siege towers and ramp. He would not presume to prove to the general that the giant existed, to correct his disbelief, but he was relieved to hear that order. To face an enemy, he knew could not be stopped from killing him—even if he had the help of the other legionaries—had been a crossing point from which Nicanor could never return.

In his first year in the army, over twenty years before, he had met an old soldier who claimed his father had served with Legio XIII Gemina under Gaius Julius Caesar. The old man said his father told stories of Caesar, and that when he crossed the Rubicō, Caesar had declared to his men, "*Alea iacta est.*" Nicanor had not understood the significance until he learned more about the history of Rome. Only age could make a man truly understand the finality of the declaration, "The die is cast." But he knew now—starkly—as he currycombed Tempestas's coat and mane and reflected upon recent events in his life. He had now gone beyond his own Rubicō.

The massive rebel was ready to die for his country. A death that would mean something to his countrymen. The story of how the man died—and what he had done to defend this Galilean town—would live on. But the bitter truth Nicanor did not savor was that his own death would not yield the same result. There would be no stories told of his life or how he died. *No one will mourn me*, Nicanor thought with a fleeting wish that there might one day be a woman—like Lady Cleo—who would. *I will do my duty for Rome as commanded*, he thought *and will fight if I must. But I will not seek it out.* There was no glory in the lonely death he faced.

"Centurion..."

Nicanor turned from Tempestas to see Vespasian, wearing a plain camp cloak and tunic riding toward him. "Yes, general."

"Saddle and mount... I want you to come with me."

"Where to, sir?" Nicanor set the brush aside, picked up a thick blanket, and draped it over Tempestas's back. Then reached down to pick up the saddle and set it in place.

"I just received a report of your giant upon the walls. The rebels are trying to fight off our ram... I want to see him for myself."

"Yes, general." Nicanor finished securing the saddle and cinching its girth strap and stepped to a post just inside his tent to fetch his armor. Waving a young auxiliary over to help, he quickly donned it.

"I'm going just close enough to see him, Nicanor—if he's that big, I should be able to. No need to go up to the siege line."

Nicanor settled the scale plates against the padded undertunic and pulled on his helmet. Gladius already on his hip, he picked up his scutum and mounted Tempestas, shifting the shield—not usually carried horseback and the sword around to not gouge the horse as he settled into the saddle. "I'm ready, general." *He might not seek battle... but if he was to be near one, he would be prepared.*

* * *

"It seems what you and the other men said was true, Nicanor," Vespasian said as he dismounted, handing his horse's reins to an auxiliary.

They had arrived behind the line as the ram's head struck, and parts of the wall around its central gate began to crumble. Nicanor heard a bellow from the enormous figure atop the wall, but it was directed inside the walls, not outward. The men at the ram must have heard it because they redoubled their efforts, shouting insults at the defenders as they increased the tempo of the pull of the ropes and release of the ram's strikes.

Vespasian moved closer. No firing came from behind the walls, and Nicanor wondered if the rebels had spent all their arrows. He walked alongside the general. The giant began hurling from the ramparts, rocks larger than what any man should be able to lift. The first broke through the shed's cover-decking over the ram. The second landed on the men beneath it.

Vespasian was still moving closer, and Nicanor kept an eye on him. The general's face held an expression Nicanor had often seen at the games when a gladiator was doing something extraordinary. With rapt focus, the general intently studied the man upon the wall above them.

"General, we should move ba—"

"That rebel... that man is a Heracles, centurion... even his armor cannot withstand his strength. Look!" Vespasian pointed as a third, then a fourth boulder crashed upon the legionaries and ram.

They were close enough now to see the giant's armor had come free, exposing his upper body. Then one... then a second javelin struck the man. But he did not fall. Tearing one spear from his shoulder and snapping the shaft of the other in his chest... he raised and threw a fifth gigantic stone as a third javelin pierced him.

Nicanor, caught up in the marvel of such bravery, even if from an enemy, no longer kept an eye on the general. He, too, had to get closer to see the giant fall, as he surely must.

But the rebel did the unthinkable and jumped from the wall and landed upon the re-forming Romans around the headless, now useless ram. The man was a raging behemoth, a lion casting off jackals. He grabbed Romans, wrenching their arms and legs as he threw them from him as they tried to bring him down.

Free of the soldiers, the giant lifted the ram's enormous metal head high and faced the Romans with a rumble of thunder that silenced all around him. A half-dozen arrows—the thick shafts of crossbow bolts—stabbed into his thick legs, most in the thighs. The man lowered the ram's head, which glancingly blocked a javelin that would have impaled him. He stooped, gripped the spear, and cast it back.

Nicanor did not know if the man had recognized an important Roman or merely targeted the closest Roman wearing the least protection. The javelin flew straight, without an arc, at Vespasian.

Nicanor's tackle took the general off his feet but saved him. Vespasian's right foot kicked up waist-high as he fell and was skewered by the javelin as a volley of arrows rose from the walls to shower them both. Rolling Vespasian under him, Nicanor covered the general with his body and shield. He felt several bolts strike his back plates and glance off, and two sliced the leggings of his breeches. Lifting the general and getting his arm underneath to half-carry him... he got them out of range as heavy infantry moved up to confront the rebels.

Dozens, if not hundreds, poured from small portals in the walls carrying lighted torches. They headed for the ram and siege towers as Roman arrows and spears rained down on them from the towers. Looking over his shoulder, Nicanor saw the giant on the ground struggling to stand. The man got to his feet, his torso and legs sprouting a dozen arrows, a javelin through his stomach and another in his back. Then he staggered and fell, facing his enemy.

As Nicanor carried Vespasian to a medicus, he wondered what story would be written of the man. And what story would be told of his friend Yosef, who fought behind the walls that would surely soon fall?

LXXXIX

INSIDE YOTAPTA

The cry came from the Romans first: "The general has fallen..." And then the men on the ramparts with Yosef and Levi's men on the ground outside took up the call: "The Roman general has fallen!"

Yosef heard the lift in their voices as the Yotaptan defenders took heart at the news. Yosef did not. He had just watched Dov die, and the murderous rain of arrows still fell on Levi and his men. They had done some damage to the Roman equipment but not enough.

Yosef turned his attention from what was happening outside to inside the walls. Ariella still comforted Dalit, and a second flash of conscience came and went—why had he not seen that Dalit and Dov cared for each other? Ariella's head came up as men—what was left of Levi's assault—staggered through the sally ports, most of them wounded. Many that had attacked the siege engines had not returned. With a last hug of Dalit's shoulders, Ariella stood and ran toward a man covered with blood, either his own or that of the torn body draped across his shoulders. The man settled the unmoving figure on the ground and fell into Ariella's arms. Levi lived, though Yosef could not tell how badly wounded he was.

That their general was wounded angered the Romans, but the shouts of the rebels celebrating it enraged them to unleash a fury not yet seen. As twilight became night, the darkness filled with the echoing clank of siege machines firing and the crash of a seemingly endless hail of rocks that fell inside the city. Within the walls, the few lighted torches needed to care for the injured drew heavy fire from the Roman siege towers. A man next to Yosef, bandaging his own leg, had his head torn from his body by a stone that then struck below, where a group of women tended to the recently wounded. Arrows rained down, and he sent teams of other women to gather the shafts— even those removed from the dead and injured—so they could fire back at the Romans. Then came the thuds and screams at the large bolts repeatedly fired from a heavy scorpio outside.

Yosef watched under the torchlight as a pregnant woman awkwardly bending to bandage a man's arrow-blinded eye was impaled by one of the thick shafts of a scorpio bolt. The metal head tore through her stomach, sending her body flying and casting her

346

dead child—ripped from her womb—alongside her. The man lying at her feet, just inches below, was untouched. The sound of bodies falling from the ramparts grew louder. The Romans' raking fire cleared the ramparts, killing men in clusters. As the men fell, others climbed to replace them.

Yosef wiped tears from his eyes, for there was no time to cry. Later—if there was a later—he would cry... for his people.

Unable to muster an effective attack outside the walls to stop them, Yosef had seen the Romans working to repair the vinca sheltering the ram. It took the labor of a dozen men—likely auxiliaries—to bring forward a replacement shaft equally large and with a neck reinforced by a broad collar of metal. They would soon have the new ram re-rigged and ready.

Yosef spotted Galon and called: "More men to the walls. Gather all you can, even the wounded who can walk and carry a weapon. The fittest men are to join me at the gate wall." He climbed down and went to where the Romans would likely make their first breach. The area in front of the wall and gate was covered with blood and dead bodies in piles. Thus, they performed a last service, becoming part of the barrier against a breakthrough by the Romans.

Soon hundreds of men were with him before the gate: "When the wall and gate are penetrated, plug your ears and do not flinch at the legionaries' war cry. Fall back at the volley of missiles, they will fire to clear the way for their infantry. Stay under your shields until the Roman archers have spent their arrows. Then rush into the breach once the Romans have pushed their gangways over the rubble."

Yosef took a breath before his next instruction. "Make your stand. Don't forget for one moment the old men and the children here, those who are about to be horribly butchered. Don't forget how bestially your wives will be raped and then put to death by the enemy. Remember your fury at the idea of such atrocities and use it in killing the men who want to commit them."

Yosef turned from the men and spotted Levi, chest thickly bandaged, directing the emptying of cartloads of more stone and bodies to pile against the gate. "I don't think we'll leave by that gate, Yosef, and we have to use what we have to reinforce it against that ram."

"You gave the right order, Levi." Yosef gripped his friend's shoulder. "I'm happy to see you."

* * *

Yosef returned to the ramparts at sunrise. From every quarter of Yotapta came the crying of women. They had no medicine to give the shrieking wounded, and the sound of everyone's suffering had lengthened the night. As daylight finally came, three ranks of Roman legionaries were assembled before the wall and soldiers covered the nearby hills. The sobs of the women grew to a horrible, hopeless wail. "Levi," he ordered, "have Ariella and Dalit get all the women into the buildings."

Levi did so, then returned to Yosef. "What are they doing?" he asked. The heavily armored Roman cavalry dismounted and moved to join the rows of infantry. The rest of the horsemen remained mounted further back.

"The heavy-armor will lead into the break to clear the way for the light-infantry. The remaining cavalry will sweep out and secure the perimeter of the battle and kill or capture anyone escaping the city once it falls. They'll attack soon—stay with me in command of the ramparts, Levi."

A Roman trumpet sounded a call—echoing through the hills—and thousands of legionaries roared their battle cry. The morning sky filled with missiles: arrows, scorpio bolts, lead from the slingers, and a barrage of stones. "There"—Levi pointed—"they are moving ladders behind the main battle line, and up the siege towers to drop as gangways onto the walls."

"Bring up the oil now," Yosef said in reply. "Get everyone to help. When the bombardment stops, they'll charge the wall." Another blast from a Roman bugle came as Yosef looked through the sentry peephole. The Roman infantry had begun moving, and many carried the thick-timbered *scalae* Levi had mentioned. "Hurry the oil!" he urged.

As he turned, Dov's crew come onto the ramparts just as barrels of oil rose on the same platform that had hoisted Dov's rocks. The men quickly moved the barrels to the bulwark. Two men to each, the Jews poured hot oil on the Romans, lifting the ladders into place. Their close-fitting armor drenched in the oil that had not burned their exposed flesh, and the ladder rungs slippery, the Romans fell away, one by one. "Keep pouring," Yosef ordered, then told Levi, "Go below, and when we run out of oil, bring up the boiled fenugreek to throw on the ladders and any gangways the Romans manage to keep in place."

* * *

Rallying men from one part of the wall to another, at any point that seemed close to being overcome, Yosef did not realize the day's passing until it was done, and the Romans still had not breached the walls. Tired beyond measure, he sat with Levi in the corner of a damaged watchtower. He listened to his lieutenant, who grimaced in pain from the wound beneath his blood-soaked chest bandage: "We failed, Yosef. Dov broke their ram, but the Roman siege towers still stand, and they've rigged them to lift scorpios up to the platform to fire directly inside the wall. We stopped them, but after all the days of fighting and being trapped behind these walls... the already-exhausted men are completely spent..."

"We still live, Levi." Yosef had to give what strength he could, not knowing how they could hold out against another assault. "We will do what we can to stay alive."

* * *

OUTSIDE YOTAPTA

"I was foolish not to believe you and the other men—especially you, Nicanor. And more foolish still to get that close without armor." Vespasian settled his bandaged foot on the cushion beside his campaign desk.

"General, we were out of reach of the throw of any man but that one... and even in armor, you would have been skewed by that javelin. I'm a strong man... but a child compared to that giant Jew." Nicanor shifted one of the folding canvas stools out from the desk and sat.

"I'm sorry to have missed seeing the man," said Titus, pouring wine and handing full goblets around.

Nicanor drank deep, set his cup between his feet, and rubbed his forearm and a sore shoulder. "It was a sight to remember... but I'd rather not have met him up close."

"He is dead now, and so are hundreds of the rebels. The attack has further battered their walls, but they still stand. The siege artillery unleashed Hades upon them, and they still will not surrender." Vespasian shook his head and turned to his son. "Titus... you think this man—who claims to be a deserter from the city—has information worth my hearing?"

"Yes, general," Titus replied. "He says he knows a weakness and a way to get through the walls, but he will speak only with you."

"What does he want for this information?"

"Not to die, for one—and to be allowed to return to his family in Gischala."

XC

The woodmen had to have traveled some distance to find a tree tall enough, but they had managed it, Nicanor thought. The limbs had already been lopped off, making it easier to drag. Two workers affixed and secured a crossbeam just below where the trunk began to taper.

Nicanor understood the general's decision about the deserter's fate, but to lead the man into divulging the information... thinking it would save his life... That was something he could never do. Of course, Vespasian's reasoning was irrefutable: "We've been here too long. The rebels have held out, but the deserter says the Yotaptan defenders are exhausted, as are most of their means of defense—their arrows and oil. Men guard the walls through the night, sleeping at their posts in the early morning hours."

The general had paced in front of them. "Some have asked about the deserter. Nothing must give the rebels hope. I want no word of compassion or compromise to leave here—nor the deserter."

Nicanor had pondered the consequences to the soul of such a decision. Were it not for the words of Yosef, then Paul, he would not have thought of the burdens that choices place on the soul—he would not have given much thought to it at all. But once he started thinking of it, he found much to consider. He did not care to add any more weight to his own soul, and though he saw the appeal that converted so many... he did not believe Paul's words about how to cleanse a soul.

But he had agreed when the general declared, "It's time to end this." The staff meeting had then turned to a plan and the choice of who would lead the attack.

The sound of a soldier's sandals—the iron hobnails scraping on stone—came to him a second before the general's greeting.

"Centurion, I hope you're not offended that I chose Titus to command the assault." Vespasian stopped and studied Nicanor's face before glancing at the woodworkers and nodding to them. "I've heard the men of the 12th Legion exclaim their need to regain the honor lost at Beth Horon, and I know your bitterness at that, too."

"I'm not disturbed, general, and you offered it to Lord Senna in any case. Rightfully so, since he is the commander now."

"Yes," Vespasian said. "I believe he thought the job better suited to one of lower rank."

"But you've chosen your son."

The two soldiers exchanged a look. Neither mentioned how Galerius Senna had blanched—his face paling—when the general had offered the command. Then Vespasian—his test complete—had moved on to the man he had already decided would lead the attack.

"True, Titus and Senna are of equal rank, but Titus is a soldier." Galerius Senna was not and never would be.

"Why did you not order me, general?"

Vespasian scrutinized Nicanor, his usually stern expression eased, and he started to say something, then changed it to gesture at Nicanor's arm. "You need to heal fully before you see more combat."

Nicanor had noted the pause and wondered if some doubt lingered about his loyalty. He had just witnessed Vespasian make a cruel decision—as Roman commanders often must—and declaim against seeming compassionate. Why had he not ordered him to command the assault that would overcome this stubborn city?

* * *

INSIDE YOTAPTA

The night after the Romans' brutal onslaught had been unexpectedly quiet—at least the Romans were quiet. Inside the town, only the dead were silent. For the wounded and dying, the moans and crying did not subside, but Yosef had managed a few hours of sleep until called to the wall.

That morning the sun had risen upon an expected sight: the massive formation of Roman legionaries was advancing, forming a battle line before the wall. But close behind them came the unexpected: a team of men protected by heavy infantry dug a narrow, deep hole. It was a man's screams—shrill in the morning's stillness—that made Yosef look beyond the Romans to see something else approach. A line of mule-carts carried the trunk of a very tall tree. As the first cart neared the square of infantry, the rear row of legionaries pivoted to let the carts enter. Men came from both sides to lift the trunk from the first cart and position it at the hole. The screams grew louder. That cart was trundled aside, and more men raised to get the second cart, then the third from under as the butt end of the pole was lowered. On the last wagon, near the top of the trunk, was the crossbeam with a shrieking man tied or nailed to it.

The Roman workmen ran out long ropes attached to the upper end and crossbeam, and another team of men gripped them. With a heave and pull, the timber slid into the deep shaft as the men walked backward, pulling and steadying until it came erect, to bring the man level with the wall. In the slanting rays of sunlight, bright blood glistened on the man's body, where the Romans had beaten him severely. Ragged wounds in the wrists and ankles proved he had been nailed to the wood.

A dying man on a dying tree; the message was clear. What stood before them was what they could all expect. Whether in the coming battle or after... there would be no survivors from Yotapta—nor merciful deaths.

* * *

"Levi, why are you awake?" Yosef looked up from his journal as his friend entered the room. "There's been no alarm—none I've heard, since this morning. About..." He did not need to finish. The man's death had ended his suffering, but it would not be forgotten.

"I could not sleep." Levi tugged at the tunic that fit tightly over a thick swath of bandages wrapped around his chest. "I think I'll check the night watch on the walls."

Levi's pain showed in the clench of his jaw. "I'll go with you," Yosef said, starting to stand.

"No"—for a second, his old smile flashed—"Keep writing, Yosef. You must record what has happened here. Don't you always say... if no one writes it down... then those that live after us will never know?" Levi half-turned and stopped. "Earlier, you wondered who the man was. He seemed familiar, so I checked with the others with us at Gabara. We think he joined there and returned to Yotapta with us. No one knows how or when the Romans captured him." Levi stood still a moment, his head down. "Write about it all, Yosef."

* * *

Yosef woke from a doze. Lifting his head from the table, he rubbed the mark it had left and wiped his mouth. He closed his journal and set it with the others on the corner of his desk. He poured a precious cup full of water into the bowl next to them and peeled off the tunic he had worn for two—or was it three?—days. The *kinyan*, the coin from Leah, on its cord, came with it. He separated the two and set the *kinyan* next to the bowl. He had just dipped a piece of cloth in the pan to wash his face when he heard the shouts.

352

Dalit burst into his room—"The Romans are over the wall!" Yosef spun around, knocking the table over. "Where's Levi?" "Getting Ariella—he sent me after you. Hurry, Yosef!" He tugged on the soiled tunic. "How many Romans?" "Levi says too many... and they keep coming"—Dalit waved her goatherd's crook at him—"He says there's no way to stop them... the city is falling. We must get to the cavern."

Yosef picked up his sword and followed her, moving ahead to lead the way once they were on the street. Clusters of swearing, shouting, fighting men—a tangle of his own and the Romans—were everywhere. The Romans in full armor cut down the half-awake rebels, and bodies and blood covered the square. Yosef shot a look toward the northern wall and gate. On the parapets, two gangways crossed onto the bulwark from where he knew the siege towers stood. An unbroken chain of legionaries coursed across them onto the ramparts and down inside the wall. His men had tried to repel the Romans and been slaughtered. Their bodies lay in heaps at the foot of the ladders.

The din now filling the town came from the same yells and the harsh clanking of metal he had heard on the training fields with Nicanor. It was an unforgiving sound; one he would always associate with Rome. Heavy infantry, in full armor, ran and roared their war cries. He had seen them charge and slash apart hundreds of man-sized targets—wood, clay, and straw men—barely slowing. A part of the force separated from the mass and moved toward them. He pulled Dalit into the alley leading to the olive-oil storage cellar where Dov had found a passage into the cavern. He could make use of that man now—he almost muttered the wish aloud but remembered Dalit in time. Ahead, down the alley, at the descent into the cellar, he saw Levi with a sword and Roman shield. Ariella sagged against the wall behind him, her robe half torn from her. Two dead Romans lay at Levi's feet.

"How many made it?" Yosef gasped as he stared into the dark stairwell to the cellar.

"Two dozen... maybe more." Levi's chest was soaked in blood. A crimson slit through the bandages beginning to fall from him showed another deep gash across his stomach. "Dalit, please convince Ariella to go in."

"I'll not leave you, Levi"—Ariella shook off Dalit's hand on her shoulder.

"Yosef is here now... we're all going." Levi's eyes shot up and over Yosef's shoulder—"Now!"

The sound echoed louder and louder from the alley. Yosef glanced back to see the first of a dozen or more legionaries closing on them.

"Inside"—he shoved Dalit and Ariella into the stairwell and followed. He felt Levi press against him as they reached the bottom, the man's hand gripping his shoulder as they raced to the wall with the hidden passage into the cavern. The men spun the stacks of empty barrels away, and behind them tore apart the covering hiding the entrance. A quick glance inside showed that Dalit and Ariella had done their duty—each day—by keeping it alight with new torches, though these had burned low, flickering in the current from the opened entrance and the narrow airshafts to the alleys above.

The clatter of Romans coming down the steps made the dozen people seem hundreds. There was no time to get in and pull the covering back into place, hoping the Romans would miss it in the dimness.

"Go!"—Yosef waved at Dalit and Ariella and tugged Levi's arm. His friend still gripped his shoulder from behind. Thirty feet in, he felt that pressure lift. "Levi?"

"Someone has to stop them, Yosef!"

"Together, then..."

They met the Romans entering the tunnel, who could only come on barely two abreast and only by quarter-turning their broad torsos. Yosef took the shield from Levi, who could not raise it to protect them as they crouched and both thrust at the Romans. The legionaries overlapped their scuta in the narrow passage and pushed the two rebels back while thrusting at their heads and feet as they advanced. Ariella yelled behind them. She and Dalit were at the final ingress, a downward slanting channel into the caves. Darting a glance over his shoulder, Yosef saw Dalit pull Ariella backward to clear the opening for him and Levi.

"The Romans are too close!" Levi bellowed in Yosef's ear. "Save Ariella!" He pushed Yosef behind him to shove him back into the entry as a Roman sword drove between his shoulders to come out his chest. "Do it, Yosef!" Levi's eyes shot to the small inset carved in the wall, the deadfall trigger Dov had crafted that would collapse both the passage and the cellar they had come through. Yosef hesitated, and Levi kicked him, his foot square on the shield, to drive him back. Then he leaped for the trigger.

The crash of dirt and stone and push of air knocked Yosef from his feet. The shield atop his body gave him some protection from the rocks falling around him. The last sound he heard was Ariella's scream—"Levi!"

354

XCI

Beneath Yotapta, the Refuge Cave

Yosef blinked up into the surrounding haze, discovering it was not the befuddling effect of the blow to the head he had suffered. Dust hung thick in the air around where he lay. He coughed and touched the back of his skull. His fingers found a large bump—he winced at the touch—and came away damp and sticky. The light was too dim to tell for sure, but must be blood. He wiped his hand on his tunic, already stained with others' blood. *Levi!* He tried to sit up, and a hand on his chest pressed him down.

"Stay still, Yosef"—Dalit used her headscarf to wipe his face—"Other than your head, I don't think you're injured. I've called for a light so I can see better."

A man brought a torch closer, and Yosef could see that under her usual scarf, Dalit's hair was dark, with a reddish tint. A lot like Ariella's. And Dalit's features caught sharply in the torchlight were also similar. He knew they were friends, but they could be cousins too, perhaps. Yosef shook his head and wished he had not. "Help me up."

"You should"—Dalit lifted her hand and rocked back on her heels when Yosef rose shakily without stopping.

"Help me up," Yosef said again, reaching an arm toward the man with the torch who gripped his hand and pulled him up.

Yosef saw now saw the man was Galon, and he turned toward what had been the entrance from the cellar passage. A mass of broken stone and dirt spilled from there into the chamber. "It's completely sealed now," said Galon, "even more than Dov planned, and some of this cave ceiling has come down. Sections near and around the air shafts must have had cracks from the men boring or widening them. They came down with the shaking from the release of Dov's deadfall."

"Levi?" Yosef stumbled even though the cave floor where he stood was clear. Dalit steadied him.

"You left him to die." The voice was low but sharp and rang off the rock walls. Ariella came forward into the circle of light. Her face was powdered with dust and dirt, as were all of their faces. Tears had formed runnels that ran down and dripped muddy drops. She roughly smeared her wet cheeks with the back of a hand. Ariella no longer cried from sadness... the wide eyes caught in the torchlight were full of hate and anger. "You could have pulled him back... you could have saved him."

"Ariella..." Yosef saw Dalit shake her head and put a hand on Ariella's arm to turn her away. "Please let's go get you cleaned up."

"I'm Levi's wife"—Ariella yanked her arm from Dalit's hand—"I will not forget, Yosef. He is dead because of you."

The glistening eyes locked on him, and he wanted to explain there was no way he could have saved Levi; the dying man had given his last breath to save his life... and all of their lives. But Dalit was right—Ariella would not listen to him now. He hoped she would later.

Yosef turned to Galon—"How many people made it here?"

"You wouldn't have if not for Dalit—she saw Levi kick you backward but not far enough. She dragged you the rest of the way, and still, you were partly caught in the fall. Including you, me, Dalit, and Ariella, there are forty. Not counting you, six or seven of them are wounded."

"How are our supplies?"

"There's enough food for quite a while... and we have oil for the lamps. But...."

"Water's the problem." Yosef knew it would be.

"Yes. Several water-skins had been stored here with the food, and there is a cistern, but it appears someone has been using it... a lot. So, now it's low."

"How low?"

"Dov found a natural well, but the water level is far down, or perhaps it has gone dry." Galon covered a sneeze and waved away from his face, something flitting around the torch. "That rope with the hide bucket doesn't reach what water is left—if any—in the well. So, after we take care of the wounded, we must lengthen the line somehow, or someone will have to climb down with a light to see."

* * *

"How does it look?" Yosef asked Dalit as Galon pulled her from the cistern, and she handed him her small lamp. She had insisted she was the best person to check the water level: "I am the smallest and regularly climb more than all of you combined. Have you ever tended goats here or anywhere in the hills of Galilee, Yosef? It's day after day spent climbing up and down." Still unsteady himself, when no one else had volunteered, he had not argued with her.

"The water level is less than an arm's length above the bottom of the well," she glanced down at her bare feet and legs wet to just below her knees. "There is only a very tiny trickle of water into the well through its sides.

"Along with what's in the water-skins, we might only have about three- or four days' worth of water for the people here," said Galon. "What do we do then?"

XCII

Nicanor was glad to see it was just General Vespasian and his son Titus. Earlier that day, Galerius Senna was already assuming the trappings of a victor over Yotapta, striding through the camp some distance from where soldiers had fought and died to win that victory. Nicanor could not stomach any sight of him now.

Titus greeted him: "Nicanor, I wish you had been with us. The deserter was right—the rebels were asleep and did not wake until we cut their throats. The heavy mist helped, so thick inside the walls that our men were on the streets assembled in units before the rebels realized it. I ordered Placidus and Tribune Sextus Calvarius and their men to cut their way through the city seeking the commander."

"Did you find him?" Nicanor chose not to say the word "kill."

"No. Most we faced were asleep or just coming awake—they were in shock at finding us within their walls. Some gathered their wits and weapons to fight back. But no one talked—other than curses—none would tell us where their leader was. That thick mist filled the streets, and it was hard to search once the city was choked with rebels trying to flee. Many of the defenders barricaded themselves in the tower by the gate and held out for a while. When we broke through and overwhelmed them, they seemed to welcome death."

"None of them surrendered?"

Titus's expression tightened. "A wounded rebel was hiding in one of the shallow gulches that scar this mount even inside the walls. Domitius Sabinus, the tribune of the 15th, reported the man had called to a centurion, Antonius, saying he wanted to surrender. The man asked for help in climbing out, and when Antonius reached down, the man stabbed him in the groin with a spear. They could not stop the bleeding.

"I knew Antonius," Titus said, "a good man, a good soldier. To die like that from a cowardly blow,"—Titus grew quiet, but his clenched jaw did not relax.

"Titus...." Vespasian leaned toward his son.

"The men did not—will not—forget that," Titus continued, "and many still suffer from the boiling oil." Titus raised his eyes to Nicanor. "And they have taken up the anger of the men of the 12th

358

after what happened to them at Beth Horon. They were driven by rage this morning and drove the rebels like cattle until they had nowhere to run—and they slaughtered them all. My men are now hunting down more of those in hiding and the ones who fled to the south."

Vespasian studied his son for a moment. "Ulpius Trajanus is moving the 10th Legion to secure the area southwest of us. Sextus Cerealis of the 5th has control of Samaria, where despite their traditional hostility toward Jews that I've been told of, the people were on the verge of joining the rebellion. At Mount Gerizim, where a militia had gathered, the 5th Legion killed 11,000 Samaritans. Galilee and the route to Jerusalem are ours.

"But I must know we've killed the Galilean military leader. I do not want him to escape and raise men to harass us as we move from Galilee." He turned to Nicanor. "Centurion, you're the only one who can identify him. Under your command, I want you to take at least a *decanus*—better two—to search the city. Check all the rebel dead and bring me his body, or capture him and bring him to me alive."

* * *

At the horse's nicker and clop of hooves behind him, Aulus stepped from the path without turning around and continued his upward climb on the rough outer edge of the trail.

"Without having me to tend to... what occupies your time, my friend?"

The *medicus* looked up as the horseman came even with him. "Nicanor! I could ask you why you've had no new wounds requiring my skill... but I'm glad you've not needed me lately."

Nicanor dismounted to walk alongside his friend. Behind him, Tempestas blew through her lips, the blubbering a sign that the horse was relieved not to carry the centurion's weight up the slope. Nicanor glanced back and half-smiled at the horse.

Aulus squinted at Nicanor and stepped over a stray rock. "You look weary, yet the fighting has been over for days."

"After three days, I tire of viewing dead bodies... I'm tired of having them rolled over, of kneeling to check them."

"Check them for what?" Aulus was puzzled.

"—To see if any is the rebel leader of Galilee."

"You mean your Jewish friend, Yosef?"

Nicanor grunted and nodded. "There are thousands of dead... it will take weeks to examine just the bodies of men. And after a few more days, I won't be able to recognize him. But that is what the general wants."

"I heard today that 1200 have been captured—could he be one of them?"

"Those are women and children—soon to become slaves"— Nicanor shook his head—"But I think there are more rebels in hiding we have not yet flushed out."

"Hiding where?"

"Like much of this region, the rock beneath the town is riddled with caves."

The two men and horse reached the plateau where the headquarters camp had been established. "Let me tend to Tempestas, and then we'll eat—if you care to join me, Aulus."

Before they reached Nicanor's tent, a camp runner intercepted them. "Centurion, General Vespasian requires you in his command tent."

"Here"—Aulus reached for the horse's reins—"I'll take care of Tempestas for you and will wait. We'll eat and talk when you return."

With a nod of thanks and a pat on Tempestas's neck, Nicanor turned to follow the runner.

* * *

Nicanor entered to find Galerius Senna and Titus with Vespasian.

"Good"—the general nodded at Nicanor and beckoned to his aide—"Gaheris, have them bring her in."

Moments later, two burly legionaries dragged in a disheveled, battered woman wearing a torn and soiled robe. "Be still, woman!" With an effort, they held her fast.

"Give your report again," Vespasian ordered.

"General, we captured two women carrying water-skins, climbing from a gully. We followed them and found the mouth of a tunnel. One woman screamed a warning when she spotted us, and someone inside brought rocks down, sealing it off to stop us from entering. They were bringing water to rebels hiding below ground."

Nicanor waited, but no one asked—or perhaps the others already knew, since this seemed a retelling for his benefit. "You said, two women..."

"The other would not be taken, and we killed her. This one"—the legionary shook the woman's arm—"fought like a wild animal." He threw to the ground the goatherd's crook he had been holding in his other hand. "I got this from her and knocked her out with it." He raised his free hand to trace a still-fresh welt on his cheek that testified to the force of her blow.

Nicanor looked down at the crook, then up at the woman between the legionaries. She lifted her head, eyes burning at him from beneath tangled strands of firebrand hair. He turned from her to Vespasian. "It seems there's more for me to hear... right, general?"

"She says the Galilean military commander Yosef is still alive, along with other rebels who survived our attack." Vespasian scrutinized Nicanor's face. "We've discovered the air shafts that must go down to this hole they hide in. Go to them and call down. Tell him to surrender, or they will all die."

XCIII

BENEATH YOTAPTA, THE REFUGE CAVE

The world—his world—had become chaos, filled only with loss. It pressed down on him until he could barely breathe. From within the chaos came a voice: *A man will come from Judea... who will restore order.*

What man? Show me, he had asked the voice.

The figure came closer, with thick arms crossed over a barrel chest.

Who is this man?

The voice answered: *The emperor of the world.* Then it had faded as another called to him.

"Yosef"—a hand had shaken him awake, and the dream had slipped from him. "The water's almost gone," Dalit had said that morning. "I checked, and since it's before dawn, there are no Romans around that I could see near the tunnel exit. Ariella and I must find water. We'll be careful."

Fogged by a shaky—broken—sleep, his head still pounding, Yosef had thought to forbid it. But they needed water to survive. So he had nodded. As Dalit and Ariella slipped into the smaller passage to the only remaining exit from the cave, Ariella cast a vicious look at him. The anger and hatred had not left her eyes. Dalit had said it would fade, and in time she would accept that Levi's death was inescapable... and that no one could have saved him. But how much time was left for them? Hours had passed, and Dalit and Ariella did not return; he knew it must be sunrise, and his worry for them had grown.

Galon had asked if he could search for the women. "No," said Yosef, "but stay near the entrance to watch for them."

He had continued to wait and worry.

A crash of stone echoed into the chamber and brought him to his feet, looking to the ceiling for collapse before a staggering, coughing Galon came crouching from the tunnel after a billow of dirt. "The Romans have Dalit and Ariella...." he gasped. "They must have caught them returning. I had to seal the tunnel, but that will not keep them out for long—they'll soon know how deep the rocks and dirt go. They can clear it with a few hours of work."

The wounded moaned and cried; the rest of the men were silent. Yosef knew their thoughts. There would be no survival... not that there had been much hope for that. He returned to his corner beneath one of the air shafts, and the small circle far above he grew brighter with the morning.

He tried to sleep. Reaching for the kinyan that always comforted him, he remembered it no longer lay upon his chest. Somewhere in the scramble to get here... to what would become their burial place... he had lost it. Eyes closed, missing the one thing that anchored him to the life that was slipping from him, he felt the beginnings of the dream forming. He was tired... and his head ached so badly. Maybe he should just let go. He slipped into a drowse that deepened, and the voice in his dreams called to him.

* * *

"Yosef..." The voice from above was faint. "Yosef"—it grew louder. A hand shook him, and he opened his eyes. "Galon... what is it... are the Romans clearing the tunnel? Why do you call me?"

"That's not me..." Galon pointed a finger up.

Is God now speaking to everyone? Yosef wondered as he sat up, and with Galon steadying him, stood. The circle of light in the air shaft had dimmed with the lateness of the day. Something passed over it, and the gray disappeared.

"Yosef, are you there?"

The voice was louder, imperative. And it was familiar, that gruffness. He had tried not to think about the man since that night when Dov had saved him—when he'd seen him in the firelight, through the blood in his own eyes. But now he recognized it was also the voice in his dream.

"Nicanor? Is that you?"

XCIV

Galilee

Beneath Yotapta, the Refuge Cave

"How is it you know this Roman, Yosef?" Galon asked, drawing closer while holding out an arm to restrain the other men. "I speak Greek, too, and understand all he said."

Yosef looked at them, rubbing his aching neck after talking to Nicanor through the air shaft. The men had been muttering, and now a few shouted curses and threats. Galon had moved them away and quieted them so he could listen.

"I met him on the ship to Rome a few years ago," Yosef replied, "and while there spent time with him learning about the Roman army."

"You sound as if you trust him." Galon's tone was harsh, unlike the respectful tone he had always had with Yosef before. "You cannot trust the Romans..."

"I trust this man, Galon. There's a difference between the man and the country... the empire he serves."

"Not to a Galilean!" shouted a man behind Galon.

"Well, I trust this man and believe what he told me—what he promised," Yosef answered quietly but firmly.

"You believe that the Romans will not kill us if we surrender?"

"He said his general, this Vespasian, respects us as soldiers. He respects that we held out for seven weeks. Few can claim to have done that against the Romans." Yosef did not mention that the offer of life Vespasian had given via Nicanor would fulfill what the voice in his dreams seemed to tell him—that he somehow would survive this war of rebellion.

"Yosef, if we surrender... we all become prisoners... slaves to the Romans," replied Galon. "Or more likely crucified! We've all seen that done...."

A man behind Galon shouted: "It is better to die than live with a Roman heel on our throat! —And their swords ready to strike if we do not do as they wish."

"Then I alone will surrender," said Yosef. "You heard the Roman—Nicanor is his name. Vespasian wants me alive. Why... I do not know. But if he does, then maybe if they take me, they will let you go."

Several of the men behind Galon pressed toward Yosef, and Galon declared for them all, "We will kill you if you try to do that."

"I can ask the Romans if they will—"

Three men pushed Galon aside and charged Yosef with drawn swords. "Coward! Traitor!" cried one, and another, "Ariella was right—No Jerusalemite will ever care for us in Galilee. You let Levi die!"

Yosef dropped the torch he had held while talking with Nicanor, and it went out. Once the scrambling men had kicked over the lamp, the center of the cave was in darkness. A blade hissed through the air, and he ducked and rolled. Staying low and stepping into the deeper shadows, he pleaded with them: "I'm neither coward nor traitor. Galon, you know this... I did not let Levi die. Dalit herself told you that."

"Stop!" Galon shouted. "You men, stop and lower your swords." His eyes sought Yosef in the dimness. "But, Yosef, you want to submit to the Romans! Levi would never... ever surrender. And Dov... think of him and how he died fighting. If surrender is your choice... these men will kill you. And then we will all die by our own hands rather than risk capture by the Romans—to be enslaved or crucified like that man outside our walls. That is no way for any man to die."

The voice in his dream had spoken of what and who was to come to bring order from chaos. "Killing ourselves is not a sacrifice that will please our Lord... he is not pleased with suicide."

A man lit a new torch. In its blaze, Galon blinked and shook his head. "Did that blow to the head unhinge you, Yosef? You talk as if you know what our Lord—"

"Let me think about it then, Galon," Yosef interrupted. "Just overnight. Let me come up with something... an alternative."

Galon shook his head, took a deep breath, held it for a heartbeat, and let it out. "I have followed you, Yosef, and Levi believed in you, too"—he glanced over his shoulder—"You told the Roman you would give him an answer tomorrow morning. I can keep you alive tonight. But in the morning, if you still talk of surrender to the Romans... I will not stop them, and they will kill you."

"Just give me tonight to think."

"Until daybreak, then..." Galon turned and waved to the other men to go with him and leave Yosef alone.

* * *

Through the night and early morning, there had been little sleep but a lot of talk. Yosef heard the low voices of the men who thought he should be killed and Galon telling them to wait and listen to what was proposed and then decide. The dream did not come again to Yosef, though it remained a clear vision and voice in his head. But he thought much of Levi, of what his friend had told him the night before the final Roman attack: "Keep writing, Yosef. You must record what has happened here. Do you not always say... if no one writes it down... then those that live after us will never know?"

If they all died, no one would ever know what had happened—not just in Galilee, but what he had witnessed in Jerusalem that had played a part in starting this war.

Chance—or was it fate?—had brought him together with Nicanor on the *Salacia*, in Rome, and even now, and he had come to know Sayid and Lady Cleo. People of such different backgrounds and culture... but they had a bond formed through shared experience. They were all good people. Nicanor would hold to his word—the word of his commander Vespasian—and see them all safe if they yielded.

Yes, they would become prisoners; slaves, likely. But he did not believe they would suffer the same fate of the man who had deserted Yotapta. He knew how Romans despised such men. Romans like Nicanor and this Vespasian admired those who fought well, even against them. God had kept him alive despite all that had happened at sea, in Rome, in Jerusalem, and here in Galilee. The Lord forbade killing themselves, but he must come up with a means to let him choose who lived and who died. The talk he had heard throughout the night—the men who now wanted to kill him—had convinced him that was the only thing that might satisfy them.

* * *

"Yosef, it's time...." the glow of a lamp cast light before Galon as he crossed the chamber.

"I'm ready." Yosef rose and followed him to where the rest of the rebels sat or lay around several other burning lamps.

The man who had talked most about killing him stood. Yosef had not known him before they took refuge in the cave. "Before you speak, Yosef, I have something to say. You wanted to surrender. Do you love living so much that you're ready to live like a slave? Have you lost all self-respect? How many men did you persuade to die fighting for you against the Romans you would now surrender to?"

He paused and drew a ragged breath that spoke of his deep passion. "You won't deserve to be called a man if you surrender, and everybody will spurn you for allowing yourself to be spared by the people you fought so fiercely. Perhaps the Roman victory has made you forget who you are, but we are here to see our forefathers are not insulted. We will give you our own right hands and a sword for the fight, and if you are ready to die properly, then you shall die as a Jewish general. But if you refuse us and continue your plan to surrender, you can die as a traitor." The man sat down and crossed his arms.

"I would not go over to the Romans because I want to betray anyone," replied Yosef, "and I would not betray myself. I would be as stupid as a deserter if I did. Deserters seek to save themselves, while I would be trying to save others. Yet if surrender ended in my destruction, that would be Roman treachery. If they kill me after giving their word to spare my life, I'll die happy, since it will show the Romans falseness and their lies about honor. Inside their hearts, they would have to recognize the truth of that, and that alone would be winning a victory. Why are we so frightened of yielding to the Romans?" Yosef looked around, making clear he asked all of them.

"Is it death?" he continued. "Why are we afraid of death when you've made up your minds, we must kill ourselves? And we only suspect the enemy might kill us. Or are we scared of being made slaves? Well, just now, we're not exactly free.

"God does not want the alternative—our death. The souls of men who act against themselves in this mad way are shut up in the darkest hole in Hades while God punishes their children, blaming them for their fathers' sin. God hates such a deed, and God's declaration of the punishment for the crime is given by our lawgiver, Moses. Our law demands the bodies of suicides should be exposed, yet we are allowed to bury the corpses of our enemies in due time. Many of our priests disapprove of suicide—you know this, too." Yosef paced, circling the lighted lamp at the center of the men.

"There is one way to serve the honor you wish and still offer what God will accept. We must draw lots and let God choose who lives and who dies." Yosef took two nearly identical stones he had found, both about the same shape and roughness. One was light-colored, one dark. He set them before the largest lamp so all the men could see them. "These—by our hands, our choice—shall be how God decides." He picked them up and put them in the skin pouch he had detached from his waist.

"Each man will reach in and choose a stone—cast his lot. Those who get the dark will cut the throats of those who get the light. So it will go until only two men remain. Those last two will live to bear witness that those who died were not murderers nor cowards... they were heroes of Israel... and of our faith. Chosen by God's hand in this.

"These last two will risk crucifixion to save your souls. And so, you see, I am ready to die with you. If I survive, it will be against all the odds. It will be God's will alone."

The silence grew as Yosef walked to stand beneath the air shaft that revealed night and day outside, the one through which he had spoken with Nicanor. He glanced up at the faintest arc of a circle forming.

"What he proposes is reasonable," Galon replied as he walked toward Yosef. "You men cannot argue differently. We will not surrender—we will stand before God as men true to our faith. We do this now. Two by two, all of you stand and pick." Galen took the pouch from Yosef.

* * *

A voice called through the air shaft—"Yosef... "

The cave was silent. The air, long grown stale and heavy with the stench of soiled humans, some with souring wounds, had become more oppressive with the coppery cloying scent of fresh blood. In orderly rows lay dead men, each with prayers and benedictions intoned over him. Dark pools grew beneath them, yet to congeal.

Most men had been conflicted—was it better to draw the white or black? Better to get it over with than to have to slit the throat of another. Yet the desire to live was always there. He had watched as many tears were shed as men embraced and said goodbye to each other with parting words that offered comfort: "We will meet soon on the other side, my friend," and "You are a hero of Israel."

"Yosef!" the voice above echoed.

The count of the living had gone down by halves, and now the four remaining men looked at each other. Two reached into the pouch and brought out stones. The man holding the black stood aside as he dropped it back into the skin bag. The man with the white did the same. Yosef shook it, reached in, and took a stone without looking at it. The fourth man stepped forward and took the last stone. The hand trembled as he opened his fist, gripping the rock. Black.

"I guess the Lord wants you to live, after all, Yosef." Galon shook his head, resigned to what was to come next. He had picked the next-to-the-last black stone.

"I'm sorry, Galon." Yosef looked at him and then away.

"I am not sorry, Yosef. I wish for this ending. You must tell our families the news of our bravery."

"Yosef... are you there?" Nicanor's voice echoed.

XCV

Nicanor had asked Yosef about the others in the cave and looked with surprise at the reply Yosef gave him. "I don't understand," the centurion said back to where Yosef was trailing on foot behind Tempestas.

When Yosef looked up, he studied his friend's face, which had aged markedly since they had last met in Jerusalem so long ago. He did not count their recent nighttime battle glimpses as truly seeing one another.

"Why did you and your men do such a thing?" Nicanor asked. "Leaving your life to such poor odds, you could just as easily be dead, too."

Wary of getting too close to the horse's tail and hooves, Yosef explained, "I offered my men an alternative to the suicide pact they wished to follow. The casting of lots is something they know and respect as a means of letting God decide." Yosef lowered his head to watch his footing on the trail as it steepened. "I trusted in what I have seen and heard in my dreams... that even against such odds, my God would somehow spare me from death. You remember my other visions that proved true." Yosef looked up again at Nicanor and stumbled. With his hands bound behind him, he nearly fell.

When the Romans had cleared the rubble from the passage leading to the only remaining exit from the cave, Yosef had stepped out and been nearly blinded by the sunlight after days in mostly dark. A grim-faced Nicanor had met him, and the legionaries with him were more than grim. Most had hands on their swords, a few with spears lowered toward him and ready to run him through... all with fierce expressions.

Nicanor had quietly greeted him: "I am glad to see you alive, but my men are not." Yosef knew their anger by the roughness as he and the other survivor were chained. The man who had been one of the strongest advocates for killing Yosef did not look at him or say anything as they dragged him away. Nicanor had gestured for Yosef to come with him.

As they crossed the near mile from Yotapta to the Roman encampment, Yosef's eyes had finally adjusted. The sun was brighter and hotter as they began the ascent to what Nicanor had told him was General Vespasian's command encampment. A breeze stirred the air as they climbed higher, cooling his face. Despite being so tightly bound—Yosef was losing the feeling in his hands—being aboveground, in the sunlit world, was a blessing.

Nicanor confirmed that his men and the other prisoner had made the turn for the path toward the camp at the base of the hill. Satisfied they were out of sight; he dismounted and untied a waterskin from the saddle and handed it to Yosef. "Here, it looks like you need this."

Yosef drank greedily, wiped his mouth, and gave the skin back to Nicanor. "It's not quite the taste of the wine in the cask you found floating near us after the wreck of the *Salacia*—how beautifully that slaked our thirst then!"

With a bark of a laugh, Nicanor took a drink. "No, not like it at all...." He clapped Yosef on the shoulder and shook his head. "I still don't understand what you and your men decided. But if in your faith or belief, it was an honorable death, then I leave it at that. Strangely, you mention being alive against the odds. Recently, I've thought the same about what's happened to me in the past few years since meeting you. Together and apart, we both have had experiences to make us think."

"And now I expect I have more to face...."

Nicanor nodded. "And I regret it, Yosef. I take you to General Vespasian, and he holds your fate in his hands."

* * *

Yosef noted that Nicanor did as he had told him he would when they reached the meeting place for the Roman general. Though bound as a prisoner, Yosef was not led by Nicanor; instead, he walked beside the centurion. As they approached, four auxiliaries finished rolling up the walls of the large tent to let in the air. Several officers and senior legionaries had assembled to see the captured Galilean military commander. They struggled among their ranks to get a better view of him, and several men called out demands to put him to death.

Yosef did not let their calls distress him, and he stood before the thick-chested man with an aquiline nose and a lined forehead that seemed broader for the lack of hair. Seeing the man shook him more than did the fear of becoming a prisoner of the Romans. The man looked familiar. Then he remembered—it was the man in his dream!

Tight-lipped, Vespasian scrutinized the prisoner with a glare and the expression of a rigid, unforgiving commander. Nicanor had told him this general was also fair, and unlike the Roman nobles who pretended over-politeness to superiors and arrogance toward those below them.

Nicanor saluted. "General Vespasian, this is Yosef ben Mathias, the military commander of Galilee, who has surrendered to you."

Yosef recognized that Vespasian sat on a *sellae curules*. Made of wood veneered with ivory, with curved legs forming a wide X, the low chair with a folding seat had low arms and no back. The general looked uncomfortable. Yosef knew why, from his study of the Romans. The chair was a symbol of political or military power and authority. And it was also meant to be uncomfortable to sit on for long periods. The official must carry out duties efficiently, and his power was temporary.

Next to the general was a man slightly younger than he, Yosef thought. It was hard to judge since he stood, and the general sat, but the nose marked him plainly as the general's son—Titus—who Nicanor had mentioned. *The son is softer than the father*, the stomach more rounded, without his father's barrel chest. But after a friendly nod at Nicanor, Titus became stern, too, when he stared at Yosef. The young man was as formidable as his father.

The clamor from the other Romans around that the prisoner grew—they insisted he should be crucified. But Vespasian raised the wooden cudgel that had been resting in his lap. All quieted as he looked expectantly at Yosef for him to speak.

Knowing the Romans for their appreciation of dignity in those they dealt with, which commanded respect, Yosef knew he must speak up and carefully consider his words. The wrong ones could cause him to become nailed to a cross: "It seems I am defeated by the man who will soon rule the entire Roman world. General, I ask to speak with you privately on this matter of great importance to you."

Yosef turned to Nicanor, who had remained at his side. "Centurion Nicanor and I know each other. And he"—Yosef gestured with a chin thrust—"knows that I have dreams that somehow come to pass. The most recent one I must share with you." He nodded to the young man, making steady eye contact, then moved to study the general. Yosef patiently waited for a reply and did not flinch at the man's unwavering scowl.

Vespasian locked eyes with Yosef for several seconds, as if trying to determine if this was an honest man who stood before him or someone carrying out a ruse. "Everyone away," Vespasian ordered, sweeping a thick arm to encompass the crowd of men—"except for you two"—he gestured at Titus and Nicanor and shifted in the chair.

The sour expression hardened, and he glanced up at a gray-haired man standing behind him. "Gaheris, clear the area and have the sides rolled down." He slapped the arms of his seat— "And bring me my camp chair. Put away this thing, Lord Senna insisted on."

* * *

Yosef appealed to the Roman general: "Lord Vespasian, you may think you've done no more than take me prisoner for your purposes, but had I not had a certain compelling dream more than once, I would have shown you how defeated Jewish generals die. I've thought you might want me captured to send to your emperor. But why send me to Nero? I believe he and those who follow him will not survive the time of this war. What I have clearly seen, Lord Vespasian is your face—as one who is the ruler of the world. That means that you will, not long from now, ascend to become caesar and emperor. You, Caesar, are not only lord of me but of the land and sea, the lord of all mankind—"

Nicanor interrupted him: "Yosef... the general is not a caesar."

No doubt, he fears I will crucify myself here, mused Yosef, aware that Nicanor sought to protect him by moderating his words.

"What are you doing?" Nicanor insisted.

"I'm speaking what of what I've seen and heard, Nicanor. You have seen that these vivid dreams of mine somehow come to pass."

"I have no wish to become a caesar nor an emperor," said Vespasian, more at ease on the field stool, but still forbidding. "There are many in Rome who would become caesars—emperors—before me. They have probably already secretly planned their ascent to the throne when the opportunity presents itself. I am only—once again—a soldier. I am content with my status, and for me to become emperor would be against all the odds."

"Yet, Fath—general"—Titus spoke up—"Nicanor has told me of this man's prescience. He foretold the shipwreck of the vessel he and Nicanor sailed on to Rome. And the great fire that almost destroyed Rome. He saw them before they happened. What if what he sees is true? We both know there are many such seers in the world with visions of future events. The Jews have stories of them through the centuries."

"Or perhaps this man lies to save his life." Vespasian pointed the cudgel at Yosef—"If you have this power, why did you not prophesy to your people that Yotapta would fall and that you would be taken a prisoner?"

Yosef spoke calmly: "I don't dream of all events. But I realized Yotapta would fall as it did. If I had told others I had seen it in my dreams, it would have disturbed and distressed them. So I was silent. You can ask my fellow prisoner who survived—he will confirm this. But I also knew it in my heart before I had the dream. It is no matter that I have loyalty to my country and people, or that most Jews are against this war. Our country has been manipulated by a handful of extremists who prevented us from making peace with you. That cannot change the reality of our fate. In Yotapta, more than once, I dreamed that I would appear before a man who would become emperor of the world. The face in my dream was yours, Lord Vespasian."

"Centurion, you know this man... what do you say about his claims?"

Nicanor moved his lips in one or two trials of a response, and Yosef knew he was aware that his words now might determine the fate of his Jewish friend. "I know firsthand he has seen things that came to pass, general," Nicanor replied. "I have never known him to lie. If he says it... he believes it is so. I do not believe this to be a trick to save himself. After all, he had committed himself to die in the cave with the other rebels."

Vespasian rose from the stool. "Titus and Nicanor, I want the other prisoners questioned about this. See if this man has talked to any about the fall of Yotapta. Has he expressed to any of them his concerns about what has caused the rebellion he and his countrymen find themselves in. Report to me what you find, and then I will decide what I do with him."

XCVI

Vespasian studied his eldest son, the one he could rely on, as he read the latest dispatch from Gaius Mucianus in Antioch.

Titus's expression never changed, but when he spoke, his voice held a note of concern. "Father, the governor, says Gnaeus Domitius Corbulo is dead—Nero ordered him to commit suicide in Greece!"

"Once he was relieved of his command," Vespasian replied, "he had to obey the emperor's command to go to him in Greece."

"But Corbulo was our finest general! He led what—three legions? And he routed the Parthians, our biggest threat in the east. The 10th is with us now, and I know you've heard those men thought him a fine commander. Why did the emperor order him to kill himself?"

"Corbulo answers that with his own final words... see what Gaius wrote: 'Axios, I am worthy.' Domitius has the lineage to become an emperor, and Emperor Nero must have feared his ambitions were too grand."

"What of you, Father? You are an equally great commander."

"I pose no risk to the emperor—I have no pretensions and little mind that our family is not well-known among the other nobles. Nero does not fear me, and that's why he chose me for this campaign."

Even as he told his son that, Vespasian felt a qualm growing within him. Mucianus had told him of a failed coup attempt by members of the Praetorian Guard only two years before that the public only suspected. The emperor had grown even more unpopular and paranoid since then. There seemed so many sides—led by a few strong and powerful men, all with agendas that rotted an empire whose people wanted simply a stable republic.

He took the scroll of parchment from his son. "We are here in Judea, not in Rome among all the conniving and the grasping for power. We must win this war, and then I'll receive no letters from Rome calling for my death." Still, he wondered at the Jew's prophecy. It had seemed a ploy, but he did believe the gods spoke to rare individuals and sent signals of things to come. And Mucianus also felt the future was full of danger. *What if Nero becomes concerned that my family and I are a threat to him?*

He set it aside and changed the subject: "Now, tell me what you and Nicanor learned from questioning the prisoners about this Yosef ben Mathias."

* * *

Nicanor found him in the same spot as when they had looked upon Yotapta for the first time—that early morning—as the sun rose to reveal it. But this was the dawn of a different day.

"Yes, general?" Nicanor stopped next to Vespasian, "Lord Titus told me you wanted to speak with me.

"Titus reported what was learned from questioning the prisoners. Many of them liked your friend and thought him a good leader. Others thought he admired us Romans too much. And some had heard rumors of his portents that the rebels and their towns would stand for seven weeks against us. They said he believes Jewish factions have played a part in forcing this war."

Vespasian paused to think about the latest report from Mucianus in Antioch—the rumors of plotting against the emperor and the growing resentment at his reign. And how the generals were relieved of command and recalled to face their fates. He had a fleeting thought again about the question of Cestius Gallus's death.

"General?"

"Yes, centurion. I've decided to keep this Yosef ben Mathias as my prisoner and not send him to Rome, though the emperor has..." Vespasian slapped his thigh and interrupted himself. He had made a decision. With what was brewing in Rome, he could, with reasonable excuse, ignore the request to have high-level prisoners sent to Rome. He would claim he had not received it. "Have you prepared any more reports to the Praetorian Prefect?"

"No, general. But a man came to our camp outside of Ptolemais before we marched here and took my first report."

"Did he give his name?"

"No, sir. He asked for me—sent a runner for me to come to where the sentries had stopped him. I went to him, and he quietly asked if I had something for Lord Tigellinus, took my report, and left without saying anything else."

Vespasian considered the news of the undercurrents of turmoil in Rome again. "We'll soon return to Ptolemais. So perhaps you should prepare another report for the Praetorian Prefect. Dine with Titus and me tonight, and we'll discuss it. Now, about the requests, your friend has made..."

* * *

Nicanor was glad he did not have to saddle Tempestas and go down that cursed rock-strewn path to the lower camp and back to visit Yosef. Vespasian had wisely ordered him held nearby—there was still a desire by many to crucify the Jew. The engineers had deepened a recess in the jutting spine of a ridge behind the command quarters, then taken long iron rods found in Yotapta and formed a lattice of bars with an opening for a crudely hinged door. The converted shallow cave became a prison cell. Nicanor hated to see his friend within, still wearing chains on his arms and legs. When he had led him to the cell, Yosef had said bravely, "At least it's not in the ground... I can see the sky and feel the wind."

As he approached, Nicanor saw Yosef sitting as ragged as they had all been when adrift at sea after the *Salacia's* sinking. But instead of being matted with sea salt, Yosef's head was a wild nest of dirt and sweat-tangled hair, his tunic and cloak tattered and soiled, stiffened with the crust of bloodstains. Yosef sat cross-legged, facing the bars that layered him with shadow stripes from the rising sun. He rose stiffly when he saw Nicanor.

"I have good news for you, Yosef."

"I'm to be freed and can bathe?" Yosef's jest was half-hearted but hopeful.

"Bathe, yes, and soon. Free... no. But you will live, and do not face travel much harsher than our last accommodation sailing to Rome to appear before Nero. General Vespasian will keep you as a prisoner until he sees how your prophecy unfolds and whether it proves true. You'll remain chained in this cell, but you will get water to bathe and fresh clothing—expect that today. And you will be let out for exercise—I will try to walk with you when I can."

"That's good... I have you to thank, my friend," Yosef said, hesitating before asking, "What of my other requests?"

"The gods—my gods—favor you. Vespasian keeps a journal and has for decades; he told me I could bring you writing materials to continue yours."

"What of my journals in my room in Yotapta... if they have not been destroyed?"

"I go now to see... but Vespasian wants to discuss them with you, so expect to do so when he asks."

Nicanor paused, uncomfortable with what he must say to his friend: "Yosef, you must know that if your prophecy does not come true... Vespasian will send you to Nero, who will make an example of you. He will show you and everyone watching the painful death awaiting those who rebel against Rome."

* * *

Vast sections of the outer walls of Yotapta had been torn down. They would never serve again as a meaningful defense. It was quiet. Much of the town was ruined, and rubble, trash, and many hundreds of bodies still littered the streets, attracting scavengers. Buildings had, at most, a semblance of street-side entries. Nicanor went through one of them Yosef had directed him to and climbed to find his friend's office and room.

Debris and trash were scattered on the steps, and Nicanor stepped inside what he thought should be Yosef's room. Everything had been upset or thrown about—legionaries and auxiliaries had searched for hiding rebels and likely any valuables they could loot. He went to the table nearest the window, where Yosef would have his journals close to where he could write by daylight. The wooden shutters had been torn from the window, and the desk's contents had been swept to the floor. With the toe of his sandal, he flipped over half of a broken shutter. Beneath, he found an overturned bowl with a leather cord trailing from it. Stooping, he lifted the cord, and a coin swung from it. *I've seen this before,* he thought, and then saw the corner and edges of what must be Yosef's journals underneath the other half of the shutter. Nicanor put the coin and its cord and the journals in his satchel and hung it over his shoulder.

On the street, he had not gone a dozen steps in the strange silence when it was broken by a braying laugh that could only be Aulus. Up from a path that followed the eastward slope, the echoing laughter rolled toward him. *What could be so funny in this desolate place?* he wondered. He followed the laugh to a street of several homes. There in an alley beside a cistern, he spotted the medicus splinting the leg and arm of a legionary and laughing at the man. He walked over to him.

"Nicanor, this jackass believed the rebels threw treasure into a dry cistern. His friends—maybe he won't call them friends now—taunted him to climb down its crumbling walls to see, and he fell. The gods smiled on him... I was nearby."

Nicanor smiled. "I had to see what you were up to, Aulus... but I'll leave you to tending to this soldier." As he passed the man, moaning and not sure which of his miseries to grip and curse about, Nicanor leaned down and spoke firmly but low: "I'd better not hear you claim this as some courageous wound from combat." He straightened to head back toward the ruined gate.

On the other side of the cistern, below its low wall, was a body, pierced so many times the pool of blood had spread in a puddle surrounding it and had long since dried to the color of brick. Next to one hand was a hand-sized piece of slate, and the other gripped a small chisel such as stoneworkers used for detailed work. Nicanor stooped to look at the slate. The man had scratched a drawing of a building with a triangular roof on a stepped platform and what looked like two small trees. Picking it up, he noted the other side had a drawing of a crab. He had seen these symbols in Patras, the Roman port on the northwestern Peloponnesus, where he had been raised by his Greek mother. The side with the crab was smeared with dried blood. He wondered at the meaning of the drawings as he set it on the dead man's chest and wiped his fingers clean.

* * *

"Nicanor, even more than the journals... I thank you for finding this"—Yosef held the coin on its cord for a moment, spun it, then slipped over his head, settling it beneath the torn cloth to rest flat on his chest.

"I found something else and wonder at its meaning," Nicanor said, describing the drawings on the slate.

"The building portrays a *nefesh*, a traditional Judean ossuary—a mausoleum for the dead. The crab is a symbol for the Hebrew month of Tammuz."

"I understand about the... what you called a 'nefesh.' But why the crab for the month?"

"That's this month when Yotapta fell... and when the man died."

"He wanted to leave a marker of his fate,"—Nicanor nodded. He understood and even admiring the man who had spent his last minutes of life working to leave something behind. He thought again of his many conversations with Paul in Rome. Had the Christian been executed, or did he still sit in that damp, dark cell? In their talks, Nicanor had told Paul of his friendship with Yosef, and the Christian had asked his god for Yosef's safety. Had that god intervened, and was that deity's power the reason Yosef still lived? Was that the same god that spoke to Yosef, as Paul seemed to imply? He hoped Vespasian's decision to keep Yosef a prisoner did not change. He did not want to witness him receiving the kind of execution that Rome was capable of.

XCVII

Jerusalem

Mathias's burst of strength had lasted long enough to defend Yosef before the Sanhedrin, then faded. Miriam and her mother were back to caring for him, but Miriam had gotten out of the house long enough to leave a message for Elazar ben Yair, telling him of what Ehud had told her father and Matthew. If the Idumeans were trading with the Romans in Alexandria, then they were likely also exchanging information. And ben Beor was in the Sanhedrin, where he could hear vital details about Jerusalem's defenses and other areas of Judea.

Matthew did not trust ben Beor, and after what Elazar had told her of the man, Miriam knew he was right not to. She heard that Leah's husband, Yonatan, had been in Alexandria just before the rebellion broke out, and he returned telling of a massacre of Jews there. Elazar and his Sicarii were probably aware of that, but still, she must soon meet with Elazar.

She paced, glancing from time to time at the back gate, conflicted in wishing she could leave and being thankful her father was sleeping on the long couch she had moved into the courtyard where the breeze cooled her flushed face. She heard footsteps on the stone tile inside the house—her mother was returning. Thankful for that, too, she hoped to slip out to check for Elazar's reply to her message.

"He's in the courtyard, Yohanan"—her mother stepped out, followed by her father's friend.

"You are getting so thin, Miriam!" Yohanan ben Zaccai exclaimed.

Miriam hurriedly picked up the robe she had taken off in the heat and slipped it on.

"I try to get her to eat more," said her mother, slipping into her habit when vexed of speaking as if Miriam were not present.

"I eat enough, Mother—you don't have to worry about me." Miriam nodded to the old priest and asked, "How is Yosef? We've heard the Roman army is at Yotapta."

"Yosef was well when he ordered me to leave when the Romans got near. I checked on my village, and while there, I heard the Romans were laying siege to the town. But Yotapta's walls are stout and well-defended, so I'm sure Yosef is safe."

"But for how long?" she asked. "They also say three Roman legions have moved from Azzah to Caesarea and then most of the

379

soldiers on to the north of Jerusalem. Matthew says the Romans have sealed off Galilee."

As Miriam spoke, her mother checked to see if Mathias still slept and then darted a look at her she knew well: *Why bring up such bad news?* But not talking about it would not make the situation better, nor drive the Romans from Judea. "There is no way for Yosef to escape, nowhere to go in Galilee." Miriam went to her father and smoothed the damp hair from his brow. "Now that you're here, Mother... I must go out for a while. Will I see you when I return tonight?" she asked the priest.

"I plan to remain in Jerusalem, here with your family, if Rebecca"—he patted her mother's shoulder—"does not mind. And I can help tend to Mathias."

* * *

"Yes, Elazar left a reply for you... days ago," Kefa said, "but he is here right now. Come." The leatherworker waved her inside his shop, which she had discovered was larger than it seemed from outside. The stench was far more potent than what wafted to Zechariah's across the alley.

"I waited, hoping you'd come by to check," Elazar said as he waved to greet her. "I have news of where Esau ben Beor will be this evening. When he leaves, you must follow him."

"Where?"

"Wherever he goes. What you told me in your message is true. Many of the Idumeans are in contact with the Romans in Alexandria. I'm now sure he is sending messages out of Jerusalem. If we find out how I hope to find out who he sends them to."

"No—I mean, where will ben Beor be this evening?"

"At the House of Caiaphas meeting with your brother."

XCVIII

My weeks of peace now end, Cleo thought as she heard Gessius Florus's voice echo with calls for Glaucio. She had glimpsed him when he came in, face sunburnt and wind-chapped as was usual after many days at sea. She wondered where he had gone and why. But mostly, she wished he had not returned. Leaving Cicero in her room, with Elian to keep him quiet, she went to listen to her husband and Glaucio in his office. His loud voice helped:

"Dead! How?" her husband asked.

"His body was found on the beach, Lord Florus. Judging by the wounds, Capito was killed with a blade—a sword."

"Where was he found? Here?"

Cleo heard the heavy footfalls that meant her husband paced his office, as he often did.

"Some distance from here, lord... it looked like he had washed up on the edge of the shore closer to town. It's hard to say where he was killed."

There was silence for several moments, and Cleo worried they would come out unexpectedly, and she would be caught. She began quietly returning to her room.

"I'll look into Capito's death." The heat in her husband's tone had cooled. "Were there any issues with Lady Cleo while I was away?"

She stopped.

"No, lord. She walked the beach and practiced archery."

"Where Capito was found?"

"No, lord, just beyond the dunes here... I don't think she goes far." Even muffled, the disdain was evident in Glaucio's voice.

"You watched her at all times?"

Without a pause, Glaucio replied, "Yes, lord, or I had Eris do so."

Cleo wondered at the man's hedging of the truth—perhaps his scorn for her was good fortune—and she was thankful. If he and Eris were as diligent as he claimed, she would have been found out, and Sayid would be dead. "Leave me"— she heard Gessius dismiss Glaucio, and hurried away before the major domus came out. Later she must send Elian to check on Sayid; her husband would expect her in the evening. Still, she prayed he would not.

* * *

Gessius Florus breathed heavily, his face flushed with too much wine, lust, and anger. "I expect you to yield to me as a wife should!"

"I will not!" Cleo gasped, pressing one hand to her side, the other pulling the torn gown up to cover her breasts. "You may take me, but I will no longer willingly give you what you want."

He lashed out backhanded, and his jeweled rings tore her lip and raked her cheek, leaving a crimson furrow as Cleo spun and fell across the bed. Florus loomed over her, and his heavy body pinned her down. "You will scream in pain if you won't in pleasure."

She bucked until another heavy blow to the head stunned her momentarily. He kneed her legs apart and moved on top. She feigned a swoon, knowing it gave him satisfaction to dominate her when she fought, and little pleasure when she didn't. *Let him be done quickly.* As he heaved and groaned over her, she turned her head and spat blood and a tooth. *But I do not give up,* she swore to herself, and her mind seethed at him: *I bide my time until I can make you pay.*

* * *

Elian had breathlessly burst into the half-buried building where he hid, reporting that Lady Cleo was being beaten and worse. Sayid knew he could wait no more. He had immediately left for the port to get news of where General Vespasian was and then to go to him—the general's protection was their only hope. The moon was full, but the gods had smiled on Sayid, for he was healed enough to move quickly and had met no patrols.

He climbed the moss-and-water-slick rocks onto the quay. Before he entered the wharf-side taberna, he straightened and tucked in the too-large tunic and pulled down the cowl of the cloak—clothes Elian had enough forethought to provide. Sayid sat down in a dark corner, planning to ask about the latest news, as sailors fresh from a sea voyage usually did. Very soon, three nearby Greek sailors—deep in their cups—boasted of the rebels' defeat and the fall of Yotapta. Their one regret was the legion's return to Ptolemais that day meant the prices at brothels and bars would rise as the owners took in a flood of Roman coin from lust-filled, thirsty soldiers.

Sayid gulped down the mug of cheap wine, hating to leave behind the full pitcher he had paid for—the cost of getting a seat at a table—and stood. He would go immediately to the legion encampment and find a place to hide and wait for sunrise. Then he would try to somehow brave his way in to see General Vespasian.

* * *

Happy with the legions' victory and focused on the celebration to be enjoyed once off duty, the sentries had not spotted Sayid well-hidden in the large patch of scrub near the main entrance to the encampment. Wrapped in his dark cloak, cowl over his head, he tried to find a comfortable position. His chest and shoulder ached, and it would be hours until daybreak.

He heard the clop of hooves grow louder on the road from the town. Sayid slowly rolled over on his stomach to peer through the scrub. The horse was a magnificent black, and its coat gleamed as if oiled in the gate's torchlight. The rider—a centurion by his gear— seemed average-sized until Sayid compared him to the standing guards. The centurion doffed his helmet, and as he stepped away from his mount, his face came full into the arc of light. Sayid knew that scarred visage before the sentries greeted the horseman.

"Ho, Nicanor... back so soon? Not enough coin in your pouch to convince a wench to let you stay in her bed overnight?" one of the guards quipped, and the others laughed.

Stunned at seeing his friend, Sayid did not catch Nicanor's response, which drew more laughter as the men moved the barricade and let the centurion pass. He watched as man and horse turned right once inside the gate to follow the chest-high perimeter wall. He got to his knees and crouched. Staying out of the glow of several campfires and lighted torches, Sayid swung in an arc outside the wall to follow Nicanor. He could see Nicanor above the *sudis* wall with his helmet still clasped under one arm. He knew the centurion preferred keeping his tent at a distance from the other soldiers, and that would help.

The gods continued to favor Sayid—the timing between the sweeps of 3-horse patrols was perfect. When Nicanor stopped, Sayid hurried to the point of the wall nearest Nicanor's tent. With a grunt, he pulled himself up between two of the sharpened wooden spikes that made up the formidable barrier.

"Nicanor... Nicanor!" he whispered urgently. In the dim illumination of a campfire two tents away, the centurion's head swing in his direction, and he dismounted. Pulling his sword, he came closer, squinting. Sayid turned his face up to the moon so his friend could see him—he prayed no other Roman was around. "It's me... Sayid!"

* * *

Nicanor shook his head at what Sayid had just told him. It seemed he had not stopped doing that since he'd helped the Syrian auxiliary over the wall. Sayid had reported that his mission for Cestius Gallus was similar to Nicanor's own—he was to take his letters and the entire 12th Legion report to Lady Octavia for safekeeping. Then Sayid had seen and saved his mother. Those events he had passed over quickly to get to the most important—obeying Lady Octavia's wish that he check on Lady Cleo, and his discovery that she was in danger.

"Florus rapes and beats her, Nicanor—we must do something."

"I'll talk to General Vespasian, Sayid, but I have to think through what to tell him. I don't know what—"

"Please do it as soon as you can... I know at some point Florus will kill her."

Nicanor rubbed his face. "You said you heard about the legion's return at that taberna at the port—the one beside the waterfront warehouses. Go back to your hiding spot near Cleo and meet me at that taberna in two nights."

XCIX

It was a Shabbat, unlike any Miriam had experienced. The *kiddush* and blessing recited over the *lechem mishneh*—the two braided loaves of challah and wine—after her mother lit the two candles was the same ritual they always knew. But it had gladdened none of them this time, and some prohibitions were ignored. Bad news does not care or respect what day it arrives; it does not wait for a better time. Yohanan ben Zaccai had brought the news from the Temple that morning: Yotapta had fallen, and the Romans had destroyed the town. Thousands of people were dead, and no survivors were reported.

Miriam looked at her father, who had turned even paler and shakier since hearing his friend's announcement. *Yosef must be one of the dead*, she thought, and that belief was in the expressions of her father, mother, and brother. Yohanan, who sat in Yosef's seat at the table, had been the only one of them to see him in months—he had kept his head bowed through the dinner. Miriam remembered happier Shabbats, sitting on the roof terrace with Yosef at sunset to watch for the first three stars to appear that signaled the end of the week's holy day. She would never do that again with Yosef at her side. The last and brightest of her stars was now gone.

The candle flames shimmered and blurred before her. Miriam wiped her eyes and caught that glisten in her mother and father's eyes—in Yohanan's too, as he raised his head: "A voice from the east, a voice from the west, a voice from the four winds; a voice against Jerusalem and the sanctuary, a voice against all the people."

No one else spoke, and Miriam did not know what he meant, but her father, mother, and brother nodded. She could not clear her throat to ask. The silence weighed on them as the candles burned down until they recited the *Havdalah*. The beginning of the new week began with tears for the dead.

* * *

"I'm glad they honor our heroes in Yotapta," Matthew commented to Miriam as the memorial parade at the Temple wound out of sight with an empty casket for Yosef. "I was nearly overcome—'A hero of Israel' indeed." He glanced toward their parents, arm-in-arm a few feet away with Yohanan ben Zaccai. "I must go now—I have a meeting. Can you help mother... with father? I need to speak to Yohanan privately before that meeting."

"Yes, I'll walk home with them." Miriam knew Matthew was meeting Esau ben Beor and Eleasar ben Ananias—she would have to hurry to change and to get where she could watch for when ben Beor left them. *Why does Matthew need to speak to the old priest, though?* Something had puzzled her at Shabbat, so she asked casually: "At dinner, what did Yohanan mean by what he said... about a voice against Jerusalem?"

"Five years ago," Matthew replied, "a man came into the Temple, shouting the words Yohanan repeated at dinner. He was escorted out but then went throughout the city, crying the same lament and warning. This angered many people, and he was arrested. The magistrates brought him before the Roman governor. Although they beat him, he would not ask them to stop, and he never cried for mercy. As they beat him, he responded to each stroke with 'Woe to Jerusalem!' Since they let him go, he has never taken his message back to the authorities. But he is still found walking the city, usually wailing those same words, even though there might not be any to listen to him. But he was right... is right. All are against us... against Jerusalem. The odds of our survival are not good, I fear."

Miriam spotted Hananiah in the fringes of a group on the street. "Matthew, give me a minute before you leave Father." She walked over to the bladesmith just as he turned her way with a grim look on his pale, thin face. Without showing it—and she was not sure how she sensed it—he nevertheless seemed pleased to see her.

"You do not visit me anymore..." he said.

"My father's been sick." Miriam expected him to offer sympathies, but he just studied her with his unblinking stare. He looked away at the people milling around on the street, now continuing their day but with downcast expressions.

"The people in the city grieve."

"All the deaths in Yotapta are tragic... and now the Romans will come for us," she replied.

Hananiah nodded. "Yes. But grief and the deaths of loved ones can make us strong—strong enough to survive many terrible things"—his eyes locked on hers.

Though the depth of the stare was disconcerting, she returned it. "You sound as if you know... from experience."

"I do."

Miriam did not know why but told him: "One of my brothers died in Yotapta."

"You loved him?"

"He's my brother, and we were very close. It's hard to believe he is no longer with us. The Romans are killing all who are important to me."

"Then, his death will strengthen you...." He hesitated, then added, "Come revisit me, and I will tell you about a death that helped me survive."

* * *

"Before Esau ben Beor gets here," Matthew sat down across from Eleasar ben Ananias and watched the door, "you've heard the reports the Romans at Yotapta have pulled back to Ptolemais. And other than patrols and strikes against surrounding villages, their forces at Legio have not moved south."

"Why do they wait?" Eleasar asked.

"I don't know, but we can't assume we have long. I've asked Yohanan ben Zaccai to go to the Essenes to see if they are ready. We must decide now what treasure to move from Jerusalem and how much will remain here in the Temple—enough to satisfy the Romans. Yosef believed—as I do—that should Jerusalem fall, and should the Romans not find enough treasure to appease them, they'll kill more people—perhaps destroy all of Judea to find what has been hidden from them."

C

Ptolemais

After leaving Nicanor at daybreak, Sayid had been forced to hide through the day. With the legions back, there were more men and merchants on the roads around the port and traveling up and down the coast. He had started out again at sundown, and with the help of the gods and the full moon, he had reached the dune-buried building in full dark just as Elian was leaving.

The boy greeted him: "Sayid! I was worried and checked to see if you were back. I did not want to have to tell Lady Cleo you were gone!"

He had told the boy to go to her: "Tell her I reached our centurion friend—she will know who I mean—and that he will help us. I'll leave at sundown tomorrow to meet with him at the port to plan our escape. Tell her not to worry—I'll return after that meeting and will have news for her."

Sayid had anxiously passed the day until another sunset faded and grayed the dunes with deepening shadows. He was about to blow out his small lamp to leave when he heard the crunch and shuffle of footsteps on the sand and stone below. Then on the steps to the second level. He picked up Capito's gladius and stood to one side of the entry.

Lady Cleo stepped into the room. Even in the dim light, the sight of her battered face shocked him. "My lady!"

"Sayid, I'm going with you to see Nicanor."

"Lady, you cannot—it's too dangerous, and you're hurt."

"My husband is dangerous... and he thinks I'm too injured to do anything but lie in my bed. He and Glaucio are gone tonight, off to meet someone—Capito's replacement is what Elian overheard. Eris began her drinking as soon as they left.... she'll know nothing until dawn, and Elian will stay in my room and keep Cicero quiet."

"But it's not an easy way to the port."

"I'm stronger than I seem, Sayid—that's what will save me from Florus. Going to the port is a risk for you, too, and I went to hear Nicanor's plan for myself."

Sayid shook his head to tell her she could not go with him, but she held up her hand—"I need some hope to draw upon... from someone who can offer it. I am going, Sayid."

* * *

"Are you both insane?" Nicanor stared at Sayid and Lady Cleo, who now sat in the shadows of one of the taberna's back tables away from the light of lanterns over the bar. Even though she wore a simple hooded cloak and plain clothing, a head or two had turned her way when she entered with Sayid.

"Nicanor, she would not stay," Sayid explained. "She—"

"—I insisted, Nicanor," she interrupted. "Do not blame Sayid. I know the risk you take, but I fear for my life and cannot remain with Gessius Florus." She paused, and the smile that so appealed to him spread despite her swollen face. "It's so good to see you—thank you for helping us."

Nicanor looked away to scan the room, then came back to her. "I'll help you both," he said as he slid a bowl of fruit and a knife to them. "Slice these and eat. You must not act as if you are here only to talk." He drank from his cup and poured more wine. "I have news that should give you hope, a good portent for what we can do."

Nicanor nodded at Sayid. "I went to see General Vespasian, planning to tell him of your circumstances, and Lady Cleo's—about the letters and evidence passing to and from Cestius Gallus. I had hoped he would take you under his protection and investigate. You still have your letters, right?"

"Sayid has them hidden with him," Cleo replied.

Nicanor continued: "And I have material and reports from Cestius Gallus, too. He tells about Roman efforts to start this war, escalate it, and undermine Gallus's leadership of the 12th Legion. When I went to meet with the general, he stopped me before I could speak. There was something to discuss first—he felt he could share since he likely owed his life to me. Then he asked for my word of honor to tell no one of what he was about to speak of. But I must tell you... so you now hold my honor in your hands."

"It is safe, my friend," Lady Cleo replied, and Sayid nodded.

"The new governor, Gaius Mucianus, has heard growing rumors of trouble brewing in Rome. Powerful men conspire to oust Emperor Nero. But the words of this unrest come from the lips of those who might have their own agendas. To ensure his own and Vespasian's safety, the governor asked Vespasian if there is anyone, he trusted in Rome who could verify what he had been told. But Vespasian does not know anyone... at least not anyone in a position that would not draw Nero's suspicion or his ire. Many wish to become emperor..."

Nicanor paused and rechecked the room. No one now seemed to pay any attention to Cleo. Several other women, similarly cloaked and robed, were eating, and one more among them apparently did not draw attention.

"Cleo, when I went to Rome, I carried copies of Lord Gallus's letters and reports, just as Sayid had a similar assignment. Some of my letters were about the suspicions you and Octavia aroused in Gallus about events in Judea that have fueled this war. The conflict has caused such death that it seems against Nero's interests with its disruption of taxes and tribute. Gallus also gave me a copy of his report questioning some of his advisors in the legion.

"Knowing he bore the blame for the pull-back from Jerusalem and the defeat at Beth Horon, he wanted this material in the hands of someone who could be trusted to use it. I remembered you telling me of your brother Otho as an honest man with a position of some power. I thought he could be the man Lord Gallus sought; a man who could help clear his name. Or at least he might prevent his execution by Nero until the truth was determined. I found and met your old major domus, Graius, and he agreed to take the material to your brother. But he would do so only if I agreed to see you were safe from harm. He was concerned—rightfully—about your treatment by Gessius Florus. And so, I decided to check on you and see you to safety if needed."

Nicanor took a bite of fruit. "So, I told the general I indirectly knew your brother, hoping he would agree Otho could be of help. Vespasian knew of Otho and thought he might be a good contact to cultivate—to learn what is really going on in Rome. So, General Vespasian has asked me to return to Rome on his and Gaius Mucianus's behalf." Nicanor did not mention how distasteful he found it playing a role in the political intrigues of Rome. But it offered a solution and means to help a friend.

"I agreed on three conditions"—Nicanor looked down with discomfort—"Pardon me, my lady, but I told him I had met a woman when I served here before. I said I did not want to leave her behind a second time. I wanted to take her—you in disguise—with me to Rome." The man-to-man, knowing look he had received from Vespasian, was not important to share, and it was too dim in the taberna for his flush of embarrassment to be noticed. "I asked the general that a pardon be granted for Sayid—who had been given leave by Cestius Gallus, but might be mislabeled a deserter—so he could return to the legion."

Nicanor took a packet of parchment from his satchel and passed it to Sayid. "This protects you when you return and is signed and sealed by the general.

"I then asked General Vespasian to please keep Yosef alive as his prisoner and to see what the future holds."

"You say that Yosef is alive?" Cleo leaned forward, nearly revealing her face. "My husband taunted me as he... as he beat me. He said that Yosef is dead!"

Nicanor looked at Sayid, who was also surprised. "I thought I told you," Nicanor said. "Yosef did not die at Yotapta. He's here... held as a prisoner at the camp."

"I really want to see him, Nicanor," Cleo said.

"My lady, that's even more unwise than meeting me here!"

"Nicanor, I pray your plan works... and that I can leave Judea alive... but I never thought I would see Yosef again. This past year, I've learned that what haunts me most are the regrets I have for the things I did not do when I should and the things I have not said to those who I... those who are important to me—when I had the chance."

Nicanor's mind had been racing at the foolishness of what they would soon attempt to do. But her words stilled it. All reasoning might warn him it was insane, but there were greater concerns. He had promised Graius he would see that Cleo was safe, and though he was not good at sharing how he felt, he was good at doing what he must.

"I will get you in to see him tonight, but we must go right now."

CI

PTOLEMAIS

Nicanor could see the connection between Cleo and Yosef even though they did not touch. Upon the legion's arrival in Ptolemais, they had secured Yosef in a guarded tent, shackled in iron at ankle and waist to a massive post anchored by cement. The engineers had tested the fittings and guaranteed the general no man could break free. Vespasian had then agreed to leave Yosef's hands and arms free, so he could write in his journals. Yosef still had a limited range of movement and slept on his side on a pallet beside the post.

Cleo had come over the camp wall with Nicanor's help in the place Sayid had crossed earlier. Nicanor still felt the softness and warmth of her body in the tingle in his hands. Getting her in to see Yosef had been as easy as dismissing the guard as he had done for previous nights' talks with at the Roman camp outside Yotapta. He told Cleo he must be inside Yosef's tent with them while Sayid kept watch outside after briefly greeting Yosef. When Nicanor had entered with her, he saw the surprised spark in Yosef's eyes and heard the lift in her voice as she greeted him. As the torchlight revealed her face, she hurried to explain to Yosef what had happened to her.

Nicanor gave them that moment, then warned them: "We have little time... Lady Cleo is in danger, and I have a way to get her out of Judea." He described the plan.

"But you cannot trust anyone in Rome," Yosef said, "if Gessius Florus has done what you believe—starting this war for his own ends. If that's true, then others are interested in his success here. When you go to Rome, Cleo, he will have you accused of treason and use his contacts to wield power—to have you found and publicly executed. You will not be safe from his reach anywhere in the Roman empire."

"I will hide and protect her, Yosef."

"But Nicanor, it will be just you, unless you can find allies in Rome... and what if you don't?"

"What else can I do, Yosef?" Cleo asked.

Yosef shook his lowered head, then raised it. "You could go to my family in Jerusalem before Vespasian begins his siege. Nicanor, you said Vespasian awaits the fall supply and replenishment ships with more siege equipment before the winter storms. He will make sure Galilee no longer poses a threat, and it will be next year before he marches on my home. Lady Cleo would be safe there for a while... We

392

know Vespasian hopes I can convince the elders in Jerusalem to surrender before that assault begins, and she could escape then." He picked up his journal and pen and began writing.

Nicanor rubbed the scar on his face. "The rebels will kill any Roman woman they see before she can even speak with your family, Yosef."

Yosef turned to Cleo and removed the page he had just written upon from his journal and handed it to her—"Take this message with you. Disguise yourself as a Jewish woman." Yosef thought quickly and slipped the kinyan from his neck. "Take this to my family... and go by the name Ya'el. My family knows both that name and the coin I just gave you. And they will recognize you from your visit last year and understand you must have come to them for protection at my request."

"The name Ya'el... it has meaning?" she asked.

"Do you remember that night, adrift after the wreck, Cleo... I told you of my wife, Ruth, and that she had died, but not how. She died in childbirth, and we named our stillborn daughter Ya'el—it means 'Strength of God.'"

Yosef's voice dropped. "How sad this is. The two of us—separated and each trapped and living with those our people believe to be our enemy. And both our peoples will think us traitors, though we do what we think is right." Yosef wiped his eyes. "Do as you and Nicanor feel you must. But please"—he held out the coin on its cord—"whether you go to my family or not, take what I offer, and remember me—as I remember the one who gave it to me."

Cleo took the kinyan, and her other hand came up to stroke Yosef's face. "We are two souls... man and woman... drawn to each other, and somehow fate has spared us. But Yosef, now we must part again." Tears glistened on her cheeks as she slipped the cord over her head. It lay above her breasts among the fallen tears and the lunula pendant Poppaea had given her.

Nicanor turned from them to give them another last moment, and then he spoke: "Lady Cleo, I don't believe that going to Yosef's people is a wise course of action. That will only put you in worse danger. I can get you safely out of Judea, but you and Sayid must go now. Meet me tonight at the taberna, and I will get you aboard the ship we sail upon in the morning. Sayid will hide you nearby until then, and I will find appropriate clothes for you."

"Wait—I must get Cicero. I can't leave without him."

"Lady, please... leave the bird."

"I will not. I leave too much behind, and my husband will kill him." Cleo smiled at Yosef a final time. "Sayid will help me get him, and I'll meet you tonight at the taberna, Nicanor."

CII

Ptolemais

Cleo had sent Sayid on to the dune-buried building: "I will join you at sundown with Cicero." Exhausted, she drew strength from the hope that in less than a day, she would be at sea and away from Gessius Florus's hands. Leaving for Rome with Nicanor was her safest option. From there, she could try to get to Otho for his protection. Darts of pain stabbed her side as she hurried to the dunes closest to the domus. She passed by her practice range, which made her regret having to leave her bow. But all she needed was Cicero. Sayid already had her letters and notes from Poppaea and Octavia and the scraps of messages she had found in Florus's office. She prayed her husband was still gone as she stepped onto the portico and then entered the atrium.

"You must feel much better. Where have you been, my wife?" Gessius Florus stood with his hands on his hips, and beside him was a tall weathered-looking man wearing a *sagulum*—a short cloak—and an impassive expression. A long scar bisected his milky right eye. He held a long dagger in his hands, and his thumb caressed the metal from hilt to sharp tip.

As the hope drained from her, Cleo controlled most of the quaver that weakened her reply: "I awoke early and walked the beach."

"I think you lie—doesn't she lie, Quintus?"

"I saw her with two men at the waterfront taberna at the port last night, Lord Florus."

"Glaucio has paid for his failures"—Florus glanced at the blade in the hands of the other man. "And now, my wife"—his voice dripped with contempt and a threat of what was to come—"the time has come for me to find out what you know and who you've told it to." Quintus stepped forward, and Florus put a hand on his arm to stop him. "No, I will do this...." He smiled at this wife.

* * *

Sayid picked up the goatskin container he had directed Elian to fill from the household's store of lamp oil and leave at Cleo's practice range.

He had been anxiously awaiting Cleo earlier, afraid something had happened, as twilight grew without her return. Then the boy had

395

appeared, staggering and falling down the nearest sandy hillock, gasping that Gessius Florus had discovered Cleo and beaten her again. She was now locked in her room.

The only way Sayid could think to get her out was to create some disturbance that would occupy Florus. Then Sayid could free her in the chaos and try to escape. *So we burn the domus,* Sayid had thought, *and maybe it will trap or delay him.*

Under the moonlight, the boy exited the house with another skin of oil and poured it up and down the portico before running to Sayid.

"I've done it, Sayid. I've poured oil everywhere, especially in Lord Florus's office and the hall outside his chambers. I soaked his door, too. He drank a lot this evening with the other man before he left, and I have not heard him stir. The passage outside Lady Cleo's room is the only one I did not touch."

"Stay here, and I'll send her to you," Sayid ordered. "When she comes out and reaches you, light your torch so I can see it and then throw it onto the portico."

"What about you?"

"I'll fire the rest of the house and then the livestock stalls and run off the horses and mules... then Florus can chase us only on foot."

* * *

Sayid snuck inside, the smell of oil so heavy he covered his nose with one hand. Elian had drawn in the sand the layout of the house for Sayid to study. Then Elian had returned to the domus to await nightfall. Sayid went straight to Cleo's bedchamber and used Capito's sword to force the door open, cutting the wood away from around the improvised lock Florus had fashioned.

"Lady Cleo..." he called quietly. He could not light a torch; he must wait for that. He found what should be the exterior wall and located the shuttered windows barred from the outside. He hewed through them with the sword—cursing the noise it made—and enough moonlight entered that he spotted her unconscious on the bed next to the window. "Cleo"—he shook her—"you must get up."

She opened one eye, the other was a bloody swollen-shut mass, her face bruised and enflamed along her jaw. "Sayid..."

"We must go now"—he began to lift her, and she cried out.

"I can walk," she said as she lurched up with a moan.

"Elian waits where you practice archery," Sayid said quickly. "When you get to him... he will light a torch, and I will start the fire inside and turn the animals loose." He wrapped her robe around her. "Hurry, go now. Take Cicero with you—no, just the bird in your arms... we cannot carry his cage." He helped her to the atrium and watched her stumble away. Soon, he saw the flare of light from Elian's torch, so he unslung the skin of oil from his shoulder and splashed the wooden columns in the atrium. Lighting the torch he took from a loop at his waist, he set the columns ablaze before heading to where Elian's diagram had told him should be Florus's bedchamber. Flames blossomed behind him as Sayid reached the room.

The man, in a sleeping tunic and pulling on his robe, came out just as Sayid got there. With a shout, Sayid shoved him backward into the room and slung oil from the still-half-full oilskin-bag on him as he fell. He tossed the lighted torch onto the man and saw the oil on the Roman's legs catch fire, and then the tails of his robe. Sayid turned and ran for the corral.

* * *

The fire had spread over the entire house by the time Sayid found Cleo unconscious on the ground outside while the boy struggled to calm the bird. "She collapsed, Sayid, and I cannot wake her!" the boy cried.

Sayid had seen that happen to men struck in the head. He would have to carry her, but there was no way to get her to the port now. He did not know how badly he had burned the Roman or whether he was still burning inside, but the port would be the first place Florus would search for her.

"Here"—he tossed Elian a canvas bag Cleo had used to hold the reed shafts used for making her arrows—"stuff the bird in carefully—try not to hurt him—and follow me." He knelt to get Cleo in his arms and staggered to his feet.

"Where do we go, Sayid?" the boy cried as he tried to close the bag on the screaming bird.

Cleo had told him of Yosef's offer... and now that was their only option. But how could he move an unconscious woman, possibly severely injured? And with only the help of a small boy. "Away from here, Elian... half the Roman army will be looking for her here in the north. We'll go inland where they'll look last, and then south to Jerusalem."

CIII

JERUSALEM

Miriam had excused herself shortly after Ehud arrived and almost regretted it when she saw the disappointed look settle on his face. But the men—her father and brother, Yohanan and Ehud—would not talk freely with her near.

Instead of going to the market as she had told them she would, she went up to her room. The air was stifling, and she wished she could do more than crack the window shutter just enough to hear them in the courtyard. But beyond the conversation with Ehud, she must be able to learn what Matthew would say when he spoke alone with their father later. The ailing man had awakened more alert than usual, and Matthew had been about to see him when Ehud arrived.

"Matthew, Mathias, I came to ask how I can help with Jerusalem's defense." As Ehud spoke, Miriam mused upon her thoughts of the past two nights. What would a normal life be like... to be married to Ehud and have his children? Ya'akov had been her betrothed... but he was her second love. Ehud had been first in her heart.

"You've never carried a sword or trained with arms," Matthew replied with a tone of impatience.

From being interrupted before speaking with Father, Miriam thought.

Ehud's voice from below, though muffled, sounded downcast: "Then I can turn my glassworks to producing them—weapons. We can cast and forge spear tips, arrowheads... whatever is needed."

"We have every arms-maker working but need more of everything," Matthew said, his voice betraying more interest. "Do you know how to produce in quantity?"

"I've seen it done and can direct my men. I just need raw material... and more men would help."

"You meet this evening with Esau ben Beor, do you not, Matthew?" asked Mathias with a touch of a weak quaver. "He could allocate resources for that."

"Yes, Father. Ehud, I will see about getting you the materials you need and meet with you tomorrow morning with details. Now, please excuse us... I must speak to my father and Yohanan."

Two sets of steps left the courtyard. Miriam heard Ehud go and one set—Matthew's—returned to the courtyard and spoke: "Father...

Yohanan, this morning Esau and Shimon ben Gamliel called me to them to ask questions."

"Gamliel can no longer interfere with Yosef." The pain of loss was in her father's tone. "But he can mock his memory and create trouble for you, Matthew."

"I know, Father, so I had to tell them we have put in motion a plan to protect the Temple treasure. I did not say how. Now they insist on knowing more, and both will be at our meeting. Then they will decide whether to present the details to the Sanhedrin."

"We won't know any specifics until my meeting in Qumran with the Essenes and return to tell you," Yohannan ben Zaccai replied.

"I plan to tell Esau and Shimon that," replied Matthew, "and I hope it forestalls my having to tell them anything else for a while. They'll know the Essenes are involved but no specifics, and I will ask that they not reveal anything to anyone else."

Miriam heard Rebecca enter the house, cross to the courtyard, and greet the men. So she hurriedly put on a plain robe and cloak, tied a scarf over her hair, slipped downstairs and quietly went out.

* * *

Miriam passed Hananiah's shop, then backtracked to stand before its entrance. The odd man's mention of a death that somehow helped him grow stronger had made her curious. It was late afternoon, but she would not don her disguise to follow Esau from the House of Caiaphas until the sun was well down. She had the time now and stepped into the shop.

It was dark inside but for one circle of lamplight. Hananiah—holding a long-blade in one hand—looked up without a sign of surprise and only a slight welcome: "Hello, Miriam." He put the metal to the disc-shaped sharpening stone that turned from the pressure of a foot pedal below and out of sight. "Is your father better?"

"He is," Miriam said. She had developed a sense of the man and a strange empathy for him. He would not tell her what most would say... that the news was good to hear. The only sound was the rasping of the grindstone sharpening the blade. Every few turns, Hananiah stopped and ran his thumb along its edge.

"You said a death strengthened you," Miriam prompted him, "that it helped you survive, and that you would tell me about it."

"When something or someone important is torn from you... and cannot be replaced," he began with no preamble, "what fills that emptiness can be powerful and give you a purpose. I sense you know that already, but I will tell you my story. My question is this—will you tell me yours?"

* * *

With practice adjusting and placing the false beard, Miriam had made it fit better and hold longer. She still hated the padding that girded her hips and midriff to just under her breasts that had been flattened by cloth wrapped so tight she was afraid a deep breath would loosen it.

She had spent her watch thinking about what Hananiah had told her of his father's death. A Jerusalemite contractor eager to earn a bonus by completing his work on Herod's massive projects quickly had forced his stoneworkers to exhaustion, and Hananiah's father had made a mistake and been crushed. His mother, before she died of grief shortly afterward, had seen Hananiah apprenticed to an Alexandrian trader in metal who abused him in ways he would not speak of. His mourning for his father and mother had fueled, strengthened, and hardened his hatred of the Alexandrian.

She had asked him what had happened to the man and had not been shocked when Hananiah said, "I killed him." Then he stared at her with his fathomless, unblinking eyes.

Miriam saw through the open window that Kefa had gestured to her, and she was saved from having to meet his expectation of hearing her story. She would have time to make up what to tell him. She had excused herself and followed the leatherworker, who moved farther down the street and pointed out Ehud near Zechariah's. "He is the man who has been watching."

Miriam had told him not to worry, that she knew the man. Then she waited with Kefa until Ehud left, then she went into Zechariah's to get ready to follow Esau.

A half-hour later, Miriam saw the light moving inside the House of Caiaphas and stepped farther from the street lantern and into the shadows. Matthew and Eleasar ben Ananias came out, followed by Shimon ben Gamliel and the burly Idumean, Esau ben Beor. The men separated into pairs, Matthew and Eleasar walking faster than the two older men. As Gamliel and ben Beor passed her, she let them get some distance down the street toward the Temple enclosure before she followed.

CIV

Jerusalem

Miriam had trailed the Idumean from his parting with Shimon ben Gamliel at the Temple to a wine stall. From the pouch, at his waist, he took out a reed pen and a sheet of parchment and a small jar with a clay stopper. Writing while drinking three cups of wine, ben Beor then folded the note in fours, sealed it, and tucked the parchment into his pouch. He continued a route through the Northern City into the New City, climbing the hill of Bezetha. The only likely place he might go there was Solomon's Quarry. *Why?* she wondered.

The entrance to the quarry was sparsely lighted. All the nighttime activity was deeper inside, where the teams of chisel and wedge men split and sheared blocks and slabs of stone for the next morning's crew of workers. Draymen and their oxen would then pull the loads out of the quarry and down to the stoneworkers' yard at the foot of Bezetha.

Miriam followed Esau inside, but at a distance. Water dripped from the ceiling onto flat-cart loads of *Melekeh* in an extensive gallery, and the white limestone slabs glistened under the light of torches. The footsteps she had followed grew fainter, and then she could no longer hear them. She kept moving in the same direction and passed a darkened passage. The sensation of someone moving fast alerted her before the sound of ben Beor's charge. She spun to the side as a blade sliced across her back, leaving a thin shallow slash that stung. Esau ben Beor's second thrust entered obliquely and ripped away most of the padding over her stomach and split the front of her tunic. The wrapping over her breasts came free as she dropped Zechariah's staff and pulled her daggers from forearm sheaths.

"A woman!" ben Beor stood flat-footed long enough for both of Miriam's blades to sink deep into his flesh. One tore through the Idumean's throat and arced down to cut away the pouch at his waist, and the other lodged in his chest. She snatched the bag as it fell from him and saw his eyes widen even more as he looked behind her. Letting go of the dagger stuck in ben Beor's chest, pulling her torn robe tightly around her with the freed hand, she spun to see what he had seen as he died.

The tall, lean man was dressed as Zechariah had told her the Sicarii were when they stalked a target at night: black tunic and breeches, with a cloak and headdress that covered the lower face,

401

leaving only the eyes free of cloth. He stared at her, and his unwavering eyes glinted as he struck without warning.

Shaken by ben Beor's attack, Miriam had let the man get too close. With a reach and sweep of a long arm, his blade slashed at her eyes to blind her or make her fall back and leave an opening for the second strike. She twisted, and the blade cut into her cheek instead. Still gripping the cloak to her torso, she brought her knife hand up to press against the slash. The false beard began to slip as the icy sting turned into a hot stab of pain through her face.

The man closed in on her. His dagger thrust struck the metal *hamsa* clasp of her cloak and deflected to cut a furrow up to her shoulder instead of piercing her heart. Not letting go of his blade caught in the cloth bunched at her shoulder, the man did not back far away. Wounded and about to be revealed as a woman, she could not fight him knife-to-knife. She kicked him where she had been taught; the blow would be sufficient to slow any man.

As the man slumped, one hand cupping his groin, she kicked again, striking the outside of one knee so that it buckled inward. She stooped to grasp Zechariah's staff and swung at the man's head, catching it with a glancing blow. Not waiting to see if he fell, she scrambled from him and ran. The downward slope told her she had made a mistake and was headed deeper into the quarry. She heard lurching—echoing—footfalls behind her that picked up speed. Too late to turn back, she surged forward, looking side to side desperately, despite the pain, to find a place to hide or at least put her back to a wall to make a stand.

Miriam was in a place of faint light and dark as the torches and lanterns were spaced farther apart. The sound of running closed on her just as she saw the shadowed cleft of an opening—darkness among stone—and prayed it was deep enough to hide her. Miriam pushed into it and discovered a passage that within a few feet was choked with rocks and sand. Whether intentionally sealed or a natural collapse, it kept her from going farther. The louder footfalls of the man searching for her made her catch her breath. She cut a piece of cloth from her cloak to wrap around her face and staunch the bleeding. The dust settled around her in the unused tunnel.

As Miriam breathed slowly—calming herself in the darkness as Zechariah had taught her, so she could face the man trying to kill her—she felt a current of air. Her mouth seemed cotton dry, but she managed to wet two fingers and passed them over the stone blocking the way ahead. Working by touch, she found the thread of air came from between smaller stones framed by larger ones above them. There must be an open space beyond the blockage. Her fingers tested the rocks, and the smaller ones the size of her fist or her head shifted when she prodded. She pulled one of the loose ones toward her, and it came free, so she set at her feet. With a push, another fell away into the other side. She quietly removed more of the smaller loose stones until the space was barely large enough for her to wriggle through. The scraping of the big rocks above gave her little warning—she pulled her staff and feet out of the opening and crawled free just as the largest rocks dropped. The opening was no more.

Miriam caught her breath and closed her eyes despite the darkness. Zechariah had often commented about her exceptional ability to know the passing of time and to judge distances and recall directions. This tunnel ran south and east. It might join with the network of underground passages near Antonia Fortress and the Temple. *It must not be far away,* she thought, and she knew she could emerge there.

* * *

Miriam was sure she was lost. It seemed well over an hour had passed as she had used Zechariah's staff—just as he had shown her—to tap her way through the darkness. But this was no longer practice, pretending blindness; the darkness was total. She had worked her way through three more sections of the tunnel, some of them lengthy. In some spots, the tunnel was partially blocked by rubble, and she used the staff always to check her footing. More rocks had fallen, so she squirmed through openings she explored with her staff that no one larger could ever pass through. Then after the third jumble of stone—when Miriam feared the maze would not end—the tunnel came to a pit whose near side descended at a sharp angle.

Tapping her way around the edges, she came to a wall of rocks so packed that she could detect no crevices to enlarge and crawl through. The stones sealed off the place where the tunnel must once have continued its level course. The pit had been part of the floor of the passage she was in and the ceiling of the one below. And it had collapsed. Feeling along its descending slope of rubble, she reached the spot where it leveled into another passage. She was farther underground than she had been before—and well past the Temple mount. She must have slowly descended and reached a spot below the City of David.

Beneath her, Miriam felt a crunch and a sharp pain as she knelt to check the ground at her feet. A splinter of something jabbed into her knee. Her exploring hand touched the haft, then the head of what seemed a burnt torch. She held the head's loose end of dried fabric close to her nose to check for oil, then opened the pouch at her waist for her sparking stones. After some effort, the sparks caught, and a small flame bloomed on the fragment of fabric. Lifting the sputtering, dying torch, she saw the pile of bones she stood among. *Two men,* she thought, judging by the skulls and the size of the bones and remnants of scorched clothing. *But why burnt?* The bones were charred by fire.

Behind the bones was a carved stone-lintel entry to what must be a chamber, the passage to it fire-blackened. The large blocks of stone fitted into the entrance to seal it had fresh chisel marks and had been loosened and one block removed and set aside. The opening was rimmed with burnt-black stone. A stronger current of air came from it—a good sign.

Thirsty, exhausted, her head throbbing with pain, Miriam was more strongly driven by a growing fear that she would die underground. She shoved the blocks and fell forward as they gave way. The torch's meager flame went out, and she toppled into blackness.

* * *

Miriam regained consciousness in the dark, finding she was sprawled upon stone steps that descended from the entrance to the chamber. Realizing with thankfulness that she still gripped Zechariah's staff, she used it to help her stand and, in the stillness, heard a steady drip of water. She tapped toward the sound until she reached a stone wall wet with a rivulet of water and pressed her mouth against it. Her hand, searching for more and failing, found a bracket holding what seemed an intact torch. Afraid to remove it without checking first—the wrapping might crumble—she raised her stones and struck streamers of sparks. The ancient torch's fabric flared and cast a faint light around her as she turned to check her surroundings. Along the wall, at the edge of the light's reach, was a gleam. On a low table sat a row of chests open to reveal their contents. Each was full of gold coins or jewelry. In the arc of light, she saw objects made from silver and gold—multi-pronged candlesticks, bowls and plates, and other sundry items.

Mathias had told his children the story of King Herod's attempt to plunder this treasure. But his men—Temple guards—never returned. Those nearby had reported a sound described as an eruption, and it was understood that the wrath of God had consumed them by fire for disturbing the place. The story had soon turned into a warning to all of Jerusalem that fate would do the same to any who

attempted to enter and steal the treasure. She did not know what could have burned Herod's men to death... but she understood that was where she must be. This was King David's tomb and treasure chamber. No one had entered it for centuries until Herod tried to retrieve its wealth back in the days of her grandparents.

Miriam could not go back the way she came, and she had no idea how to get out. The light wavered, the torch's shreds nearly exhausted, as she looked around the chamber.

Her life had been ruined when two Roman soldiers had raped her in flickering light and shadows like those that surrounded her now. Zechariah had saved her that day in the tunnel near the Temple with the staff she now carried. He had taught her how to overcome fear... to turn fear and hatred into strength. But what good would that do her now? What good would come of this vast wealth that lay before her? As despair grew from questions she could not answer, the last flicker of the torch went out, leaving her in darkness with only the sound of dripping water.

CV

Ptolemais

Nicanor stood on the harbor quay and studied the sky as it shaded from pink-orange to red at the horizon. Yosef had often told him onboard the *Salacia* heading to Rome that the shepherds of his country considered that a good sign... a sunset portent of good weather the following day. And some of the sailors hearing him had nodded at the wisdom, having their own version of that saying. And that's how he and his friend had parted not an hour before. Both watched the first coloring of sunset, and Yosef said he prayed the saying held true, and the weather would be fair all the way to Rome and beyond for Nicanor. The centurion did not look forward to what was expected of him in Rome, but it was the best way to save Cleo.

Before saying goodbye to Yosef, he had met with Vespasian and Titus. The general had given him letters and instructions: "Before Rome go to Falacrine, Nicanor. Give these to my wife Antonia Caenis, and she will understand how to help you. She is wise in the ways of Rome's politics and has resources that can aid you. You may wish to leave your woman there and not take her to Rome. I've mentioned this to Antonia in my letters—she will care for her." Vespasian had given him a second batch: "My personal orders—under my seal—for you to meet with engineers to discuss improvements to the siege equipment you have commented on before. I want the works shipped directly to Caesarea for our use against Jerusalem. You will see to this and your chief purpose." The last item Vespasian handed him was a single sheet of vellum. "This tells you how to send reports to me—and to carry copies to my wife. I will share the reports with Gaius Mucianus. Read and memorize these instructions and then shred this and cast it into the sea before reaching Ostia."

Titus's goodbye had relieved Nicanor of one worry and regret: "I'll see that your mount—Tempestas—is cared for, and I look forward to when you can rejoin us both."

Nicanor turned from the darkening sky and entered the taberna. The back-corner table where he had last met with Sayid and Cleo was empty, and he sat down, calling for a pitcher of beer from the barkeep. Now he must wait.

* * *

Hours had passed, and the tide of patrons into and from the taberna had flowed and ebbed from a throng eating evening meals and drinking noisily to the few sitting silently alone at a late hour with drink and their thoughts. Nicanor had switched from beer to water as the evening turned into night. The coins he gave the barkeep kept him unbothered by any demands or attempts by others to join his table when seats grew scarce early in the evening. Now the tables were nearly empty in the early hours of the morning. The barkeep slept sitting on the floor, leaning against the door to the wharf. There he would know when his last—very generous—customer finally left.

The sinking feeling in Nicanor's gut had increased hour by hour. Something had gone wrong, or perhaps Cleo had decided to go to Jerusalem—to Yosef's family—was better than returning to Rome with him. He stood and went to the door, nudging the barkeep aside with his foot and tossing a last coin onto the man's ample belly. He swung the door open to gray dawn, the ship's masts touching a sky that was just losing its darkness. Men walked the quay and opened warehouse doors, beginning their busy day.

Further down the dock, men were readying the vessel he would sail upon soon. He headed toward the ship, but his eyes continued to sweep the waterfront even as he put a foot on the gangplank.

The ship's master near the brow called to him. "There you are, centurion, just in time. They put your gear and the chest for your companion aboard last night. Where is the woman joining you? We must sail now with the tide."

"She... is not coming."

"Ahh... well, there are plenty of women in Rome." The captain turned away to curse a clumsy line handler. "Board now, centurion... we're casting off."

It did not seem long before the first shuddering roll once the ship passed the port's breakwater and the sea current and a gusting wind took hold. Nicanor's heart sank as the sails lifted, billowed, and the lines grew taut. The skies were darkening again—a reversing of dawn—over the land behind him and the sea ahead. He had kept watch on the waterfront for any sign of Cleo or Sayid. Now, though they were too far out and the strengthening wind was pushing them farther away, he still searched for someone he would likely never see again.

Last evening's sunset has lied, Nicanor thought, *I sail from a storm in Judea... into another in Rome.*

# # #

407

THE STORY CONTINUES IN BOOK THREE.

FOR UPDATES, PLEASE VISIT THE AUTHOR'S WEBSITE AT:

WWW.CRYFORJERUSALEM.COM

ABOUT THE AUTHOR

Dr. Ward Sanford is an internationally renowned hydrogeologist who has spent over thirty years studying and writing journal articles on the availability and sustainability of groundwater around the United States and the world. He has given professional advice on a number of sites across North America, Europe, and the Middle East, as well as undertaken missions with the International Atomic Energy Agency to Thailand and the U. S. State Department to Libya.

More recently he has developed a keen interest in the first century history of Israel through the writings of the contemporary historian Flavius Josephus. His desire is now to bring those recorded events to life through dramatization in a series of novels entitled *Cry For Jerusalem*. Dr. Sanford is a member of the Historical Novel Society of North America. He and his wife, two grown sons, and daughter-in-law live in the Virginia suburbs of Washington DC.

Made in the USA
Monee, IL
25 September 2020